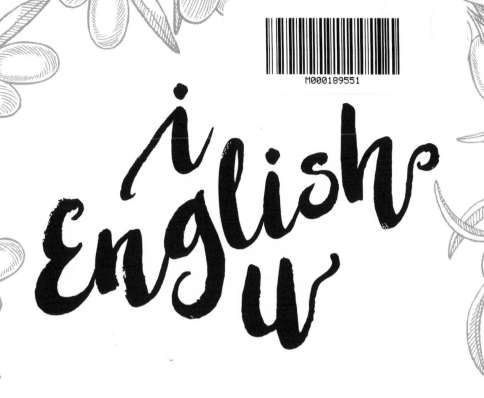

i English

JR LAURENCE

Publisher's Cataloging-in-Publication data
Names: Laurence, J.R., author.
Title: I English U : an international romantic comedy / by J.R. Laurence.
Description: Silvermine Bay, Hong Kong: Top Floor Books, 2022.
Identifiers: ISBN: 9789627866572 (hardcover) | 9789627866589 (pbk.) | 9789627866596 (ebook) | 9798200939312 (audio)
Subjects: LCSH Online dating--Fiction. | Man-woman relationships--Fiction. | English language--Study and teaching--Fiction. | Italy--Fiction. | Romance fiction. | Humorous fiction. | BISAC FICTION / Romance / Romantic Comedy | FICTION / Humorous / General | FICTION / Romance / Contemporary
Classification: LCC PS3612.A9326 I46 2022 | DDC 813.6--dc23

The following excerpts appear by kind permission of the respective authors:

"Four Stages of Acculturation" from *Keep Your Life, Family and Career Intact While Living Abroad* by Dr. Cathy Tsang-Feign (Top Floor Books, 2014)

"36 Questions" from "The Experimental Generation of Interpersonal Closeness: A Procedure and Some Preliminary Findings" by Arthur Aron, Edward Melinat, Elaine N. Aron, Robert Darrin Vallone, and Renee J. Bator (Personality and Social Psychology Bulletin, April 1997, vol. 23 no. 4, p. 363-377)

Cover design by Gabriella Regina

ISBN 978 962 7866 58 9

Top Floor Books
PO Box 29
Silvermine Bay, Hong Kong
topfloorbooks.com

i English u

AN INTERNATIONAL ROMANTIC COMEDY

J.R. LAURENCE

TOP FLOOR BOOKS

for Xiao Fei

Chapter 1

*T*oo late to pull on pants.

Dead phone meant no alarm and the kitchen wall clock gave me two and a half minutes to shove a half-stirred coffee in the microwave and squirm into a cleanish ivory blouse. A splash at the bathroom sink, greeting the unlovely image in the mirror. Flat chin, too-narrow nose, pleading blue eyes swept by a storm cloud of smog-brown hair. No time to fight it with a brush. I tied it back while tripping through the hall.

A peek through the curtain: orange-fringed powder blue sky. Hello, perfect southern California morning, and goodbye. Time for my daily trip around the world.

I gulped coffee while sliding behind my desk in the corner of the living room, tapped the laptop awake, and clicked the video button, catching a pudgy twelve-year-old Chinese boy mid-yawn.

"Good morning, Bieber," I said. "I mean good evening. Sorry I'm late. What time is it in Shanghai?"

"Good evening, Teacher Serena. Time is"—eyes rolled up while brain computed grammar—"two minute after eleven o'clock, pee em."

"Two *minutes*—plural, remember." I checked my notes from yesterday's session. Lesson 14: Writing a Letter. As if anyone knew what a letter was anymore. "So. Homework. Did you write—"

"Why two *minutes* and not eleven *o'clocks?*"

"That is a very smart question, Bieber."

He offered a lipless smile, eyes aimed sideways. I loved pronouncing his name: Bieber Bao. Kids in China choose their own English names, lucky things. If only Americans could choose theirs. I'd have picked something more suited to my life, the antonym of serene.

I rolled my eyes in return. "It's because English is crazy. Homework?"

A document icon flashed in my school inbox.

"Please read it out loud, Bieber."

Behind him in his cramped little room a blue slipper popped into view, then arced off-screen again: a woman uncrossing her legs. Poor kid. Bad enough to face tutors five days a week, from the moment he returned from school until me, English, his last lesson. But his mother standing sentry as study cop was humiliating. No life for him. Or her. Or me for that matter, though for other reasons.

Bieber narrowed his eyes and recited, his natural singsong Chinese tones turning every other word into an oral speedbump: "Dear *Moth*-er. Hello. How *are* you. Did you eat *yet?* I *want* to eat ice *creams* and candies and *beans*. I *want* to less study. I *want* to motor-*cycle*."

A lump filled my throat. I felt like answering, *I want to motorcycle too.* Right now. Gun it out of this bland apartment and fly.

They didn't prepare us for this in college. Between all the language acquisition theories, deep syntax and tongue diagrams, suffering through Chomsky and Piaget and impractical eastern European teaching methodologies, the entire pedagogical approach was rooted back in the twentieth century, when English was taught with textbooks and chalk. They never mentioned needing to dress only from the waist up because your entire career would be spent alone in front of a webcam in an empty living room with a cheap blackboard at your back to create the illusion of an actual classroom, contracted to a tightwad online language school hundreds of miles away that was the only option left for English majors. No staff lounge to take breaks in and let off steam, no handsome chemistry teacher to exchange flirty wisecracks with in the hall. Not even one flesh-and-blood student to offer an encouraging pat on the shoulder to—or, in the case of this Algerian I had for two lessons, a deserving slap in the face. Only the electronic image of a tired, bespectacled boy on the other side of the planet with an off-screen mother breathing down his neck.

"That letter is very good," I said. Then I had an idea. "Hey, Bieber, let's try reverse translation. I say English, you repeat back in Chinese, okay?"

He cocked his head like a puppy, eyes darting toward his maternal overseer.

"Okay, loud and clear in Chinese: *My teacher says...*" I waited for him to translate. "*...I am her smartest, favorite student...*" He took a deep breath and relayed my words. A blue toe blipped in and out of view. "*...And teacher says my mother probably is tired and should go to bed.*"

His face broke into a grimace and froze.

"Go ahead," I said. But his image remained stuck, unblinking, unbreathing. "Bieber? Do you hear me?"

I clicked every control on screen until the cursor stopped dead, hammered ESC and ENTER and the space bar until I worried they'd snap off. I lifted the laptop and shook it, then spanked its bottom. The monitor went black. Now the power button refused to respond.

I slid over to my roommate's door, knuckles poised to knock. Or would she kill me? She worked late shifts and often stayed up until dawn. "Only time I ever see eight a.m. is when I run into its ass from behind," she liked to say.

"Zuzie..." I tapped her door, gentle but insistent.

3

Waited, then raised my voice: "Zuzie? I need help."

My fist flipped back to knock harder, when the handle clicked. A buzzard's nest of dark copper dreadlocks fixed me with a droop-eyed, screw-you-for-waking-me-up glare.

"Zuzie, I'm so sorry. Network died, screen went blank, middle of a lesson. Do you know anything about—?"

"Hell if I know how to fix that shit. Good day, madam."

The door slammed. An angry rattle of the lock.

Each tick of the clock triggered an ice shower down my spine. Two minutes must have passed already, meaning I had thirteen minutes to fix the situation before my pay would be automatically docked. The head office knew by now: the feed was routed through their server, logged, and recorded at random for review. I unplugged and replugged the computer, gnawing my thumb as it lazily restarted. At least the screen worked. Another two minutes before it informed me that no network was detected, not even after changing every setting I could find, one of which turned the user interface into Spanish.

Nine minutes. Time to call the school's tech support. I grabbed my phone from the bedroom before I remembered the battery was dead. Another minute gone while I located the charger, meanwhile composing excuses for my supervisor: Chinese government censors had hacked the lesson, sewer workers accidentally severed the cable, the student's robot dog ate his homework. An unfamiliar man's voice told me to hold. He came back a full lifetime later—though the clock had advanced only forty seconds. "Guy'll be there in three, four minutes."

"Who'll be here?"

"Tech dude. Lessee...name's right here...*ah*...Elias."

The Biblical miracle worker. A good sign.

I paced, reminded myself to breathe, and considered a splash of vodka. If only I had a better computer, better-paid work, a tech-savvy boyfriend, *any* boyfriend.

The doorbell chimed. Four minutes, as promised. I flung the door open so fast the tech guy recoiled in fright. He was tall, verging on pudgy, and wore an orange t-shirt that read *E-Nerd-gency Services*. His gray chinos were so wrinkled they'd pass as igneous rock.

His eyes, behind black-framed glasses, fixed somewhere on my legs. "Sailor Moon. Cool. More into Doraemon myself."

He was referring to my Japanese cartoon pajama bottoms, an "ironic" gift from an old classmate, since the title character was also named Serena.

"Just fix my Internet, please." I pointed to the desk. "You have four and a half minutes."

He put down a rattling canvas bag, settled into the chair and tapped keys while bobbing his head like a pianist performing a jazz improv. I peeked over his shoulder at dialog windows filled with indecipherable scrolling text.

"Truckloads of junk on this thing. When's the last time you ran a virus scan?" he said.

"Uh..."

"Yeah, what I figured. I have to ask this, 'kay? So, like, don't shoot me, 'kay? You frequent any cybersex or porn sites?"

"Jesus Christ!"

He smiled. "A grown-up chick in little girl jammies. Lotta guys'll pay big money for that. Just sayin'. Trying to rule out some badass malware."

"No, I do not do porn, damn it."

Was the clock running faster? In movies the bomb's count-down timer always slows down so the lead actors can trade wisecracks in between ticks and tocks, but in reality, the more panicked you get, the more time accelerates.

"Have you found the problem?"

He didn't respond. I asked again.

"Listen, Sailor Moon, know how you can help? By staying calm, whaddaya think?"

Two minutes.

I couldn't bear watching the lack of progress. I dashed into my room and changed into a pair of khaki shorts, whose button popped off. Would nothing go right today?

The repairman's voice resounded down the hallway.

"I said, you got a puppy?"

"What the—? No dog here."

Praying the zipper would hold, I stepped into the hallway. At the other end he held up a severed gray cable.

"Even worse, then," he said. "You got rats."

No. I didn't have rats. Not exactly.

The carpet burned my heels as I spun back into the bedroom. Two hamster cages stood in the corner, linked by a maze of colorful plastic passages. One wire mesh doorway lay wide open. I dropped to my knees, calling: "Laurel! Hardy!" Their wheels, the passages, their little wooden shelves, all empty. A telltale lump in the sawdust revealed one tiny creature cringing behind his food dish. I brushed him off, saw the lighter tan fur, and knew that Hardy was the fugitive.

He wasn't in the bathroom or kitchen. I searched under the couch, lifted the coffee table, spilling Zuzie's *Cosmo* collection, and crawled beneath my desk, where Elias was propped on his elbows, doing something with wires.

"We have to stop meeting like this," he said.

He flicked a switch on the router. Green lights flashed.

"Aaaaand...we have contact."

I backed out from under the table, craning my head toward the clock. Four or five minutes too late. Maybe they wouldn't notice. I restarted the school interface; everything appeared normal. All except Bieber's student icon—a photo of the Canadian pop star whose name he'd borrowed—grayed out as offline. He'd given up waiting.

A cheerful tinkle; a message popped up in the Admin panel:

Lesson terminated. Please contact Administration.

My forehead struck the desk and stayed there.

"Um..." Elias's tools clanked into his bag. "I mean, it's not my business, but if you want my advice—of course you don't, but, ah...your laptop is running kinda slow. I mean, this model is, what, seven, eight years old, and anyway the Wi-Fi adapter seems wonky, as you obviously know. I mean, you might want to consider a new computer."

"You're right about it being none of your business." I clawed my hair with both hands. "How am I supposed to afford a new computer? I can barely feed myself, and now maybe I can't even do that this week."

I knew I should shut up. It wasn't this guy's fault. He was just some poor tech-head, doing his job. But my mouth had a mind of its own. "I've got this piss-paid job, hardly step outside my front door or see real people, not that I can even spare four bucks to sit in a coffee shop. If things go on, I'll have to move back home with my mother the drunk—"

"Um. Don't think I'm the right person to—"

"And now my sweet baby hamster ran away! Maybe when you came in." My sobs sounded like an antique bicycle horn.

"Hey, hey, I'll help you find it. But you gotta chill first, okay?" I sensed him hovering behind me. "I mean, you're really, majorly stressed right now and I'm guessing you got a student in ten, twelve minutes? So, like, um..." He cleared his throat. "Not sure if I'm overstepping boundaries here, but, like, I know some shiatsu—well, my Mom taught me—and there are these meridi-an points. Is it cool if I show you?"

I shrugged, then felt a light touch on my shoulders.

"Right here and here," he said. "Sure you're okay with this? Because—"

I nodded hard. Strong, fat thumbs sank into my upper back.

"Cool," he said. Fingers bored into the tops of my shoulders, but they may as well have been daggers.

"Oww!! By the way, how did you get here so fast?" I said.

"Me?" He kneaded inward toward my neck. "My house is literally around the corner. Two-minute walk."

I'd never seen him before. No surprise, though, considering how seldom I left this apartment complex except to drive to the supermarket. "If it's a two-minute walk, how come it took you four minutes to get here?"

The pressure moved down between my shoulder blades. I screamed, certain that he'd severed my spine. Then it was as though a spring lock popped open. A deep, fuzzy tingle spread across my upper back and wrapped around my chest. I must have moaned with pleasure, because at first he chuckled. Then his fingers froze. Then they let go. He sucked in his breath in a panicked sort of way.

A slash of color in the corner of my eye. I stretched out the shoulder fabric for a better view.

There, where his fingers had been, my ivory blouse was scored with day-glo orange streaks.

"Were you eating, like, *cheese puffs* before you came?"

"Um..." He shuffled sideways around my desk.

"*Cheese puffs?* For *breakfast??* All over my frigging blouse!"

He held his canvas bag in front of his face like a shield. "Look, I'm sorry."

"Thank you for fixing my computer, but I think you'd better leave now."

"There's a paper you need to sign."

I stood up and felt my shorts threaten to drop. "Get out. Now!"

The front door clattered shut after him. One hand supporting my pants, the other tearing open the buttons of my soiled blouse, I took one step toward my bedroom, when the computer began chirping its perky ringtone: my next student calling. A door opened and Zuzie shuffled into the living room in a terry bathrobe, supporting a hamster on her open palm.

"Found this sewer rat in my room. Whoa, look at you! No wonder I heard some dude's voice, and you moaning like a horse. Shoulda sent him in to me when you're done."

Chapter 2

Here's what I love about my job: a student like Yasmin Okay. Yes, her real name; in Turkey people don't make up their surnames. She was seventeen and looked like a sweet little mouse, appearing every lesson in a different colored headscarf framing enormous, earnest eyes. She claimed she was working on her English to help her family's immigration application to Australia, but she had other motives, which she made no secret of in her homework, including today's assignment from Lesson 24: write examples of future perfect tense.

"I will...have...had...no boyfriend, because Father and Mother will...have...met me husband."

I nodded. "The first verb is correct use of future perfect, but the second verb, *met*—"

"Shit! I knew," she said. "Father and Mother will have...ah... met me *to* husband."

"Will have *introduced* me to *a* husband."

"I will have had no boyfriend because Father and Mother will have...introduced me to...hus—*aiee!*—to *a* husband. Fat, ugly husband, I think also lazy."

"I think you will have met a boyfriend—see how I use 'met'? You can meet someone, but you can't meet *to* someone—you will have met a boyfriend before next year."

I watched her process this information, quickly type something into her notes, then fix me with an inquisitive stare. I've trained myself to point my eyes at the little lens above the screen when speaking, so the student gets the impression I'm looking directly at them, but like most students, Yasmin looked straight at my face on her monitor, so from my viewpoint she seemed to be gazing downward.

"Have you a boyfriend yet?" she said.

She asked me this about once a month, as if I were the elder sister who must find a match before the younger sisters were allowed. Sometimes I did feel that way toward her.

I shook my head. "Next month I won't have had—hear that? I am using the negative. Next month I will...not...have...had...a boyfriend for one year." Of course, I wasn't telling the truth. It had been closer to three years, unless you counted an incoherent one-nighter after a drunken house party in Huntington Beach last fall.

Yasmin blinked dark eyelashes while my syntax sunk in, then broke out smiling. "You come my home. We go to Europe, speak English to handsome foreign boys. Together find boyfriends."

When she said "go to Europe," I knew she meant cross the waterway dividing Istanbul over to its European side, where tourists and foreign businessmen congregated. Yasmin's family lived in an apartment somewhere on the Asian side, visible now through the window behind her.

That was another thing I loved. Every day I traveled the world. I knew that sounded like a hokey recruitment pitch for what was essentially a cheapskate, exploitative language factory. Yet it was true. Sometimes I leaned in, peripheral vision faded, and it felt as though I were sitting face-to-face in an office or living room or across a dining table in Slovakia or Uruguay or China or Egypt. Or, right then, in the ancient city of Istanbul, where the sun was setting over a rolling hillside crammed with tiled roofs, like a red carpet pinned down with spiky minaret towers and a white dome that must have been a mosque. Behind them sparkled the waters of the Bosporus, where Jason and the Argonauts once passed in search of the Golden Fleece. I imagined going for an after-work stroll through the bazaar, stopping in a crumbly-walled cafe to hang out with my circle of witty, sophisticated local and expatriate friends over backgammon and a cup of sweet, thick coffee. All dreamlike and so very real, until the ten-minute warning icon reminded me that it would soon be time to move to Estonia for an hour.

"Have time for special words?" Yasmin asked. This was part of her lesson plan that she'd made up herself. I waited for the red signal, indicating the five-minute interval when I was supposed to prepare for the next lesson: the only time when there was no danger of being caught in one of the company's random recordings, their Orwellian means of keeping teachers on our toes.

"Go ahead," I said.

Yasmin's face darkened, whether from the setting sun or her blushing I couldn't tell. "What is difference between 'give a shit' and 'take a shit'?"

This, too, is what I love about my job.

HERE'S WHAT I HATE about my job. The moment I signed off from my eleven o'clock student, looking forward to my lunch break, a notice popped up from Marisa, my supervisor at iEnglishU.com.

Message received this morning in what appears to be Chinese. Ran through translate program. Hope you can offer a spectacularly good explanation...

I PAY BIG USA MONEY TO ENGLISH ONE DAY ONE HOUR BUT THIS DAY FIVE MINUTES! IF SON'S TOEFL SCORE AFFECT EVEN ONE LITTLE, SO HE CAN NOT ENTER HARVARD OR OXFORD, FOLLOW-UP WORKING INSIDE BIG-FIVE INVESTMENT BANK WITH MILLIONS ANNUAL BONUS DOLLARS, I SUE YOU VERY BAD SCHOOL EVERY $4000 MILLION.

Marisa's head formed on my screen before the first ringtone faded. "So? Got a better translation for me, sweetie?"

Her plump brown face and pillowy bosoms fooled you into thinking she was a sweet-tempered Latina *madre,* until you realized she had a heart of gold only in the pure mineral sense of the word. If you were making money for the company she was your best friend on earth, but if your student numbers were down, your free lesson conversions dropped below thirty percent, or, God forbid, you messed up a session like I did, you might as well have been one of those hoopball players that her Mayan ancestors beheaded after losing a game.

"My Internet broke down. I got it fixed," I said. "Won't happen again."

"Oh, really? You can guarantee that? Because I can understand three minutes for a reboot, five maybe. But *forty-five minutes?*"

"I was down eighteen minutes. But by then the student—"

"Eighteen is past the limit. We had to offer that crazed woman two weeks extension, so she doesn't pull her son. You know I have the authority to dock your full day's pay."

"Please, Marisa!" I didn't want her to see me cry, but maybe it would help. "I made sure it can't happen again, I swear."

How was I supposed to tell her that I fixed the source of the problem with a paperclip through a hamster cage door? Just then a blonde head appeared over Marisa's shoulder and waved her fingers.

"Hey. Serena, right?" Victoria, gorgeous in a Teutonic ice queen sort of way, was iEnglishU's star teacher. Her snub-nosed features graced the homepage twice: the masthead featured a dreamy head shot with her teacher's microphone headset; when you scrolled down, a little video auto-played of her flipping her creamy vanilla hair and purring to the viewer, "I English U." Total whore tease. What was she doing in the office, instead of preening in front of a camera being the shampoo model of online English tutors?

"So how many students you got these days, Ser?"

My name's not 'Ser.' I couldn't lie about my numbers in front of Marisa, and she knew it.

"Eight," I said.

She raised a plucked blonde eyebrow. "Single digits. Cute. Hope you reach puberty someday."

Marisa turned to her. "Oh, Vicky, that wasn't nice."

"Sorry. Guess I'm just sugar and spice, then."

Marisa laughed at the wretched joke. "Have you told Serena your good news?"

Of course she hadn't. It wasn't as if one ran into other teachers in the hallway, when the office was 370 miles away in San Jose.

"Vicky will be starring in—"

Victoria interrupted, "Not starring, dear. Educating."

"Vicky will be the face of our first series of subscription video lessons. DVDs too. Hope to launch by September. We have to, that is. Already booked this year's Geolingua in Milan."

"Lucky this year it isn't in *Shanghai*," Victoria said with a rub-it-in tone. So she knew all about the Bieber Incident.

"But that's not the only good news, is it, Vick? Come on, tell her. All right, I'll tell. Vicky is engaged! To a Swedish prince!"

"Not a prince," Victoria said, fake-annoyed. "He's a count."

"One of her former students. Isn't that grand?"

Grand? Were we speaking like royalty now? "Vicky" spun around and wagged her butt at me on the way out. My middle finger rose off-camera in salute to the incipient countess.

"How nice for her." My words oozed between gritted teeth. "Victoria's so busy, maybe you can send some more students my way?"

Marisa resumed her familiar business countenance. "Serena, look. You know you just don't get the requests she gets. It wouldn't kill you to do something with your hair. And I'm afraid this little, ah, network failure will cost you points."

"Come on, Marisa. My schedule looks like Swiss cheese! You've got to give me more students. This month I'm dying from rent and car payments and student loans, much less having a penny for a goddamn hairdresser. Please. And while you're at it, I call dibs on the next Scandinavian prince."

"Count. And kindly watch your tongue."

"Sorry, Marisa. Today's been... The router thing really shook me up. You're not going to dock the whole day?"

She clicked her tongue and sighed. "What kind of person do you think I am? I wouldn't pull such a thing on my dear, dear teachers. You're my family." She gave me that bee-sting pout which meant as far as she was concerned the discussion was over. I tried one last tactic.

"Thank you. But please think about sending me more students. You know how much I love working with iEnglishU and I'd hate to have to take employment elsewhere."

"Sure, sweetie. I understand." Her smile was warm for once. "I hear the pizza place in the mini-mall across is hiring dishwashers." The screen went gray.

This, and a little bit more, was what I hate about my job.

Chapter 3

*M*y final lesson of the day went better than expected. Not my favorite student: Thierry, a forty-ish Belgian petroleum engineer working in North Dakota, who claimed to speak six languages, all, it seemed, with a French accent as gooey as mayonnaise. He'd been badgered by his American supervisors into studying remedial English pronunciation, and made no secret of his reluctance, nor of his disdain for any word that ended in a consonant. There were times when I wished I could reach into his throat with a wrench. But today I tried something different—we reenacted the scene from "My Fair Lady" which every English teacher loves to hate.

"In Hartford, Hereford, and Hampshire, hurricanes hardly happen."

It was a breakthrough. His R's thinned, vowels flattened, didn't drop a single H...after around the twenty-fifth try. He met my whoop of delight with a grin. "Perhaps I am ready for to graduate, yes?"

No. No no no no NO! I wanted to say. *Don't even* think *about depriving me of your weekly tuition.* I flipped my hair, Victoria-style, to which he raised an eyebrow.

"Next week we'll work on the rest of 'The Rain in Spain'," I said. "Very important out there on the Great Plain."

He whistled the tune as he signed off.

A last check for messages, then I staggered to the sofa. The light outside was fading. I considered escaping for a short walk, but I was limp with exhaustion. Besides, I was in no mood to be reminded of the homogenized suburban monotony that characterized my neighborhood, and indeed my life.

I could drive someplace in my clunky Toyota, but that meant spending money on gas, and where to? A shopping mall? Drive ten miles to the beach? A solo evening stroll along the pier among groping couples was not the mood-enhancer I needed. I considered dosing myself with television, but I'd stared at screens long enough today.

I forced myself off the couch, sliced a carrot, and went to inspect the troops. Laurel was jogging on his wheel. Hardy lurked in a corner, poor little thing, as if guilty for his earlier crime. Both came running at the sight of carrot slivers pushed through the mesh. Happy hamsters receiving orange manna from heaven. I wished someone would do the same for me.

I switched my phone off airplane mode. Immediately it chirped about a voice mail. It was my mother's number. No need to listen; I'd phone later, when she'd be too bourboned-out to offer her usual monologue of well-meaning advice about my life.

There was also a text from Zuzie:

Girl we gonna play tonite? G&C!

Where my roommate found the money to go out drinking on a barista's salary, especially at a hipster joint like the Grove & Chicken, I never quite understood. We'd lived together for eight months now, ever since I graduated from college and responded to her Rooms Shared posting for a "lady non-smoker, clean, neat, employed, fun-loving, repeat: clean." Technically I met the requirements: never smoked tobacco, showered daily, and I loved fun; I just didn't have much of it. I'd offered to pay more than half the rent, since my movie-set "classroom" occupied a corner of the living room, but Zuzie told me to save my money for nights on the town. She'd somehow latched onto me as her project, her suburban white girl Pygmalion.

The bed beckoned, silvered by moonlight melting through the window. When I closed my eyes it was no longer the plain, dry Orange County moon, but a million sparkling diamonds on the Marmara Sea, against the silhouetted backdrop of Topkapi Palace in Istanbul. I was sailing on the ancient waters joining Occident and Orient on a brilliant white yacht packed with international lawyers and investment bankers, all gorgeous and single and under thirty. An olive-skinned, athletic Greek led me to the railing and confessed that his English needed so much work that he hoped I might offer private training in where to place his lips and tongue. Muscular arms encircled me while Istanbul's city lights reflected in the adoring eyes of my lover from Mount Olympus.

A hand clamped my shoulder. The glare from a naked ceiling bulb stung my face.

"Where you been? I been texting and messaging, and—and even tried *calling* you for God's sake, for like the past hour." A dark blur coalesced into Zuzie towering over me in a skimpy leatherette skirt and sheer colorburst silk blouse. I sat up, rubbing my eyes, and wiped spittle from the corner of my mouth.

"Guess I fell asleep."

"You mean to say your ass been parked here this whole time?"

"I've been cruising the Mediterranean with a Greek billionaire."

She retreated into the bathroom. Drawers slammed. "Well, I hope you did him a quickie, cause right now, Miss Harlequin Romance, you and me going to cruise down exotic Irvine Boulevard to hook up with some prime American meat."

"Sounds romantic." I shuffled into the kitchen, feeling a slight headache coming on, and grabbed orange juice from the fridge. "I had a tough day. You know they docked me for that missed lesson?"

Zuzie came out of the bathroom aiming a hairbrush at me like a pistol. "Hey, you know how much you piss me off? *I had a tough day, so I'm gonna make sure it stays shitty,* that's you. Now park your butt on that stool and I'm gonna fix your hair, then you're gonna put on that cute turquoise satiny thing—yeah, the one you never, *ever* wear, gives your boobs a nice lift—then you are going out and have a few laughs if it kills me! Mindy'll be there, says she invited some college guys, just your type. Now, sit!"

In her car, Zuzie's head, strobed by passing street lights, bounced to something that blended Gypsy dances with hip hop. Just as I was starting to like it, she turned down the volume. "You're strung tight as a mousetrap. Smoke a joint before we're there?"

"No, thanks."

"Suit yourself. You got about three more miles to come out of that pout."

We passed a sad 1960s strip mall, half its shops boarded up; only a chain drug store and a Thai restaurant were open. Across the boulevard stood a big box store, its half-full parking lot jaundiced by tungsten lamps. I covered my face with my hands. Istanbul beckoned. Shanghai. Somewhere teeming with people and lights and spice and history, where a special someone would be so entranced by a girl from exotic Tustin, California, that he'd swoon at my feet.

"Look, Serena, I know where you're coming from. I do," Zuzie said. "How many times I can't sleep cause I feel like I'm standing on a cliff—always verging on broke, living in a crappy little apartment, no prospects except serving overpriced coffee to assholes who bark in my face if their soy milk separates—and all I wish is that Spiderman will swoop down and whisk me off that precipice to some better place. I mean, am I off base here?"

This was something new. Zuzie had never confided in me. "Not sure about Spidey. But, yeah. I mean, no, not off base."

"So here's my personal philosophy, if you wanna call it that. You can look for Mister Right all you want, but meantime, maybe Mister Hunk will do for a laugh."

"You mean plural *Hunks* from what I've seen."

"Hey, It's called multi-tasking, my dear. Keep a few channels open and eventually happiness will find its own groove. I mean, I got to believe that, otherwise I'm *really* screwed."

"Never really thought about it that way. Anyway, right now I'm not in the mood to invest much money searching for Mister Anybody."

She turned across the dark street into a driveway between spindly orange trees and found a parking space by the side of the building.

"Know what you need? Some spice in your life. And spice doesn't cost much," Zuzie said. "Anyway, to misquote one of your dead white men poets: 'Tis better to have been laid and lost money than never to have been laid at all."

The Grove & Chicken was a British-themed pub in a restored plantation manor which once oversaw an empire of citrus and avocados, now long buried beneath tract home developments and shopping plazas. Inside, among the Union Jacks, London Tube signs, and the requisite dartboard, hung framed photos of the area's history: sepia Mexican cowboys and treeless cattle ranches that predated citrus planting, beside old colorized images of groves and packing houses. The place was only half-full, but the air buzzed with voices and cheerful clinks of glassware. Suddenly I was glad I came.

Zuzie's friend Mindy waved from a table between a pointing Lord Kitchener and the karaoke stage. As promised, she shared it with three guys, whose eyes focused in unison on Zuzie. They wore denim jackets over t-shirts, not like any college students I'd ever known. One was kind of good looking, though his long smoky blond hair could have used some conditioning. He slid aside, patting the seat beside him. Then he offered to buy a round for the table. Nope, definitely not a student.

He returned from the bar with a splashing pitcher and held it aloft in a heroic pose, while everybody but me snapped photos with their phones, followed by an orgy of sharing, posting, tweeting, feeding, and storying them around the known universe. His eyes pointed at my hands' notable lack of hardware.

"Bandwidth-impaired," I explained. He poured for Zuzie and me, then himself, passed the pitcher and sat beside me. We clinked glasses. I took a long, icy swig of beer while he studied my face and I tried to think of something, anything to say.

Everyone else at the table was showing off this or that on their phones, saying things like, "Oh, that's so funny," without actually smiling. The entire conversation sounded like a transcript of a random social media page. I half expected people to mutter, "Like." At the next table, where they were doing the same thing, somebody shouted.

"Did that guy really just say, *'rotflmao?'*" I asked.

"Sure did," said Zuzie, leaning so far back in genuine hilarity that every male eye swiveled toward her chest in anticipation of a wardrobe breakout. All except the guy beside me.

"Hysterical," he said.

"Mindy says you're at the university," I ventured.

He ran his hand over his hair. "Yeah, working there for the time being."

"Nice work if you can get it. What department?"

He laughed. "I guess you might say I'm multidisciplinary. At the moment I'm in the Biology Department."

"C'mon, tell her," Mindy said.

"Yes, ma'am." He nodded to her, then to me. "I'm a painter." His thumb pinched against his first two fingers made a brush-wielding flourish.

"So you teach scientific illustration?"

"Not this term, though I suppose I'd give it a shot if they asked."

"Oh. That's interesting." I was about to ask what medium he worked in—what else did you ask a painter? The twinkle in his eye told me he'd played me for a fool.

"About this time, most gals ask if I paint watercolors or acrylics, and then I come back at them with, 'No, ma'am, I stick to mold-resistant premium emulsion.'" He hoisted his glass with a crooked smile. "Seems you're smarter than that."

I mirrored his glass-raising, mainly to hide the blush spreading across my face. I knew I should have been a good sport and laughed along or made a wisecrack about my education. I pressed the glass against my cheek. What was wrong with me, that I couldn't take a joke?

"Sorry," I said. "I've had a rough day. Maybe after a few more beers."

"No, I'm the one who's sorry. I'm kind of tired of that joke anyway. Shouldn't have set you up like that. Sorry for being a jerk."

"The only true words he's uttered all night!" Mindy said.

His own embarrassment looked genuine. We both focused on the karaoke stage, where a pub employee with a beard like a grizzly bear laid out the song book and a sign-up sheet. My companion, whose name I didn't remember hearing, refilled his own glass. "So Mindy says you're a teacher."

I nodded. "Sit home teaching English online. It's like every day I travel around the world without leaving the dull confines of my living room."

"That's hysterical."

That word again. A voice inside my head warned me not to say what I was about to say, but my lips missed the message.

"Funny how *hysterical* became synonymous with *hilarious*. Did you know it shares the same linguistic root as *hysterectomy?*"

"Wow. Guess I probably could use a few English lessons myself. People always picking on my spelling, I mean like online and stuff. Must be worse with foreigners."

The head-voice: Say no more, Serena.

"Actually, you'd be surprised that second language learners"— *shut up now, girl, you sound like a jerk*—"particularly East Asians, tend to make fewer spelling errors than native English speakers"—*stop it, dummy, before he walks away*—"such as distinguishing between the adverbial *t-h-e-r-e*, possessive *t-h-e-i-r*, and, um.... Know what? Maybe I'm just gonna shut up now."

He laughed. "No doubt about it. Us Americans are dumber than Japanese or Chinese, especially at our own language, am I right?"

"Oh God." I rested my head in my hands. He had warm hazel eyes and a cute chin, but all he saw in me was a jackass. Why was it that when I was staring at someone eight thousand miles away through an LCD screen I could be in perfect control, charming, quick with a compliment or a joke; yet put me in the same room as a warm-blooded human being, and I became a stuttering, misfiring heap of flesh?

"I'll tell you what," I said. "I am so stupid right now that I don't know what I'm saying anymore and I am going to be quiet and not speak another word. I'm sorry."

He patted my forearm. "No, I understand. All is cool. You're honest. I like that."

I was saved from the necessity of an insincere reply by the blaring notes of a fuzzed guitar and a pale Asian girl who looked like she'd just crawled out from the back stacks of a library, belting out "Rebel Rebel" in a grating squeaky voice, which made further conversation impossible. We all sat back with drinks in hand and watched a succession of mainly execrable singers take the stage. Two men far too handsome to be straight performed

"I Am Woman" in an amazing operatic duet which brought down the house. Then Zuzie gave in to everyone's nudging and took her turn, posing in the spotlight, hair sparkling like some 1980s soul diva until she opened her mouth and wailed a country western number in a perfect Texas twang, to a room full of whistles and *yee-haw's*.

My companion and I traded judgmental looks toward the singers. The music and the alcohol were making him cuter by the minute. I stood up, excusing myself to pee, when Zuzie grabbed my arm, pulled me onto the stage, and shoved the mic in my hand. This was going too far. Hadn't I suffered enough humiliation for one day? I tried to hand her back the mic.

"Don't be such a shrew," she whispered, leaving me alone on stage. The entire pub stared up at me like a crowd in the Roman Coliseum waiting for a Christian to be fed to the lions. I ran my finger down the list and stopped on the easiest song I could find, a mushy old favorite of my dad's. But instead of the lush opening strings of "Sentimental Journey", horns blasted and a funked-out crotch-grabbing guitar. The monitor flashed the title, "Sex Machine/James Brown". The crowd hooted.

No sooner had I croaked the first, "Get on up, like a sex machine," than a gunshot-like pop exploded from the speaker, the music stopped, the screen went blank. People cheered as if it were part of the act. What was it about me and electronics today?

I dashed toward the toilet, some guy trying to grab me as I passed: "Whoa! Be my sex machine!"

The woman in the bathroom mirror looked like she'd seen a ghost, in fact was staring at one right now. Was this how that guy—God, I hadn't even paid attention to his name!—was this how he saw me? A nervous wreck grammar snob frightened little troll. The consolation prize after the other guys latched onto zexy Zuzie. Though come to think of it, he'd been kind of nice, seemed smarter than he made himself out to be, not bad looking except for the hair. Maybe not Spiderman or a Scandinavian count, but I was no prize either. Bonus points for being the first man—the first *flesh-and-blood* man, not a screen image—to pay attention to me in how long? What harm would it be to get to know him?

I splashed my cheeks and smoothed my hair. Better get back before he switched to someone else.

I'd barely stepped out the door when a big bushy-haired guy rushed past me. I recognized him by his canvas bag: the orange-fingered slob who'd fixed my router. I waited until he reached the karaoke machine and was talking to the bartender before I returned to my seat.

"Took you so long?" Zuzie said. "Here, you earned this." She slid over a shot glass of high proof rum which could have melted steel.

My blond house painter friend was in deep discussion with the guy beside him, though he raised an eyebrow my way. On stage, Elias had the karaoke machine opened up. He yanked out a circuit board, then took a deep breath, blew inside, and was enveloped by a dust cloud. He put the machine back together, pushed a button, and it started right up, to cheers and applause.

"Gotta clean this baby once in a while," he said, then picked up the microphone and spoke in a deep baritone: "One for the money, two for the show. Whose turn was it up here, serenading you all with...according to the log—*Sex Machine?*"

Mindy shouted, "Serena!"

First our table, then the whole pub chanted and stomped their feet, "Serena! Sex Machine! Serena! Sex Machine!"

Zuzie forced me to stand. I was too drunk to resist.

Elias grinned when he saw me. "Oh. Hey, *that* Serena." Then he said into the mic for the entire universe to hear. "First time I've seen you with all your clothes on."

The entire building erupted into drunken guffaws like a barn full of donkeys. All by itself the unfinished glass of rum in my hand transformed into a projectile. Elias ducked. The glass struck the karaoke machine. A mist of seventy-five-point-five percent pure alcohol burst into a blue corona of electric flame.

I nearly tripped over my chair, dodging a meant-to-be-reassuring outstretched arm of Mr. Blond Painter, who called to my fleeing back: "I'll friend you!"

I ran out into the chilly night, and kept running down the dark empty street.

A car pulled alongside. Zuzie held up the purse I'd left behind and told me to hop in.

Chapter 4

Life wasn't supposed to be this way.

I wasn't supposed to end up spending my days in an empty living room facing a cheap acrylic painting and a wall clock, and an ugly green carpet that made my nose itch no matter how often I vacuumed, with only hamsters for living company.

My parents always exhorted: "Don't be anonymous!" They never coaxed me toward one profession or another, so long as it was one I could excel in. "Find your heart's mission, and you can't help but stand out and make a name for yourself," Dad always said. "Don't be a consumer, be a creator," Mama added. Grand advice from a generation who all dreamed of being rock stars or actors or globe-trekking authors back in the days when those kinds of success stories might have been real. Long before the era when being a "creator" meant watching your work pirated online or done cheaper by some Bangladeshi villager. In a way, my generation's attitudes toward creative work were purer than my Dad's hippie-dippie notions, since we couldn't even fantasize about making a living from it. Heart's missions were for rich kids.

Not that Dad practiced what he preached. I doubted his dream was to sell house alarm systems for an Asian conglomerate. But he did excel at it, meaning he was gone most of the time I was growing up, making sales calls throughout the Cal-Ari-Nev tri-state territory. Mama used to practice a New-Age-meets-the-suburbs organic lifestyle, but now all she mostly did was drink.

My little sister took their words to heart and became their favorite practically before she could walk. She sniffed out challenges the way dogs sniff utility poles, butting heads with life—literally: the more violent the sport, the more she threw herself into it. At sixteen she was already weighing offers for rugby scholarships. No anonymity for her.

Dad and Mama were half-hearted in support of my choice to major in English. Mama hoped it might lead me into publishing, having instilled in me a love of books, and she half-joked about me becoming her source of free advance reader copies. But I was drawn to the language itself.

Delving into English vocabulary and grammar, I felt like Alice entering the looking glass, twisting and turning through an eccentric historical epic: Greek roots wrestling with Latin conjugations, ravished by monosyllabic Germanic nouns, whirlwind invasions of Angles and Saxons, Celts and the French, before streaming to America and feasting on Spanish and Algonquin and West African Creole—what we now knew as English. I was intoxicated by languages and syntax. For a while I dreamed of being a United Nations interpreter, until I discovered that all the theory in the world didn't make up for the fact that my hopelessness at learning other languages was more likely to trigger a war than prevent one.

Yet I had a knack for helping foreign students with their English. It started informally, hunched over a corner table in the central cafeteria, correcting their writing or tuning their pronunciation for oral presentations. Though I never asked for compensation, hardly a day passed that I wasn't offered tasty Asian or Latin American snacks, even a pair of hand-embroidered shoe liners from Mongolia.

Word spread, and one day I found six Taiwanese students lined up at my door, then a gaggle of laughing Micronesians. I began to charge a token fee. My students reported better grades than I was receiving in my linguistics courses. I'd discovered my calling.

During a Christmas visit home, I found my parents more resigned than delighted, which infuriated me. After all, I'd fulfilled their expectations: I'd found my heart's mission, one in which I seemed to stand out. It wasn't artistic, nor achievement-oriented, like my sister's dislocating shoulders on a rugby pitch, but it was doing good for mankind by bringing cultures together and helping others to interact with the world. Wasn't that hippie enough for them? Their flaccid approval had me crying into my pillow.

Back on campus, I was determined to finish my degree as soon as possible and dive into my new-found career. I imagined standing before a classroom of multi-hued faces in a wild medley of colorful clothing. I played out lessons in my head: students taking turns giving oral reports about their home countries—one week the subject would be traditional desserts, another week public transport. Together we'd improve not only their English but international understanding. I would strut before the blackboard—the ringmaster, the conductor, their instructor, their friend. And each of them, so different, from so many places, sharing a united identity in English. "Don't be anonymous," I would proclaim.

Then came graduation; reality struck with the force of a lead pipe. School budgets shrinking. Vying for teaching positions against desperate unemployed PhDs and every other freshly-minted English major in America. One of my classmates ran off to teach in Thailand, for which I had neither the guts nor the airfare. Most others used their considerable English composition skills to scrawl customers' names on coffee cups.

As I watched my classroom dreams evaporate like spilled soup on a hot stove, I knew I had three choices: drag myself starving and bleeding through the bed of nails that was graduate school, beg a job as an online tutor, or move back in with Mama and Dad to a chorus of *tsk-tsk's*.

Online tutoring companies were less like schools than language brothels, with wages adjusted down toward the lowest common denominator of what some bright-eyed graduate in the Philippines might expect. Yet even among these new bastions of education, I was in a cat fight to land a job. Application after application produced either crickets or more pillows dampened with tears. Then Dad's ridiculous mantra appeared one night like a neon sign in the dark. That was my trouble. My job applications were no more remarkable than everyone else's. I was anonymous.

I gathered as many of my tutoring students as I could find, snuck them into an empty classroom, duct-taped a selfie stick to a chair and recorded video testimonies about my qualities as an instructor of the English language—including countless retakes to correct incriminating flubbed grammar—edited down to a 90-second infomercial with a light hip-hop beat.

Twenty-two days, five form rejections, and three non-responses later, I was down to one last place on my list, the bottom of the barrel, my final resort before I completely gave up hope.

I clicked send.

Five minutes later I received a call from Marisa at iEnglishU.com.

I was an English teacher, the calling I'd dreamed of.

I was an English teacher—low-paid, underworked, stuck by myself in the corner of a barren living room.

Maybe life was supposed to be this way.

Maybe dreams that come true in bits and pieces are the only dreams worth having.

Chapter 5

*A*fter the pub night fiasco I didn't step out of the apartment all week, aside from one late-evening supermarket run, where the cashier eyed me curiously as if he might have been witness to my karaoke meltdown. I occasionally passed Zuzie on the way to the bathroom, but we exchanged hardly a word. Not that we were avoiding each other, but Zuzie was caught in her own melodrama with some mysterious manfriend, who she confided was "sweet as heaven but married as hell."

At least the International Incident of the Chomped Ethernet Cable had a positive outcome, or so I thought. Bieber's mother insisted that my pay not be docked for the missed session. What's more, her slippers had been conspicuously absent from his lessons.

On Thursday I couldn't hold back from asking. I typed in the message window: *Is your mother there?*

Bieber hesitated, then typed: *Not*

NO, not NOT, I typed back, answering his baffled look out loud: "I asked a yes-no question, so you answer *yes* or *no.*"

"You don't ask yes or no, you ask mother here. Not here, so I write *not.*" He checked his online dictionary, then regarded me with a satisfied smirk, his most genuine smile in days. "Logical."

"Logical. Very good use of that word. English not—*tsk!*—English *is* not logical sometimes."

I sent my warmest smile to the opposite side of the world. Without his mother breathing down his neck, I'd expected Bieber to be more at ease, yet I'd never seen him so tense. Then realization struck. I knew I shouldn't say the next words, which might be recorded by iEnglishU, but I could defend them as continuing the theme of yes-no questions.

"I made your mother lose face, didn't I? Answer yes or no."

Bieber bobbed his head side to side. "Maybe yes."

"Then I don't understand. Why does she want me to teach you? Why didn't she make you change to a new teacher?"

His lips silently repeated my words, constructing their meaning inside his head. Meanwhile, my mind raced with various theories of Chinese notions of blame and shame: by not changing instructors, by asking for my pay to be reinstated, his mother demonstrated power over me, since I would of course be aware of her magnanimity. Kind of a passive-aggressive victory with Chinese characteristics. Maybe I'd find it in Sun Tzu. Of course, asking Bieber to explain would have tied his basic grammar into knots. Then he hit me with a look that made me flinch—a half smile, eyebrows stretched to the ceiling, as though he'd read my thoughts and considered them the most foolish thing in the world.

"I am not..." Again he checked his dictionary. "... accept—*accepting?*—new teacher."

I turned aside, dabbing my watering eyes as inconspicuously as I could. He'd fought with his mother. Over me.

He also looked away, embarrassed at my embarrassment. I cleared my throat. "Let's review Lesson 14, dialogue part three. You're Jerry, I'm the Post Office Clerk."

I HAD THE NEXT hour free, having received notice only this morning that my Thursday morning eight o'clock, a Mexico City business woman, had not renewed at the end of her three-month package. She'd hardly needed English lessons anyway, a compliment I'd lavished on her perhaps once too often.

Note to self: praise students at one's own peril.

I used the opportunity for a bathroom break and half a pear. When I returned there was a pop-up notice in my personal inbox: a random friend request from somebody named Steve. Not being infected with Chronic Friending Syndrome—my miniscule social media network was strictly limited to people I'd genuinely met in the flesh—I was about to delete, when something made me lean in and squint at the tiny profile photo: the house painter from the Grove & Chicken. So that was his name. I clicked *Accept*.

The school's Admin page indicated that the office manager was online. Marisa picked up on the second ring.

"Morning, sweetie. Was about to call," she said. "Package came for you a few minutes ago." She reached under her desk, her silver loop earrings tinkling like wind chimes, and came back up shaking a small box tied with twine. "From *Mexico*"—she pronounced it the Spanish way—"Goodbye present, I suppose."

My dropout's kindness warmed me. The fact that students sent gifts didn't hurt my reputation among the administrators, though I wished they earned me points on my ranking. "Forward it when you have a chance, okay?"

"Absolutely, sweetheart. I should get a cut of these treasures you guys are sent. That's what I told Vicky—I want a room in her Swedish palace."

"I'm glad you brought her up, because that's what I want to talk to you about."

"I believe she's still taking applications for bridesmaids."

I bit my tongue. I'd as soon be Victoria's bridesmaid as her pallbearer. "Look, Marisa, I know you think I nag you, but when Victoria's on leave, honeymoon, whatever, maybe you might have me fill in with some of her students?"

Marisa rattled my packet close to her ear, trying to divine its contents. "Sure, baby, I'll forward your request."

"Come on, Marisa. I just lost one. You've got to send more students my way."

She folded her arms on the desk and leaned in. "Serena, don't you think it hurts me, too, to lose them right and left to every new so-called school that pops up offering five dollar lessons in an Islamabad accent? I've got fifty-eight hungry teachers to look after. You're like my children! I'd give my right arm to see every one of my children fat and happy."

"I'm not asking to get fat. Please—"

"Try my best." Her lips puckered like a sea anemone: meeting over.

"I call dibs on the next Nordic royalty."

"You got it, honey." She clicked off.

I USED TO THINK I was hopeless at learning languages. After struggling through two required semesters of French, I forgot every word *tout suite*. But when it came to linguistic pig-headedness I was no match for Vlad, my Tuesday and Thursday nine o'clock. He ran a heavy equipment rental yard somewhere in southern Bulgaria. Maybe a wrecking ball had struck him in the left temporal lobe, the area of the brain responsible for verbal language skills, or maybe it was a lifelong overindulgence in vodka or whatever Bulgarians drank, but he'd driven his English language tractor into a ditch somewhere in Lesson 8 and remained stuck in the mud of vocabulary drills about Dining Out two weeks later. A beefy fortyish man, all black eyebrows and paintbrush mustache, he claimed he needed English to expand his business into Europe, but I got the impression that his evening (Bulgarian time) lessons with me were rather a twice-weekly escape from after-dinner conversations with his wife.

Vlad greeted me with an impish grin that turned his mustache into a horizontal bracket.

"Hallo how are you lovely teacher?"

I'd taught him the meaning of *lovely* last week and it had become his favorite word.

"Hello, Vladimir. I am very well. How are you today?"

"Today I am..." He leaned into the screen. "...*hot* for learn English! Can say, yes? Hot?"

"Yes, you can say." I considered whether complimenting his ingenuity in looking up slang would violate my new resolution not to heap students with praise. But I couldn't help it. "Very clever. But maybe *passionate* is better. Today I am passionate about learning English."

"*Hot* more easy saying."

Fifteen minutes into the lesson, I interrupted his fourth botched attempt to identify pictures of hard-boiled, soft-boiled, fried, scrambled, and poached eggs. I wished the lesson, the whole day, were over, but I still had three more students.

"Vlad, I think you're bored with Lesson 8. Bored." I tipped my head and shut my eyes to indicate the meaning.

He nodded his head, which in Bulgaria meant *no*. "Not bored. Having beautiful lovely teacher, never bored."

"Maybe today we begin Lesson 9. Okay?"

Again the negative nod. "Finish Lesson 8." He tapped his temple. "Stupid man. But I not...*ay!* Moment." Dictionary time, then he gazed into the camera with priest-like sincerity. "I am not hasty bitch."

"What?"

"In Bulgaria, we say: Hasty bitch make born blind puppies. You don't know? Meaning—work too fast, bad finish."

"Haste makes waste."

"I think." His head swiveled side to side, meaning *yes*. A bushy eyebrow ascended like one of his forklifts. "Also I think lovely teacher bored Lesson 8. Yes? No? I see your..." He patted his mouth. "Today sad."

I tried to erase whatever mood had tainted my features by forcing a laugh, but it came out more astonished than amused. I made a point never to reveal my personal life to students, but at the same time the teacher in me couldn't pass up an opportunity for unscripted dialogue.

"Today I am a little bit worried," I said. "But not about you."

"Worried?" He searched his memory for the meaning of the word. "Ah. Why you worried? Is—?" He mimed coughing, making a sick face.

"No, it isn't my *health*. I am very healthy. Are you healthy?"

He waved aside my question. "I know! Beautiful hot fox chick—"

"Foxy, not fox." Where was he finding these words?

"Beautiful *foxy* chick worried, problem is money, yes?" He shook his head, *yes,* then his face brightened. "Tell me PayWallet account, I give fifty dollars."

The little image of me in the corner of the screen showed my mouth hanging open. I clamped it shut.

He tapped his ear. "Internet working? You hearing? Tell me account number, I send fifty."

"Yes, I heard. That is a very kind offer, but I can't accept..."

"Can. Is business offer. I give fifty dollars. You—" He mimed unbuttoning his shirt and pulling it open, then wiggled his chest.

This time I didn't bother re-fastening my jaw. I wondered if he saw my face turn red.

"I like looking. You like fifty dollar. Two person happy. No problem!"

I crossed my arms over my chest, anger tempered only slightly by the almost naïve innocence in his face. Unwilling to lose yet one more student today, I composed myself before I spoke.

"Vlad, listen. Please never ask me that again. Never ask any woman. Do you understand? It is not appropriate. It is not—" What was a better word that he would comprehend?

"It is not *cool,* yes?" he said.

I nodded, which must have confused him. "Yes. A very good word. It is not cool. I am your teacher. I like to be your teacher.

36

You are a good student. You're a nice man, but...please, never ask that again. Okay?"

"Okay. No problem."

Miraculously, he flew through the egg section of the vocabulary drill without error, and only twice had to repeat the exercise about asking for the check, bringing Lesson 8 to a weary and triumphant end. He slapped his textbook shut with a fat, satisfied grin.

"I give one hundred dollars, is cool?"

My face burned with rage that could have fried one of Lesson 8's eggs. Was there some cultural issue at play here, or was he just being a scumbag? Or was I?—because deep down I was calculating what I could do with the hundred bucks.

"Before, fifty. Now I am two-timing you!"

Teacher Serena overruled Pissed Off Serena and Desperate Serena and took a deep breath.

"That's the wrong word," I said, watching his face fall. I explained the meaning and usage of *two-timing,* as in cheating on his wife.

Vlad brightened again. "Ah! I am doing that, too!"

By the time I finished my last lesson of the day, with a woman fitness trainer in Ecuador, I felt dizzy and stuffed up as though a dust devil whirled inside my skull, while something—an octopus—squeezed like a vice around my ribs. My personal inbox overflowed with eleven messages from Steve the painter. I almost didn't notice the blinking light in my work window. A message from Marisa.

Check your Friday 12:00

I glanced at my schedule. Sure enough, it had been booked. She knew damn well that was my lunch hour. Worse, it was a freebie introductory lesson, for which I didn't get paid. Worse yet, Friday freebies usually lost interest over the weekend and never signed up for paid lessons. I was about to click Respond to ask her to reschedule, when I found a follow-up note from her:

You owe me, honey.

Chapter 6

*Y*asmin wasn't thrilled with Lesson 25.

"Why I need to learn 'Shopping for Clothes' in English? Dress is too expensive in America. Fabric no good. In Turkey cheaper and best. Don't need English."

"Because," I explained, "we're learning comparative modifying clauses. For example: Clothing made in Turkey is better than that made in America."

"Say again?"

She was in a touchy mood, something else on her mind. It was one of the rare days that her headscarf was solid gray, nearly matching the color of the sky through the window behind her.

"I'll try another sentence." I brushed back my hair, which I'd conditioned that morning for an extra bit of bounce to impress the free intro student at noon. "Guys who wear glasses look smarter than those who wear none."

"I don't understand." Yasmin moaned. "When I can skip to Lesson 32?"

"When *can I* skip to Lesson 32?" I corrected. "The answer is: you can not. Eight more lessons. Starting with modifying clauses. Please turn to page 91."

I didn't know whether to be amused or annoyed at her agitation. She forged through such admittedly useless textbook constructions as, "The woman wearing a purple dress is older than the one wearing green," but was sloppy in coming up with original examples. The lesson finally over, a relief to us both, she slapped her book shut.

"Special words?" Her whole demeanor changed when I nodded; her eyes brightened. "I join online dating site, many nice boys! One, he is from Australia, very handsome! He wants be my boyfriend."

Hairs prickled on the back of my neck. She was only seventeen. I wondered which website, how much personal data she'd revealed. With four minutes until my next student, I had little time to advise or give out warnings.

"Which special words?" I said.

"He ask many questions I don't understand."

"We have time for one."

Her keyboard clacked. "He ask, 'Are you spitter or swallower?'"

I bit my lips. A little snort escaped from my nose.

"What, you also don't understand?"

"Oh, I understand," I said.

I had two and a half minutes. I cut to the chase, explaining as delicately as I could, while Yasmin's big dark eyes popped wide, nostrils flared, her face flushed, and she held a hand over her mouth as though about to be sick. Then she let out a whoop and vanished from the screen with a loud thump. I instinctively stood up, and was about to call her when I heard gulping laughter. I couldn't help but burst out laughing too. She picked herself up, headscarf askew, both of us struggling for breath in between horselaughs.

"I think I," she gasped, "I look...new boyfriend." Then she clicked off, leaving me about twenty seconds to pull myself together for an owlish fifty-something property manager in the capital of Estonia.

MY ELEVEN O'CLOCK, IN Sao Paulo, ended right on time. I dashed to the kitchen, gulped down a yogurt drink, and returned to my desk, where I opened the files for introductory lessons. The content hardly mattered; the trick to hooking a fish was to lay the encouragement on thick, maintain constant eye contact, and repeat their name as often as possible. Skills I could have employed standing under a street lamp on Harbor Boulevard on a Friday night, for much higher pay.

I glanced through the trial student's information form. Name: A. Buonaventura. Gender: male. Country: Italy. Reason for learning English: business. I imagined some stubble-faced guy with heavy lids and thinning, slicked-back hair, working out of a cluttered office in Naples. Except it was nine o'clock at night in Italy. He'd probably be at his kitchen table with chest hair billowing out of a tank top.

A yellow circle turned green. He was online, waiting. I clicked the call button. Hair, eyes and chin came into focus on the screen. My mouth went dry as a fossil.

"Buonasera, signorina."

Facing me was Adonis, Romeo, Michelangelo's David, and half the Italian national soccer team—the sexier half—all rolled into one granite-jawed living sculpture. From the black curls cascading over a marble-smooth forehead, to yearning dark eyes, a nose that deserved a place in a museum, and lips which made my mouth water, he could have been a movie star, a fashion model—he couldn't be real; this was a setup, Marisa's idea of a practical joke!

"Signorina? Hallo. Are you hear me?"

His voice had a cello's silken resonance. Mine in response squeaked like a chair scraping across tiles.

"I...oh. Um. Start again. Hello. I am happy to meet you. My name is Serena."

He held out his hand as if inviting me to dance. "Serena. *Un bel nome.* My name...is...Alessandro. English no good."

"You look very clever." I accentuated each word with my

hand: pointing first to him, then to my eyes, then touching my head; straight out of the company guidelines. "For you, English is easy."

He responded with a smile that made my groin sizzle like Pop Rocks.

"Alessandro, how old are you?" He didn't seem to get it, so I tapped my chest. "I am twenty-three years old. How old are you?"

"Ah, *si si si*. I am, ah, twenty"—he counted on his fingers—"five years."

"You are twenty-five years old. Very good! Do you have brothers and sisters?" He didn't seem to get it, so I typed *brother* in the chat window.

"Broe-ther," he said, nodding. "No have broe-ther."

"You do not have a brother?"

"No have—ah! *Che cretino!*" He performed an elaborate hand pantomime, slapping his cheek and flapping his wrist. "I do not have a brother."

I gave him a thumbs-up. "Excellent, Alessandro. You learn fast."

"Excellent teacher." He returned my thumbs-up and pursed his lips in a way that set fire to those remaining parts of my body that weren't already engulfed in flames. Forget asking about sisters and parents. Cut straight to the bone.

"Do you have a wife?"

"Wife...wife..." He held his hands together like in prayer, then flung them apart. "Ah! *Wife!* Yes, I know." Without thinking, my hand went to my throat and I stopped breathing. If he was married, I swore I would kill myself right on the spot. His mouth curled at one end. "I do not have a wife."

My lungs took in air. "Excellent," I said, meaning it most sincerely. My hand slid down, discreetly unfastening the top button of my blouse.

"You have a 'usband?" His head tilted with a wicked grin. "You ask, I ask."

"I do not have a husband."

"Excellent."

I had to get hold of myself before I wet my chair. I checked the guidelines file. He was beyond novice level, so I clicked on Elementary 1: good–better–best, using dialogues about work and hobbies.

"Do you have a job?" I typed the word *job*. He looked it up.

"Yes. Have a job."

"Is it a good job?"

He laughed. "Now good, now bad, now–" His hand rocked side to side.

"So-so. Ha. What is your good, bad, so-so job?"

"Olive oil."

"Mm! I love olive oil. Is Italian olive oil good?"

"Is good!"

"Is Greek olive oil good?"

"Oil from Greek? *Pipí di gatto!* Italian olive oil more more good."

This was where I wanted him. "Italian olive oil is *better* than Greek olive oil." I typed better. "Please tell me."

"Italian olive oil is better than Greek olive oil."

"Good–better–best," I said. "What is the *best* olive oil?"

He pretended to think. *"Pool-ya* oil is best in...in...*ai!"*

"The world, right? Pool-ya olive oil is the best in the world."

"See? You know! Why you ask?" His laugh spawned thoughts of bright green fields under a golden Mediterranean sun. Though I had no idea what "Pool-ya" was. A brand?

"How do you write *Pool-ya,* Alessandro?"

A word appeared in the chat window: *Puglia.*

"All person, they know. Oil to Puglia is best," he said.

I guessed it was a place. *"From* Puglia," I corrected.

"Oil from Puglia is best."

"Excellent, Alessandro. Let's practice good–better–best." In the white panel on the right of the screen I shared cartoons of customers in a shop: a lady making a small purchase with coins, a man handing over a fistful of cash, and a third buying sparkly jewelry with a credit card, each to a progressively happier shop-keeper. I typed the word *customer*.

"Can you see? Mrs. Green is a good customer, but Mr. Garcia is a better customer, and Miss Chow is the best customer. Can you tell me about your customers, Alessandro?"

He pursed his lips in thought. I finally relaxed, treating him like a student, keeping it professional and businesslike. But, damn, he was hot!

"O-*kay.*" He raised the second syllable like an eager little boy. He counted on his fingers. "Argentina is good customer, America is better customer, and Japan is best customer."

"Ah. So you are an exporter." I typed the word, and he nodded. "Who is your *best* supplier?" I typed the last word and waited while he looked it up.

"One supplier," he said, pointing to himself. "Family have the farm. Fifty-eight *hectare.* Two thousand and six hundred of trees."

My mind spun. He'd said he had no brother. Even if he had sisters, Italian family businesses were strictly patriarchal, weren't they? At least they were in "The Godfather". That made him sole heir to an international olive oil business. Not only was he handsome, young, charming, and single. He was rich!

I reminded myself to stay focused, keep my mind on the lesson. Good–better–best, good–better–best. Or in Alessandro's case, out of the ballpark all the way to the moon. I hoped he couldn't hear my guts gurgling.

"You are not well?" he said.

"No no no. I'm fine. I'm good. I'm better. I'm best!" We

both laughed. "Let's do one more practice. Cars from America are good. Cars from Germany are better. But cars from Italy..." I nodded.

"Good, some not good. My think, from Germany cars are best."

"Excellent, Alessandro. Now you."

"I?" He appeared scared at having to come up with an original sentence. But he quickly recovered, stroked his chin, then one end of his mouth curled upward. "Girls from Sicily are good, girls from Puglia are better. But American girls maybe are best."

That smacked of a cheap pickup line, though at least it answered the crucial question of whether he preferred women. I conducted the rest of the lesson smoothly and professionally, moving through other comparative-superlatives—big–bigger–biggest, far–farther–farthest—while scooping up more information about him. He lived far from Rome, farther from Venice, near the farthest tip of Italy's boot heel. His nearest neighbors had a big vineyard, but his olive farm was bigger, the biggest in his area.

As the session neared its end, panic crept in. Would I see him again? What if he wasn't impressed with the lesson? Or what if he was, but he requested a time for which I was already booked, and they assigned him to someone else? If Victoria nabbed him, I'd drive all the way to San Jose to personally scratch her eyes out. I thought of which students I could juggle. Yasmin would understand. Bieber I could move to one in the morning his time if necessary; his mother wouldn't care.

"Well, Alessandro, our time is up."

He combed his fingers through his hair and exhaled as if he'd just completed a race.

I sent him a pre-prepared document which listed the word sets we'd covered. "This is for you to keep. Alessandro, I hope you enjoyed—"

"Sandro."

"Excuse me?"

"You, me, friends. You say me Sandro."

"You and I are friends. I call you Sandro. Now you say it."

"Ai! Lesson finished! But o-*kay*. I say. You and I are friends. I call you Serena?"

He could call me bitch if he wanted and it would sound adorable in that musical accent, that sonorous voice which echoed in my ears for the next hour while a Belgian mangled the *r's* and *th's* in "The Rain in Spain".

Chapter 7

I was wrestling ancient Greek style—naked and slathered in olive oil—except that my opponent wasn't Greek, but an equally buff and oiled Italian man. He had me pressed against him in a nelson hold until I flipped and pinned him to the mat in a full body scissors lock, thick green drops of extra virgin dribbling from my chin and breasts onto his face. Never mind that in ancient Greece only men wrestled.

The apartment doorbell called an end to the match. I glanced at my phone: who would be visiting at 8:45 on a Saturday morning? Should I wait for Zuzie to get it? No, that wouldn't happen. I shrugged on a robe and padded to the door.

"Oopsy, did I wake you?" Elias said. "Oh, man. I'm sorry."

"Wait!" I shut the door in his face. No more cracks about seeing me half-dressed. I pulled on jeans and a pink long-sleeved jersey top. I gave up brushing the tangles from my hair and tied it back into a tumbleweed pony tail.

When I opened the door again Elias was leaning on the door-frame hugging a canvas backpack. His pants looked like they'd been ironed sometime in the past 72 hours; apparently his idea of dressing up.

"Hi." He spread all ten fingers. "See? No synthetic cheese residue. Ah...oops." He sucked one fingernail clean.

"I didn't call in any computer problems," I said.

"Look, I came by to apologize for, you know, the other night?"

"That was a week ago. Not that I care anymore."

He stared at me, as awkward as a human being could be. Then he patted his bag. "Can I show you something?"

I stepped aside. Elias swept hair from his eyes and set his bag down on the couch. "How are the hamsters? Laurel and Hardy—see? I remember. Any new attempts to bring down the global information network?"

"They're good." I stepped into the kitchen and took orange juice from the fridge without offering any. "So you were saying, you came over to apologize for—let me see...wrecking my clothes? Or is it for making me out as a slut in front of the entire world? Or did you say something worse after I left?"

"I was a total asshole, okay? I'm so sorry I could...*um*...what I want to say is...in mitigation I must point out that I'm an engineer, which means the people skills lobe of my brain atrophied at birth. Which means—oh, hell, I don't know what it means. Here."

With that, he tipped his bag onto the kitchen counter, and out slipped a pink laptop computer with a Hello Kitty logo.

"For you," he said.

I nearly spat out my juice. I could understand a guy I barely knew, who had pissed me off and publicly humiliated me, trying to make amends. But an expensive computer, even a girlie one, was treading way over the line.

"I know, I know," he said. "Doesn't quite match your pajamas. But it's what's inside that counts."

"I can't accept this."

"Sure you can. Last time I was here, you were crying about your dying laptop. If anyone desperately needs a computer, it's either starving kids in South Sudan or you. And this doesn't have a Sudanese keyboard."

"I can't possibly pay you back."

"I'm not asking you to. Look, if it makes you feel any better...I wasn't going to say, but...it didn't cost me a dime, okay? Got it from a company bankruptcy blowout. They owed me for some consulting, and in lieu of cash, slipped me a couple computers before the creditors got wind. So I figured in exchange for some nastiness you didn't deserve, a computer that I didn't pay for."

"Wow."

"Think it mighta been meant for the boss's mistress. But don't worry—certified free of communicable diseases." He nudged it toward me. "Fair?"

I palmed my forehead. "Wow wow wow. Fair, I guess."

He carried it to my desk and raised the cover. The screen, the keyboard, everything looked brand new. He grinned at the shock on my face. "Want me to set it up for you?"

"Can I get you an orange juice?" I replied.

He sat at my desk installing programs and transferring files from my old computer, while talking non-stop. "Course I swapped out the hard drive. So you got in here a next-gen solid state drive, boots up so fast it'll give you blisters. Two-point-four gigs throughput Wi-Fi, no more cables for hamster snacks. UHD touch screen, eight gigs onboard graphics, so if you do any gaming..."

"My whole life's a game. Excuse me a minute." I needed to compose myself before I said something stupid and ruined the moment. Anyway, he was still busy. I made my bed, fed and watered the hamsters, fixed my hair in front of the mirror, thinking what an odd and lucky girl I was. Thinking too of Sandro. How much cuter he'd look in my new high definition eight gig screen, or whatever it was. If he signed up for lessons. Which I wouldn't find out until at least Monday or Tuesday. An excruciating wait, but meanwhile I had this incredible surprise from Elias. I had to introduce him to Hardy, whose antics had led to this change in my fortunes.

"Ready for a test run?" Elias said. "Hey, who we got here?"

"The criminal who started all this." Hardy sniffed around on my palm, then raised his head in Elias's direction. "Want to hold him while I try the computer?"

Elias flinched when Hardy scampered from my hand into his. "Tickles. Hey, don't jump. Do they respond to commands? Sit! Hear me? Sit!"

I sat down and admired the computer's sleek lines, its pearly pink keyboard, the almost liquid gloss of the screen. I was hesitant at first to touch it, as though this was a momentous occasion: first contact between mother and newborn, explorer and newly discovered planet. Elias pointed to the Start icon.

I tried my e-mail, but of course had forgotten my password, which I'd have to rummage in my panties drawer to locate. My login for iEnglishU was burned into my brain, so I tried that next. The window opened so quickly I flinched. The teacher interface had never appeared so crisp on screen, each word as though seen through a magnifying glass. I checked my inbox: two students changing lesson times, the in-house company blog. And one with the subject line: *Bingo!* From Marisa, sent last night.

You hit the jackpot, babe. Italian signed twelve months Fi5, paid in full. Specified you. Congrats.

I re-read the message two or three hundred times. Our "Fluent-in-Five" package, that is, five lessons a week, paid in advance for a year. With me. That face, that voice, five days a week for a whole year!

Above it, a second message from Marisa, sent minutes after the first:

Bonus $150 in your account end of the week.

I typed Marisa a reply:

I owe you so bigtime

Then I screamed.

Could this day get any better? I'd forgotten how it felt to be so happy.

"Good news, I guess?" Elias said.

Then he screamed, a full-throated, blood-curdling howl.

A small brown furry object arced through space and bounced to a landing on the other end of the couch. Elias hopped around on one foot, hand clawing the air overhead, blood streaming down his wrist like in a horror movie. He ran to the kitchen and opened the faucet full-force over his finger.

"That little vermin better not have rabies!"

I scooped frightened, shivering Hardy from the couch, ran him back to his cage, then stopped in the bathroom to pick up antibiotic ointment and bandages.

"Oh my God, oh my God, I'm so sorry," I said. "Let me see."

The wound looked like a leaking semicolon at the tip of his fourth finger. I squeezed on ointment and wrapped it in a gauze strip. "Don't worry, he's clean. Do hamsters even get rabies? I don't know why he'd bite you. Unless—"

"Manicurist must have missed a spot of cheese powder under the fingernails."

I couldn't help but laugh. And laugh. "I'm so, so sorry. That must have really hurt. Here, let me do what my Mom always did to make it better."

I held his wrist, raised the bandaged finger to my lips and gave it a kiss.

His whole body seemed to melt. Maybe the kiss had been overkill.

"Wanna go get a coffee or something?" he said.

After Marisa's message, I felt rich. "I'm paying," I said.

My green Toyota sputtered like a horse for the whole five-minute trip to Frannie's, a genuine 1960s coffee shop retaining its original Formica tables, each with a plastic rose in a vase, and flower print wallpaper. In other words, a hangout for old ladies and bleary-eyed young hipsters. I indulged in one of their chocolate bomb brownies. Elias ordered scrambled eggs and toast. They offered two choices of coffee: black or white.

"I remember when I was little, my mom sometimes took me here," Elias said. "Still gave free coffee refills then. Can you imagine that nowadays? Waitress comes over, 'Can I top up your low-fat blueberry soy Frappuccino, sir?'"

"You grew up here?"

He swallowed half his coffee in one gulp. "Who'd move to this place by choice?"

I cocked my head and twiddled my fingers at him.

"Oh, man!" He scrunched his eyes, pounding his forehead. "Think I'll shut up and eat."

I laughed. "Yeah, I guess I moved here by choice. I mean, for college. Moved down from the Valley, so I can't say I went through culture shock. I call them North and South Suburbatory."

"Parents still there?" he said through a mouthful of runny scrambled eggs, little yellow globs spattering his t-shirt, already peppered with toast crumbs. His sloppiness was so unself-conscious it was almost charming. More big-boned than chubby, a few pounds less might tighten his cheeks. Add to that a desperately-needed haircut, new glasses—wire frames, definitely—a grown-up shirt, a bit less hunch to the shoulders...and he still wouldn't be my type, but hopefully somebody else's.

"My mama still lives there," I said. "Yours still around here?"

"Nope. Desert retirement community. Dante's Inferno with old people."

He washed down his eggs with the rest of his coffee, hoisted his bag onto his lap and unlatched a small side pocket. "Something else I wanted to give you." He winced when the bandaged finger caught on something, then slid a tiny memory card across the table.

"For the laptop?" I said.

"Nope. Took it from a guy's phone. You can keep it or cut it up. I recommend the latter."

The caffeine and sugary chocolate bomb were setting off sparks in my brain. I shot him a questioning look.

"So right after you ran out that night? The Grove & Chicken?" he said. "I see these guys—not the table where you were sitting. They're kind of bleating like mules while this one schmucktard's showing them something on his phone."

I dropped my fork onto the floor. "Oh, crap."

"Yeah, he videoed the whole thing—your little number before I got there, and my lame attempt at standup comedy. I probably shouldn't say this—you can watch it if you want—he kind of stalked you while you were running out, close-up on your butt. His best shot, to be honest. Um, I mean, the picture, not your— uh...I mean—know what? Maybe I should stick to the story."

"Good idea."

"So the guy sees me watching over his buddies' shoulders, holds up the phone, says to me, 'Hey, dude, you're a star!'"

I buried my face in my hands. "He didn't! Oh, for Christ's sake! He didn't!"

"Nope. Hasn't uploaded it. Not yet. So I'm thinking fast. I laugh along with him, then put on this big serious look and tell him there's this little shudder in the video that indicates his phone has some config issues. I kind of shrug and say, hey, I could fix that for you. So he hands me the phone, moves aside, invites me to sit. But I tell him I need better light near the bar. Jerk's wasted enough to believe me. Make a long story short, I swapped out the SD card for a blank."

"Which you conveniently happened to have."

He patted his bag. "Geek. Guilty as charged."

"And he couldn't tell?"

"I powered off the phone before handing it back. Then excused myself to the bathroom. And ran the hell out of there."

I wanted to throw up. Me and that embarrassing song, the exploding karaoke, and Elias's filthy joke—lesser things had become viral sensations online. I'd been saved in the nick of time from becoming an international laughing stock, which—who knows?—could have cost me my job, just when Sandro had come along.

"You okay?" Elias looked at me with concern.

"I'm okay. I'm fine. I'm great! You saved my butt. I'm so—" I picked up the chip on the tip of my finger and considered whether I wanted to watch, maybe even keep the video as a warning to self. Then I plunged it into the remains of my brownie.

"Good choice," Elias said. "Though he has some awesome music files on there you might like. Want me to...?" He reached for the brownie.

"No." I let out a deep breath. Disaster had been averted. "Thank you."

I smiled and sipped coffee. He smiled and sipped his empty cup.

"So..."

"So..."

"So I guess you're off today?"

"Um, yeah," I said. "You?"

He tapped the bulge in his shirt pocket. "Always on call. But, you know...weekends. It's either nothing or a major five-alarm catastrophe."

My rear end fidgeted on the seat. Elias had been very nice to me this morning, but I didn't want to give him any ideas. "I guess I need to answer some messages and plan for my new student on Monday," I told him, though said plans had more to do with slithering Greek wrestling fantasies than language tutorials. We stood up, and I paid at the register with my debit card. We drove back in silence.

I switched off the engine, listened to it tick.

"Yeah, well. Thanks for breakfast," Elias said.

"Oh, oh, thank *you* for the computer. I can never repay you enough. And the memory card thing. I'm just so..." I patted my chest.

We stepped from the car and faced each other as if about to head opposite ways, even though we had to walk the same direction out of the parking lot. His eyes, enlarged through smudged lenses, couldn't hide their pleading. I opened my arms and we exchanged a back-patting, no-strings-attached hug. His big body was soft in a memory foam mattress-like way.

"Thanks again," I said, then pulled away. All the emotions of that morning, the stresses and surprises and elations, welled up through my chest and throat. My eyes must have glazed over, because he asked, "You sure you're okay?"

"Fine. Just, um, allergies." I sniffed.

He nodded at his feet. "So if you have any problem with the computer, like, give me a shout."

"I will. And if you..." I didn't know what I was trying to say.

"Sure. If I ever need my nails clipped by a hamster, I know where to go."

Chapter 8

*M*onday morning I barreled through Bieber's lesson, as if pushing the pace would speed up time.

Then came Yasmin, as full of haste as I was. She'd spent her weekend getting a head start on Lesson 26, and shredded through two pages of new vocabulary without error. Not a peep about online dating adventures, and no special words. I worried why not.

My next two lessons were brisk and professional. I was saving all my personality for *him*.

The icon by his name turned green a full three minutes before the hour. The next 180 excruciating seconds were longer than all that morning's lessons combined.

Then there he was. Lips slanted up at one end, jaw so smooth that it practically outshone the brilliance of his eyes. Behind him a bookcase overflowed with file binders beside a small curtained window. I must have seen him before he was able to see me, because suddenly his smile spread, his cheeks creasing like the f-holes on a violin.

"Good evening, Sandro," I said.

He raised a hand in greeting. "Good evening, teacher."

"Please call me Serena."

"*Si, bene*. Good evening, Serena."

Had he forgotten already, "We are friends?" Never mind; we had time. An entire year.

"Where are you now, Sandro?" I carefully enunciated each word.

One eyebrow lifted. "Now I am on the Planet Earth."

"Me too!" I laughed. "But...I want to know: where are you sitting? I see books."

He looked behind him, then turned back. "Ah! Yes. Books. Where I am now? I am in...ah...*ufficio, ufficio, ufficio*..."

"Office?"

"Yes. I am in the office."

"Is the office in your house?"

"Your house...? *Si*. Yes. Business office in your—ah, *my* house." He shrugged; this was hard for him.

Of course his office was at home, to run his family's olive plantation. I imagined an ancient stone mansion ringed with stout, grandfatherly trees, a stucco-walled study with an oak table covered in leather-bound ledgers and quill pens.

Then he caught me off guard. "Your office is where?"

I was supposed to maintain the facade that I worked in a modern, air-conditioned hive of busy English teachers, each in his or her own soundproofed little cubicle facing a state-of-the-art terminal. In other words, an English factory. I always wondered why, when the truth sounded more personal.

"My office is in my home," I confessed, imitating his shrug.

"You go my home, I go your home."

"You...*come...to*...my home. I go...*to*...your home."

"Yes."

"Please say it," I said.

"You come to my home." His eyes shot heat-seeking needles through the webcam deep into the animal lobes of my brain. How soft his voice was, steeped in gentility, as though bred to speak this way.

I stifled my unprofessional thoughts and plunged straight into the lesson. Sandro's student profile indicated his textbook was in transit, so I uploaded Lesson 5, a good starting point for him: present and past progressive tenses and the word *so* as conjunction and adverb, all wrapped inside a dialogue about sports. As we navigated through such engaging repartee as, *"Are you working all day? No, I am leaving early today, so I can play tennis,"* I studied the contours of his face and its few endearing flaws—one nostril slightly flatter than the other, evidence of an old scar on one cheek. Sparks of panic stung my brain: did the webcam make me look fat? Did the ceiling lights heighten the freckly birth spots near my chin? I scribbled a note to myself:

Look up lighting tricks.

After about twenty minutes I had a new worry. Maybe I'd been through this lesson fifty times too many, or maybe the sentences were as dreary and banal as they all of a sudden seemed. *"The music was playing so loud that he did not hear the phone."* Boring to the max! Sandro's contract gave him one week to drop out and claim a full refund. At the end of Exercise 3 I closed the lesson plan.

"Teach me is difficult? Am *stupido*." He tapped his forehead.

"No, not stupid. Very smart! Now we do conversation. Using the grammar." I was winging it. Why did I feel so nervous, like a schoolgirl on a first date? I asked him to describe his work, his house, his family, using the conjunction *so*. I prompted: "Now it is July, so the olives..."

"Now it is July," he repeated, "so olives fly die."

I asked him to explain, sticking to the grammar.

"July sun very hot, *so* fly it die. Fly die, *so* olive is happy."

I guessed that fruit flies died off in the heat, allowing the young olive fruits to mature. He was delighted at my understanding. This was teaching at its best, both of us learning something and enjoying the conversation. I learned that he lived outside a small town and that Puglia, the region that encompassed Italy's boot heel, was covered with olive farms like his.

"I am thinking that it sounds beautiful," I said, making a lame example of present progressive.

"Here is like..." He looked away, then leaned forward, lowering his voice. "Is olive *Purgatorio*. You know Dante? Up, down, front, back, right and, ah..."

"Left."

"Left...you are seeing only olive, some little grape, no other. Purgatorio." He drew back, embarrassed, as if he'd confessed some private secret. "Is *scherzo*..." He looked it up. "A joke."

In my peripheral vision Zuzie's bedroom door creaked open. A tall, scholarly, very dark man tiptoed across the living room, tucking a white dress shirt into his slacks. He gave me a half-wink, held a finger to his lips, knelt to tie a shoe, then let himself out the front door with barely a sound.

"Serena? Teacher? You are fine?" Sandro said.

"I'm fine. Sorry."

"Okay, I use word *so*." He tapped his head. "New student is *difficile*, so teacher is feeling tired."

"The student is definitely not *difficult*," I said. "But our lesson is finished, so I must go."

"O-*kay!*" He raised a thumbs-up to the camera. "I say goodbye."

"Goodbye. See you tomorrow?" I said, making it a question. As if I was unsure.

"Tomorrow."

He lingered on screen until I clicked off.

As though waiting for her cue, Zuzie staggered out of her room in a yellow terry cloth robe, hair like an exploded shag carpet.

"Hey. Could hear you through the door, cooing like a pigeon. Hope he's a hottie."

My face flushed. "Yes, he's a hottie. I suppose that cat burglar I saw is your married friend?"

She ignored the question, spotting my bright pink Hello Kitty computer apparently for the first time. "That is so cute-tastic! Where'd you get it? I want one!"

Sandro's lesson had left me both drained and buzzing, like my heart had been bungee jumping for the past hour. Sandro was funny and charming, and required lots of help with his English. He was my project. He needed me. He was mine!

Fortunately, it was my lunch hour. I was in the mood for tagliatelle and grilled Mediterranean flounder smothered in garlic and of course olive oil, but settled for leftover chicken salad, sliced bread that was beginning to curl, and a clinically depressed tomato.

"Mindy says Steve's been messaging you." Zuzie emptied a container of shrimp fossilized in orange gelatinous goop over a bowl of cold elbow noodles and condemned it to the microwave. "Dude's sweet. You gonna reply?"

I carried my makeshift sandwich to the counter and sat on a stool.

"Zuzie, I wonder whether there exists a remote possibility somewhere in another dimension that we can for once talk about something other than men?"

"Gotcha." She ran her sizzling lunch over to the counter. We ate in silence, exchanging occasional glances, until she couldn't hold back any longer. She licked orange gloss from her lips.

"Okay, Serena, I've got to clear the air once and for all. You think I'm always trying to turn you into the slut you believe I am. So first we need to clarify one thing, okay? Honey, I don't need men to validate me. I don't chase after guys, never have. But they sure as shit chase after me, ever since I lost my baby fat, even before then. Like flies to honey. Can I help it if I'm gorgeous?"

I choked on stale bread crust. Was she joking? Her face didn't look it.

"It's all I ever hear—'Oh, you so pretty, baby, you just so beautiful'—like I'm going to say, 'Wow, nobody told me that since this morning. Sir, you deserve a fuck.' Know how I learned to scare them off?"

"Say it."

"Guy tells me, 'You beautiful,' I say straight, 'I know I'm beautiful. Tell me something interesting.' They back off quick, like I'm some snake poised to bite."

I laughed, which I regretted instantly. She looked away.

"Cause I do know it," she said to the wall, then to me: "I know I'm beautiful, outside and in."

"You say it as if it's a curse."

"Funny you should mention that." She picked up a noodle between her fingers and sucked it in. "You know the guy you called cat burglar? Associate Professor of Neurophysics. Comes into the coffee shop, I serve him a caffè americano, and he pulls a line, 'You so beautiful baby I don't need no caffeine.' So I hit back with, 'Tell me something interesting.' And guess what? He does exactly that. Tells me about some new research about caffeine's effects on the polarity of brain synapses."

"Which isn't really that interesting," I said.

"Guess what? The way he tells it, it's *damn* interesting. Dude keeps standing there while I'm working, telling these stories." Zuzie carried her empty bowl to the sink, squirted in detergent and turned on the faucet, then stood with her head bent. "How come the first asshole with any substance to come along has to be goddamn married?"

She leaned back, toweling her hands. "But we were talking about you."

"You were, not me." The wall clock told me half an hour had passed. I itched to go to the computer and search about the olive business and Italy's boot heel.

"I shouldn't, I know I shouldn't, but I worry about you, Serena. All I'm saying is, maybe you can consider, for once in your life, grabbing an opportunity to be happy that's being shoved right in your face? You're beautiful too—well, if you did something with the hair. Maybe you need to believe it a little."

"I'll work on the hair," I said, glancing deliberately at the clock.

"Steve's a good dude, and he ain't married, all I'm saying." Zuzie strode toward her room. "Time for me to head off to the trenches."

That afternoon, Vlad repeated his offer of a hundred dollars. Maybe if I'd said, 'Tell me something interesting,' he'd have upped it to two hundred.

Another message arrived from Steve, his only one so far today. Poor guy. In my excitement over Alessandro I'd let him slip my mind. He was asking me out. All right, Zuzie, I will grab. I clicked *reply*.

Chapter 9

Taking on a new English student is like *The Art of War*.

*To assess the enemy's situation and create
conditions that lead to victory, to analyze
natural hazards and proximate distances,
this is the way of the superior commander.*

Or teacher.

This was where I was with Sandro, scoping out the other side's strengths and weak points, the vulnerabilities in his defenses, while targets came into focus. After a week of daily lessons, he and I had settled into the roles of student and teacher, trading salvos in the Battle of the Gerunds.

I fired the day's first volley: "I eat bread. I like..."

"I like *eating* bread," he shot back, straight from the textbook.

"I drink milk."

His mouth twisted as if tightened with a wrench. "I do not drinking milk?"

"Use the word 'like'. I do not like *drinking* milk," I said.

"Since I am child, no milk. I can say, 'I do not drinking milk?'"

"I do not *drink* milk."

He flung up his hands. I quickly tapped the keyboard for a screen capture. The image was partly blurred but adorable. I saved it to the folder where all that week I'd been collecting his portraits.

Watching him was my daily pleasure—his lopsided grin, the crinkle around his eyes, the carefree way he moved his hands and inhabited his chair, made him seem the easiest man in the world to get along with—yet I couldn't quite get a grasp on how to teach him. He was cheerful enough throughout each lesson. But I had the strange sense that he wasn't studying English because he cared about the language, and that each time he struggled to get a word or phrase correct, he did so in order to please me. If he wasn't serious about English, then why, after one sample lesson, had he committed himself to seeing me five days a week for a year? What did that make me? Some cut-rate language harlot? I shook the thought from my head.

"I do not *drink* milk, because *drink* is the main verb, preceded by the auxiliary *do*. I do not like *drinking* milk, because *like* is the verb, while *drinking* is the gerund form, which acts as an object."

Even I was confused when I said it. He screwed up his face as if I'd been speaking Mongolian.

"No more textbook today," I said, which he greeted with undisguised relief. I suggested we make our own sentences based on the lesson.

"I'll go first. I like..." I was going to say *I like cooking,* which was so banal that my lips refused to form the words, not to mention untrue. *I like running?* Not even the lofty goal of education justified such falsehood. But when I tried to think of something I genuinely enjoyed that could be turned into a simple gerund, nothing came to mind. Outside of work and the four plain walls of this apartment, my existence was so spectacularly dull that the only *–ing* construct I could think of wasn't even a verb: *I like nothing.* So I lied after all.

"I like singing karaoke."

Sandro performed a hand gesture which I interpreted as Italian for, "No way, not me."

"I like..." he began. I nodded encouragement. He checked a word and looked up at the camera. "I like looking stars."

"I like looking *at* stars," I said, then, "Movie stars or, like, planets?"

"*Momento.*" His keyboard clicked. "I like looking at..." His eyes and a finger pointed upward. "Heaven."

Another screen shot, posed like some dimpled Roman philosopher. I guessed that *heaven* and *sky* were probably the same word in Italian, just like Spanish.

"Tonight, Saturno is—how you say?—brilliant." He raised an invisible telescope to his eye. "You like look? *Ai!* I'm mean: you like *looking?*"

"Tonight Saturn is *bright.* And yes, I like looking at the stars." Though the last time I'd been near a telescope was on a Fifth Grade field trip to the Mt. Griffith Observatory.

My only other student that day was the Ecuadorian woman fitness trainer, who as usual treated English lessons like high-impact linguistic cardio drills. Before signing off I checked my payroll account at iEnglishU and found my $150 bonus duly credited, a lovely end to a trying week. I celebrated with a glass of chilled wine for myself and Japanese rice crackers to be shared with Laurel and Hardy. Then I lay down, slightly dizzy, imagining my stucco ceiling as Alessandro's star-filled Heaven.

I must have dozed off, because my eyes blinked open to darkness. I tapped my phone awake, then sprung up in panic. I had fifteen minutes to get dressed for my date with Steve!

I'D EXPECTED A PAINTER—HOUSE or any other kind—to drive a dented pickup truck missing at least one window handle. But Steve arrived in a tidy Honda whose interior was so immaculately groomed that I suspected he always kept it that way. He'd done a corresponding job on himself: blonde hair tied back in a neat masculine pony tail, while oncoming headlamps highlighted cheeks and chin so clean-shaven they looked cartoon-like. We drove the back roads toward the beach, curving around tidy neighborhoods and dormant agricultural land. Barely audible pop-jazz saxophone meowed from the car speakers.

"So, what do you call what you do?" I asked. "I mean, it's not house painting."

"Ha. Most folks never ask. Industrial painter. Sounds high-tech, yeah?"

"I'm guessing you're not just standing on a ladder with a brush and a bucket, right?"

"Hey, you really get it." He slapped the wheel. "Yeah, we got these fancy programmable sprayers, can practically play games on them. So what do they call you?"

"My job?" Tugging the strangling seatbelt from my neck, I must have looked nervous. Maybe I was. "Teacher. Or language tutor."

Steve frowned.

"You expected something else?" I said.

"I dunno. Everyone's got a fancy title these days. I thought maybe something like *linguistician*."

We both laughed. Something—a twitch of the brow—told me he'd prepared that remark, like a card up his sleeve.

The restaurant was, Steve assured me, his favorite crab place in the whole world. "Better'n any place I know in Alaska, Chesapeake Bay, or Shanghai...having never actually been to Alaska, Chesapeake, or Shanghai." Card number two, played as he held the door for me at the Claw Cooker.

I instinctively read the menu from right to left, though it turned out not to be the pricey extravaganza I'd feared. While he considered his choices I had a chance to look him over for the first time under normal lighting. He had one of those permanently youthful faces that could pass for 17 as easily as 30, with high cheeks and fine wrinkles around his eyes that made him appear always on the verge of laughing. An off-white cotton shirt and tan sports coat enveloped a frame that looked naturally muscled rather than gym-sculpted. It was clear he'd carefully deliberated every detail—the place, his outfit, even the way he tied his hair—not too formal, not too casual, but just right. Like I was dating one of the Three Bears.

As soon as the waiter took away the menus, Steve reached inside his coat with half a wink, "Brought you a little something."

A present on a first date? This was no Baby Bear; his porridge was too hot.

His fist unrolled and out fell a small stack of wet-wipe packets. My relieved laugh drew looks from the young family at the next table.

"Food here's great, but all they give you is little cloth towels that get all sticky. Be prepared, like the Scouts say." Card three. His tricks were working. I was starting to like him.

He was right about the food. The chowder was the best I'd ever had, though to be fair, I couldn't remember ever eating chowder that wasn't from a can. In my family, "dining out" meant a drive-thru, or an all-you-can-eat salad bar, and once every year, the same Chinese restaurant. I used to joke that I inherited stinginess from my father and penny-pinching from my mother. So this bowl of chunky, steaming clam chowder, which cost more than an entire Happy Meal, was the height of decadence.

I voiced my delight to Steve. His face smoothed, his shoulders spread out and relaxed. He was trying so hard to make it look like he wasn't trying hard, and appeared so happy just to make me happy, that I couldn't help but feel moved. He mopped up the last remnants of his soup with a biscuit, not wasting a micro-drop, same as me.

"Glad you enjoyed that," he said. "Old family recipe. Not my family, unfortunately. We're more the franks-and-beans type."

"From cans, yeah? That's how we ate too. If it didn't require ketchup, it wasn't a meal."

He pointed a finger at me, pistol-like. "There you go. *Cuisine américaine.* Ha! Like my French?"

"*Très bien.* Though to speak proper French, you have to gulp down half your syllables and slur the rest. The test is if your English then becomes incomprehensible."

"I take it you got some French students."

"Only one at the moment." I took one of the hard sea biscuits from the basket between us and worked it between my fingers like a worry bead. "French and Japanese, they're the toughest accents to crack. But anyway, I don't want to bore you about my work."

"You kidding? From my limited impression so far, I don't suppose there's anything boring about you."

He was moving a bit too fast for me. Fortunately, a bus-woman took away our bowls and the waiter loaded the table with food: skewered shrimp and scallops, plates of lobster cakes and potatoes and coleslaw, and an enormous platter piled with crabs. The steamy aromas conjured images of fishing boats, not that I'd ever been on one. The waiter placed a nutcracker in front of each of us, then stepped behind me and tied a plastic bib around my neck.

"Last time I wore one of these I was in a high chair," I said.

"It becomes you, my dear," Steve said in a fake English accent. I half-smiled at his cleverly squeezed-in little endearment.

It was all so delicious and fun. Steve instructed me how to correctly crack a crab claw, though I narrowly missed squirting crab juice all over his sleeve. The waiter returned with hand towels and asked whether we wished to order wine.

"She's the worldly one," Steve told him, then to me: "Choose us a nice bottle."

"Only if you go easy. You're driving." I scanned the list for any Italian wines, then felt as though I were cheating on him. I put on a discerning sneer and chose the second-cheapest California Chardonnay.

I wasn't entirely comfortable with the concept of an old-fashioned guy-asks-a-girl-out-and-he-pays kind of date, and now that we'd settled down to the meal, I panicked about my usual social ineptitude in close company. What to talk about without being boring or making a fool of myself? I fell back on my teaching methods: I asked him about himself.

He'd grown up in Oklahoma. His father owned an appliance sales and repair shop, and took Steve's elder brother into the business.

"Love my Daddy and my brother, but darned if I was going to be their employee."

"Did you think about going to college?" I said.

"You bet! For all of three and a quarter minutes. Nobody I knew did that, except one gal who became a nurse. Spent a summer in the Texas panhandle herding cattle. Mexican guy I got friendly with, Ferdi, was moving to California to join his cousin in a house-painting business, invited me along. My Daddy and Ma could have thrashed me when I told them. They expected me to settle down with some girl and fix washing machines somewhere within two hours driving distance, three tops."

His laugh contained a clear dash of bitterness, which he muffled with a forkful of lobster cake. The wine came. Steve went through the show of sniffing and tasting, and let the waiter pour for us. We clinked glasses.

"Think you want that?" I said. "Not the washing machines, but settling down back home?"

He considered a moment. "Put it this way. Where I'm from, you find the best thing within arm's reach and that's what you stick with. And from outward appearances, folks seem happy about it. My Daddy sure is. Happiest gentleman I ever knew. Loves his work, plays ball with his buddies, blows harmonica with a bunch of guys, twice a year drives down to the gulf to go fishing. Him and Ma, even after all these years, they're crazy about each other. Embarrassing sometimes to watch. Whoa, this wine's making me talk too much."

"No. Go on. I like to hear."

"Sure? Okay, so the answer to your question is—yeah, I kinda want that too. But maybe I also want a peek past the horizon. So I came out here, learned all this fancy equipment. My job is cool and believe it or not, even a painter keeps learning new things. Saving up to buy a house, maybe close to the beach, even though my family still thinks I'm going to be like that Prodigal Guy in the Bible and run home. But I think home is where you've hung your hat. What do you think?"

The question took me by surprise. "I–I never thought about it that way. I suppose for me it's a bit weird. I sit in my apartment all day, cut off from my surroundings, while entering other people's spaces around the world. And I could do it from anywhere— Greenland or Samoa." *Or Italy,* I thought. "It's like in quantum physics, where a particle can be two places at once—home is everywhere and nowhere."

His body settled like liquid into his chair, regarding me as if the world around us had faded. I pictured him twenty years from now: the jaw a bit softer, hair receding and probably cut short, maybe a small gut peeking above his belt, though I couldn't imagine him ever not being in shape. A kid at the next table shrieked. We both glanced that way—thirtyish parents good-humoredly breaking up a scuffle between their little girl and boy. Steve looked back at me and smiled, his thoughts practically scrolling across his forehead: that family was the picture of what he longed for.

"You haven't tried the scallops," I said. "They're wonderful."

"You know what's wonderful? Having an honest conversation. I don't get that much. But all I'm hearing mostly is me talking about me. You're the college grad, you should be doing the lecturing."

It took no time to see that tales of college life and English Department shenanigans didn't fascinate him. So I talked about growing up in the Valley, my parents, tearing through the hills with friends on bicycles. He laughed at my most mundane stories.

I was telling him about my first driving lesson, stalling the car in a busy intersection, when a biscuit struck our table and rolled onto the floor. The mother at the next table snapped, "Ginny!" The little girl's lip trembled like a shivering slug. I waved away the mother's apology. Then she leaned toward us, eyes flicking between Steve and me, cupped a hand beside her mouth and stage whispered, "If you lovebirds are thinking of kids...*don't.*"

I must have blushed as red as the crab shells on my plate.

"Want more wine?" Steve offered. "Or we can get out of here and walk on the beach."

We passed between vacant holiday homes and emerged onto the sandy shore. Cackling teenagers tried to topple each other in the darkness into knee-high waves. A quarter mile to our right, people strolled on the lamp-lit pier jutting out to sea. A light breeze sprinkled sand at our legs.

"I'm stoked that we could get together," Steve said. "Was worried it might never happen."

"Worried? Why's that?"

"I dunno. I mean, you spend all your time talking to people online, I thought maybe you weren't so keen on being with people in person. For a while I thought I'd be better off if I bought a webcam."

"Your computer must be old if it doesn't have a camera."

He kicked an empty drink carton. "Maybe. Never had one, and my phone's lens is scratched. Anyway, just as well. I'm more a people person than a LCD person. Somehow it doesn't seem real when you talk to someone on screen."

He gulped and pressed his thumb and forefinger into his eyes. "Um...sorry. That's me I'm talking about. I'm sure you—"

"You know, I sometimes wonder the same thing? I'll be talking to someone in Istanbul and seeing stuff on their shelves and hearing birds out their window. And it's like I'm there and not there, but I'm also not here, know what I mean?"

A trio of pelicans passed over the water. I watched Steve watch them vanish behind the pier. I saw him for the decent, hardworking, respectable man he was. A guy who wanted to settle in the suburbs, start a brood, do his job, have a beer after work, cuddle his nice little wife. And that was it. Stability and security, what was wrong with that? Plenty, I thought, though I couldn't explain it to myself.

"What else do you do? Play music like your dad?" I said.

"Not music, but, hey, you like the theater?"

This was something unexpected. "Sure. I don't go all that often, since college at least."

"I guess that's my little hobby," Steve said. "None of my family gets it. But I love going to the theater."

If one were to plot my interest in Steve on an EKG, it would have just surged into life.

"That's cool," I said. "I used to go in college. The Theater Department put on some interesting stuff. Chekhov, pre-war Germans, contemporary ethnic playwrights." I told myself to shut up. Just because the Theater Department had performed them, didn't mean I'd attended. "So what do you like? Classics? Or more modern American?"

"Dinner theater."

I let out a doubtful little chirp. *Dinner theater?* How blandly middle class suburban could you get?

"I know. It's fun, right?" he said. "I just kind of love it. Sometimes, you know, they have a murder mystery, where the actors are running around, and the waitress turns out to be one of the cast. But I like the song and dance ones best. You know, from the classic musicals?"

I shook my head.

He sang: *"Oh, what a beautiful morning...*Or should I say evening? *Oh, what a beautiful day..."*

We crossed through the inky shadow beneath the pier, Steve's voice echoing from the planks. On *"Everything's going my way..."* he "accidentally" brushed his hand against mine.

I slid it away, pretending to scratch my leg. "What's that song from?"

"'Oklahoma!', my favorite, what else? Man, I'm crazy about that song and dance. Turns all the troubles in the world into a tune. Hey, you teach English, probably know this one. *'The rain in Spain stays mainly in the plain...'"*

"I used it in a lesson just the other day. 'In Hartford, Hereford, and Hampshire...'"

"'*'Urricanes 'ardly 'appen.* Yes!" He whirled to face me and took my hands. "We gotta go sometime."

His silly, innocent enthusiasm swept over me. I almost wanted to hug him.

"What about pie and coffee? There's a great place I want to take you," he said. "You have not lived until you've tried their macadamia nut cream pie."

"I suppose I do want to live," I said.

We walked back to the car while he sang "Some Enchanted Evening" and I couldn't help but hum along.

WHEN I ARRIVED HOME the apartment was dark except for the clock's glow: ten minutes to one.

Zuzie's door opened. Her head peeked out. "How's your hot date?"

I flicked on the kitchen light and filled a glass at the sink.

"Nice."

"Nice?"

"Yeah." I settled at the counter and sipped water. "We had

a nice time. A nice restaurant. Nice food. He's a really nice guy. So...it was nice."

"Ew."

Zuzie's door clicked shut.

Chapter 10

*S*aturday morning my inbox contained a rare genuine message sandwiched between the phishing invoices and crypto get rich schemes.

A photo of Saturn.

Jessie and Miko were divided as to its meaning when I met them for cupcakes and tea. Outrageously mismatched roommates during our first college semester, we held occasional Watson Dorm Room 307 reunions ever since. Today Jessie looked almost ordinary in a powder blue skirt and plain white knit top, her homage to having settled on one guy and a steady job with an eyewear retailer. Back in college we'd called her The Pollinator, the curvy redhead from Hemet who liked tight, flower-patterned tops, trailed by swarms of guys like drone bees craving her nectar.

Like antimatter to Jessie's matter, Miko had never been observed in the wild with a man. Or, to be fair, a woman. Whenever the subject of her sexual orientation or the state of her hymen came up, she dodged all questions until we finally quit asking. She also never aged: a straw-shaped body topped by a round face that could be drawn with three lines and a buzzsaw haircut which had earned her the nickname Broomhead. Today I was pleasantly surprised to see her wearing something purplish with short feminine sleeves over her narrow shoulders. One thing hadn't changed: half the things she said needed footnotes.

"Checked the EXIF data. I can tell you this photo was taken

at ISO-800 at one-half second. But no hidden keywords or other messages." Miko passed back my phone, then sipped her scorching tea in a way that only Japanese seemed capable of.

"You expected to find a secret message in the data?" I said.

"Not really. But we have nothing else to go on. It's just a nice photo of Saturn. From a decent telescope, I'd guess."

And it was nice. A fuzzy-edged ball banded in orange, yellow, and blue-gray. The rings were awesome in their detail, concentric colored stripes like a set of hoop earrings.

Jessie chimed in: "Are you kidding me? Don't you guys see how Saturn resembles a diaphragm? Hel*looo!* How unsubtle can you get?"

"Come on, I'm serious. It's got to mean *something*. I've spent all morning on this," I said, opening a note on my phone. "Okay. First, he knew I'd get it on Saturday—*Saturn Day*. Ha! Anyway, then it struck me. Alessandro is Italian. Saturn was a Roman god, right?"

Miko's thumbs tap-danced on her tablet. "God of agriculture. God of wealth, of time."

Jessie nodded. "God of wealth's cool. Can we just order? What cupcakes we having?" Her finger ran down the menu under the table's glass top.

"Interesting." Miko read from a wiki page: "'*Saturnia tellis,* a mythical golden age when Saturn, deposed by Jupiter as King of Olympus, fled to what is now Italy, his presence celebrated in antiquity with public banquets, intoxication, and orgies during the annual Saturnalia rites.'"

She tapped an image. The screen filled with a painting of a full-frontal Roman orgy.

"Love it," Jessie said. "What do you guys think about Pink Mint Frosted Bacon Cappuccino Dream Cake?"

"Gross," Miko said, though she may have meant the painting.

"I know. Has to be great, right? Serena?"

My eyes sprang from ancient Roman genitalia to the cupcake menu, pre-ordaining my choice. "A Chocolate Double Orgasm, what else? Miko?"

She raised a finger. "Make it two."

Jessie's perfect butt and five-alarm hair swished toward the counter, men's eyeballs rotating out of their skulls as she passed. Artisan Cupcakes was a small island of color in a refurbished outdoor mall, tucked between a lingerie outlet and a dollar shop. Incredibly, I'd almost never seen any oversized bodies in this place. Artisan Cupcakes was a hangout for guilty pleasures rather than indulgence, a subtle distinction which may have explained why it had a reputation as a pick-up joint.

Miko reclined into her chair with both hands cradling her teacup. "Anyway, Jessie says you're already dating someone."

"Oh, he's just a plain old American. Went out once," I said, rubbing my eyes. "So, what are you doing nowadays?"

"Not much. Bit of database development. A monkey could do it." Her mouth almost verged on a smile, which was as close as Miko ever came to full-blown rapture. "But in about three weeks I'm doing a coding bootcamp in Palo Alto."

"Wow, Miko, that's great!"

"Mm-hmm. Wasn't going to tell you. You think I've gotten even more boring, as though that were possible."

"No way. What's great is—aren't those tech bootcamps like ninety-nine percent men? That's going to boost your chances of—"

"Of employment, yes."

"Oh, come on." I raised my tea cup—now tolerably hot—and clinked hers. "Level with me already. This isn't a weaving retreat. Tell me that being surrounded by so many guys with similar interests isn't just an eensy-weensy little attraction?"

She gave me an unamused sniff. "Let's make something clear, Serena. Yeah, maybe I don't have the experience, or obsession, about getting laid like you and our hormonal friend there. Maybe that makes me actually *less* stupid about men. *Or* women. That's why I'm pretty sure your Italian's a pervert."

"What?" I wasn't sure whether I was reacting to the words *getting laid* coming out of Miko's mouth for the first time ever, or her unprovoked remark about Sandro.

"I mean, you're trying to analyze whether there's any hidden meaning in this photo of Saturn," she said, "and we've pretty much figured out that if anything's implied there, it's either: a) disgusting; b) toxic masculine assholery; c) a juvenile prank; or d) all of the above."

"Romantic isn't on the list."

"Not unless your idea of romantic is the planetary equivalent of dick pics." A smirk informed me this was one of her rare jokes. "Like I said: pervert."

"Or it leaves us with no hidden meaning," I said.

Miko nodded. "Anyway, Saturn might even be a bad sign. Know the word *saturnine?* Means gloom and doom." She pointed past my shoulder. "Like that cake."

Jessie returned with a tray bearing a concoction of bacon strips protruding through a glossy pink shell like zombie arms from a confectionery grave. "Yours are coming soon, fresh. I watched the guy pumping out hot chocolate goo. Ooh yeah! Meanwhile, yum yum."

Miko wrinkled her nose. "Disgusting."

Jessie wiggled into her seat. "I'm disgusting; therefore I am."

I winced as she bit into her meat-and-sugar vulgarity. Her jaw paused mid-chew, evaluating whatever odd flavors were consummating inside her mouth, then gulped down the result.

"Interesting," she said. "But, oh yeah, your Saturn photo? I'm thinking—Saturn's all about rings, right? So there you have it. He's proposing."

"We abandoned the search for meaning while you were gone," I said. "How's your bacon bun?"

"Kinda gross, to tell the truth." Jessie wiped her mouth and pushed the plate aside. "So, you gonna show us the goods or what? Got pictures?"

I hesitated to admit that I'd photo-stalked a student. But my friends had earned a peek. Jessie and Miko craned their heads across the table as I swiped through five or six stolen portraits of Alessandro.

"Slow down! Oh, my heart!" Jessie said. Even Miko seemed transfixed.

"I know. He's cute and, like, kind of playful in our lessons. But, I mean, I don't know..." I set down my phone and leaned back. "Seriously, I've thought about this—I mean, my whole *life* is dealing with people on video chat—but sometimes I feel it's not real, like it's all just a movie. Can you really, truly get to know somebody through an effing webcam?"

Jessie frowned as though weighing the deepest existential question of the universe, then proclaimed, "True. You have no idea how his butt moves."

"I'm serious!" I said.

"The Hawthorne Effect," Miko said.

Jessie—and I guess I did, too—looked at Miko like a pair of retriever puppies regarding an alien.

She rolled her eyes at us ignoramuses. "It's when a person modifies his behavior when he knows he's being observed. Everybody does it. Then add to that the webcam effect."

Jessie glanced at me. "Uh... meaning...?"

"Distorted optics, pixelation, compressed audio," Miko recited. "You don't get it, do you? A phone or a webcam lens stretches your face, detail's blurred out, voice gets distorted. Plus, there's no other sensory input, like smells. No pheromones, no body language below the neck—yeah, like butt wiggles. All you're seeing and hearing is a low-res approximation of the real person, and that's how he sees you."

Jessie and I gave her stink eye like we always did when Miko went off onto one of her tangents. She hunched over and dropped her head onto her hands. "Sorry. My body urgently requires sugar."

"Hey, that selfie lens stuff can be a good thing, you know," said a flutey voice behind me. A girl wearing an Artisan Cupcakes apron balanced a tray on one hand. "I got this kind of lip fuzz, you know, and some old acne scars, but nobody can tell on those online hookup sites. And by the time a guy sees me in person, he's more checking out my boobs, know what I mean?"

Her check-outable breasts brushed my shoulder as she placed our cupcakes on the table. Moist, almost black cake dripped with thick, luscious chocolatey goop, encrusted by a hailstorm of chocolate chunks. I couldn't wait to bite into one.

Cupcake Girl's eyes zeroed in on my phone. "Whoa! Tell me that's your brother and he's single."

"He's my student," I said.

"Who just sent her a photo of Saturn, and she thinks there's nothing behind it," Jessie added.

"Are you kidding me? That is like..." Cupcake Girl hugged the empty tray to her chest. "The most romantic thing I ever heard!"

"A third opinion," Miko said. "Maybe we should vote."

"He live around here?" the girl said.

"Italy," Jessie, Miko, and I spoke at once.

The party of six at the next table turned around. One man said, "You're dating a dude in Italy?"

"Yes!" Cupcake Girl squeaked. "And he sent her a picture of Saturn! And she thinks he's not in love with her."

"I never—"

The guy who'd spoken nodded knowingly, stroking his chin.

"That's heavy," another guy said. "I mean, I never thought of sending a chick a planet before."

"Smooth," said the first guy.

Cupcake Girl placed a hand on my shoulder. "Girl, I was you? I'd book the next flight to Vienna."

"That's Austria," Miko said.

"You should definitely go," Guy One said. "*Romeo and Juliet*. That's Italy, right?"

His friend whacked his chest. "Shut up, man. The dude dies and the chick kills herself. Or the other way around maybe, I think."

"Who cares?" said a sun-bleached blonde who'd joined the growing throng. "I'd grab him before he loses interest."

I felt like an accident victim surrounded by gawkers. How did I get myself into these situations where the entire world invented a sex life for me and then debated about it at the tops of their lungs? I glanced around to make sure nobody was video recording with their phone.

Then Miko gave me the shock of my life. She stood up. She banged a fist on the table, nearly upsetting my tea.

"Everybody! Hey! *Hellooo!* Will everyone kindly return to your seats and allow us ladies to enjoy our Double Orgasms in private!"

Our audience dispersed, leaving us to consume as much ul-tra-chocolate cake as we could stand, which was about half for both Miko and me, sharing the rest with a grateful Jessie, who was still going on about the meaning of the photos.

Miko tapped the table. "Do you trust him, Serena?"

Good question, if there was more than a chicken's chance in a nugget factory of my ever meeting him in person. But he was my student, on the other side of the world, whom I'd only seen through the—what was it?—Hawthorne Effect. "How do I know? Why not just have some fun with it?"

"That's what I thought about these cupcakes." Miko downed the remainder of her tea and leaned back like an irritated cat.

81

Chapter 11

*M*onday morning my inbox opened to an ochre ball. Caption: *Venus.*

It took two nights of experimenting with a cheap camera perched on a sofa arm before I finally had my "appropriate response": a silhouette of me posing by the window contemplating a crescent moon. The next day I received a crisp, haunting closeup of lunar craters, in such searing detail that I could count the boulders littering the surface. At first I felt humiliated, as though he meant to mock my cheesy selfie. Between my limited imagination and my limited camera skills, I couldn't conjure up a fitting astronomical response. A couple days later he sent photos of two star clusters with colors I'd never imagined existed in space. I replied with a picture I'd taken years ago of Judy Garland's star on Hollywood Boulevard.

We were like students passing notes in class, never mentioning our intergalactic dialogue during lessons. The closest we came to discussing stars and planets was during Lesson 7's "Visit to the Doctor", a vocabulary dump of human body parts featuring a diagram of a naked genderless body. We got into a silly discussion about butts, and I taught him the phrase, "to moon someone".

Steve texted me almost daily. The university job finished, his painting crew was camped out near the Mexican border, doing over a government building in Calexico. The tacos were great, he said, but there was nothing to do at night except sit in his motel room watching TV. Old musicals on classic movie channels, I presumed. He was sweet, but without a lot to say, our exchanges usually devolved into goofy emoji hieroglyphics.

These days I almost never saw Zuzie. Sometimes her married professor would steal in early, other times they'd be shut inside all evening, sounding like a muffled documentary about mating chimpanzees.

Often when my last lesson finished, running for the last hour on adrenaline fumes, heart racing a million beats per second, I'd realize that all day I'd consumed more of my own fingernails than food. Other days I felt like one of those inflatable punching bag clowns that had lost half its air. Was this some variant of the Hawthorne Effect, talking to images of people all day long, and at the end feeling like I'd had no human contact?

Maybe I needed to join the Peace Corps or a kibbutz and work with real people all day.

Maybe I needed a dog.

One solitary evening I let the hamsters run around the living room while I lay on the floor beaming a flashlight around the stucco constellation on the ceiling, wondering if Sandro would make the connection if I sent a photo. Hardy climbed onto my belly, curled up, and let me stroke him until he fell asleep for one of his hamster flash naps. A tear rolled down my cheek, moved by his unreserved trust, his innocence, the heat of his tiny body. Then he gnawed a chip in my shirt button.

I DECIDED TO STAGE my own little revolt.

Monday would be No Textbook Day. I would chat with my students like regular people, same as if we were meeting over coffee. In fact, I'd tell them to get a coffee or tea to set up the atmosphere. They'd all love it. We'd get to know one another better.

Bieber's eyes went wide as bowling balls when I told him. He excused himself, checked outside, then locked his door, lest some mama tigress suspect that he might be one hour less advanced toward acing his English proficiency exam. A juice carton with bold purple Chinese characters stood in for a latte.

"So, how's it going, dude?" I said. His one eye squinted while the other looked like it might pop, and I had to laugh. "It means, how are you, friend?"

"I know its mean," he said. "I see in American TV show. But, *aiya!* Teacher call me *dude*..."

He made another funny face and slapped his cheek. Questions about his friends elicited restrained replies. I gathered that he didn't have many. I had better luck asking about his favorite musicians, which he rattled off in a gleeful litany of Chinese and Korean names that I couldn't latch onto long enough to repeat a single one. I asked about the last name on the list.

"What do you like about this guy's music?"

"Not guy. Girl. Has pretty looking. I show you."

A glittered baby doll face with an explosion of whitish-yellow hair popped up in the corner of the screen—how did he do that? I thought only the teacher could share images through the school interface.

Bieber beamed at me. "She is very, how to say, *ke-ai*." His keyboard clicked as he looked up the word. "Cute. She is very cute. I like."

She was hideous. Starting with the dandelion hair, made creepier by contact lenses with giant irises the color of lime Kool-Aid. I suddenly felt old for even thinking such thoughts about a teen pop idol. Behind the pose and glitter and baby girl pout, a genuine—or, more likely, surgically reconstructed—wholesome prettiness shone through.

"And her songs? Are they cute, too?" I asked.

Either Bieber's camera suddenly changed contrast or he was blushing, with a hand over his mouth and one eye squeezed shut. "Songs very...ah...naughty."

So she was a little tramp. And he was a typical teenager. Thank goodness for that. I shared some of the musicians I liked, surprised to find he'd heard of several and could even name a few songs. It was my turn for embarrassment, that a sheltered thirteen-year-old in a Shanghai housing block would be familiar with my culture's pop icons, while I couldn't pronounce, much less remember, the names of singers whose fans outnumbered those of American stars by the hundreds of millions.

"What about girls in your school? Is there one you like?" I said, then added with mischief, "Or maybe a cute girl likes you? You can tell me, dude."

I expected him to glow red as a beet. Instead he turned deadpan, as if we were back to repetition drills. "I do not have a girlfriend," adding matter-of-factly, "Girls at my school not interesting."

"Oh." I couldn't think of an answer.

Then he gave me that nervous wink again. "But I know you have boyfriend."

"Um, not really."

He grinned like he was holding back a secret. "You can tell me, Teacher Dude. I see his picture."

"What are you talking about?"

He tapped at his keyboard. All of a sudden one of my screen shots of Alessandro materialized. "He is very handsome."

"What the—? Where did you—"

Bieber recoiled as if the force of my shock had knocked him back from eight thousand miles away. The photo vanished.

"I mean it, Bieber. What is going on here? Where did you get that?"

"It's...I..."

"Did you hack the company software or something?"

"Not hack." His voice cracked and he looked set to cry. "Maybe little. I am so sorry, Teacher Serena. Please no be angry."

"Omigod, omigod, omigod. Listen, Bieber, I'm, I'm, I'm...I'm not angry at you. But, God in heaven, how did you manage to...?" Where did he even find the time?

Worries tumbled over each other inside my skull: Bieber would be too ashamed to continue with lessons. And another: that a manager would randomly audit this lesson and try somehow to prosecute him. And a bigger worry yet: That then they'd fire me for collecting screenshots of a student, like some kind of sick stalker. Which maybe I was.

I took a deep breath and spoke straight to the camera. "Good use of computer slang to make jokes, Bieber. We'll play with more computer vocabulary in Lesson 29."

He got the signal. We diverted the dialogue onto safer topics. I put on a smile the whole time, all the while feeling like a pressure cooker about to explode. At the end, I made Bieber stay during the five-minute break when I was sure not to be audited.

"What else did you access?" He didn't understand, so I rephrased as gently as possible, "You saw my pictures. Anything else?"

"Nothing, Teacher. I tell true!" His voice cracked, his head shook urgently side to side.

"Bieber, listen to me. I am not angry, just surprised a little. No, a lot. Do you understand? That man is another student. Bieber, stop shaking your head and listen." I leaned toward the camera, forcing my sweetest smile. "Bieber, between you and me—a little secret, okay?"

He wiped his nose and nodded, though clearly wary.

"I like him," I said. "But he isn't my boyfriend. Our secret, you and me! You don't tell anyone, okay? I don't tell anyone that you, uh..."

"Hack."

"Hacked, yes. Okay? Secret?" I pressed a finger across my lips. Then I held a fist toward the lens, little finger curled outward, the way I'd sealed secrets when I was his age. "You know this? Pinky promise." I spelled it for him.

"Mm. I see on American TV show."

"No one can ever break a pinky promise."

He relaxed at last and held his extended pinky to the lens.

"Pinky promise," he said.

YASMIN WAS EXUBERANT AT the chance, as she put it, to "go off book" and spend an entire lesson on her favorite topic: boys. Her huge eyes were electric beneath her golden yellow headscarf. I'd never heard her speak English so fluidly.

"New guy works in butchery shop near to my house. Is, like, real hot stuff! Or, how you say—*hunk!* Oh, baby!" She patted her chest with a theatrical swoon. "Mother asks me why every day I'm going out for buying meat! Like ha!"

My delight at her slang repertoire, complete with proper use of the interjectory *like,* rinsed away my stress and I relaxed into a giggly fifty-five minutes of girl talk. She was in fits when I gave her an abridged version of my evening with Steve, breaking every rule about not discussing my personal life with students. After I answered approximately a hundred questions about him, she leaned toward me like a judge.

"I think he is for you not the right boy."

"Oh, really?"

"Yes, I think. You are a smart chick—can a girl call other girl *chick?* Yes? I think better for you is clever boy with high class. Not Turkish! Maybe French man, or Italian. Ah, you smile!"

Had Yasmin hacked my private screen shots as well?

Her "special word" at the end of the hour was tame for her: *scumbag,* which she'd heard some American woman shout at her husband outside a tourist café while beating him around the head with her purse.

Next came Vladimir, who seemed lost without the textbook

structure. I had him describe, with much assistance and prodding, the heavy machinery his company leased throughout southern Bulgaria, learning to my surprise that bulldozers come in many varieties. Then he took advantage of the lesson's casual tone to raise his offer to a hundred and twenty dollars to see my boobs.

I was on a roll, in the zone, cruising with ease through a free trial lesson with an aristocratic older Polish woman in Krakow. Of course, I had to stick mostly to the prescribed materials. But even with her I threw in more general chatter than I normally would have, especially because her English wasn't terrible. By the end of the session, we'd warmed to each other like a niece and her favorite aunt.

The pleasant glow lingered through my lunch break. Bieber's little misdemeanor still nagged, but I'd partially convinced myself that it was nothing more than harmless, boyish mischief. The incident had made me reveal something of my real self to him, and him to me. I'd truly bonded with people today, from teenagers in China and Turkey to a horny Bulgarian steam shovel dealer to a mature lady in Poland, who I welcomed having as a student, and not purely for the income. It did seem possible to reach into people's souls even through a webcam, without having to share the same air or inhale their pheromones.

I finished my lunch—a quick salad with garlic ranch dressing, topped with shaved parmesan—and, with five minutes left, dashed into the bathroom and frantically brushed my teeth. I looked in the mirror at white foam dribbling down my chin and laughed at myself. I'd forgotten that nobody could smell my breath.

ALESSANDRO WAS APPREHENSIVE AT my announcement of No Textbook Day. While he'd been doing fine with Lesson 10's grammar exercises, he struggled to assemble an English sentence of more than eight words (I'd counted).

"Today is a fun lesson," I told him. "We pretend—understand *pretend?* Okay, pretend to sit in a café on the *piazza* drinking cappuccino." I held up my mug, in which long-cold instant coffee had formed a milky crust.

That made him laugh. "What time for you?"

"Um. Here in California it's twelve o'clock noon."

He flicked his hand, smirking, "Americans!"

"What?"

"Middle of day, nobody drink cappuccino! Morning only." Eight words, but two sentences.

"What do you drink at this time?" I asked.

He tilted his head, scratching behind his ear. No more screen-shots, I warned myself. "Here, now is after the dinner time. Maybe drink little grappa, maybe wine." Seven words, times two.

"Okay, you get yourself a glass of wine, here in our café." In fact, alcohol might loosen his tongue. One of my linguistics professors had once told the class, never mind language acquisition theories, beer had been indispensable to his speaking fluent German.

"Yes, I do that. But I can not drink—how to say, *solo?*"

"Alone." I hoisted my mug. "You're not alone."

He touched his forehead in what I guessed meant crazy. "I drink wine, you drink *caffè*, is not—*ai! Non è civile.*"

"Not civilized?"

"Yes, not civilized. You must drink wine with me."

I would be burned at the stake if this lesson was ever audited. But maybe not, if I explained that I'd filled a wine glass with water. Which I did. Then added just enough cheap generic boxed burgundy to color it plausibly red.

When I returned to my desk he was in his seat, holding a thin-stemmed glass whose content was such deep scarlet I could nearly taste it.

"Cheers," I said.

"You, me, in *trattoria* or American bar?"

"I think I prefer your trattoria."

"*O-kay! Salute!*"

"*Salute!*" We clicked glasses against our screens.

"So, how are things on Saturn?" I said.

"Saturn, very good. You like my, ah...my photographs of Saturn and stars?"

"And Venus and the moon. They're all so beautiful. You must have a very big telescope."

"My telescope, he is not so big, but he—" Sandro slapped his forehead. "*It!* My telescope, it is very, how you say, it has special, ah, *specchio, specchio, specchio*...mirror! Very special mirror, motor, gyroscope, camera. Too much money. But photographs..." He kissed his fingertips and flung them open.

"Wow. I would like to see that. Do you have clear skies this time of year?"

He sipped his wine, deciphering my question, then leaned toward me. "You know, where I am living is very—tsk, how you say?" His hand traced a horizontal line.

"Flat," I said.

"Flat. My region is very flat, and dry. Sometimes much, how do you call this, dirty in the air?"

"Pollution?"

"No. Not pollution."

"Dust, you mean."

"I think so. Dust, yes. Sometimes pollen." Another deep sip of wine and he hooked his elbows over the back of his chair. "Sometimes I drive to the mountain. It is three, four hours. No city, no light, no dust. Air is like diamond. All night I look to the stars. It is—" He gazed upward, at a loss for words, not just English ones.

"You go by yourself?" I asked, expecting accounts of girls, wine, all-night Saturnalias.

"Always go alone. But I tell you something. When I am look at the stars, millions of millions of stars, I am never feel alone, you know? Internet—you, me, very far away, across the world—I see you, you see me, can see many, many countries, many people. But with telescope, alone on the mountain top, I see the whole universe. Sometimes maybe I think—ah!" He slumped down, waving a hand. "I talk too much! Sorry."

Sorry? I'd been as carried away by his words as he was, almost like I was next to him on that mountain. Whether it was the alcohol or his passion welling up, he'd just had a major breakthrough in conversational English, though it would spoil the mood to point that out.

"Sometimes you think what? Tell me." I raised my watered-down wine, to pull us back into the charade.

He pressed his lips in thought. At last he spoke, as though to himself. "Sometimes, when I am looking up at the heavens, sometimes I think I am standing next to God."

If I could have reached through the screen and taken his hand, I surely would have. "I would love to stand next to God," I said, though of course I meant Sandro.

He raked his hair with near-violence. A curl fell over his eye. "Speaking too much English, my head, it hurts. Ha! You must talk now."

"Sandro, you're the student. You do the speaking, not me."

He raised his glass. "No student. Now sit in *trattoria,* you remember? Please say me you like, you no like... I remember, you like karaoke."

I leaned back and laughed, nearly toppling my glass. "The truth? I hate karaoke!"

"You hate? But why?"

It seemed such a petty topic to follow his revelations. But even half a glass of watery wine on an empty stomach had lightened my head. "Well, a few weeks ago, my friend took me to a karaoke bar. Understand? Okay. I didn't want to sing, but they made me. And my singing was so bad, the machine exploded."

"No!"

"It's true," I insisted. "I opened my mouth and *ka-boom!*"

"What song?"

"I—I don't remember."

He wagged a finger at me. "I think you remember, but you don't like say to me. I thought you are my friend."

Oh my God, was he teasing me? "You don't know it. American song."

"I know American songs. Tell me."

My face flushed. I tried to think of any other song title, but a whirlwind was spinning my brain synapses into cotton candy. I muttered, "Sex Machine."

If I'd dared to take a screen shot of his face at that moment, it could have gone on a magazine cover and broken women's hearts around the world: all heavy-lidded seductive grin, thumb and forefinger fondling his stubbled chin, and that curl over his eye. "Maybe I don't know. You sing for me?"

The dialogue had entered uncharted territory. I was about to suggest a change of topic, when he said, "A joke. You sing, maybe my computer explodes."

He asked about my friend: A girl? Was she pretty? Did she teach English? I offered brief answers to questions about my family, then changed the subject back to him. I learned about his parents and grandparents, uncles, and sister. He was coming out of his language cocoon, though as the questions became more probing, he paused more often to look up words. I didn't realize that we'd gone overtime until a notice popped up simultaneously on my computer screen and phone. From Marisa at the office:

> *Where are you? Your 1 oclock*
> *says you dont pick up*

AT THE END OF the day my brain was reamed out. This must have been how standup comics felt, improvising on your feet, riffing on different topics, keeping the energy high without losing momentum. Sticking to the textbook turned out to be something of a crutch. Every one of my students had responded with enthusiasm, even my dour French Belgian oilman, who shed some self-consciousness about his accent and had reached a tentative truce with the letter H.

I expected to find a message from the office, but my inbox remained stubbornly empty. Sometimes free trial students never called back, and sometimes they took a week or two to make up their minds. But the Polish woman and I seemed to have hit it off. I clicked a call to Marisa.

"Yes, darling? What can Mama do for you?" Marisa wore a starched white blouse and a gold chain, rather formal for her. A new perm and dye looked like surf swells.

"Love your hair, Marisa. Highlights! You going out tonight?"

She patted her hairdo with affection. "No such luck. Needed a little change is all. Anything I can help you with?"

"Well, um, sorry about my one o'clock. A rare case of running overtime to, uh, complete a drill."

"No harm done, hon. Just keeping the customer satisfied, yeah?" She glanced aside and raised a finger, signaling someone to wait.

"Sorry if I interrupted something, Marisa. I was wondering if you heard from my ten o'clock trial? Polish lady?"

"What was her name?" Marisa typed and leaned into her screen. "Uh huh. Mrs. Rozanski. Yeah, she signed up for two days a week."

My heart leapt. A new student, new income. And she seemed so nice. One of those people you have a warm gut feeling you're going to be fast friends with. I scanned my schedule for the most likely time slots.

"Vicky squeezed her in," Marisa said.

My hand plummeted onto the keyboard. The video window disappeared. My trembling fingers needed several tries to click the restore button. "Um, she was my freebie."

"Honey, I can see right here that she didn't specify a teacher. Victoria had an opening."

What about me? I had a million openings! Mrs. Rozanski belonged to me! Maybe she hadn't seen the Request Instructor box, or she'd assumed I'd be her teacher. I knew it was fruitless to argue. New student allocation was all based on a point system I didn't fully understand. Had she gone to any other teacher I wouldn't feel such swollen rage. But Victoria? That bitch had everything—bursting full schedule, face on the homepage, the video series, engaged to a count. Two lessons a week meant nothing to her—table scraps! But for me it was a full student loan payment.

"I sense you're a wee disappointed," Marisa said. "I get it, sweetheart. Don't worry, first of the month coming up, we usually get a rush of prospectives. Vicky'll take good care of your Polish lady. Won't you, darling?"

I couldn't believe it. The twat hole had been sitting there the whole time.

"Come here, Vic. You two be friends, now." Marisa beckoned until that blonde head leaned into view. Victoria's fingers wiggled hello.

"Hey, Serena. How you doing?"

Pale skin, pale hair, pale blue eyes—she reminded me of one of the ghost brides in old German fairytales. For the sake of my job, I had to pretend to be nice.

"Hey, Victoria. How's the wedding coming?"

"Great. Uh-huh. Hey, yeah, I need to ask you. Did you receive an invitation?"

I would have remembered receiving such a thing, and watching it burn in the sink. "Ah...no, I don't seem to have gotten one."

Victoria turned to Marisa. "See? I told you my wedding planner wouldn't make a mistake." Then back to me: "Toodles!" Her other hand panned past the camera to show off a monstrous diamond engagement ring: a bunch of small stones surrounding one huge rock in the center, all set in white gold—a gaudy slut-fest of white, suited to an Ice Queen about to move to the frozen north.

I clicked off the call without saying goodbye to Marisa. Then I slammed my fist down.

Parades of Z's marched across the screen. The Z key protruded from the keyboard like a crooked tooth. I used a pen cap to pivot it back into place. The plastic cover shot into my eye.

When I returned from the bathroom with a wet cotton ball eyepatch, the Z's had multiplied into a standing army. And I found the new message icon flashing. I clicked it open.

An image of stars. Lots of them, like a celestial soup.

I shut the window shade, turned off the living room lights, and maximized the picture so it filled the screen. It was crisp and clear, a cross-section of the Milky Way, millions and millions of stars. One or two blobs may have been other galaxies billions of light years away. He was sharing the universe with me.

I only noticed the caption when I opened the image later, a second time.

You come to Italy, I show you God.

Chapter 12

"Looks like somebody has a grievance against the letter Z," Elias said. Using a tiny screwdriver, he probed the gaping hole in the keyboard like a dentist.

"I was aiming for V."

"I'm not even going to ask." He'd taken nearly an hour to arrive due to another job a few miles away, fixing some old lady's ancient desktop machine. In the meantime my pink Hello Kitty laptop had started beeping like it had hiccups. The only way to stop the noise was to open a blank text document and watch irregular outbursts of Z's form lines across the screen. I was ashamed to let him see how I'd damaged his gift to me.

"Thinking something's a little bent, hopefully an easy fix," he said. "Got the proper tools at my place."

Elias looked me, not in the eye, more like at my left ear, making no sign of moving. *So go get your tools,* I thought.

Instead, he said, "Maybe you wanna come over? Just around the corner."

"I, um...probably it's better you fix it without, you know, distractions? Bring it back when you're done? Obviously I'm paying you for the repair job, your normal rate."

He slipped the Z key into his shirt pocket. "Hey, no charge. Any computer I give away comes with a full one year warranty against crashes, defects, and random violence. And pizza. The warranty comes with pizza and a beverage."

"No, I won't let you—"

"Let me guess. Vegan? No carbs, no gluten?"

"No, none of that. It's just—" *Well, why not,* I told myself. "I insist on paying for the pizza."

"Normally that would invalidate the warranty. But in your case I'll make an exception."

We walked two blocks to a tidy house overlooking a weary lawn. But instead of heading to the front entrance, he led me around the side and unlocked a door to the garage.

It was set up like a studio apartment, with a kitchenette in one corner and a mattress in the other. The space in between reminded me of an art installation I'd once seen, in which what looked like the entire contents of a city dumpster had been spilled onto a gallery floor and someone had given it a title like Urban Magma 3.0. Stained dishes, socks, crumpled shirts—fortunately no underwear—magazines, open books, and fast food cartons covered every possible open space. Huge hairballs of computer cables lurked beneath a glass-topped patio table, while a red plastic laundry tub brimmed over with prehistoric game consoles and remote controls. The garage door supported shelves crammed with CD cases, books, more electronic detritus, stacked sweaters, and an umbrella. Yet in the middle of one wall an oasis of tidiness surrounded a work table which, while covered with tools and electronic parts, appeared to possess some sort of organic logic.

"Um. Yeah. Looks like the downstairs maid ran off with the butler again. If I'd known you were coming, I'd have, like, burned everything. Come in." He swept clear a space on a black leatherette sofa.

"This place is spectacular," I said. "And I don't mean that in a good way."

"That's what I tell my aunt. It's her house, she lets me live here free. Which I guess explains her refusal to provide cleaning service."

I dusted off the sofa cushion and sat, while Elias negotiated a path to his work bench, where he put down my computer and snapped open a tool box. On the wall facing him he'd pinned up a red square paper with a single Chinese word printed in gold.

"What's that say?"

"That? It means *home*. Present from a Taiwanese work buddy. He says the Chinese character for home is a picture of a pig under a roof. Can't imagine what he was implying."

He voice-dialed a pizza place, turning to me. "Mega cheese? Hawaiian? Okay, cheese. While you're waiting, help yourself to hors d'oeuvres."

He indicated an open bag of cheese puffs curled on the glass table in front of me.

"Sorry I don't have anything fancier. Suppose I don't have many women visitors. In fact, you're the first."

"I would never have guessed," I said.

His place was a chaotic, dirty mess, but it expressed something about him, kind of a mad energy. Better than I could say about my airless apartment with the landlord's taste in durable furniture.

Elias pried open the pink casing around the laptop's keyboard, exposing what looked, from where I was sitting, like black gridwork over a dense sandwich of circuit boards and metallic blocks. While he probed and tested, my eye wandered, settling on a carton filled with strange electronic gizmos. I picked one from the top, the size of a cigarette box, with a narrow screen across the middle.

"What's this?"

He peered over his shoulder. "You never seen one? A pager. They used them back in the Stone Age."

"But a carton full?" As if his place didn't have enough junk. I pointed to another box, full of disembodied electronic screens. "And what are those?"

He regarded his cave of treasures, Aladdin surveying his lair. "Hey, I like stuff. Better than throwing it away, especially when it still works. Anyway, one of these days pagers and stuff'll become retro cool, like vinyl records, and I can sell them for big bucks."

He returned to his task, probing and twisting with needle-nose pliers, humming a thumpy tune, while I tried to find a comfortable position on his sagging couch. Maybe I was wiped out after a day of nonstop talking. Or maybe I was simply ill at ease, alone in this pig-under-a-roof place with a guy who was a little too interested in pleasing me.

I tried a cheese puff. I hadn't had one once since I was ten years old. I didn't remember them tasting like over-salted Styrofoam, though I was sure they always had. Orange granules encrusted my fingers, which I licked clean and was about to wipe dry on a faded throw cushion beside me, until I thought of the thousands of times he must have done the exact same to this exact pillow, and I imagined generations of microbes whose evolution had been mutated by subsistence on synthetic flavoring and dyes. I cleaned my hand with my shirt tail.

Leaving the computer's guts exposed, Elias slouched back while it booted up. "I suck at conversation starters, in case you hadn't noticed."

"Funny, that's what I do all day. So in my time off, I'm not really up to it."

"We are a sad pair," he said.

We watched the laptop come to life. He tested the keyboard, wasn't satisfied with it, and tinkered some more.

"So what upset you so badly that you'd take it out on a defenseless Hello Kitty computer, if you don't mind me asking?"

"Oh, it was me being stupid." I told him about the motherly Polish woman, how much I'd liked her, and how Marisa and Victoria had conspired to take her away from me—at least, that was my version of events. He restarted the computer while I went on about the unfairness of Marisa's teacher point system and Victoria's charmed life and charmless attitude.

"Sounds like a bitch," Elias said. "Let's see." He called up iEnglishU's website and there she was, in a poured-on sky blue skirt, swishing her long blonde mane and purring, "I English you."

"I guess she's pretty hot, if you don't hate me for saying. But that web design! So 2009! Sorry, can't bear to look." He clicked the browser off.

"So you're saying you wouldn't consider my school because of the graphics?"

"Maybe if it was you on the homepage..."

I opened my mouth without a retort to fill it, but was saved by the bell; rather, a knock at the door. I got up to pay for the pizza, then balanced the box on the couch arm while I cleared the table, found a paper towel, and wiped the whole thing clean. Elias shut down my computer and reassembled it. For some reason I was surprised when he walked to the kitchen and washed his hands at the sink.

"Ah, smell that! Magnifico!" He put on a silly accent that sounded more Russian than Italian. "What shall-a we drink with...how you say dinner? *Dinero?* I'm-a sorry, the only alcohol in the house is of the rubbing variety. May I interest you in a selection from my soda pop cellar? Sprite, Vintage 2021? A very good year."

Elias dragged his work chair to the table. He and I shared a giggle while hot, gooey cheese flowed like lava over our fingers. We ravaged our first slices like wolves.

"So what was the damage?" I said.

"Like I suspected: bent spoke and contact. All better now. But next time some blonde pisses you off, take it out on something inanimate, like your bathroom door."

"Mm." I reached for another slice. "Are you trying to imply that computers are *not* inanimate objects?"

He spoke through a mouth full of cheese and dough. "Put it this way: some machines right now, with AI running touch screens and mics and gyros and accel—" he gagged, holding his throat to help swallow—"accelerometers and visual recognition, they have all the architecture in place to be programmed to feel pain."

"Yeah, sure."

"I mean it. Computers talk back nowadays, right? It ain't fake, nor is it magic. It's crude intelligence, but it's going places. Heck, even your dishwasher uses fuzzy logic these days. It's like we're in the Proterozoic Age of computer evolution—I mean, think about how DNA evolved and little creepy blobs started moving around on their own. Do amoebas feel pain?"

No, I thought. Though my stomach did, from eating too fast.

"Come on, you're not serious," I said. "Computers don't feel. They *can't* feel, I don't care how far AI evolves. Even if you can program it to respond to something like me punching it, it's pure simulation. Metal and plastic and code. You hit it, it doesn't hurt. It just breaks."

"Ooh, that's cold," Elias shook his head, causing a mozzarella suspension bridge to snap over his chin. "This coming from someone who just beat the crap out of a helpless little pink computer. You're a goner when the cyborgs attack."

"Not funny."

"Sorry."

We drank soda and shoved pizza in our faces in silence while darkness fell outside the single tiny window. With only the kitchen light and a lamp clipped to his work table, the room took on the impression of a cavern, mounds of objects solidifying into rocky contours. The dim light and shadow chiseled his face into someone a bit older and more pensive.

"You'd look better with a haircut," I said. "I mean, find someone to actually style it."

The look he returned reminded me of an attention-starved puppy who'd heard its name called. I bet I was the first woman since his mother to comment on his looks.

"You think so?" was all he could come up with.

My phone buzzed: Zuzie asking if I wanted to go in on an Indian takeout. I tapped a negative reply, but started thinking about how to excuse myself to go home. Elias must have noticed the way I shifted on the cushion, because he wiped the back of his hand across his lips, covered a burp, and almost pleaded, "Don't go yet."

"I wasn't going to." I intended it as a lie, but in fact I had nothing to rush home to.

He leaned in, removed his glasses and polished them with the hem of his t-shirt. He looked like a big teddy bear with little button eyes. "Confession time," he said. "I don't know anyone else who might understand. Maybe you won't either, but maybe you will."

"Try me."

"So, we were talking—at least I was—about computers having feelings?" he said. "Okay, that's going a bit far. But I'm being Scout's honor serious now. Sometimes I really do start thinking my machines have a kind of consciousness. You know, like some cultures believe in rock spirits?"

Tempted though I was to make a joke, I held my tongue and let him continue.

"I mean, I deal with people every day—run around to their homes or offices. Sometimes have to play the shrink to calm them down when they panic about losing files, or I need the patience of the Buddha to teach them how to do simple stuff like switching browser tabs instead of reopening the same web page fifty-seven times. So it's not like I don't know how to talk to living human beings—though you might disagree. But when the problem's fixed, they pick up where they left off, and I cease to exist in their life. Know what I mean?"

"Sure."

"I mean, I get it, I'm just some dumb slob repairman," he continued. "So I come home, the people part of my day's over. I walk in the door and who's there to welcome me? Conan over there—the red laptop? And Van Damme, my very own home-made desktop. It's like I hear voices—*Me! Me! Turn me on!*—*No, me!*"

I wasn't sure whether he intended me to laugh, so I raised an eyebrow as a sign to continue.

"It sounds a little nuts, I know," he said. "But I been thinking about this—your brain forms a thought and emits electromagnetic waves, which travel through space like radio signals. Maybe that's what clairvoyants pick up from other people. Then you read about people who supposedly pick up radio programs through their fillings. And computers are like beehives of electromagnetic energy. So maybe in some way, my nervous system can receive machine thoughts."

I didn't know what to say. Ask for a demonstration? Or should I tell him to see a therapist? Or maybe an exorcist.

"Do they have different personalities, Conan and, um, Van Damme?"

"Now you're making fun of me. I thought you of all people would understand."

"Me?"

"Sure. You talk to a computer all day."

"I talk to *people*."

"I fix code, you fix grammar. At the end of the day—"

"You don't know what you're talking about." I wasn't in the mood for this. I was tired. I was grouchy.

A pulsing bass melody erupted from somewhere, the same tune he'd been humming earlier. I recognized it now: the opening bars of "In-A-Gadda-Da-Vida".

"Sorry, my phone's bluetoothed to my speakers," Elias said. "Gotta answer a client. Please don't go. Please?"

My turn for the phone to buzz. Another text from Zuzie.

Out late chick tikka in fridge if u want

Another solitary evening ahead, reading or streaming a movie. In a way, Elias was right. He fixed machines all day and came home to more machines. I fixed people's English all day, and when I finished I was already home with...what? Was it so bad staying here a bit longer, in the company of a real human, however weird?

He finished his call.

"My turn to confess," I told him.

"Wait. Am I playing priest or cop?"

"Quiet. I'm serious." I leaned forward, cradling my chin in my hands. "You're a guy."

"Glad you noticed."

"Then let me ask your take, 'cause girls and guys think differently."

"I'm listening."

"Speaking of speaking at computers. Do you think, like, you can get to know somebody—I mean, really *know* them—from just being together online?"

He scratched the back of his head. "Uh. You'd be the expert on that."

"I'm asking you."

"Someone's been hitting the dating sites?"

I glared.

"Sorry. Okay." He settled back and gestured in a professorial manner. "Let's approach this from different angles. First, you don't smell their farts. Probably don't hear them either."

"I ask you a serious question and the first thing you think of is farts?"

"Well, it's one point in favor of online relationships."

"Come on, Elias. What I mean is, you don't see the way they walk, the way they eat, the things they shout at the TV, if they avoid dogs or stepping on sidewalk cracks, or tap their toes to some tune in their head."

"Or if they sweat a lot. I mean, that's something you want to know."

"Will you quit it with the body odors?" I said. "So you think you can't know someone through online contact alone."

"I didn't say that."

"You said there were different angles."

"Guess I did. Trying to figure out what they are. But hold on, what's your angle? Why are you asking me? Oh, wait. Think I get it."

Maybe this had gone far enough. Time to slink home to my empty apartment, feed rodents, and slug down the rest of the generic burgundy I'd shared that morning with Sandro. Though of course we hadn't shared it. We'd shared compressed digital approximations of wine. "I think I'm gonna go."

"Uh uh. You're not leaving me hanging like this. My guess is you're hot for one of your students."

I dropped back onto the couch, relieved that he was the one who said it. "I'm that transparent, huh?"

"No. But it doesn't take a genius. Anyway, you started this whole discussion by referring to my, uh, *manhood* as my main qualification."

Now I was in deep. I'd never talked to a guy about another guy. What did you ask? A guy's advice on how to get into another guy's pants from halfway around the world?

Elias stood up and strolled to the kitchen. "Where's he from?"

"Um. Okay, I'm telling you this stuff. But you promise never to breathe a word!"

"Who would I breathe to?" He returned with glasses of tap water. I gratefully accepted and downed half mine in a single gulp.

"He's Italian. I've been seeing him six weeks. Not the best student, but lately he's been dropping all these hints."

"Like what hints?"

I thought of showing him, but decided against it. "Photos of Saturn and nebulas and stuff."

"Let me get this straight." Elias reached for the bag of cheese puffs and munched between sentences. "This guy sends you Saturn pics and it's supposed to be like valentines? Could have at least sent you Venus."

"He sent that too."

"What about verbal clues? Drop any hints during lessons? Come on, Serena, give me something to work with."

"I don't know. Maybe I'm making the whole thing up. Never mind. Forget it."

"Sit down. You wanted advice from a guy. So, tell me if I'm wrong." He counted on his fingers. "The dude's charming, good-looking, gainfully employed, all the base requirements. Am I on track?"

I crossed my legs, hitting the table and nearly spilling his water.

His chair squeaked as he leaned back, clutching the cheese puff bag between his knees.

"Okay, let's do the math: a hot Italian guy you've probably seen only from the sternum up, face forward, for six weeks—every weekday? Yeah? So, thirty hours—whose English communication skills leave something to be desired or he wouldn't be seeing you in the first place. Then he sends you snapshots of frozen gas giants, and you're wondering if these are the signs of a budding romance. I'd say that's about on the same level as me hearing voices from my computers."

"He invited me to Italy. Sort of. Does that help?"

As I uncrossed my numbed legs, my foot got caught on the table, this time knocking the water glass right onto the cheese puffs bag in his lap. Orange sauce dribbled onto the carpet.

He dashed to the kitchen and rummaged under the sink,

returning with two sponges and a Tupperware bowl. We both got on our knees and mopped up the mess.

"I'm sorry," I said.

"Not the first time it's happened. But first time caused by some crazed chick karate kicking my table."

"Anyway, that's the whole story. As long as I asked, might as well tell me. What would you do?"

Elias tossed his sponge into the bowl and sat up on his knees, taking his time to form an answer. "Serena, I don't know beans about how people work. So I'm going out on a limb here. I think it all sounds really cute, yeah? And if I was a girl I'd probably be falling all over this dude. But seeing as I'm a guy all I can say is..." he sighed "...wish I'd thought of it first. In fact, just a sec—"

He reached for his phone, thumbed and scrolled like he was searching for something, then tapped and out came a tiny beep. Two seconds later, my phone's incoming message tone sounded. I looked.

A photo captioned Jupiter.

Elias leaned back against the chair, grinning, while his eyes simmered with sadness, or hope, or even jealousy. "For what it's worth, mine's bigger."

I'd had enough of talking computers and lonely men for one day. I gave him a peck on the cheek, then tugged a lock of his hair, heavy as a spring. "Thanks. Night. Get a haircut."

I had my hand on the door handle when his voice crossed the room.

"Wait! Don't forget Kitty."

"Who?"

I turned around. He held out my computer with both hands.

BACK HOME MY NEWLY healed computer, which I was already starting to think of as "Kitty"—*damn him!*—balanced on my lap as I leaned back in bed waiting for a web page to open.

The site hadn't changed since the last three hundred times I'd checked it: Masseria Buonaventura, olive plantation and oil maker operated for generations by the family Buonaventura. That matched Alessandro's surname, and it was in the right region, but no mention or pictures of individual people, only photos of olive groves and oil bottles, a watercolor of a country manor, and descriptions in Italian. A general image search of his name produced, for the three hundredth time, a 16th Century painting of a dandy with a feathered cap, and a sepia photo of a man in a three-piece suit who looked like the Monopoly banker.

I ran through the other searches I'd done before: Capracornea, the town named on the website, and the Puglia region in general. Once more I scrolled through touristy pictures of churches and piazzas and little white cone-shaped houses that looked like homes for elves. And of course, olive groves. It was all starting to feel familiar.

At last I performed a new search, one I hadn't dared yet.

cheap flights italy

Chapter 13

The rules of grammar are nothing more than lists of patterns that can be heard in proper speech. The fact that there are so many exceptions proves that they aren't rules at all, but a blurred-around-the-edges, evolving consensus about what sounds right. Children learn their native language by imitation, and trial and error, without ever knowing there was such thing as laws of syntax. It seemed obvious to me that grammar isn't the cause of proper speech, but the outcome.

That was why sometimes my job made no sense. What was the point of teaching grammar? It was like teaching someone to ride a bicycle by drilling them in the laws of momentum and centrifugal force. The moment you start worrying about the cosine of the angle of attack of your front wheel, you fall off your bike.

I was coming to the same conclusion about men and relationships. All those do's and don'ts ingrained in me by my mother and girlfriends, and preached in glossy magazine articles like "Ten Surefire Ways into a Man's Heart...and His Bed", were more hindrance than help in trying to figure out my personal feelings, much less guessing a man's. It seemed I had to make up my own rules. Or, more likely, there were no rules, only outcomes. I was on my own.

Which was why I tried not to analyze too much when Alessandro sent me a private message near the end of one lesson, asking whether I'd like to "share another wine" after work. I responded that by the time I finished my last student it would be one o'clock in the morning for him, to which he replied that was a perfect time for stargazing. My contract forbade me from contacting students outside the school's mechanisms. But some rules, like those governing auxiliary verbs in the simple present tense, were born to invite exceptions.

Plus, we had traded phone numbers. No one needed to know.

I sat cross-legged on the couch with my phone inches from my face. The connection appeared at first not to work: static-like rustling noise and a totally black screen. Was it my data problem? Then a light came on, saturating the video until his camera adjusted. Sandro's face floated in the darkness, lit from below by a flashlight.

"You see me?" His voice was thin and dissipated.

"Are you outside?"

"Yes. Outside. Wait." The image went dark again, then refocused on a cylindrical device budding with attachments.

"That's your telescope? It's so short. Are you on your mountain?"

"It is sp–*mirror* telescope. Not on the mountain. Now stand outside my house." He moved the phone so that I saw shaky squares of yellow light from what must have been windows, though I couldn't make out the building's details. Then he turned the camera back on himself, wearing an exaggerated frown. "But sky now is not, ah, clean."

"You mean not clear?"

"Yes. Not clear. We are not fortunate."

The base of my spine tingled when he said the word *we*. Then he surprised me again by holding up a glass of wine. I dashed into the kitchen, and discovered that someone had left about eight drops in the box of burgundy. I found an unopened bottle of Pinot Noir, then spent an eternity scrounging for a corkscrew, shouting "Wait!" at the phone on the counter. By the time I sat down again, I really needed that drink.

"Slow service in this trattoria," I said.

"Ah! Must be Italian." We laughed and clinked cup images.

"I am sorry, we don't see stars. But I see Serena. So I am happy."

The way he said my name, drawing out the second syllable like he was caressing it with his tongue, stopped the wine halfway down my throat. I desperately wanted to pull an Alice in Wonderland, step through to the other side of the screen, stand in his garden in the cool of the night, where I would lean into him, parting my lips...

And dribble wine down my chin.

I wiped myself and gulped down the rest, triggering a choking fit in me and a look of alarm on him.

"I'm okay," I said. "I...wine went...wrong place." I stoppered the cough with my hand. "Sandro. I'm also happy to see you."

"Look. Cloud is open. Can see?" He aimed the lens at a tiny bright spot, my first sight of the southern Italian moon, though it wouldn't sit still long enough to focus. I heard more rustling footsteps and his face came on again, lit only on the edges. "This night not good for to looking stars. Now we sit."

"Outside? On the ground?"

"Ground...yes, I think so. We sit, we talk. How your work?"

Jessie texted me. I replied that I was busy talking with my Italian. Her response was instant: an emoji with hearts for eyes.

I told Sandro in simple English about my day, working at home, pretending to be inside a classroom. He rested his chin on his palm, regarding me as though I were revealing the profound wisdom of the ages.

"I'm question...I pay money for lesson, how much you get? I think half?"

"I wish."

"Smaller?"

All I could do was shrug.

"*Oddio!* Why you do this job?" He looked as scandalized as if he'd learned I'd just been mugged. It occurred to me that Sandro had grown up with an oil-filled silver spoon in his mouth, in a prosperous family business he would inherit one day, and that probably everyone in his social circle was the same. He would have no concept of what it's like to leave college mired in debt, having to grab the first thing that comes along in order to barely cover rent on a crummy shared apartment. And someone raised in an ancient family business might not appreciate how shameful it would feel to go back and live with your mother.

I tried to change the topic. "I like my job. And you?"

One eyebrow shot up and a smile filled his face, teeth sparkling like stars. "I like you too, Serena."

It took a couple seconds for my mind to click: he'd heard my "And you" as a statement, not a question!

"I didn't mean—No. Wrong. I didn't actually say—Oh, shut up, Serena!" I slapped my cheek and leaned my chin on my hand, mirroring his posture. "I like you a lot, Sandro. Yeah. So, um..." What was I supposed to say? We both seemed stuck for words. If we'd been in the same hemisphere, I might have lowered my head onto his shoulder or inched forward until he kissed me.

Another message from Jessie. I didn't even read it, just replied:

He likes me. Talk later.

She came back immediately.

*OMG careful pull back now
gotta hold the tendon*

I guessed she meant *tension.*

"What about your job?" I asked him. "How does it work? Do you get a salary?"

"Ha! For me, no money."

"What? You're telling jokes."

"Not jokes. No salary. If I need money, I say Papà, he give, no problem. Almost."

"Almost what?"

He swallowed the rest of his wine, then the picture blurred again. "We go foot."

I corrected: "We walk."

"Yes, teacher! I walk, you walk, he she it walks. We walk."

Light shifted across his face as the flashlight changed hands, while his footsteps sounded louder and harder, crunching on gravel. "Okay. Now I say you...I don't know English: *verità.*"

"The truth?"

"I say you the truth. The truth is, I don't want to learn English."

The picture faded in and out as his phone camera struggled to adjust to the unsteady light. The image froze for a moment, a side view of his head, eyes turned toward me, maybe to assess my reaction.

"Papà want me to learn English because for the business. I am not interest. But Papà..." He rolled his eyes. "I say him I am no good to learn, don't want, but he..." A rolled fist filled the screen.

"He hit you?" I said.

"No. But he very very angry. So I look your school."

Our eyes met across eight thousand miles and I suppose spoke to each other, because what was inside me at that moment couldn't be expressed in any language.

"Then you are there," he continued, "and my thinkings change. If I learn English, every day I see you."

I blinked hard, guessing that on his tiny phone screen he wouldn't notice the tears welling up. The picture bounced as he continued to walk. Dark treetops passed in the darker night. The scrape of his steps: dirt again. I felt as though I'd crossed through the glass into the picture, actually walking beside him, until my phone's buzz rudely pulled me back.

A message popped up from Steve:

*Back next Friday. You won't believe what's
coming to LA: Oklahoma musical! Want to go?*

I poked the screen until the message vanished. The shift from
a romantic stroll under a Mediterranean night sky, to watching a
peppy song-and-dance show with a nice All-American Guy, was
too much of a cognitive jolt at that moment.

I asked Alessandro about what it was like growing up on an
olive plantation. He told me how he'd known from a very young
age that his life would revolve around this work, this venture, this
land, speaking as if he'd recited these same words many times to
visiting buyers or tourists. He sounded bored, his voice coated
with a rich layer of sadness, something I couldn't fully grasp. My
lot in life gave me little choice at this present moment other than
to do the job I was doing, live in the place I was living; it was
the hand I'd been dealt. Maybe he felt the same: his life laid out
for him, his challenges prescribed in advance, dealt a winning
hand without the thrill of earning it on his own. Or maybe I was
inventing things. He could afford all the toys he wanted—simply
ask Papà for money.

Argh. Another message popup. From Jessie. How to turn
them off?

*So what's the score with the
man in the moon?*

I tapped back: *Discussing olive oil*

Jessie: *Kinky!*

Sandro cocked his head. He could tell I was texting.

"Sorry," I said. "I think I understand. Sometimes I feel like
I'm stuck in a nice, warm prison."

His head tilted the other way. "I do not know this
word, prison."

I held up my finger to wait, and did a quick online translation.

"*Carcere,*" which I pronounced *car-SEE-ree.* I spelled it out for him.

He smirked at the stupid American and said it properly: *CAR-che-ray.* "Also me! I sometimes feel I am in beautiful— what is English?"

"Prison."

"Yes. I sometimes feel I am in a beautiful prison. We together in prison."

Text to Jessie: *OMG*

Jessie: *What what what he invite you home yet*

Another knowing look from Sandro. I turned off notifications and ignored the next few buzzes. I'd fill her in later.

"I think your prison is much nicer than mine," I said. "And better food."

"Food is good. Mamma is good...ah...cooker."

"Cook," I said.

"Mamma is a good cook." He fixed his attention on something in the sky. "Now is more clear. Can see the moon. Maybe we go to telescope, I can show you."

"I'd love to!"

His face turned to alarm. "Ai! No can. My, ah, *batteria.* Too little."

"That's okay. Next time. Or one day I can see it in person." Hint! Hint!

"Serena, come to Puglia, I show you my beautiful pris—"

The screen froze and went black; his phone had died.

I repeated his last sentence in my head. Was there a comma after my name the way he'd said it? Without a comma, it was a neutral conditional clause. But with a comma—I was sure that's what he meant. There was no doubt this time: he'd invited me! I punched a reply to Jessie:

OMG! Yes yes yes yes!!!! :D

I stood up from the couch, as though my body might keep rising and float among the clouds. I danced around the living room with an invisible Alessandro as my partner, grabbed my half-full glass, threw my head back and tipped in the wine, just as the front door squeaked open.

"Whoa! Somebody's either had a real good day or an incredibly crappy one," Zuzie said.

I put down the glass with a grand *ahhh*. "The former."

"Cool. Seeing as that is such a rare occurrence, how'd you like to go out and have Mexican?"

I didn't see the connection, but, "Why not?" I said. "Live large! Margaritas and nachos supreme?"

"With bacon. We going all the way, sister."

"With bacon!"

Zuzie went into her room to change out of her barista outfit. My phone buzzed where I'd left it on the couch.

So? Did he invite you?

From Jessie. Thought I'd already told her. But checking the message thread I couldn't find my reply. Hadn't I just written, "Yes yes yes yes"?

I had. In reply to the last message which had come in.

From Steve. Who'd re-sent his invitation to see *Oklahoma!*

Chapter 14

I lost track of how many late nights I spent registering at each and every travel website in the western hemisphere, and several in Hong Kong, hunting down the elusive bargain ticket to Rome. The cheapest return ticket was always the same thousand-plus dollar price, give or take pocket change. If I found one for a hundred bucks less, seconds later it was gone. I studied articles, blogs, and discussion groups which advised the precise times to beat the airlines' pricing algorithms. I set my alarm to 3:30 in the morning, but my phone must have sent stealth Wi-Fi signals, because the moment I found an unbelievable bargain, the cost would leap skywards as though the "Select Flight" button had really read, "Sucker!"

The first of the month came and went without any new enrollments. Marisa shrugged her shoulders, claiming they were having a slow period.

"Even Victoria—"

"Please, Marisa, enough about Victoria."

"Gotcha, sweetie. Let you know when something comes up."

I drove Zuzie mad by watching every travel show about Italy, and there were plenty—a gluttonous feast of scrumptious landscapes, architecture and art, and of course food and wine. I could taste phantom pasta and marinara sauce even while slouching on the sofa spooning cold baked beans from a can, while Zuzie bellowed from her room: "I hear one more happy frigging host say

'Mamma mia' just one more frigging time, I swear I'm putting my foot through the frigging screen!"

I envied the refugees on the nightly news who set out in leaky boats and the Italian navy would deliver them for free to some southern port with a gorgeous name that rolled off the tongue. If only the Italian Coast Guard would show up off Huntington Beach!

Then one night there it was: Los Angeles to Rome, round trip for $538! Oh my god oh my god oh my god what to do? Did I even have that in the bank? I hadn't thought through what I would actually do if some buy-in-the-next-five-minutes flash special appeared. Up until now it had all been a fantasy. One side of me screamed: *Go for it, girl!* The other cautioned: Now you know such bargains exist. When the time comes that you're truly ready to make the trip, patience will reward you with another pop-up bargain.

Patience? I was running out. My life was like a car stuck at a broken stoplight. Waiting, always waiting, for more students, more money, a better job, broader horizons. Walking hand in hand through olive groves heavy with fruits, sipping wine amidst laughter and ancient ruins, none of that was going to happen by being patient.

I clicked "Book your flight". Chose some dates—six weeks from now seemed "sensible"—and scheduled myself a three-week trip to Italy. Trains, hotels, time off from work, I'd figure that out later.

A little wheel spun forever in the center of the screen. Then there it was: a real itinerary, with flight departure and arrival times—at Leonardo da Vinci International Airport. Oh. My. God.

I clicked "Accept", which brought me to the next screen, where I typed in my name, nationality, contact information. I nearly ripped my purse and wallet apart to get at the debit card. When all the little numbers and check digits were entered, there was only one thing left to do.

I patted my chest, told myself to be brave. Nobody succeeded in life if they were afraid to throw caution to the wind.

I clicked "Pay now".

A bit too quickly, a new screen appeared:

This fare is no longer available.
Please try another booking.

I fell back in my chair, limp with relief. What had I been thinking?

SANDRO TOOK ME ON another after-work midnight stroll through the family acreage. He acted cheerful as usual, talking about some nearby music festival and asking what concerts I'd attended. Yet even through the grainy image his pensiveness showed, his shoulders stiff. It must have been as hot there as in California, because he kept reaching inside his shirt collar and wiping his neck.

I asked him about work today—was he out in the groves, in the refinery, behind a computer? I didn't understand his explanation and asked him to repeat. He struggled to find the English words. When I attempted to complete a sentence for him, he snapped, "No lesson!" Then instantly apologized, tapped his brow and shook his head. I understood—it was mentally exhausting to maintain a real conversation in a language you barely knew.

He continued walking past stands of trees which looked like pointillist paintings in the moonlight. The background rotated and I guessed that he was lying down. He turned the lens to the tiny white moon, then back to himself. He lay and I lay on my bed, looking at each other, his breathing rustling my phone speaker.

After what felt like ten minutes, but was probably less than two, he nodded and said, "Is good."

I nodded back.

"Buona notte," he said.

"Buona notte."

The screen went dark. My chest burned like I'd swallowed the seed of a bright fiery star.

IN THE MORNING I discovered Laurel huddled on his side in the corner of his cage. It was hard to tell the difference between shivering and a hamster's normal hyperactive fidgeting, but when he refused a cucumber stick and a green droplet spurted from his rear end, twenty bells clanged inside my skull.

With ten minutes until my first lesson I thrashed a brush through my hair while checking online hamster forums. I had Laurel's symptoms narrowed down to congestive heart failure, bowel cancer, or tummy infection, when I had to log off and torment Bieber with a review of his less-than-successful preposition homework.

Between lessons I moved Laurel to a quarantine cage and force-fed him water with an eyedropper until he nearly bit me. The apartment's front door latch clicked and Zuzie's boyfriend let himself in. I grabbed him.

"What do you know about hamsters?"

"Odd way to say good morning. Believe I had hamster stew once in Peru. Or was it guinea pig? Too greasy for my palate. Zuzie up?"

When Yasmin heard why I was two minutes late, she panicked, insisting I call off her lesson and rush to the doctor, which I might have taken her up on, except that the nearest vet didn't open until her lesson finished. She forewent "special words" at the end and practically screamed at me to phone the animal clinic.

A flat male voice picked up the phone and told me to call again in ten minutes; better yet, fifteen.

"This is an emergency! Are you the vet? My hamster—"

"Just the humble kennel minion. Ten minutes, someone'll be here, all right?" He hung up.

I called right back. Before he could dismiss me, I blurted,

"I've got three minutes before my next...uh, client. Please just help me make an appointment."

"Calm down now, Miss. Soon as someone—oop, here's Kristin. I'll hand you over."

I heard him whisper "nutjob" before a woman's voice came on. "Hi. Do you mind terribly calling back in around—"

"Please! My hamster's dying!"

"You could come in right away if you like. Doctor should be here half hour."

"I can't. All I need's an appointment before your schedule fills."

I heard the fanfare of a computer booting up. "I can pencil you in for...hmm, doctor's in surgery till...how's one thirty suit you?"

It didn't. My last lesson didn't finish until four. "How about four thirty?"

Kristin sniffed. "Didn't you say it was an emergency? Hamsters can very quickly—"

I wasn't in the mood to be patronized. "Four thirty, okay? The earliest I can get out."

"We close at five, so our last scheduled appointment is, like, four fifteen."

"Oh, come on!" I caught myself shouting.

A sigh hissed in my ear. "Anyway, we always run a bit late. Make sure to keep him warm and hydrated. What's the name?"

"Laurel!" I hung up, then put on a huge smile for my Estonian property manager who was on Lesson 27—or was it 28?

My performance was off for the rest of the day. Sandro noticed right away. "Is something that sads you? Is me?" I explained that my hamster was sick, and asked whether they ate hamsters in Italy. He responded with a disgusted face and encouraged me to rush to the doctor. As did my Belgian French student in North Dakota, though probably because he too felt unwell, having come down with a slight head cold that wreaked havoc on his already gelatinous accent. It was like someone speaking under water.

Lessons thankfully over, I checked that Laurel was still breathing, grabbed his cage, and ran out. My Toyota decided to put up a fuss about starting. One day I needed to break down and get it looked at, but not this month, not with less than eight hundred dollars in the bank, my next payday earmarked for rent and student loans, and having promised my grandmother another payment toward the $4500 she'd fronted me for the car.

I headed down Seventeenth Street to the freeway, then squeezed into the early rush hour stampede. Traffic was heavy, but things were moving fast enough that I'd get there in time for the clinic's precious 4:15 cutoff. Laurel appeared calm in his cage, strapped beside me in the passenger seat.

This was the last thing I needed right now. A previous visit to the vet had cost eighty dollars to treat Hardy's gummy eye infection. Ten percent of my current net worth, for rodents who had cost me five bucks a pair in a moment of impulse late last year. I shook such heartless thoughts from my head, hair whipping my face, which earned me a fist-pump from the fat bearded slob blaring death metal in the next lane. His eyes lingered on me like I was an ice cream cone to be licked. I tapped the brake to let the jerk pass. A horn blared to my rear.

Laurel pressed against his cage bars, nose and whiskers twitching in alarm at the noises and vibrations and unfamiliar smells. Or maybe he felt my tension. He'd spent nearly his entire nine-month life with me, so perhaps he could pick up my—what had Elias called them?—my brain's electromagnetic waves. I told him, "Hang in there. I won't let you suffer."

Even if it meant me suffering. I tried to skew my thoughts toward the positive side, as preached by all the self-help books I used to stuff into my head. It was okay to blow eighty bucks on someone I loved, no matter how tiny. I'd earn karma points, or I'd meet some rich benefactor at the clinic, or find a note on the board there: someone giving away a flight to Rome. According to the books, everything we considered as setbacks or bad luck should be viewed as a cosmic lesson to guide one onto the right path. Normally such passages read like mumbo jumbo to me. But now, with time to think in the slowing traffic, I struggled to extract whatever lesson the Cosmos intended me to learn.

I had to let go. I had to stop feeling as though my guts were being ripped out every time something broke or got sick that would cost money. Look at what had happened with my crappy old computer: without my asking, Elias had come along like a knight in—not shining armor exactly—a cheese puff-stained t-shirt. See? I *was* lucky sometimes. I would get through this. I would spend without resentment whatever it took to rescue my hamster. Something would balance it out. I would get a new student, I might even freelance on the side like I used to with exchange students, maybe start a blog for English learners and bring in crowdfunding or write an e-book. I would make enough money to stop worrying, so that I could do whatever I wanted: fly to Italy, or Tahiti, or Mongolia. I had it in me! I was smart, I was competent with words. I would live the life I deserved to live.

I pounded the steering wheel. That was it! The lesson the Cosmos was giving me. I was no longer a victim of circumstances. Good things were going to come to me. Because I deserved them! Didn't I, oh God or Buddha or spirits up in heaven? Prosperity and...and...*love* were coming my way. Starting today! Starting this moment! Tears of jubilation streamed down my cheeks.

I wiped my eyes with the back of my hand, then reached for a tissue.

A pair of red lights glared too close ahead.

Jerked the wheel.

Slammed brakes.

My head and neck came apart. Blinded and smothered in fabric, choking on powder. I clawed at the airbag, desperate to free myself, to see around me, to leap from the car in case it caught fire. A sharp pain dug into my belly. *Oh my God, my spine's been severed!* I moved my feet, successfully wiggled my toes. It was only the seat belt constricting me.

What had happened? There'd been skidding, brake lights looming larger, but no impact, no sounds. Maybe I was all right. Nothing had happened. Except for a loud hiss and ticking and car horns blaring, a siren in the distance. But I wouldn't be able to see a thing until I got this airbag out of my face. Weren't they supposed to automatically deflate? I felt around for valves, or maybe some button on the steering column. I gasped for breath, like a yawn that wouldn't finish. Then the bag suddenly collapsed. I fell back against the seat, struggling to catch my breath, my vision spinning like a pinwheel.

A tap at the half-open window. I guess I didn't respond, because the door handle rattled and somebody said, "You all right?"

A man in a rumpled business suit reached in and opened the door, undid my seatbelt, and helped me out of the car. Then I saw, and my knees gave out.

My entire front end was smashed in, the hood crumpled like an accordion. The ticking I'd heard was louder outside. The car in front of me, a dark blue German-looking thing, had its trunk hood skewed at an angle, its front inserted into the back of a minivan.

"You hurt anywhere?" the man asked, helping me stand. "You nailed me pretty hard."

I patted myself down for fractures and bruises, but nothing felt broken. "I don't think so. You?"

He rubbed his neck and my breath caught in my throat. He was probably a lawyer. Yes, he looked like one. Who else in southern California wore a suit in the summer? He would sue me for whiplash. I'd lose everything, my money, my car, my license.

"Nothing that won't come out in a hot bath," he said.

"Not so sure about our rides, though." He told me an SUV had broken down in the far left lane. Someone about three cars ahead swerved into our lane to avoid it, and Newton's first and third laws of motion, allied with driving too close, had kicked in. Now six of us, including the breakdown, were spread over three freeway lanes, with mine last in the pile-up. A traffic jam stretched out behind.

Somehow a Highway Patrol car emerged through the mess. An officer directed traffic, while his fat partner took down my name, license number, and address. He smelled strongly of onions. He grumbled, "Gotta get off this road, lady."

I indicated the wrecked state of my engine. "I'm not sure I—"

"Next exit's two'na half miles." He pointed ahead. "Can't have you sittin' here, not safe." He walked off to interrogate other drivers. The minivan started its engine.

I got back in my car and tried the ignition. It turned over once, twice, then popped like a knife blade snapping, followed by an ear-splitting metallic scrape. Sure that Laurel and I were about to become toast in an automotive mushroom cloud, I reached toward the passenger seat.

The hamster cage was gone.

It lay overturned on the floor, shrouded by a limp airbag.

I picked up the cage; its door dangled open. My hand shot inside, but found nothing warm or furry. I shook its contents onto the seat. A hill of sawdust, but no hamster.

"Laurel!" I scrambled outside and knelt to peer under the seats. No sign of him.

Oh my God! Why hadn't I checked? Why had I left my door open?

I lay sideways on the gritty asphalt and searched beneath the car. A lake of shiny liquid pooled almost its entire length.

"The hell you doin', lady?" Two hands dragged me by the shoulders from under the chassis. Onion Cop looked more like a mustached tomato. "You lost something, I give you thirty seconds to find it, then you get your butt and your vehicle off this road."

"Get your hands off me, jerkwad!" I squirmed free and accidentally head-butted his belly as I got up.

"Listen to me, lady. If you ain't in that car and moving off this freeway in thirty seconds, I'm gonna—"

"My car's busted and my hamster's missing!"

"What'd you say?"

"My hamster! I was taking him to the vet. And now I can't find him!" I licked tears from the ends of my lips.

"Whatever. If your vehicle's disabled..." His meaty fist grabbed my arm and pulled me toward the freeway divider. "I'll need you to stand to the side while I call a tow and—*Jeebus!*"

I dug fingernails into hand and spun free.

"Laurel! Laurel!" I dashed between stranded cars and nearly ended up in the one moving lane. A horn-blaring blue Prius squealed to a stop, nearly causing a third pile-up. I moved in front of the car.

The driver shouted through the window: "Hey!"

"The hell you doing?" Onion Cop shouted.

I stood my ground in the center of the lane. "No one's moving till I find my hamster!"

"What's going on?" a woman shouted. A discordant symphony of horns broke out.

"I mean it!" I said, my hands on the Prius's hood.

Onion Cop held his police radio to his mouth. "Got a hamster on the loose. Close the lane and find the damn thing."

The Prius driver opened his door. "What's your buddy's name?"

"Laurel. Like Laurel and Hardy."

Soon the freeway swarmed with people calling, "Laurel! Here Laurel! Come to Mommy!" A little girl stuck her head out a window. She was crying for my missing hamster. For a moment I forgot the accident itself, knowing only that I was crawling on asphalt, Laurel was missing, some people were nice enough to help.

A whistle cut through the freeway noise. I banged my head on an open car door.

"The fugitive has been apprehended!"

Another policeman held up a fist, from which a tiny head poked out. Cheers broke out, a few horns beeped congratulations. Onion Cop said someone had found him huddling behind a tire. He made sure Laurel was firmly shut in his cage, then patted my shoulder. "Now get off my freeway. I'll call you a tow."

I thanked him and told him I'd write a glowing recommendation to his commander, and to the newspaper, for stopping traffic to save a hamster's life.

"You do that and I swear I'm toast. Let's just keep it between you and me and about a hundred pissed off drivers."

I sat on the concrete divider with the cage in my lap while vehicles zoomed past. My fault. My stupid fault. If only I hadn't rubbed my eyes.

Stupid Cosmos.

The tow truck finally showed up. The driver winched my car onto the bed, then Laurel and I joined him up front.

"Where am I taking you, lady? You got a regular body shop?" He had a light Hispanic accent and a wrestler's build.

His dashboard clock read almost five-thirty.

"Can you bring me to the animal hospital? My hamster's dying."

He looked at me like I was crazy.

"Second exit," I said. "They close in like five minutes."

He crunched the shift into gear. "You lucky. I got no other calls right now."

The nurse put up a big argument until I explained what happened. She buzzed the veterinarian to come out, then made me tell the story all over again. Twenty minutes later, Laurel was pronounced suffering from a common intestinal infection, jabbed with an antibiotic, and I was handed a little dropper bottle of medicine. My debit card was sixty-five dollars lighter.

I stepped outside, scrolling my phone for a car hire app, when a light tap of a horn made me glance up. The tow truck sat in the convenience store parking lot across the street.

"Like I said, no other calls right now," the driver told me. "Your, uh, animal okay?"

I thanked him and climbed into the cab.

"So, you gotta call your insurance now, talk to them where to drop this wreck." He saw the alarm on my face. "Yeah, well, while you're in there I checked her over. Looks pretty bad, I think. Hope you got good coverage."

I crept along the edge of the truck bed to get the papers from my car, then sat again in the cab to call the insurance company. I gave the agent my policy number, described the incident, and waited two or three minutes while he put me on hold. When he came back and told me I wasn't covered, I dropped the phone in my lap and cried.

"Hey, hey, what's goin' on?" the driver said.

"They told me my insurance won't cover collisions."

"Huh? They still on the line? Gimme that phone."

The driver did a lot of listening and a lot of *uh-huhs*, then started arguing, gently at first, escalating into Spanish expletives, many of which I understood to be directed toward the insurance agent's mother. He hung up and returned my phone.

"Short version is, you got comprehensive. Don't cover collision."

"What are you talking about? I'm an English teacher. Comprehensive means 'everything included.'"

"Then you better teach some English to these insurance sons of bitches, cause in their lingo, 'comprehensive' means it covers shit. But they paying for the tow at least, after I threaten."

"Now what? I don't know what to do," I blubbered so hard even I barely understood my own words.

"Here's what. I gonna drop you home. Then take your car to a body shop my cousin works at."

"Then what do I do?"

"Was me," he said, "be a tossup between a stiff rum or a quart of tequila and orange juice."

Chapter 15

I missed Steve, but for selfish reasons. I knew how mechanics played tricks on women. Steve probably spoke their language, but he was still in Calexico. The only other guy I knew was Elias, not exactly a manly match for some hulk packing a welding torch. Nevertheless, Elias was male and had a car and agreed to drive me to the body shop after work.

For good measure, I begged Miko, the walking anti-bullshit monitor, to meet us there, which also let me play matchmaker between the two biggest nerds in my life. When I texted Elias that we'd be meeting my Japanese girlfriend, he replied with a thumbs-up emoji and arrived wearing a Doraemon t-shirt still showing creases from the packaging.

Miko was waiting outside the Car Clinic with a look that spelled tragedy. My eyes watered at the sight of my poor car in a lineup of wounded vehicles in the alley beside the shop. The entire front end was squashed, the bumper hung by a wire, and one side panel stabbed into a tire.

Elias raised his phone to take a picture, but couldn't miss the condescending sneer unrolling across Miko's face.

"Hey, I know what you're thinking. Looks like an iPhone, right?"

Miko spat a dismissive puff of air.

"Well, it ain't," he said. "It a Fan Yin—Chinese brand that comes with stock dual boot Linux."

Miko looked impressed. "Forgive me for doubting your manhood."

"Came damn close. Apology accepted. Want to check it out?"

I sighed with relief. "Elias, meet Miko. Miko, Elias."

Miko gave a stiff nod. "How do you do."

"Doobie doobie doo," Elias said.

Were my eyes playing tricks? Miko actually smiled. Then she looked at me and back at the car and turned somber again as she peered under the crumpled hood with her phone flashlight. Elias jiggled the passenger door, but it wouldn't budge more than a couple inches.

"Maybe you should get a bicycle," Elias said.

"Or a hoverboard," added Miko.

I walked a big circle around the vehicle, trying to swallow my sobs.

"Looks like the Sad Avenjahs." I recognized the mechanic's Boston accent from our earlier phone call. A grizzly bear-shaped guy with slick black hair strode down the alley, extending a bear-sized paw. "Hey, I wanna picture," he said, pulling out an iPhone, a real one. "Look sad, everybody." He showed off the photo; Miko's and Elias's eyes had rolled halfway to the backs of their skulls.

"Lemme guess which one a you's the proud ownah." He pulled a tissue packet from his pocket and handed it to me. "Serena, right?"

"How much to fix it?" I said.

He offered his hand to shake. "Vince. Thanks for asking. I'm the owner here, so you're talking straight to the top. So, look, lemme ask you first—how much ya pay for this chariot?"

"Six thousand, round about."

His lips jutted, he scratched his nose. He tried the hood release, but it wouldn't pop. "Gotta get one of my boys out here."

"So, how much?" I said.

"No insurance, right? Like ya said on the phone?"

"Does that make a difference?" Miko said.

Vince narrowed his eyes at her. "No difference." Then back to me: "Listen, honey, I'm an honest man. But I gotta level with ya. Run three thousand easy, and that's with my nice guy discount."

Miko folded her arms. "Based on a full, detailed appraisal, I assume."

Vince's friendly-bear act dropped long enough to reveal the East Coast street punk behind the mask. Elias side-stepped toward Miko, a protective reaction that was kind of cute.

Vince asked Miko, "You work, sweetheart? What job you do?"

"I'm an engineer."

"I'm guessing not choo choo trains or ya might know something about engines. How's about big guy here? Engineer, too?"

"Computer technician," Elias said.

Vince nodded at him. "Okay. Guy like you probably gets it. Know how you see some computer on the blink, most times you sense what's wrong before you even moved a finger, am I right? No need to open it up—you just *know*."

"You got a point."

Vince slapped the front side panel. "I don't need to peel this off to tell you the chassis's bent. And the hood looking like my grandpa's accordion? Yeah, you noticed. Impact like that, the block might be cracked. Or maybe not, though I wouldn't let my mother drive it to find out. Your radiator's history, and right in there's where you got your electronics. Toast, I'd wager. Drive shafts, axles, could be okay, lemme take a peek." He looked behind a tire.

"Enough," I said. "Can you please get me a repair quote?"

"Itemized," Miko said, blinking hard behind her glasses. "Essential mechanical repairs separate from cosmetic work."

Vince raised his eyebrows to Elias. "What planet your girl from?"

Elias blinked at Miko.

"Burbank," she said.

"Kay, lemme level with you," Vince directed his speech to me. "In the real world—maybe not in Burbank, but in the real world—this car ain't worth fixing. What I'd have to charge, if you add a grand on top, can buy yourself something that'll give you another hundred thousand miles, easy." He slapped the hood. Something rattled and hit the ground. "In fact, you find a car you like, bring it to me. Yeah, I'll check it over for nothing, make sure nobody's try'na cheat a nice young lady."

My stomach sloshed around my knees. Four thousand dollars that I didn't have. Sure, I didn't need to drive to work. But to be without a car in southern California? As practical as losing a leg. No shopping, no trips to the beach, no obligatory visits to Mom or Grandma. Not that I often did any of those, but a car offered the promise, at least, of escape. And I still owed my grandmother over three thousand for what was now a steaming pile of metal. I wanted to die right there.

"You mean I should just abandon it? I can't even afford to have it towed away." I pulled out a tissue which fell to the ground. I took another and dried my eyes.

"I know some chop shops would buy it for scrap and parts," Vince said.

Miko stepped forward. "Excuse me. With all due respect, you've hardly looked at my friend's car, yet you seem more eager to sell it to your chop shop accomplices than to repair it."

"Hey, cool it." Elias put a hand on her shoulder. She flicked it off.

"Sweetheart, you think I don't wanna take your friend's money, see her drive away happy, car like new? Just telling it like it is. Don't believe me, fine. Pick another shop, they won't tell you anything different."

"A cartel, in other words," Miko said.

133

Vince handed me a card from his shirt pocket and walked off, waving over his shoulder. "Call me tomorrow, gimme till two, yeah? I'll have your estimate."

Miko pulled the card from my hand. I wasn't entirely sure Vince was out of earshot when she said, "Another Italian pervert trying to screw you. Metaphorically, of course."

"You didn't have to insult the guy," Elias said.

Miko peered through the car window. "I didn't hear you exactly challenging his manipulative little sales pitch."

"Let's see the estimate first. He's just doing his job."

"Snow job, is my estimate," she said.

"Sheesh. Bet you're loads of fun at parties."

"At least I questioned him. Not that Mister Sweetheart-tellin'-it-like-it-is would pay attention to an adult man wearing adolescent manga characters."

I covered my ears. "Come on, you guys." Not only was I car-less for the foreseeable future, not only was my world peeling apart, but I'd miscalculated badly in bringing them together, like magnets of identical polarity repelling each other. "Want to get a coffee? On me."

Miko glanced sidelong at Elias and clicked her tongue. "Another time. I want to do some searches." She pointed her phone at the car and took pictures. "Message you later."

Elias and I were lost in our own thoughts on the way home, mine composed entirely of deep pity not only for myself, but for Miko, and her awesome, uncanny gift for making men hate her on the spot. At a stoplight, Elias drummed his fingers on the steering wheel and said, "She's like..."

He'd been thinking about her, a hopeful sign. I imagined one of those silly romantic comedies where the two lead characters argue and snark and appear to loathe each other at first sight, but it turns out they've lit a spark in one another.

"She's like what?" I said.

"Like some sort of...*insect*."

We passed through two intersections, then he added, "But maybe she has a point."

He dropped me off, saying a work order had come in, and made me promise to keep him informed.

The apartment was empty and dark. Laurel was late for his medicine. I pulled the vial from the fridge egg tray and squeezed an antibiotic droplet between his sharp little teeth. Then I lay on the couch, staring at the ceiling while random thoughts popped like gunshots inside my skull.

It was nearly six o'clock, but I wasn't in the least bit hungry. I tried smothering my mind with television and fell asleep in front of some overbearing talent show. When I woke it was dark. Zuzie had switched off the TV and was shut inside her room. I showered, changed into a nightgown, and went to bed. The squeaking hamster wheel, cars parking and doors slamming, explosions from a movie in the next apartment, all conspired to keep me enveloped in a waking storm cloud of gloom shooting out lightning bolts of panic.

I gave up on sleep, fetched my laptop from the living room, then slid under the covers and propped the computer on my belly. The social sites didn't help: all cute animal videos, angry political memes, and worst of all, pictures of sweet, happy little activities—weaving or dessert-making or gardening—that people I sort of knew had the peace of mind to actually set their hands to. I scanned used car listings, but they only deepened the pangs of self-pity. For the first time in my life I didn't immediately delete all the get-rich-quick messages from my inbox.

I was about to power off when the cursor slid across the little video chat icon at the bottom of the screen and a bubble popped up with the list of contacts currently online. One long name stood out: A. Buonaventura.

I checked the time: eleven o'clock, so late already! What time was it in Italy? I should know this: nine hours ahead, wasn't it? I consulted my time zone widget. Yes, eight in the morning there.

Should I or shouldn't I?

My finger hovered over the touchpad, while some little imp spirit perched on my shoulder, whispering in my ear: *Go for it!*

One tap was all it took. I raised the pillow behind my back and sat up straighter, pulled the blanket over my chest, quickly finger-combed my hair, and counted ring tones up to five.

"*Pronto?*" His voice crackled. There was no picture.

"Alessandro?" I said.

"*Chi è?*"

"It's Serena. Did I wake you?"

Muted shuffling and scraping filled the speakers. The picture came on, shaking and blurred, then settled into focus: Alessandro sitting against a wooden headboard, a powder blue sheet pulled up to his navel, displaying a bare, well-muscled chest. His hair was a mess and stubble darkened his chin and cheeks. His smile was a bolt of heavenly light.

"Buongiorno," he said.

"Buona sera," I replied, two of my five words of Italian. "I woke you. I'm sorry."

He rubbed his eyes, saying, "No, no, no. Today I am, how you say...lazy."

The picture lurched closer. I guessed that the phone was pinned between his knees. I took in every detail of flat pectorals dusted with dark curls. My mind spun—here we both were, facing each other—in bed!—me in a nightgown, him wearing nothing that I had any evidence of. My nipples hardened at the thought, hidden behind the blanket, thank goodness! In the little thumbnail image in the corner of the screen I saw myself grinning like an idiot. His own expression was pretty much a mirror of mine. Before I could stop myself I clicked a screen shot.

I asked, "You went to bed late?"

"Yes. Late."

"Looking at stars?"

He shook his head, wrinkling his nose. "Family—how you say it, *vicini*—they living close our house..."

"Neighbors."

"Yes, neighbors. They come for eating. After, Papà and neighbor talking business. For me not interesting. So I drink wine and grappa with girl and boy neighbor."

"A girl and boy? How old?"

He laughed. "Old like me."

"Do you have to work now?"

"Work..." A dismissive flip of his hand. "Now talk to you. Work can later. How are you? What time now?"

I told him and shrugged. "Can't sleep. I must look awful."

"I don't know. You too much far." He twitched his fingers, bidding me closer. I leaned toward the computer, the blanket dropping from my chest, though I made no effort to retrieve it. So what if he saw my nightgown? It wasn't as if it was transparent. His head tilted side to side in a lampoon of a doctor's examination, then pronounced, "*Sei bella,* very beautiful. No need sleep."

His look could have made my screen steam up. My hand slid under the blanket to a place where it had no business being.

"Tell me why you not sleep," he said, his voice a brandy-toned whisper, as though no screen separated us, alone together in a bedroom.

I told him the whole story of the accident. I had to repeat many details in words he could understand, which took some of the sting from the memory. He bit back laughter as I recounted shutting down the freeway. But when I told him about Vince the Car Clinic owner—omitting the arguments with my friends, too complicated to explain—anger took over his face.

"You say this man, he is Italian?"

"I think." I reached for the card on my side table. "His name is Canicatti."

"Siciliano," Sandro said with pungent contempt. "Next time, you call me, I speak with him."

"He might not speak Italian."

"Is good! So he not understand all bad words I say him!"

I wanted to laugh and cry. I shook my hair loose, already feeling better. "I'll do that," I said. "But maybe I won't fix the car."

He nodded. "Better for you buy new car, yes?"

I pressed my fingers into my eyes and pushed the computer away, ashamed of appearing like a weepy, weak little girl. When I opened them, I saw that he understood without my having to say another word.

"I want to see the, the, the...*criceto*. You know, the little..." Sandro joined his thumbs and forefingers together to form an oval shape about the size of—

"My hamster?"

"Yes. Please, I want to see."

"Okay. Wait." I slid the computer aside and crawled out of bed. Laurel shivered with fear when I set him on the blanket and aimed the laptop camera his way. "This is Laurel."

"Laurel. Girl?"

"No, Laurel is a boy."

"Okay. I want talk to Laurel." Sandro sounded very stern, being ridiculous. I sat cross-legged on the bed, tugging my too-short nightgown toward my knees, then placed Laurel on my open palm in front of my face. He fidgeted and turned around twice, looked over the side like he might jump. I stroked him until he settled down, though his nose twitched warily.

"Laurel, a big scary Italian man wants to speak to you." I gently maneuvered him so that the furry hamster face was centered in front of the camera.

"This is the little thing that break your car?"

"He's the one."

"Yes, he looks very bad. *Criminale!*"

I made a kissing noise at Laurel. "Did you hear that, Laurel? He says you're Mafia!"

"Mafia? No. More bad than Mafia! You hear me, Mister 'amster? You listen! You are too much power! First you make Serena go in car for buy you drugs! Then you break car. Then you run from police! Because you, all cars in California must stop. And now big bad *Siciliano* wants all her money!"

He had me laughing so hard that my hand shook Laurel onto the bed.

"I am not finish!" Sandro said. "Come back!"

Laurel wouldn't sit still any more. I wrapped him in my fingers, holding him so close to the camera that his face nearly filled the video frame.

"I am not afraid you," Sandro said in a most sinister tone. "Do you know, Mister Mafia 'amster, what you did? Serena gives you house, gives you to eat, and now because your *crimini*...ah, your bad doing...you make Serena can not have no car. She must stay home with you! That is your plan, yes? But this is not so. Now Serena must come far away to Italy so I can borrow her my car. In Italy she must eat only pasta, not hamburger. And she must never, never, never drink cappuccino after morning! See? Because you, now Serena must—ah...she must—*soffrire.*"

"Suffer?" I said.

"Suffer, yes. She must suffer."

I lowered Laurel into my lap. Sandro and I looked at each other for a long quiet moment. I heard a knock on his door, a muffled woman's voice giving orders, his mother probably.

He shrugged and rolled his eyes, meaning he had to go, then held the phone closer and whispered, "If you do not come to Italy, I also must suffer."

Chapter 16

The next day's lessons seemed sixteen hours each, while two o'clock decided it never wanted to arrive. At five minutes to I phoned Vince at the Car Clinic.

His first words were, "Your buddies listening in?"

"No."

"Good. So I'm just checking over your estimate. Want me to e-mail it?" He sounded relaxed and friendly today.

"Um. Sure." I gave him my address. "I've got three minutes before my next appointment. Can you maybe just quickly tell me the total?"

I held my breath for about three years, or three ticks of the kitchen wall clock, before he finally spoke.

"So I told my guy Ernesto to do what your skinny friend looks like a walking toilet brush said, and come up with two estimates, one for making your car drivable but ugly, and the other—"

"Just tell me, okay?"

"So we're looking at two thousand six thereabouts."

I sunk down until my skull hooked onto the chair back. "Thereabouts?"

"2685.50. And to hammer that side panel into shape—I mean, you're replacing the hood no matter what—add another four."

"Thousand?"

"Ha. I wish. Hundred. Listen, sweetheart, I ain't charging you markup on parts. Labor straight by the book. Giving you my best offer without wifey getting on my ass for doing a pretty girl a favor."

Was I supposed to believe him? I wanted to, despite Miko's venomous skepticism. Maybe there was room for bargaining, not that I had even a third of the money. Perhaps some arm-twisting?

"You speak Italian, Vince? Nah, forget that. Gotta go." I was starting to speak like him.

AFTER WORK I HAD an hour to freshen up and get dressed before Steve arrived to pick me up. Zuzie had talked me into borrowing the slutty, clingy yellow dress that she insisted would transform me, just like in the movies, from Plain Jane into nuclear sex bomb. And why not? What harm was there in letting loose to release the frustrations of the last two days?

I hardly recognized the hottie in the mirror. It fit my body like...the word that came to mind was *like a condom,* leaving little to the imagination. Perhaps a bit too much for a downtown Los Angeles theater event. Or any event outside of a brothel, for that matter. I felt cleaner when I peeled it off.

I tried almost everything in my closet, tossing each aside until my bed resembled one of those Mongolian sacred prayer piles, finally settling on a snug peach cashmere tunic that flattered my contours, matched with never-worn-since-college skintight black faux leather pants. Who cared what some old biddies at the theater might say? I thought I looked damn good.

Steve obviously thought so too, the way he mimed wiping sweat from his forehead once I opened the door. I'd guessed him correctly: he was dressed neither too formal nor too casual, in tan trousers and a camel hair sports jacket over a pale blue dress shirt. Though it wouldn't have surprised me if he had a tie in the glove box, in case I had out-swanked him.

It was my first time on the freeway since my mishap. I didn't mention my accident; not while I was in a car. I let Steve regale me with amusing anecdotes from his two weeks in Calexico. He played coy about a couple of cross-border excursions until I goaded him, though these turned out to be about excessive drinking rather than anything wild like seeing a donkey show. No, Steve didn't do wild.

He'd predicted the traffic so precisely that we arrived at the restaurant within six minutes of his reservation time. He'd chosen a steakhouse, to "get us in the mood" for a musical about ranchers and farmers. All tasteful wood and leather, a few steer horns on the walls, the kind of venue that was adding up to be Steve's trademark date feeding place: enough on the expensive side to make an impression, but not so costly that it gave a girl pressure.

Over shrimp salad I told the story of the freeway accident in what I thought was a lighthearted, funny way. "I was sure the cop would charge Laurel with resisting arrest."

Steve put down his fork, more concerned than amused. "I'd a thought you'd be all shaken up right then, not much mood for jests."

"Well, yeah. Of...of course. Just, you know, trying to talk myself into seeing the bright side. Haven't found it yet."

"I'll keep an eye out for it," he said, though he clearly thought a car wreck was no topic for humor.

Our steaks arrived. I kept the Car Clinic episode short, without attempting Vince's Boston North End accent. I described the costs and Miko's insinuations about Vince's possible motives. Steve sawed angrily at his meat.

"Gets my back up the way these guys treat women like they're morons. Wish I could have been there."

"Me too," I admitted. "But anyway, done is done. Nobody got hurt. I'll deal with it."

"Let me find you someone to do the job. Hector on my crew is handy with engines, I'll ask him who he knows does body work."

"Thanks, but I can handle it. You just said that women aren't helpless, right?" I said, despite the fact that I wanted to lean across, grab him and plead, *Yes! Please save me!* I bet his friend Hector would find some blowtorch artist and together they'd fix everything and have the car all shiny as new as a favor to Steve, and no one would ask me to pay a penny. And Steve, in all his overwhelming niceness, would genuinely, down to the core of his being, not expect anything in return from me, no obligations, even if I never saw him again. But I, raised on a heavy diet of guilt, would feel practically obliged to have the guy's baby if he got my car fixed for free. It was me that I was afraid of.

"Cool." Steve raised his glass of sparkling water. "I like a gal can take care of herself."

The average age mingling in the theater lobby was somewhere between my grandparents and the extinction of the dinosaurs, though I did spot a few closer to my generation, androgynous skinny eels in fashionable tight denim, heads pirouetting in our direction to size up whether we were rival struggling dancers, until my tripping over my heels put their fears to rest.

Our seats were near the front of the mezzanine. Watching the rows below us fill, I let Steve know how impressed and excited I was. Finally, the lights dimmed, the audience murmur dissipated, and Steve settled back in his seat like a believer awaiting the rapture.

The curtain rose on a handsome guy with a gorgeous voice singing about what a beautiful morning it was, then hounding some woman to go to a dance, while she played hard to get for reasons apparent to no one except her feisty old aunt. So he lied about owning a car, cueing the next bouncy song about a surrey with a fringed roof. And all I, the university English major, could think was, *What kind of dramatic setup is that? Where's the inner conflict, the psychic wound behind her coy refusal?* Pretty songs, pretty people, pretty sets, but the story had all the depth of whip cream topping. Twenty minutes into the play and still no sign of the Aristotelian Inciting Incident.

143

Steve hunched forward, engrossed in the fantasy. I caught him sneaking glances to gauge how I was enjoying it. I smiled straight ahead and nodded in sync with the music. I wanted to love it, I really did.

While perky cattle ranchers traded wry barbs with perky farmers like musical Montagues and Capulets, my mind wandered back to the accident. If only I'd braked sooner, harder, swerved right. The audience laughed at the lead woman's tarty friend, the 'girl who cain't say no', while I considered how much force was needed to crack an engine block yet spare me from whiplash. The friend traded kisses for baubles from the conniving foreign peddler. At least those two characters were cynical enough to be interesting, and I was able to focus attention back on the stage.

Steve's hand lay strategically on our shared armrest—forearm bent inward like so, leaving just enough territory for my elbow to rest, daring us to touch. My suspicions deepened when his arm "accidentally" brushed mine as though to test my response: would I recoil or allow the contact, encouraging further prospecting toward the ultimate prize of holding hands? My first reaction was irritation at this juvenile game; everything he did always so planned, so deliberate. I decided to surprise him and placed my hand on his arm just behind the wrist and kept it there. Not quite holding hands, but a show of appreciation for this thoughtful and costly evening.

Our hands stayed parked this way while the spunky old auntie shoved a couple giggly girls aside and danced with the young men. Steve leaned slightly forward, reached behind with his other hand and tugged his collar, unsticking his shirt from his back. Somehow this touched me. He was sweating, though the theater was as cold as a walk-in refrigerator.

My hand slid forward and held the back of Steve's, an involuntary reaction. More than an hour into the performance, I was gripped at last by the action on stage. Handsome protagonist

Curly confronted Judd, the farmhand who lived out back in the smokehouse, who was also courting the leading lady. We knew that Judd was the bad guy because he was a stubble-faced, brooding loner who lined the walls of his unkempt room with girlie pictures. Which made him by far the most interesting, sympathetic, and nuanced character in the entire cast. The actor playing him clearly relished the role.

Maybe it was the English major in me, or maybe my own life felt so messed up, that I desperately trawled for something deeper in the narrative, some metaphor I could apply to my own situation. The scene rose to a boil; Judd tore the girlie cards from his wall, shouting that he was tired of being alone, tired of having only pictures for companions. He wanted a real flesh-and-blood lover.

No wonder I liked Judd. Judd was me. Or was I Annie, the girl who couldn't say no—shuffling between the nice, persistent local working guy and the seductive, accented foreigner?

Out of nowhere a gun appeared and I almost blurted out, "No!" I knew right then the end of the play, long before the curtain fell. Chekhov's rule: a gun which appears in Act 1 must be fired by Act 3. The supposed bad guy who'd never had any luck, desperately starving for love and companionship, the character most deserving of a happy ending, would probably die, while the bland but nice, clean-shaven good guy would get the flighty girl.

I hated her for that, for not giving Judd a chance, maybe because he was awkward, or because he smelled bad, but mainly because the script told her to. Didn't she see the passion burning within him like a prairie fire? Didn't she hunger for some of that same intensity and abandon, to cast aside all horizons and break free of her staid, flat, predictable existence? No, she would go for the one with achievable ambitions, promising her a life of easy comfort.

The lights came up for intermission. I knew what I needed to do.

IN THE CAR ON the way home Steve joked about his own Oklahoma upbringing being "not nearly so exciting. Though they got the windmills right." He went on a bit about Oklahoma statehood, one of the play's running themes. It was easier to listen to him than to wrestle with my own churning thoughts.

"But I'm blathering too much," he said. "Almost afraid to ask what you thought."

"I was quite impressed by the actor who played Judd. He was incredible."

"I know. Really made you hate the guy, right?"

After turning onto my freeway exit, we both went quiet. At a red light I caught him rubbing his eyes, then shooting a nervous glance my way. One mile to my apartment; to invite him in or say good night? It had been a long drive, it was past midnight, and he lived another twenty minutes away.

"Come in, I'll make us some tea," I said. He accepted gratefully.

Steve settled on a barstool while I filled the kettle. "So glad you finally got to see this musical," he said. "Rare these days to meet somebody our age who appreciates that sort of thing."

"Well, rare is the operative word when it comes to me and musicals." I retrieved cups and teabags from the cupboard.

"I get the wee impression that maybe you didn't like it all that much. Hope you enjoyed the experience anyway."

I sat across from him at the counter. "Oh, Steve, don't take it like that. I don't know much about musical theater. But I'm so happy you invited me. I mean, it was a wonderful experience. Really. I did enjoy it."

"Yeah, well, maybe you're the type'd go for something more arty, like 'A Chorus Line'. Though that one," he wrinkled his nose, "you can't even whistle the damn tunes."

I nodded sagely. "Mm. Whistleability is important. I'll take that into account next time."

"Next time. Like the sound of that."

A door flung open and a thunderhead of marijuana smoke poured into the room. Zuzie traipsed into the kitchen wrapped in a man's shirt, her hair clumped over to one side.

"Sorry, guys, but all this banging around in the kitchen, I can hardly— Know how late it is? Just go in and bonk this guy already, so we can all get some sleep."

Her married professor joined us in the kitchen, wearing nothing but a white fluffy towel around his waist. He and Steve traded nods and nice-to-see-you's.

"You know each other?" I said.

"In passing," Steve said.

"Steve painted my office at the uni. Superb plastering. An artist!"

"Thanks, man."

Zuzie's friend—I'd never learned his name—swayed on his feet, stoned off his rocker. I was afraid his towel might drop. "Let's go, Zuzie, back to bed. You two also, if you want my advice."

"You listen to him. He's a doctor," Zuzie said.

"Neurophysics, not Medicine. But let me tell you"—the guy was more than stoned, he was in another dimension—"we're all composed of particles. And recombination—that is, atoms pairing and swapping charges—is one of the basic principles of the universe. So let's all get on with it."

I must have blushed beet red. I looked to Steve for support, but he sat rigid on the stool, as embarrassed as I was.

The kettle whistled. Zuzie followed me to the stove, then pulled me out through the hallway and into the bathroom.

"Listen here, girl. I don't know what you're leading this guy on for..."

"Leading him on? It's what, a second date?"

"Two and a half, if you count the time in the Grove. Round up to three."

"So what?" I said. "Third, second, what's it matter?"

Zuzie nudged the bathroom door shut with her heel and leaned into me, her eyes pointing different directions. "Because, Miss Tease Queen, here's how it works, in case they didn't teach you in college. You can put a guy off on the first date, no problem. Second, maybe. But by the third, if you're not ready to put out, you're sending the wrong message."

"What wrong message? I don't get a word of what you're talking about!"

"That you're his shipoopi."

"His *what?*" I seriously did not understand a word. "Zuzie, are you just a little high or majorly whacked out right now?"

She leaned on the sink, stroking her chin like she was considering. "What comes right before majorly?"

"What was that word you called me?"

"Shipoopi. Weren't you guys, like, just at a goddamn musical? Ain't you seen 'The Music Man'? No? Shit, girl, for someone went to college, you know shit about shit. So, like, Buddy Hackett—he's Robert Preston's homey—he's got this song goes like: a chick puts out on the first date, she's a slut. On the second, she's having fun. But a girl who waits for the third time around is making it such a big deal that when you finally do it, it's a show of commitment. That's a goddamn shipoopi. Serena, look at me. I know you ain't serious about this guy. So you either bonk him a few times starting tonight, or you might as well be pointing your ring finger at him and scare off a good-looking piece of tush! Got me?"

"No, I don't got you. You're nuts. You're stoned. Go to bed."

Back in the living room, Zuzie's companion fixed me with his professorial gaze. "You two come to an understanding?"

Zuzie blew a razzie and giggled.

"Then there's nothing left but to vote on it," the professor said. "All in favor of...of..."

"Serena," Zuzie prompted.

"All in favor of Serena doing the deed with Steve, raise your hand."

Two hands shot up. Zuzie lifted Steve's arm, making it three before he yanked it away.

"Settled!" Zuzie said, steering her partner back toward her room. "Thank God we live in a democracy!"

The door slammed.

My eyes swept the floor, avoiding Steve's. "Sorry, I didn't mean..."

"No, Serena, I'm sorry too. I mean, that was...*whoo!*"

He didn't know what to do with his hands, nor did I. If there'd been any chance of me sleeping with him, it was less than zero now, and he knew it. The whole evening had been awkward, and he knew that too.

He squeezed his eyes.

I scratched behind my ear.

He pressed his cheek.

I bit a fingernail.

Then he touched my arm. "Serena, you're the greatest. Smart and beautiful and funny and...I mean..." His voice cracked, his hand withdrew. I thought for a moment he might cry. "But maybe you and me aren't...I don't know..."

"Oh, Steve, don't say that. You've got to be the nicest guy I've ever met in my whole life."

He rubbed the back of his neck. "Yeah. Guess I've heard that line before. Nice guys finish last and all that." With a little grin that was almost a wink, he added, "Except in musicals."

I hated to see him go away feeling like this. And it pinged my heart that he'd finally gone off-script and given me a glimpse into his sad side. I needed time to think.

I kissed him on the cheek. "Call me some time, yeah?"

Chapter 17

*S*aturday morning, my phone alarm woke me promptly at eight. I dialed the Car Clinic. As I'd hoped, Vince was already in.

"Decided to let me fix that chariot for ya, babe?"

"Listen, Vince. You told me someone might buy my car for scrap?"

I heard him slurp a cup of hot something. "Friend runs a chop shop, yeah. So, not scrap. But you ain't gonna get Blue Book neither."

"Can you ask him, please?"

A short silence at his end. "Sure. Call you on this number? Wait, don't hang up. I'm leveling with ya. You ain't gonna buy new wheels with what he's gonna give you. But I don't take nothing off the top, believe me? 'Kay. I'll call you."

I sprinkled sunflower seeds through the bars of the hamster cage, then opened my laptop on the bed.

Ten minutes later Vince called back. "Nine," he said.

"Nine what?"

He grunted. "Whaddya think, gonna tell ya nine thousand? Nine hundred."

My heart sank to my ankles. Nine hundred for a six thousand dollar car. "Let me call you back in a little while."

"Sure thing, babe."

For the next forty minutes I logged onto every travel website

I'd already visited a dozen times before. It must have been a low algorithm time of day, because prices were generally cheaper.

Then I struck gold.

Round trip to Rome, via London. 859 dollars. Plus taxes, airport fees, and fuel surcharge.

I called Vince. "Tell him I'll settle for nine hundred sixty four dollars and twenty cents."

He must have put his hand over the phone. I heard his muffled shout at somebody nearby to shut up. Then he came on again. "You sure about the twenty cents? Not twenty-two or twenty-seven maybe?"

"That's the price." My voice told him I was serious. "Nine sixty-four twenty."

Vince clicked his tongue. "Hey, so I'll ask."

"Not a penny less."

"Gotcha. Lemme give him a—"

"Wait wait wait. And tell him I need the money transferred to me in, um, the next fifteen minutes, or, or...or I take it off the market. And Vince?"

A sigh. "What else?"

"You're a doll."

"You 'n me both, babe."

Chapter 18

I deleted and rewrote a message to Sandro at least ten times. I'd booked the trip without consulting him, so I didn't want to come across as pushy or backing him into a corner.

> *I will go to Italy for a holiday.*
> *I hope I can visit you.*

I added the itinerary dates.

An Italian autoresponse came back, which translated that he was away on a business trip. A business trip without e-mail? Where was he selling olive oil? On the moon? Knowing Sandro, that wasn't unthinkable.

The only person who needed to know about Italy at this point was my supervisor. But come Monday morning, I couldn't hold back. I told Yasmin, without explaining why. Her big dark eyes burst open like popcorn.

"You go to Italy, also must come to Istanbul!"

"I'm so sorry, Yasmin. I don't think I'll be able to."

"Why you say? Not far! Only stupid Greece between!" Then her mouth dropped, her eyes shrunk back to size. "I know why you go Italy."

"Why?" I said.

With a knowing smirk, she tipped her head back and said, "Is a boy."

I made the slightest, teeny little nod.

Then Yasmin did something unimaginable: she tore off her headscarf and waved it like a banner, hooting and shrieking. For the very first time I saw her full head of hair: parted in the middle between thick black shoulder-length waves. I heard a book plop onto the floor.

"Yasmin, keep it down. Your parents..."

She clutched her heaving chest. "Tell me," she said between gasps, "he is rich? Show me photo. Has he brother?"

I hesitated. Sharing his photo felt like crossing a line. I lied, "No photo on this computer."

Yasmin replaced her headscarf and smoothed it down. We attempted vocabulary drills about going to the movies, but not a single word stuck. Even I was lost when trying to explain the word *blockbuster*. Finally we both burst out laughing and I told her a little bit about Alessandro—where he lived, his work, his eye and hair color. She kept prying for more, shrieking at each new detail. I worried that if I told her about our bedroom video chat, she'd spontaneously combust.

She was so caught up in her romantic imaginings that I had to tell her three times that the day's lesson was over.

"Moment! Moment! Almost forgot special words! Only one minute, please?"

"One minute," I said.

A piece of paper appeared in her hands. "So. This I look in dictionary and Internet, but do not understand: how can a man be *douchebag?*"

Only then did I notice a message that had been lurking all morning in my work inbox: my twelve o'clock had cancelled that day's lesson. Alessandro! No reason was given. The first time he'd ever missed a lesson, today of all days!

Why hadn't he told me on Friday? Perhaps his business trip had been a last-minute obligation tossed at him by his father. For someone like him, a business excursion was routine, so of course other things got cancelled. Besides, he was seeing me every day. One missed hour was no cause for apologies. I reminded myself ten times that nothing was wrong. Hadn't he told me that if I didn't come to Italy, he would suffer?

I was the one suffering now. What if he had business travel coinciding with my visit? What if I'd just thrown away my car for a trip to see nothing but a bunch of old buildings?

At least my supervisor was available. That woman was always available. Marisa appeared on screen with the same hairdo for once, though the highlights had grown out, and had on some sort of South American patterned silk blouse.

She favored me with her I'm-busy-but-for-you-I'll-make-an-exception pinched smile.

"What can I do for you, sweetheart?"

"Is Victoria in the room with you?"

"No, she's working. But I can tell her you—"

"I don't want to talk to her."

Marisa clicked her tongue. "All I can say is: glad I'm running an online school, don't have to break up cat fights in the hall. So, whatcha need, my dear?"

I brushed my hair behind my ear, took a deep breath, and broke it plainly. "I'm taking two weeks off next month, just wanted to give you notice."

Marisa's maroon lips shriveled to the size of a penny. She looked down and scribbled something before returning her attention to me.

"I employ you to teach English, so I shouldn't have to correct your grammar. But shouldn't your auxiliary verb be, 'I'd *like to* take two weeks off,' followed by—I don't know what the *diablos* you call it, an independent clause or something—'Just wanted to ask for approval?'"

"I had to buy the tickets over the weekend, before the price jacked up. Oh, please, Marisa."

She performed a long, slow blink and twirled a pen in her fingers. "Dates?"

I read out my departure and return dates and waited while she did some calculations. Finally, she said, "I count three weeks, not two."

"No. Leaving on a Tuesday, back on a Thursday. That's two weeks and two days."

"'Kay, let me lay this out: week 1, you work Monday, then *hasta la vista*. Week 2 you're off somewhere, chugging tequila on a beach. Week 3, back Thursday, one hung-over work day on Friday. Sounds to me like three weeks off, minus two days."

"Those were the only days I could get that deal. You know how airlines are."

"All I know's your contract, honey. And it says there in black and white, not tropical colors like where you're probably going, but plain black and white: two weeks annual leave."

"Unpaid," I added. "I know the contract. So what difference does it make if I take another few unpaid days? Please, Marisa, this is the chance of a lifetime."

"And if you don't mind me asking, where is this lifetime op- portunity paradise you're headed to?"

I hesitated, but figured there was no harm in at least the out- lines of the truth. "Italy."

"An Italian holiday...on what I'm paying you?" One plucked eyebrow levitated. "Kidding, sweetie. I suppose if you're clever enough to stretch your money that far, then maybe you deserve a break. Don't know why I'm so nice to you. Am I nice?"

We both laughed. Relief poured through my body. "I'll bring you back a pizza."

"Extra anchovies. Don't you dare forget."

"Thank you, Marisa. I really need this break. I've had so much crap happen lately. My computer, my car...."

The pen spun in her hand again. "Okay, don't let's get

weepy. No like weepy. Especially when you got a lesson in twelve minutes. And now I need to start juggling some schedules."

"Um, yeah. That's another thing. Marisa? Uh...I really, truly would appreciate it if you don't pass any of my students to Victoria."

She mimed a theatrical headache. "Don't test my world famous patience, darling. I mean, I get it. I do. But you put me on the spot once already today—"

"Okay, okay. Never mind. I'm sorry. Just...just think about it."

"I always think about what's best for my babies, don't I, darling?"

She gave me her conversation-over-and-out look, then the screen went blank.

I pumped my fists, once, twice, three times.

AFTER WORK A NEW panic set in: what to pack for the trip? In a full closet, all I saw were racks of tired, lintball-infested duds—literally, *duds*. There were maybe three pieces that might not get me laughed out of hyper-fashion-conscious Italy. Duty called for an emergency trip to the mall.

I thought of asking Jessie to take me, for companionship and advice, though she'd have to drive all the way down from Long Beach. Besides, she'd probably talk me into bankruptcy for fashion's sake. I looked up the bus schedules: depressing, but I had no choice.

During the endless ride on two buses I checked messages so often my phone heated up. Each time I saw no response from Alessandro, the bus felt bumpier, the seat more lumpy, my heart climbing the back of my throat. Shutting my eyes, I tried to make myself relax, to no avail. What if he told me it was a bad time to come? My ticket was nonrefundable, non-changeable. I'd simply hang out in Rome, sit in trattorias and toss coins into fountains, let myself be swept off my feet by a cute guy on a Vespa, like Audrey Hepburn in that movie—the guy in that case being

American, but if he looked like a young Gregory Peck, then why not? Maybe I'd even apply for an English teaching job and live the exotic expat life!

By the time I reached the mall, I'd already planned out my next ten years in Italy. I would teach in a six hundred year old building where Da Vinci went to school, go home to my sexy, simmering lover (please let him be Alessandro). Together we'd prepare lamb and pasta and rainbow-colored salads, followed by evening strolls along cobbled boulevards filled with well-mannered Europeans outfitted in all the latest cutting edge fashions. On weekends we'd dash to Milan or Florence for shopping or drive the Alfa out to the olive plantation (so he *was* Alessandro) and sip wine and nibble goat cheese under trellises heavy with grapes.

Then I stepped through the mall's sliding doors and found myself surrounded by dumpy suburbanites sporting gag t-shirts like, "Warning: I fart on a first date." Feral children blared like truck horns, dripping glop from frozen hyperglycemic confections, while their parents shouted at them to get back in there and try on some goddamn shoes. Half the shops I passed had faux-clever, cloyingly American names, like Church of Cheese, T-shirt Inferno, or Rite of Whey Health Emporium. Every window shrieked "Sale! Sale! Sale!" I bounded up the escalator to the second floor, lined with the same stale brand name shops that occupied every other retail purgatory in America. Pods of sneering teenagers slouched in the corners.

I already felt like a foreigner in my own country. Which, in a way, cheered me.

I skipped the overpriced boutiques and plunged through the glass portal of the department store, an overwhelming sea of stuff. The cosmetics sales vulturesses hardly gave me a glance as I passed. Was I so obviously unable to afford their exorbitant vials of goop?

I resisted the siren call of the shoe department. Sandro lived in the countryside. Read: mud and dust. Did women there even wear six-inch pumps? After an hour of dashing from one display rack to another, congratulating myself on my taste—every item I liked cost at least twenty percent of my bank balance—I narrowed my choices to three relatively inexpensive tops.

The first blouse had looked good on the hanger, but in the changing room mirror, too fuzzy and spangly. The second was a blue and white silk blend with a soft floppy collar that I imagined wearing on the deck of a Mediterranean yacht. Finally, something cottony, earthy-urban stylish, in marbled maroon and gold, perfect for an olive plantation. I had it stretched around my head, one arm tangled in a sleeve, like a human cat's-cradle, when my phone hiccupped. A new message.

Extruding my free arm through the bottom, I fumbled in my purse, knocking it and half its contents onto the floor. With the garment blocking my face, I kicked the phone out from under the little bench and bent over to pick it up without ripping the fabric. It took two tries to swipe my lock pattern, then a tap on the message icon.

From Sandro!

It contained no words.

Just emojis: a chorus line of every variant of happy expression, from open-mouthed grins to crazy protruding tongues and thumbs-ups with stumpy legs. And at the very end of the final row, a plain and simple heart.

I pulled on the blouse and pirouetted in place, imagining wearing it on a romantic hand-holding stroll through the groves. Then I changed and told my debit card to prepare for a celebration. I dropped the first item on the re-shelf rack and, hanging the other two over my arm, negotiated my way through the maze of displays toward the cashier island. Big fat numbers filled my head: forty-nine dollars for one, not too outrageous; an iffy sixty-eight for the other. A shiny red $117 hopped around inside my skull like the animation in a used car commercial. And that was before sales tax. Plus I needed at least one skirt and a suitcase and some sort of day bag and sunglasses. And I had to save some cash for trains and food and whatever. All this with slightly over eight hundred dollars in the bank.

My steps slowed. I laid the silk blouse on a nearby shelf, making myself sixty-eight dollars richer, plus tax.

The cashier sign loomed closer, the goal post at the end of a race. The woman pushed aside a box of tags she'd been sorting and with a smile took the gold and maroon top from me.

"I'm sorry," I said. "Do you mind getting someone to rehang this? I didn't want to mess it up."

I walked the mile and a half to a Goodwill warehouse.

Back home I spread my purchases on the bed and congratulated myself for my savvy shopping: skirts and blouses, some fashionably retro chic, others bearing obscure but European-sounding labels, an adorable floppy-brimmed hat, plus a gorgeous and probably counterfeit Gucci rolling suitcase, all for under a hundred and fifty dollars. Even a guide book from 2003. Same century, at least.

Then I tore apart my room in a mad search for my passport, obtained long ago in misplaced optimism for a college year abroad. At last I found it, tucked among yellowing term papers in a carton under the bed: valid for another six years, not a stamp anywhere. I pressed it to my face; it even smelled new. The lucky thing was about to lose its virginity.

I cleared a place on the bed and spent the evening loading my phone with Italian dictionaries and phrasebooks. I even memorized my first expression:

Posso baciarti? Can I kiss you?

What else would I possibly need to say?

I was ready for launch!

Chapter 19

*E*xcept for one thing. Two things, actually: Messrs. Laurel and Hardy, Esquires.

Zuzie got home around midnight. I called her into my room and showed off the clothes littering my bed, most of which met her discerning approval.

"Though I don't know about these," she said, examining a shoe with layered wood block heels. "Like 'Mod Squad' throwbacks, goes with striped polyester bellbottoms."

"You don't think I should wear them?"

"No. 'Cuz I want 'em, bad." She hugged the shoe to her chest. "Anyway, what's gotten into you to buy all this—" She reached for my Italy travel guide. "What's going on around here?"

"I got the tickets, got my passport. Sixteen glorious days! Can you believe it?"

"You never told me! Wait." She put down the shoe and took a step back. "This got something to do with that Italian Stallion student of yours?"

"It might."

She shrieked and threw her arms around me. "You crazy bitch, keeping this from me."

"I only just decided this weekend." We did a little dance together, then sat on the bed.

"So I guess you and Steve aren't a thing, yeah?"

"Not a thing."

"I hope that ain't 'cause of me, the other night...I was really bat-faced wasn't I? Truly sorry."

"Not because of you, Zuzie. Steve's a great guy. But Sandro..."

"I can imagine." She patted my hand and held it. "I hope this guy is your Mister Right, Serena. I truly do. So, when you leaving?"

"That's what I needed to talk about."

I could almost hear the *Uh oh's* clanging inside her skull.

"Flight's two weeks from tonight," I said. "I really, really need you to help feed the hamsters while I'm gone. Change their sawdust once a week—"

Her hand went up. "Hold on. So if you're leaving in two weeks and...let me see..." She pouted, counted on her fingers. "No, won't work. Sorry, we're off to Hawaii, middle October."

"We?"

"Yep. He's giving a paper at some Neurophysics conference. Taking me along as his aide. Kind of aide pushes the buttons for his Power Point in return for him pushing my buttons for three coconut oil-slathered nights."

I pretended to be as excited for her as she was for me, but inside, my panic thermometer rose. Why did every little thing lately have to have a crisis attached?

SANDRO SHOWED UP FOR his Tuesday lesson, his face raccoon-like from wearing shades in the sun.

"I was on the boat on the *Adriatico*. For business. I am very apologize."

"I am very *sorry,*" I corrected. "Either 'I apologize' or 'I am very sorry.'"

"Okay." He nodded. "I think you are angry to me."

"No, I'm your teacher." How to explain that his news exhilarated me? Yachting excursions on the Adriatic, entertaining clients—if I'd caught myself imagining such a life only a few months ago, I'd have slapped my own face. But soon I would be with someone for whom such things were routine. I wanted it so badly I had to stop myself from breaking into a giggle fit. And made a mental note to pack sun block.

"Today you are my teacher. You come Italy, I am your teacher. In Italy you must speak Italian."

"Are you a good teacher?" I said.

"Very bad. But you know, Italian people talk too much. Maybe better we do things not always talking."

I couldn't have felt more drunk at that moment than if I'd downed a case of vodka.

Everything seemed like a dream, except for the one detail. That morning I'd already received replies from two former classmates in the area, apologizing for not being able to look after my hamsters. One had a cat, the other lived in a no-pet building, as if a landlord would evict her over a pair of contraband rodents. I knew Miko was going to her tech bootcamp. And Jessie, well... she was too much the type to hop off for a wild weekend in Vegas, then come home to shriveled hamster corpses and say, "Oops."

I used my lunch break to research other options. Several kennels offered services for "pocket-sized pets", at giant-sized prices—close to four hundred dollars. The other alternative was my mother. She couldn't refuse me. But it meant a four-hour round trip—with what car?—and at least that long a lecture about wrong choices I'd made with my life and which of my former high school classmates was now a banker or ad agency executive or pregnant and when was I going to give her grandchildren already. Four hundred dollars was by far the better deal.

I had one final resort. At the end of my last lesson I messaged Elias:

You home?

Thirty seconds later his response:

Finishing a Jon in Newport.

Then: *Job, not Jon.*

Then: *Sup?*

I wrote back:

Call me when you're done.

The phone rang three minutes later. "Done," he said. "Just throwing crap in the car. What's going on? Beat up your computer again?"

"Funny." I leaned back in my chair. "We're friends, right?"

"Uh oh."

"I'm not asking a favor," I said. "I want to hire your services. But not for computers."

I heard his car door click shut and the engine starting. "That's cool. But my gigolo business doesn't open until eight p.m. Though in your case—"

"Come on! I'm being serious. I need someone to take care of my hamsters while I'm in Italy and I'm offering to pay you."

A mechanical clunk came through the phone. His engine noise ceased. "Wait. Start over. *Italy?*"

"Didn't I tell you? Guess not. I'm flying to Italy in two weeks and I need someone—"

"Off to see Romeo, huh?" His voice thick with disappointment.

"*Tsk.* Oh, never mind. I'm gone sixteen days, and I'm offering ten dollars a day to babysit my hamsters. It's really easy and—"

"Apiece?"

"What? No way. Ten dollars for the pair." I paced circles around the living room while giving him a primer on the ease and joys of basic hamster care.

A heavy sigh graced my ear. "Let me clarify something," he said. "One of those creatures sabotaged a computer network. The other single-handedly shut down the entire southern California freeway system. And one of them, I don't know which, nearly amputated my finger. You don't need me to watch them, you need a SWAT team."

I plopped onto the couch, clenching my eyes shut.

"Hey, you still there?" he said.

"Thank you, Elias. You don't know how much I appreciate this."

"What? Wait wait wait wait wait! I don't remember saying yes."

"You didn't say no."

"So the absence of a negative equates to a positive?"

"Does in binary number systems. That's your specialty, is it not?"

I swore I heard him smile. "Touché. Where'd you learn this stuff? Thought you were a digital ignoramus."

"I had a nerd roommate, remember?"

"Oh. Her. It. Whatever."

"Not that I could count to three in binary. But if you're interested in a comparative analysis of negative truth-value propositions in Japanese, Navajo, and Yoruba, I wrote a paper on it for Sociolinguistics."

"Yeah? What grade you get?"

"I don't remember. A minus?"

Another long silence, then, "Woman, you are such a total dork, and I mean that in almost the best possible way. Just for that I'll do it."

Chapter 20

Then I was high in the sky, crammed into a window seat, glimpsing a cracked empty landscape—Utah? Wyoming?—between gaps in the clouds while the plane bounced through pockets of turbulence. I tried reading a novel set in 1960s Italy, but the combination of dry cabin air, fear of flying, and the guy sitting in the aisle seat holding a full-throated conversation with people three rows behind us in what I guessed to be Hungarian, made concentration difficult. Then the obese jerk in front of me assault-reclined his seat in my face like he was felling a tree. I attempted studying Italian phrases, flipped through my guide book, finally gave up and scrolled through the movie choices on the tiny seat-back screen, so close now my breath fogged it up. I settled on a frothy wedding comedy that wouldn't require brain function.

Yet thinking was all I could do. After a year of telling other people, and even myself, that I "traveled the world daily" through my computer screen, for the first time in my life I was traveling the actual world. Other than a few day trips to Tijuana, I'd never left the borders of the United States. And now here I was, about to enter Canadian air space on the way to the opposite side of the planet. Well, not quite the opposite; nine time zones away, if one wanted to be a dork about it, as I'd been branded by Elias.

He had taken in the hamsters with some trepidation—wearing ski gloves!—until he saw how quickly they settled into their routines of gnawing and wheel running. They'd moved right in! I gave him their see-through hamster balls with the warning to monitor them at all times if he let them loose. And no human snacks! He'd rummaged through a huge carton stuffed with cables and found a cord for my computer charger that would fit an Italian socket, pointing out that he could outfit me next time I visited Australia, Korea, or South Africa as well. Maybe one day I would visit such places. Traveling to Italy was just the start. I intended to be a world citizen from today on.

Unable to sleep, I watched movies back-to-back without recalling a single plot or even title. As I semi-dozed through the third or fourth wild car chase of the evening, the pilot announced that we were flying over southern Greenland.

In the Arctic night the edges of the world glowed pink and gold, casting faint shadows across blue moonlit glaciers. I pressed my nose against the window to hide my tears from my neighbor. Scarcely a week ago I'd never once thought about Hudson Bay or Greenland; yet here was I, a girl from the manicured California suburbs, voyaging over the untamed lands of Inuits and Vikings, on my way to cities thousands of years old. Though I sat in a many-times-occupied ergonomic cushioned seat, traveling like millions before me on a computer-planned route inside a modern machine tracked every inch of the way by satellites, I was at that moment a lone explorer hurtling toward new, uncharted territory of my own life.

A FEW HOURS LATER I was at London Heathrow Airport handing my passport to a woman immigration officer.

"Destination?" she said. She looked to be late thirties, pale skin and mouth, whatever humor she may have once possessed long drained from her soul.

"Italy. Rome. Puglia, actually."

"And may I ask what is the purpose of your journey?" Her

eyes were locked on mine in a manner obviously trained to spot suspicious twitches and pupil dilations. I had no experience with border officials, much less the stiff-upper-lip British variety, facing thousands of tired, grouchy travelers all day. How much detail did they expect?

"Romance," I replied.

Her stare lingered. An eyebrow twitched. Now I was frightened. Then my passport slid back across the tray. I mumbled thanks.

I'd taken two steps past her booth when I heard her voice again.

"Don't let him break your heart, love."

By the time I looked back, she was saying, "Destination?" to a towering Black man in a brilliant African smock.

THE REST OF THE trip proceeded like a stop-motion film. A shuttle bus and miles of corridors to reach my connecting flight to Rome. Stuck in an aisle seat with nothing to do except invent worries about getting lost in Italy, boarding the wrong train, ending up sleeping somewhere under an ancient aqueduct. At last, out of my mind from lack of sleep, I emerged into the teeming expanse of Rome airport.

I congratulated myself for finding the express train to the downtown terminal, and spent the half-hour ride staring at the ticket I'd bought online for the trek across the country, memorizing the train's destination, car and seat numbers, whispering over and over to myself, so I wouldn't forget: *"Dov'è il treno per Lecce?"* Where is the train to Lecce? Though I had no idea what I would do when someone answered.

I staggered off the express into the human maelstrom of Rome's Termini Station. People of every color filled every space, every bench, every doorway. One arm hugging my purse to my ribs, the other clutching the handle of my rolling suitcase like an eagle its prey, I wound a path around Chinese tour groups, western backpackers, brawny men in identical shirts who might have been a soccer team, and too many people who looked like they weren't going anywhere. Someone patted my butt—they really did that here! I pressed through the mass of humanity to the information booth, where I finally grasped the futility of waiting my turn to reach the lone woman at the counter. I hoped that at least the station clock had a sense of order: twenty-five minutes until the departure time listed on my ticket. I eventually squeezed to the front and without waiting for the information woman's eyes to settle on mine, called out, *"Dov'è il treno per Lecce?"*

She thumbed to my right and replied in bored but musically accented English, "Binario number four."

I hauled my heavy suitcase onto the train, checked once, twice, three times—car 12, row 7, seat D. I was disappointed at its charmless modern cleanliness rather than being the cramped, smoky, distinctively Italian tin can on wheels described in my outdated guidebook. I melted onto the firm padding of my window seat, looped my purse strap around my arm, and shut my eyes. I'd made it. I could relax until I reached my destination, conveniently the end of the line, six hours and thirty-two minutes from now.

Or until someone hammered my shoulder and a short, round shrunken apple of a woman shrieked at me in machine gun Italian, waving her ticket in my face. She made a broad sweeping motion as though to cast me out like a dead roach from under a couch. I replied in English that I'd paid for this reserved seat almost two weeks ago, raising my voice to repeat myself, which enraged her even more. I was afraid she'd next go for my hair.

A mustachioed gentleman stood up across the aisle and said something to the woman, indicating a number of unoccupied seats, but this only made her turn on him, brandishing her ticket like a dagger. He raised his silver eyebrows to me and asked in English if he could help me. I showed him my ticket, which he handed back after a cursory glance, then told me, "Signorina, you are in the correct seat, but the wrong train."

"How? The information woman told me binario 4!"

The man shrugged. "Three, four, five...who knows? In my country, if somebody informs you platform number or departure time, it is not a scientific conclusion. You must check the board."

The metal snaps on my suitcase raised sparks as I dashed across the tracks, making it through the doorway of the express train to Lecce just as the platform conductor sounded his whistle.

I must have fallen into an exhausted sleep, since the next thing I knew an old woman dressed in black had occupied the seat beside mine and was gently nudging me. A conductor stood in the aisle with his hand out for my ticket. Only when I turned to open my purse did I realize we were moving. Hilly countryside slid past in crimson twilight. I nodded thanks to the woman, then leaned against the window, determined to soak in every inch of the land I was now traversing.

And fell asleep again.

It was dark when I came fully awake. My neighbor had been replaced by a young man with licorice black hair, wearing a leather jacket over an orange polo shirt. I had a hunch that it wasn't his reserved seat.

He leaned on our shared armrest and tobacco-stained breath formed a word that sounded like, *"Way,"* then, *"Ciao."*

"Ciao," I said back. I had no idea where we were, how long until I reached my destination, and less idea how to ask. My phone with its language apps was switched off deep in my purse. I tried from memory: *"Perdone. Dove sono?"* Excuse me, where am I?

The only word I understood of his reply was *treno:* train.

I pointed out the window. *"Dov'è?"* Where?

"Ah!" He pointed behind him. "Bari." Then he counted on his hand, folding back one finger, then another. "Brindisi. Lecce."

I tapped my chest and nodded. "Lecce."

"*Bene!*" He threw his arms up, then pointed at me and guessed: "*Olandesa? Inglesa?*" Dutch? English?

"Americana."

The boy spent at least the next thirty kilometers entertaining me with words and gestures, not a single one of which I understood. I must have had a stupid grin locked on my face, which only spurred him on. All I could think was: I'm a stranger in a strange new world.

At Lecce station the boy carried my suitcase onto the platform and offered to pull it for me.

"*Grazie,* no," I said. But he wouldn't leave me alone; I heard his breathing over my shoulder me as I walked.

"'Otel?"

"No. No hotel."

He dashed in front of me and patted his chest. "*Casa mia?*"

I knew from Spanish what that meant. The little devil was inviting me home!

"*Grazie,* no."

Three cars further down, bathed in lamplight, I spotted a familiar face. He was taller and slimmer than I'd pictured him. But his beaming smile was unmistakable. He raised a hand and started toward me. I waved back. The boy beside me laughed and said something I didn't understand, then patted my shoulders and nudged me toward Alessandro's outspread arms.

Chapter 21

Zooming through the night in his quick little car. Our first words in person: meaningless but dripping with feeling. Are you tired? Are you hungry? I'm so happy to be here. I am happy to see you. I can't believe it. I can not believe.

Happiness wasn't the word; I was inside a dream. What was I doing across the world, at the far end of Italy, beside this tall, radiant man I was seeing for the first time in close detail: the slight bump halfway down his nose, the downy fuzz on his ears? Hearing his breath, the body heat from his welcoming embrace lingering on my chest, on my cheeks.

Shops were closed, while windows glowed in restaurants and bars. Sandro made sharp turns into narrow streets without signaling or slowing, which every other driver seemed do as well. At a red light he made a token tap on the brake and barreled through. He heard my gasp and looked at me—in the middle of a left turn before an oncoming car!

"Here we are anarchists," he said, pronouncing the *ch* as in cheese.

We passed dim neighborhoods of multi-story apartment blocks. Then the lights thinned out and we were in the country-side on a straight, unlit highway barely wide enough for two small cars. We accelerated around a truck, my heart plugging my throat. Then we turned onto a smaller road with potholes deep enough to qualify as archaeological digs. In the headlights, glimpses of low stone walls, cactus, and shrubbery. Silhouetted trees huddled together in the dark.

When I'd announced I was going to Italy, he'd insisted I come straight to his family's home for the full length of my visit. Better to experience real country life than breathe the filthy air in Rome or Florence. So here I was, on a dark rural lane on my way to a strange house to stay with a family I'd never met, as guest of this man I'd only known through a glowing screen; nothing about it could possibly be real. He turned into a path so narrow that foliage scrubbed the doors. I did something I used to do when I was a little girl.

I slapped my face.

The car swerved. He said, "Eh?"

"Proving to myself this isn't a dream."

"You come here is a dream. For me," he said. Then he slapped his own face. "Ah! It works! Now is not a dream. Is true!"

"No dream," I said.

"No dream." He caressed his cheek with the back of his hand.

The lane curved for a long stretch, then straightened again. He braked before a stone-framed wooden gate.

"My home." He reached for his door handle.

"Let me." I was eager to move after my butt had suffered more than twenty hours sitting in planes, waiting rooms, trains, and this bumpiest of all car rides. I stepped outside and breathed in the Italian air for what seemed the first time. Clean and bone dry, tannic like old leaves. Night creatures chirped. I raised an iron latch and swung open the heavy doors, discovering nothing but darkness on the other side. Sandro drove the car through and waved me to shut the gate and get back in. We followed an unpaved drive round a bend, veered past a parked tractor and into a graveled courtyard, where I caught my first sight of the Buonaventura estate.

In the moonlight the main building appeared more plain

than the grand plantation manor I'd expected. Three stories built of stone blocks, pierced with rows of double casement windows, a few of which leaked light from behind heavy curtains. Sandro hurried me through an archway into an inner courtyard, then through a side door.

He switched on a light. We were in a small wooden-floored vestibule, where he set my suitcase against a wall. Voices rang out on the other side of the inner door. "Have you hunger? Now we eat," Sandro said.

"No need," I said. "Maybe just some water. It's so late already."

"Not late. Now is time for eat."

A brass clock on a little table showed a quarter to ten. Had they really put off dinner for me? I damn well better make a good impression. "Let me change first. I must stink." I plugged my nose for emphasis.

"Stink," he repeated, new vocabulary for him. Then he took my elbow. "No problem. All stink. Working today under sun, collect olives. Very stink work."

The door opened into a room stuffed with people. Without warning I was passed around like a basketball, introduced to *zia* this and *cugino* that—Lucia, Alberto, Francesca, Massimo—receiving kisses and kissing back eighteen or twenty pairs of cheeks. Not only aunts and uncles and cousins and a grandmother, but even the employees—the oil press master, the tree master, and their wives—had come over, bubbling with enthusiasm to meet the visitor from America.

Over and over I answered how long was the flight from Los Angeles and no, I didn't know any famous actors. But I myself felt like a rock star, underscored by the fact that everyone addressed me as *Maestra*. I wondered if Sandro had lied that I was a musician, until he whispered in my ear that *maestra* was a respectful address for a teacher. Wonderful; I could live with such respect.

A well-rounded woman in an apron was last to moisten my

cheeks: Sandro's mother. I saw the resemblance in the eyes and cleft chin. With one arm around my shoulder, she snapped her fingers and shouted what must have been a command for everyone to be seated. Then she directed me to the middle chair at a wooden dining table massive enough to seat two soccer teams.

It was laid out with a multitude of plates and wine glasses, big round loaves of bread, and, naturally, numerous glass beakers of yellow-green olive oil. A painting of the Virgin Mary and another of a saint watched me from heavy frames. A silver crucifix glistened on the wall beyond the end of the table, where Sandro's father presided over his guests. He was a thicker-around-the-chest, middle-aged version of his son, with the same laughing cheeks and full head of untamable wavy hair, his sun-darkened olive skin reminded me of surfers; an excellent advertisement for a future Alessandro. At the other end sat a fat balding man whose cheeks I didn't remember kissing. He paid attention to nobody, least of all me.

Seated beside me, Sandro caught me looking. "My mother's brother. Also living this house. He do not talk."

I joined in the general *oohs* and *ahhs* as Mamma delivered *antipasti* to the table: dishes brimming with eggplants, mushrooms, peppers, and clam-sized pasta shells that Sandro called "little ears", bathed in tomato sauce and diced olives. A pyrotechnic torrent of words and laughter swirled around the table, of which I couldn't decipher a single word. It didn't sound like the Italian in my free phone apps. The linguist in me sniffed a local dialect.

Those within reaching distance took turns loading my plate with food. Nods of approval followed my baptizing my vegetables with olive oil, and, after trying a sauce-drenched little ear and discovering it to be one of the most luscious experiences my tongue had ever had, I trilled the word I'd rehearsed a thousand times in private, *"Buonissimo!"*

Sandro nudged me. "Louder. They do not hear."

I hoisted another little ear on my fork and proclaimed a full-throated, *"Buonissimo!"* The whole table roared the word back. All except the silent uncle and a young girl across the table, who merely smiled. She'd come in too late to exchange kisses, but Alessandro had introduced her as his younger sister Olimpia.

Sandro's father went into another room and returned with a huge glass jug of red wine.

"Wait. I almost forgot," I said. Ignoring Sandro's questions, I rushed into the vestibule, fumbled with my suitcase zipper, and took out a bottle of wine, ashamed now for having brought only one. Of course, I knew nothing about any wine that didn't come in three-liter boxes, so I'd grabbed a random Pinot Noir with a pretty label from the supermarket. Returning to the dining table, I presented it to Sandro's father.

"Vero vino di California." I hoped I'd just said, "Real California wine."

He cradled the bottle, pretending to read the label and nodding in polite admiration, while someone else went in search of a cork-screw. Eventually one was found, the bottle passed around, a splash finding its way into each glass. Papà stood and raised his in toast. *"Amica dalla California, vino dalla California."* Everyone drank. I beamed. He had just called me *friend*.

Sandro's silent uncle loudly spat his back into his glass, then wiped the back of his hand across his mouth, beckoning with the other for the jug of local product. No one seemed to pay him any attention.

"My uncle is little bit crazy," Sandro's sister Olimpia said. "He comes out from his room only for eating."

I was taken aback, though not by her explanation. "Where did you learn such good English?"

"I learn in the school."

"How old are you?"

"I am thirteen."

I turned to Sandro, twelve years older. He tapped his forehead, having read my thoughts.

"I teach you an Italian word," said Olimpia. *"Stupido.* Very important word if you know my brother. In fact, he is my sister because he is so pretty. You think? *Che bella femmina!"*

Sandro threw a bread chunk at her. An aunt or cousin swatted Olimpia's arm and muttered something scolding. Two women went to the kitchen and helped Sandro's mother bring out bowls of soup, thick with meat and green vegetables and a strong chicory fragrance. Everyone in turn anointed their portions with oil. When the beaker reached me, I drew a heart on the surface of my bowl.

Mamma shot a dark look to Sandro. His sister hid a laugh behind her hand. Sandro rose from his seat, picked up my soup bowl and brought it into the kitchen, returning a minute later with a fresh bowl, now with a perfect cross drawn in oil over the surface.

"Tradition. For lucky," he explained.

I looked at Olimpia and tapped my forehead. *"Stupido."*

"Stupida for a girl," she corrected without a trace of humor.

I managed to survive the rest of the meal without another incident, consuming half my weight in pasta, mussels, cheese-stuffed pastries, and little meat pies, while drinking the other half my weight in wine. People insisted with a name like Serena I must be Italian. An uncle feigned offense when I claimed Scottish and Dutch ancestry; another said I had clearly been switched at birth, since I was too pretty to be Scottish.

By the end of the meal, when I could eat no more but was expected to sample a plate of stuffed figs, I felt like I'd been adopted by this loud, arm-waving, warm-hearted family in a sea of musical language. I wasn't sure if it was the wine, the jet lag, the almost total lack of sleep since leaving home thirty hours before, or just the general sense that I was still dreaming all this, but I also felt like passing out.

Sandro escorted me up a flight of stairs and down a long hallway to a guest room set up for me. I kicked off my shoes and fell back onto a scratchy woolen blanket across a bed as soft as a cloud.

"Did I pass the test?" I said.

Sandro looked at me, confused.

"The exam," I said. "Did I pass your family's exam?"

He rubbed his stubbled chin. "You eat food, drink wine, make laugh. To Mamma and Papà, you pass the exam. I think ninety-nine points."

"Only ninety-nine?"

"Zio do not like your wine."

"And your grade for me?"

He tugged the blanket and sheet from under me, then covered me to my shoulders. "My exam, you pass one hundred and ten."

He leaned over and kissed my forehead. "You sleep. Tomorrow work!"

Chapter 22

$\mathcal{S}$leep surrendered to a sputtering engine outside my window, ending in metallic shrieks of badly worn brakes. I desperately needed to pee and change my rancid clothes but had no idea where to find a bathroom on this floor or even what time it was, other than that it was pitch black both inside and outside and the house seemed asleep.

No matter how lightly I stepped, the floorboards creaked an account of my journey from bed to door. Unsure which way down the endless dark hallway to prospect for a bathroom, I crept along the wall, where the planks were quietest. A door clicked open at the far end. Out stepped the rounded figure of Silent Uncle in a thin white robe. Paying me no attention, he walked straight across and through another doorway. I heard the squeak of a water tap, then a toilet flush. Mystery solved.

Back in my room I changed into jeans and my plainest cotton shirt for whatever work Sandro had in mind. I unlatched the tall wooden shutters and welcomed in a cool breeze. Voices murmured somewhere out of sight. Church bells tolled in the distance. I counted five deep rings, followed by two higher-pitched tones. Five thirty in the morning. Another motor; a scooter sped around the side of the building.

I leaned on the windowsill, brushing my hair, listening to the chatter of waking birds and a far-away donkey lowing. What a lie I'd been telling myself, that I "traveled the world" through my computer screen. When had my feet felt century-old floorboards, when had my ears experienced a church bell, a puttering Vespa, an Italian donkey, when had my lungs filled with a dry bouquet of leaves and pollen and dust in all those so-called travels? As a little girl I'd often laid in the grass of our suburban backyard and reached toward the clouds, imagining that they would pull me flying across the earth. Now I'd finally ridden those clouds, here to the boot heel of Italy. It felt like a long-ago destiny fulfilled. It felt right.

Men's and women's voices carried up the stairwell over the scrape of chairs across timber. I tucked in my shirt and padded downstairs to the dining room.

"*Ah! Buongiorno! Buongiorno!*" Sandro's mother looked as though she'd been wearing her apron for hours. She poured coffee for two men. One was black-haired, young and tough. The other might have been his father, with thick salt-and-pepper hair and matching mustache. I discovered that it was never too early for cheek kissing, though the younger man seemed to drag his out longer than protocol required, until Sandro entered the room.

"*Filarsela, tu!*" Sandro friendly-punched the young guy's shoulder. Then to me: "Sleeping good? Now we eat a little-little. Then this lazy men pretend to work."

"I'm ready. No pretending," I said.

"O-*kay!* Hard dirty work. Money no good. Ah, but boss is very good looking, eh?" He repeated in his language for the men, who jeered and slapped the table, followed by what sounded like an exchange of friendly insults. My linguist's ears perked up: again that dialect, deeper and more guttural than Italian. Mamma returned and boxed each of them on the ear, insisting they speak Italian in front of me, as though it would have made any difference.

His family's idea of "eat a little-little" included bread loaves as large as car tires, mountains of cheese and sliced meat, boiled eggs, potato dumplings, and endless rounds of espresso, everything except the coffee receiving liberal dollops of olive oil. Papà and Olimpia joined us, and more workers came in to finish off the feast. Olimpia left with her school bag, then everyone else besides Mamma headed to the side door.

I stepped into a world of muted color, thinking at first the sun had blinded me. The main house and two large side buildings were all pale yellow stone blocks, their terracotta roofs a darker version of the rusty soil which extended across the land. An enormous oak in the courtyard was thick with autumn-faded leaves. Then there were the olive trees, an endless formation of dark lurching trunks and silvery green leaves shimmering through the morning haze. Except for a few clusters of prickly cactus flaunting a richer hue of green, it was like viewing an old sepia-tint photo, infused with nostalgia and a kind of proud, stoic beauty.

Sandro's father led us along a path between the orchards. Most trees were maybe double my height, in evenly spaced rows. Those in one field were massive in comparison, all thick swirling trunks out of a Middle Earth fantasy, with no order to their arrangement.

"Some trees more than three hundred years," Sandro explained. "You see big one there? With black?" He indicated a particularly wizened tree with a huge lightning scar. "My grandfather say he is five hundred years."

A group of men smoking beside a tractor followed Papà into one of the orderly groves, while Sandro pointed me and Valerio, the young guy from breakfast, toward a cluster of older trees. I dropped back and admired Sandro's easy horse-like stride. And his tight, perfect butt which Jessie expected a report about.

"You have luck. Now is early season, not many workers," Sandro said. I helped him spread black webbed ground cloth around the roots, while Valerio, lighting his second cigarette of the morning, ran off and returned with wooden stepladders.

Sandro tapped my shoulder and swept his hand toward a tree. Two trunks formed a V from a massive gnarled base.

"Me?" I said.

"You. I teach you pick olives. Two euros one kilo. Big money, yes?"

Valerio made some sarcastic remark with the word *soldi:* money.

Sandro flicked his thumb on his teeth toward Valerio. "Him I pay only one euro fifty, because he is too ugly."

"Anyway, I have a university education," I said.

"Esattamente." Exactly. Sandro translated for Valerio, who pointed his nose up and spread his hand on top of his head in what I took to be an imitation of a scholar's cap, swiveling his hips as he carried a ladder to the next tree.

From the top, what first struck me was how flat the land was, as though I was seeing halfway across the world. The vast sea of trees was interrupted by a field that might have been wheat, then more olive groves, and nestled in the distance, a stone turret and peaked roofs: the village of Capracornea, if my orientation was correct. But it was the olives that awed me. Up here I was surrounded by millions of plump fruit, from pale yellow to rich velvety green, to many the color of plums. Sandro climbed up behind me, his hand reaching around and taking my wrist. I leaned ever-so-slightly against him. This was what I'd come here for.

Then he pressed into my hand a plastic miniature rake which looked like a children's beach toy.

"We look this color." With his free hand he pulled a branch closer. "I don't know how you say."

"Violet."

"Violet, yes. Or this." He plucked one and turned it in his strong fingers: purple with streaks of green. Then he guided the rake in my hand in a combing motion through the bunch. Olives popped free and rained onto the black cloth below. *"Delicato.* Not hurt fruits or taste will be bad."

I tried it by myself. An olive flew in my face, which set us both laughing, though it kind of stung. He stroked the place where it had struck my cheek. "Now you are *una professionista."*

He demonstrated how to hand-pluck isolated ripe olives from bunches of green ones, leaving the latter to mature. Then he squeezed my shoulder and backed down the ladder. Just as his face was level with my hip, Valerio made a loud kissing noise. Sandro leaped the last distance and threw an olive at him.

I combed and plucked, combed and plucked, descending only to move the ladder, while Sandro worked other trees. Valerio moved from tree to tree, singing and puffing away, shaming us both with full baskets of ripe olives in his wake. My arms ached, and I decided I'd earned a treat. I plucked one black fruit, rubbed its glossy skin between my fingers, and bit off a piece.

My mouth imploded with bitterness. I spat until I had no saliva left, but nothing relieved my tongue. The guys howled with laughter. Sandro jumped to the ground and handed up a bottle of water. "Not for eating," he said. "For eat, first must—how you say—bath salt water many days."

"Sounds like you have to pickle them," I said.

"Piccolo?" Valerio said, Italian for *small.* He patted his crotch, pointing at Sandro. *"È piccolo!"*

My scratched and aching arms were grateful when Sandro ordered a break. Valerio gathered olive twigs and built a fire. He pulled bread from a rucksack, sawed off thick slices and seared them over the flame. He passed one to me with all the solemnity of a religious rite. Sandro signaled me to wait while he uncorked an oil bottle and drenched my toast until my whole hand dripped. A cool breeze swept the orchard while the three of us sat eating bread and oil in silence, violating the gravity of this sacramental meal with loud sucking of fingers.

As the morning wore on, my output increased, arm muscles burning. My ears grew accustomed to Valerio's off-key singing and the bells clanging in the village. I was reaching for a high branch, posed precariously with one foot on the top rung, when something struck my butt. Two trees over, Valerio winked at me.

I tried to take it as a joke, but was kind of annoyed; what if I'd lost balance and fallen? I plucked a handful, not caring whether they were ripe, and flung them at him. Sandro thought we were playing, because he began his own barrage toward Valerio. We were soon engaged in a full-fledged olive war, Sandro and me against Valerio, shouts and laughter probably carrying all the way to the village. Valerio dropped to the ground, scooped up fistfuls of ripe fruit and bombarded Sandro, until he himself leaped down and they chased each other around the trees.

Another voice joined the fray. Sandro's father sprinted after them yelling like a demon. Catching Sandro by the elbow, he spun him around. Perhaps only my presence saved Sandro from being slapped. After his father stormed away, I helped gather the scattered fruits into baskets and carried them to the side of the path for collection.

On the walk back to the house Sandro said, "You are good olive picker." Then he put an arm around my shoulder. "And crazy fighter."

We joined the workers at a long table beneath a grape arbor, where they were busy leveling mountains of spaghetti, bread, and vegetables.

"You are bored?" Sandro asked me. "You want we go to the village?"

His father, getting the gist, put down his fork with a sharp thwack, his meaning obvious. The tension between them since this morning was palpable.

Sandro's hands went up in surrender. "Today make new oil. Maybe tomorrow go to village, okay?"

His mother refused to let me help clear the table, shooing me to follow Sandro and his father to a building of the same yellow stone as the main house. Inside the air rang with grinding, humming, and pounding. The first room was full of men and women squatting around the olive baskets removing twigs and leaves. In the next, olives were crushed whole beneath a mammoth stone wheel, sounding like bones crunching. Sandro explained that oil had to be extracted the same day as picking to capture the full flavor.

"When I am child, here have donkeys walk round, round, make wheel go. But now, machine. Smells better!"

I wasn't sure how anyone could have smelled donkeys over the heady aroma of crushed olives. He guided me into the next room and offered a pair of rubber gloves. "Now you make oil."

Between the morning's exertion, lingering tiredness from my travels, and the generous lunch digesting inside me, I would rather have laid down at that moment. Instead, a woman handed me an oar-sized spatula, demonstrating how to spread the olive pulp onto round woven mats, which others then stacked on a cart. The work was more grueling than I'd thought. By the time I was on my seventh mat, my shoulders were burning. My slippery gloves lost their grip and oily mush plopped onto the floor. People laughed while I tried to shrug off my embarrassment.

"Guess I'm fired, right?" I said.

Sandro's reaction struck me cold. While others scraped up the mess, he glanced nervously at the door to the next room, as though expecting his father to appear with a renewed outburst.

A man wheeled my stack of mats to a hydraulic press, where with an explosive puff the machine bore down, squeezing oil into a collecting basin, from which it flowed through a pipe into another room. My crime had gone unpunished, but I decided I was through with that job and turned in my gloves.

Finally we reached the inner sanctum, dominated at one end

by a steel centrifuge which sounded like a Godzilla-sized dentist's drill. Sandro's father waved me over, his smile reserved for me alone. At work, Sandro and his father were pure business, stiff and taciturn.

Papà tapped the steel drum. *"Questo è il tuo olio."* This was "my" oil. The olives I'd plucked with my own fingers just hours before coursed now through transparent tubes as sunny green liquid. Maybe soon some Seattle hipster foodie would be dribbling my hand-picked *olio d'oliva* onto their charcoal-toasted zero-carb nut-free gluten-less bagel.

Papà opened a spigot and drained oil into tiny plastic cups for each of us. I mimed surprise at finding it cloudy. *"Olio nuovo,"* he said—new oil—with a raised thumb. Papà swirled his beneath his nose like a wine taster, then sucked the contents into his mouth with a disgusting, frothy slurp. He swished the mixture between his cheeks, finally swallowing it with a satisfied, "Aah!"

I did as shown, expecting a revelation of sorts. But it was olive oil: light, slippery, leaving a slight burn at the back of my throat. I touched my throat and made a face.

His father tapped his Adam's Apple, then kissed his fingers.

"Extra virgin must be bitter," Sandro said without a trace of irony.

The oil master entered from a side room bearing a large glass jug full of oil, from which he refilled our cups.

"From south orchard," Sandro explained.

I was tasting my way into a new world. The flavor stretched across my mouth, and the bitterness as it went down was ever-so-slightly broader. I told them I was beginning to get it. Sandro's father clapped me on the shoulder, said something and made a spitting sound.

"My father say, now you are destroyed. You go America, next time taste cheap olive oil..."

SUPPER WAS FAMILY-ONLY, PLUS me. Signor Buonaventura was in an expansive mood, cheered, no doubt, by the quality of his early harvest. He even teased a little about the faces I'd made when sampling the oil.

"*Buonaventura olio, numero uno!*" I said with kissed fingers, which earned me a firm round of nods.

Mamma fussed over me, making sure I ate more of every-thing. Olimpia and Sandro traded jokey insults, partly in English for my benefit. Silent Uncle never once glanced up. It seemed a normal evening at home.

Afterward, Sandro took me for a walk. The world had gone quiet again, an autumn nip spiced the air.

"I am sorry," he told me. "Today only work."

"It was great. The most fun I've had in years!"

Further along the track, away from the house lights, I nudged my shoulder against his. "I want to see your telescope."

His eyes pointed up, and I felt stupid. The sky was thick with clouds, the moon a blur. "Must wait until stars want to...*ah...*"

"Want to *be seen,*" I enunciated.

"Ah, yes, I forget. Now is time for English lesson."

"Did they offer you a temporary teacher?" I said.

"Offer. But...you know, what if new teacher is not so pretty? How I can learn?" He looked at me, worried. "Joke."

I opened my mouth to ask who they'd assigned him, but shut it again. No need to find out. I edged closer, hoping he'd put his arm around me. Instead he pointed me off the path.

"Come. You remember we speak, I am sitting outside? Here is my place."

We settled on a tuft of soft grass, facing each other in the weak moonlight, knees nearly touching.

"Your parents are very nice," I said.

One eyebrow shot up, his head rocked side to side. "My father like you very much."

"I'm happy to hear that."

"He likes women. Sorry. I don't mean like that. Or maybe. He is traditional Italian man. If woman is beautiful and intelligent, he likes."

"So you aren't traditional? You like stupid and ugly women?"

He laughed, twirling his finger in the grass so close to my ankle that the smallest move would have made us touch. He seemed nervous as a little boy—breathing a bit hurried, shoulders frozen. I was sure he wanted to lean forward and take my hands, maybe kiss me, yet something held him back, some old-fashioned chivalry. What if I were to lean in and surprise him with a kiss or drop back onto the grass and invite him into my arms? In this society would such a move tar a woman as too aggressive, even a slut? I didn't know if I was facing culture clash or just a shy, respectful man.

"With your father you seem..." How did I put this in simple English without insulting him? "...worried?"

"He is my father." He shrugged as though that explained everything.

"Does he get angry at you a lot?"

"I am his son." He counted on one finger, then the next. "And his—what word?—his employer."

"His employee."

"Aiee! Employee. Later time I will be the business boss. So if I am do something stupid, he must angry."

"And that's what you want? To take over the business?"

His grass-twirling became more intense, blades ripped from the ground. I placed my hand on his. The twirling ceased. He entwined his fingers with mine.

"Seven, ah, *generazioni*—you understand?—Buonaventura family grow olives. My—*aiee!* I don't know words—father of grandfather."

"Great-grandfather. In Italian?"

"*Bisnonno*. Bisnonno make this house. Grandfather makes bigger, buys more land for trees, makes the...the...stone for break the olives."

"The millstone?"

"Yes, he make himself. My father makes modern, with centrifuge, laboratory. Export to Argentina, South Africa. So..."

"So. What will Alessandro do to make it better?"

He looked for a moment like a helpless boy. "Yes."

We twisted our hands together without speaking. I couldn't imagine taking over my father's work, selling house alarms in suburbia. But an olive plantation? Words almost left my mouth: "I'll help you." *Slow down, Serena!*

He made to stand up. "Time is late, now becoming cold."

We walked slowly, hand in hand. As house lights reappeared through the trees, he let go, scratched the back of his head, and put his hands in his pockets. Rounding the bend, I spied an upstairs curtain quickly pulled shut, after a glimpse of his mother's face.

BACK IN MY ROOM I was too wound up and jetlagged to even think of sleeping. I flipped through my phrase book, but the words blurred before my eyes. I checked the time in California— mid-afternoon—and checked my phone. The Wi-Fi had no password, praise the Madonna on my wall.

Elias picked up on the third ring, hastily brushing off his t-shirt and knocking something off his desk.

"Hey! The world traveler! Buenas...uh...dias, or whatever."

"That's Spanish. *Buonasera*. No, that's good evening. I don't know how to say good afternoon."

"Thought you'd be fluent by now."

"How are my babies?"

"I'm fine, glad you asked. And you?" His smirk was almost charming. "Oh, you mean Ham and Cheese. Lemme get them."

He looked like he was clipping the phone to a desk mount, then he disappeared. The camera focused on the sofa across the room. Did I detect a slight reduction in sloppy mess? Then his voice—"Say hi to Mommy"—and a pair of fists filled the screen, each wrapped around a hamster. My heart pinged with motherly joy until—

"What the hell?" Both snouts were bright orange. "You've been feeding them cheese puffs? I told you very specifically: no human food!"

His lower jaw came into the picture. "Aren't you the one who said cheese puffs aren't fit for *human* consumption? No, that was me. Hey, look, I'm just bonding with the kids, right?"

"Please don't poison them after I wrecked my car getting one to the vet."

"Hey, these guys never been happier. I let them run around. Advantage at my place is you can't tell if they pee on the carpet."

"Spare me the details."

He put them away, then returned and sat down. "So how's Italy?"

I did one of those Italian finger kisses. "It's like, oh my God, I don't know how to tell you. Like a crazy fairy tale dream I haven't made sense of yet." I described my day picking and pressing olives, the food, the landscape, the five-hundred-year-old trees. Elias nodded through my speech. I must have sounded like a boring relative boasting about their cruise holiday.

"Glad you're having fun," he said, though he didn't sound awfully glad.

I settled back against the headboard. It felt good to speak in complete English sentences. "Have you ever had the feeling that you're just meant to be in a place?"

"Uh..." He glanced down like he was checking something. "You've been in the country for, what? Thirty-two hours by my count. Which means—"

"What do you mean, *by your count?*"

He shrugged like a kid caught with his hand in the cookie jar. "Okay, maybe I tracked your flights. So, as of this moment, thirty-two hours in Italy. Airport to train station plus your most likely train ride, total six hours thirty-two minutes, and I'm guessing max five hours sleep, what with jet lag. Hence, twenty waking hours in the actual target zone. Which means by my calculation right now you are experiencing the travel equivalent of a sugar rush."

"Come on, I'm serious. You should see it: the house, the farm. I mean, it isn't so gorgeous in any picture postcard sense. It's just, like, I'm sliding right into it, not even feeling culture shock. And the people. Like it's meant to be."

"Why? Cause you picked olives? Maybe that means you're meant to be in Salinas, or wherever it is they grow them here."

"Quiet! You're saying you never had a gut feeling about a place being just meant for you, like it's no coincidence the universe led you there?"

"I dunno. Have I? Yeah, I suppose maybe once. Isn't it late there? Aren't you kind of tired?"

"No. Tell me your story."

He removed his glasses, polished them on his shirt, and put them back on, his expression serious now. "Yeah, so after high school me and my friend Randy took this trip to Hawaii, right? So I'm carrying some bento box take-outs across to Ala Moana Beach to meet him, and there's the sun setting through the palms and a perfect sea breeze and all these long-haired Hawaiian chicks in short shorts, and you can hear some guy singing Hawaiian songs with a guitar, and it floored me. I stood there thinking, like, this is the place. I could live here, I really could."

"And?"

"Few seconds later some guy bumps into me, grabs my wallet, tosses it to another asshole on a moped. Kinda popped that bubble. They got mopeds there?"

"Vespas."

"Enough said."

I clicked my tongue. "Go away. I'll check back in a couple days, see what else you're feeding my darlings. Bye."

"Yeah. Miss you too."

I clicked off, then noticed a message icon. It was from Sandro, sent three minutes ago.

Sei sveglia?

I copied it into a translation app: *You're awake?*
I replied:

Vieni. Come over.

Moments later, there was a light tap at the door. I turned off my phone and put it on the side table. Sandro stood in the doorway like he was unsure what to do, the shy little boy.

I opened my arms.

My fingernails stabbed into the flesh of his shoulders. His stubbled cheek scoured mine. I walked him backwards to the bed and let him fall on top of me. In an instant, we were entwined like tangled rubber bands, lips and tongues wrestling and leap-frogging, swimming in each other's heat and smells.

I ran my hand under his shirt, stroked the smooth curve of his back, trying to wear away the wall of nerves we each pretended wasn't present. A tiny voice inside me narrated where I was, who I was with.

OMG, I'm in bed with my student!

I clenched my eyes shut to squeeze out the thought. This was the culmination of weeks—months!—of built-up desire coming true before my very, um... But my brain still wouldn't shut up. *If the school finds out...* I reminded my busybody brain: *See? Phone off, computer tucked safely in a drawer.*

He rolled onto his side. Again that little boy embarrassed

smile, as he reached behind and switched off the lamp. Was he really so shy? The thought flittered that Sandro might be as extra-virgin as his oil.

Maybe this was just too soon for both of us. Here we were, cavorting in my bed barely twenty-four hours after we'd first met in person—what did that make me? But we *hadn't* just met. We'd seen each other five days a week for the past nearly three months. Or didn't those count, those neck-up, pheromone-deprived encounters at work? Even the extracurricular walks—were they less real just because they'd taken place through a pair of selfie cams?

Shut up, brain, and kiss him. So I did.

He had one leg stretched over me. I undid the top two buttons of my shirt, then guided his hand to the next one down.

Out of nowhere, I imagined my high school history teacher, whom I'd once had a crush on, undressing me.

Shut up, brain! Lobotomize me, somebody! Shut the hell up!

My eyes sprang open. It wasn't Mr. Pollard, it was Alessandro. The dim light through the curtained window rendered his face into one of those Carnival masks, black on one side, white and almost featureless on the other. Like a mask, his expression was unreadable.

His hand slid to the opening in my shirt, then the other hand. Maybe I should tell him to stop. Maybe it *was* too soon. We had another fifteen days—two days, actually, according to Zuzie's Shipoopi Principle.

His hands moved higher. He refastened my shirt buttons, smiling sadly.

Chapter 23

I woke to the five o'clock bells, alone and fully dressed. I felt beside me where his body had been, pulled off the scratchy blanket, and stretched my arms.

Three hours later those same arms encircled Sandro from behind, saddled on an antique motorcycle whose muffler didn't muffle and shocks didn't absorb, over a long, straight, bumpy lane. With no helmet to contain it, my hair whipped my neck, eyes watering in the chill morning air. His father had given him a couple days off to show me around, though I'd caught his mother appraising me with a slight frown this morning while she loaded our breakfast plates.

I still couldn't believe what I was doing. A few days ago, scraping beans from a can in my boxy white-walled apartment. Today, cruising past orchards and vineyards through a sun-drenched ancient land which had once been traversed by Greeks and Romans, Crusaders and Ottomans, holding tight to a gentle, warm, and sexy man.

Without signal or warning, Sandro turned sharp right past a boarded shack. Trees gave way to whitewashed walls, and straightaways to zigzag alleys of mismatched paving stones which conspired to shatter my spine. So this was Capracornea, Alessandro's home town.

Cars parked on sidewalks and next to doorways transformed already narrow streets into snaking obstacle courses. Sandro wound the motorcycle through a kids' soccer game, the players not even pausing the action as we careered around them, before emerging into a cobblestoned square. He skidded sideways to a stop like a skier.

My ears buzzed so loud I barely heard myself. "That was...oh my God, do you always ride like that?"

He shrugged and combed a hand through his hair in a single motion. "Here is my city."

It was an exaggeration to call it a city. Capracornea was a farming town, understated and plain compared to the quaint hamlets in Mediterranean travel shows. We'd stopped in front of what looked like a small castle, whose reddish stone parapets had been patched here and there with gray concrete. Across the piazza—an expanse of paving stones devoid of fountains or statues—was the turret I'd spied from the groves, crowning a stone church. Its bells came to life; I recognized them, only now they were deep, thunderous clangs. Women in black rounded a corner and scurried inside. Cars, motorcycles, and Vespas crossed the square in every direction with no regard for lanes or traffic etiquette.

Sandro led me to a table fronting a tiny restaurant without a name, just the word "Bar" on its awning. The woman proprietor greeted Sandro by name. No sooner had he introduced me, than I was cheek-kissing not only her, but her husband, their adult daughter, even an old man introduced as Nonno—Grandpa— though I wasn't sure whose. They plied me with little cakes and question after question: How long did it take to fly from Los Angeles to Puglia? Did I know any movie stars? How could I possibly not be Italian with a name like Serena? Had I ever happened to come across their cousin Mauro who'd moved to New Jersey in the 1980s?

I had a question too: "Is it early enough for cappuccino?"

They looked to Sandro. As he explained how Americans

drank cappuccino any time of day, their curiosity turned to head shakes and tongue clicking. I knew I'd risk a war if I dared request soy milk. Minutes later I was watching the town come to life, while enjoying my first genuine Italian cappuccino.

"You must love it here," I told Sandro. "Everyone knows you, you know everyone."

"Every person knows what I have breakfast, even before I eat. I go here, all people say, 'Ah, today you eat lemon marmalade—why not like yesterday, grape?'"

I laughed. "So the whole village must know that I'm here, yes?"

He set down his tiny espresso cup and pointed around the square. "This moment, every house in Capracornea, no need newspaper, no need radio or Internet, all hearing the news. Crazy American girl say she drink cappuccino after the lunch! *Scandalo!*"

There was something behind his smile, though: it bothered him that the whole town was watching me. Which they certainly were. Other customers stopped in and shared gossip, smiling in my direction while the owners dropped the word *Americana* into every third sentence. There was even a near mishap between two opposing Vespas as the riders snapped their heads aside to gawk at me. I didn't object when Sandro suggested we visit another town.

We took the back roads, passing groves and vineyards and shorn wheat fields and ranch-like *masserie*. After thirty or forty minutes of bumps and turns, competing with vehicles in both directions over the less cratered center of the road, my butt was numb and I was grateful that I'd barely eaten. Entering the outskirts of Lecce, it was a relief to be back on evenly paved streets, though these led through an urban wasteland of run-down housing blocks. The people there looked and dressed like they came from everywhere except Italy, and beggars occupied every corner. I was pleased when Sandro ran four red lights in a row.

The city center was a different world. Sandro double-parked

in a side street and passed money to a nearby news vendor without taking a magazine. He winked at me. "Here we say, he is 'a friend of the friends.'"

We passed through a baroque fantasyland into the Piazza del Duomo. Block after block seemed whittled out of one massive creamy white stone. Life-sized carved figures peered down from balconies. Every door and window was embossed with ripples and swirls, Madonnas and angels, mermaids and dragons. Even churches were covered in a phantasmagoria of animal faces, fish tails, paws, and wings. I couldn't look up or down without some character leering at me out of the stone. The overwhelming whiteness was splattered with bright purple bougainvilleas.

I tried—I really did try—to pay attention to his explanations about the history and symbolism of this building and that carving, but all I cared about was his hand in mine. It was obvious he'd led this same tour too many times. I put him out of his misery, pointing to a cozy cafe and insisted that I pay.

"You must have brought a million visitors here," I said.

"Not million. Maybe only three hundred thousand. Are you boring?"

"Bored...*no!* Not bored. You're just like me. When I was growing up in California, I always had to take visiting cousins to Disneyland."

Our coffees came, black, bitter espressos with tiny cookies on the side.

"Sometimes cousins, yes," he said. "But most are customers come Italy for holiday. Since I am twelve it is always, 'Sandro, you take important friend see Lecce.'"

"Including maybe a few beautiful foreign girls?"

"Only one time," he said, and my heart stopped. "When was? I try remember. Ah, yes. Was today!"

I set down my empty cup and slid my hand onto his. "Sandro, listen. You don't need to run me around to tourist sights. I'm here to see you, get to know you. I'm just so—" My voice cracked. The struggles and stresses of the past couple weeks, the past year, all the wishes and hopes, welled up in me at once. "I'm just so happy to be here. You don't know how happy I am."

Sandro held up my hand, his eyes surveying my fingers. "Me, too. I am happy you are here."

The passing waiter, hearing English, asked, *"Inglese?"*

"Americana," I said.

He asked how long was the flight and whether I knew any movie stars or his great-aunt Orabella in Seattle.

HUGGING THE COAST GOING south under a sapphire sky, past rocky coves with a smear of beach sand, whitewashed houses clinging to slopes over the sparkling blue Adriatic Sea. Tiny settlements saturated with smells of fish and brine and cries of seafood vendors who beckoned us to try their squid, mussels, and round and spiky sea creatures I'd never seen in my life. At Otranto we walked along castle walls. Sandro pointed out the distant hills of Albania. We watched a ferry depart for Greece while Sandro made a hilarious but vain effort to explain Italian politics.

We zigzagged out of town and turned onto a country lane. A minute later he let out a curse, *"Merda."*

Two black-uniformed policemen by the side of the road flagged us down with a baton. The shorter and fatter one casually held a submachine gun at his side, pointed at the ground, at least.

"Carabinieri," Sandro said, though the word meant nothing to me.

"Why are they stopping us?"

Before he could explain, the tall one was beside us, rapping the baton on his leg, other hand gesturing for papers. *"Documenti, per favore."*

I hadn't thought to carry my passport and I had no other identification, not even my driver's license. So close to a ferry port, I supposed they were looking for refugees. But a young couple on a motorcycle?

While Tall Baton Cop examined Sandro's papers, I had my eye on the one with the automatic weapon. A bulletproof vest peeked from his collar. He offered a cold smile, as if they were checking tickets to a county fair.

Tall Baton Cop pointed his bat at our heads, indicating the lack of helmets, then at a front signal light which I knew to be cracked. He twitched his fingers toward me. *"Documenti."*

Ignoring my wide-eyed, innocent shrug, he beckoned me off the bike. Short Round Gunner Cop stepped closer.

Sandro dismounted beside me and with lots of hand language, rattled off a lengthy explanation. I caught the term *turista*—annoying but forgivable in this circumstance—then another torrent of words, among which was Hollywood, minus the H.

Both carabinieri grinned like mules. The little cop let his gun dangle by its strap. Of course I guessed the next question. I was about to recite my prepared answer, when I felt Sandro tap my toes. *"Si,"* he said, pressing harder.

"Si," I repeated, with all the confidence I could fake. *"Conosco* Al Pacino *e...*ah...Tell him Leonardo DiCaprio and I sometimes go out drinking."

The officers knew I was lying but enjoyed the story. The tall one tucked the baton into his shiny leather boot and offered cigarettes, then insisted we take pictures together. I handed my phone to Sandro and posed between them, making sure the machine gun was in the picture. This was worth posting online!

Short Round Gunner slapped his thigh and rattled off a question, the only word of which I caught was Boston.

Sandro translated: "He want to know if you ever went to Boston, maybe meet his neighbor's cousin Luigi."

"Luigi Calavari," Short Round Gunner added.

Sandro half-winked at me.

"What a coincidence! Luigi Calavari? With the mustache?" I said, holding my finger across my lip.

Short Round didn't need a translation. His squat body bobbed like a dashboard mascot. *"Si! È lui!"* That's him!

"Of course it's him," I said, and Sandro translated. "Everybody in Boston knows Luigi!"

"How is he? How is he looking?"

I patted my belly. "He's gotten a bit fat, and his hair, well..." Best to leave that vague.

Short Round's voice rose to high pitch, grinning at Tall Baton Cop, gesticulating at me, pointing somewhere in the distance, maybe at America.

"He ask of Luigi's children," Sandro said.

I was getting nervous lying to an armed policeman. "Um, the...the daughter..."

"Anna," said Short Round.

"Yes, Anna. She married a local Italian boy."

If Short Round was pleased before, now I thought he was going to split his trousers and launch to the moon. He couldn't wait to tell the neighbor, he said, who hadn't heard from his cousin in a decade. "And Pietro?" he asked.

My mind churned like a washing machine. Was Pietro the son? A brother? I said to Sandro through a frozen grin, "Can we get out of here? Just tell him anything."

He said something that made both policemen go bug-eyed and elbow each other. The gunner asked one last question. Whatever Sandro replied set Short Round into a foot-stamping rage, while Tall Baton Cop spat on the asphalt, growling curses.

"Sit on motorcycle," Sandro said calmly. I obeyed. He leaped on in front of me, gunned the engine, and we tore away, leaving the two cops to their spitting and swearing.

I shouted in his ear, "What did you tell them?"

"I tell them, Pietro he marry his boyfriend."

"Ha! So that's why they were angry."

He shouted louder as we closed in on a truck farting black clouds of exhaust. "Not angry! This they surprised only."

He veered onto the grassy shoulder, passing the truck. "Then I say them the boyfriend is Greek."

EARLY AFTERNOON, THE SKY turned steel gray; a light drizzle spread across the landscape. Sandro detoured onto a farm road through a massive olive grove, partly shielding us from the weather. We came out the other end into a sleepy town which looked yellowed by centuries of sun. We left the bike and dashed through intensifying rain into a little white-walled restaurant, empty except for a few old men smoking in the back. Raindrops smeared the windows while we lingered over a massive late lunch of peppery seafood and pasta, trading childhood stories. Maybe it was the pitcher of full-blooded local wine we'd finished, but I fell into a hysterical laughing fit when he commented how exotic I was, to have grown up in the California suburbs, with neat lawns, and swimming pools in every back yard.

"So sad! Every family swim by alone!" he said. "Why not one big swimming pool for the whole street, everybody plays together, and use gardens for grow food?"

"Because don't you know? In America, food doesn't come from the ground, it comes in cans and plastic. Did you know in America you can buy canned pasta shaped like little O's that you zap in the microwave?"

"No, this can not be true. And you ate?"

"All the time when I was a kid. And we have pizza with bar-becue sauce instead of tomatoes."

"If this is true, we must make war against America."

I gulped my last drops of wine. "If there's war, then what happens to me?"

"You must be my prisoner," he said, gripping my wrist.

Together we shouted, "Let there be war!" The smokers in the back flicked us curious looks.

WE RETURNED OVER SLIPPERY roads, through dips like reservoirs. By the time we passed through his home gate, we were caked to the waist in mud. Rounding the shed where the motorcycle resided, I spotted Sandro's father and a man in a tweed jacket. The latter quickly slipped an envelope into his pocket.

Sandro stopped me from leaving the shed. I thought he wanted to kiss me, until I saw the tense set of his jaw. I didn't ask. It wasn't my business, but Sandro seemed compelled to explain.

"He is the government man."

"Inspector?"

"*Si*. Inspector. Agriculture department."

He didn't need to—he *shouldn't*—tell me a thing. This was Italy, *southern* Italy. No need to elaborate. But he stopped me at the door.

"We are honest oil makers. Not like some big company, buy Tunisia oil and write Italian. Or mix lamp oil, make chemistry and color, say it extra virgin. You see us, how we do. We are pure."

"You don't have to explain, Sandro. It isn't my—"

"I must explain. It is my father's honor. It is my honor. Inspector can write one word—*grossolano* or *inacetito*—and... *pfft!*" He slapped hands together as if to say *finished*. "Now we go inside and drink wine with him."

The inspector was ebullient, puffing out words and pungent cigarette smoke in equal proportions. Sandro gave a brief account of our run-in with the law. His father reacted with annoyance, flicking his hand at me, clearly scolding Sandro for putting me in such danger. The inspector leaned toward me, the envelope protruding from his jacket, and asked in broken English whether I really knew Al Pacino.

"Mi dispiace, non so niente." I stumbled over the words. Sorry, I know nothing. Sandro and his father shared a glance over my bad choice of words.

NEITHER POLICE NOR INSPECTORS were discussed at dinner. Sandro's father was in a teasing mood. He asked who was handsomer, father or son, to which I replied, of course the son is more handsome but the father is smarter. He laughed and called me "dangerous". I liked him, I liked his family, and I especially liked his son. I wasn't so sure his wife and daughter returned my regard. Sandro's mother was friendly and attentive as usual, constantly sliding food onto my plate, but I got the feeling that her hospitality was more ingrained than inspired.

The after dinner pastime went on forever, family conversation that was only occasionally translated for my benefit and listening to classical music, when I wanted to play my own duet with Sandro. Late evening, when he stepped through my door, I leapt onto his back until he deposited me on the bed, where we rolled around with our mouths clamped to each other and hands went places they hadn't considered the night before. We heard footsteps down the hall and held hands over each other's giggling mouths.

Our chaste love-making had deepened, as though we'd each discovered some secret passage into the center of the other's being. We knew where we were headed, but we weren't ready to arrive. At least he wasn't. The voices inside my head had gone out for the evening, leaving me calm enough to have patience with my bashful Old World gentleman.

I felt him leave in the middle of the night. Afraid of being found out by his parents, this man of twenty-five years.

He needed me to free him. I was sure of it.

Chapter 24

*A*t breakfast the next day Sandro's mother seemed unhappy with me. It wasn't anything I could put my finger on—a pout, a puff of breath. For once she let me help clear the table without comment.

Sandro needed to spend the morning helping his father prepare newly-bottled oil for shipment. He invited me to help at the label machine, the cleanest job available. I told him I preferred to take a walk by myself. He didn't disguise his look of relief. It was hard enough to deal with his father without me around.

We both needed a little time off, not from each other, but from words. It was exhausting for him to speak English all the time. And for all my teaching experience, it was also a struggle for me to consider every word, every sentence, every grammatical construct—put bluntly, I had to dumb down my English in a manner that wasn't obvious enough to make him feel stupid.

After only two days, I was able to recognize a surprising number of Italian words, but my speaking ability was limited to *ciao,* please, thank you, sorry, delicious, not tired, how much, and the all-important, *Non conosco nessuna star del cinema.* I don't know any movie stars. At least it was something. If I were living here, I was sure I'd pick it up quickly.

It was another dazzling jewel-like day. I walked along the curving driveway toward the main gate, kicking up pebbles, listening to the racket of birds.

I sat on a tuft of grass and gazed up through the canopy of leaves at the azure sky.

Living here. Maybe Sandro's mother was clairvoyant, because the idea had already implanted itself in my head. Laugh-filled evenings over wine and pasta. Weekends in Naples. Countless days like this.

WHEN I RETURNED, SANDRO was loading equipment into the car while arguing quietly with his mother. She threw her hands up, pleaded to some saint for mercy, and pinched his shoulder. I ran inside, stuffed a jacket and spare clothes into a bag, then followed his mother's beckoning into the kitchen, where she handed me a large basket packed with food. At least she'd lightened up since this morning. Before I got in the car, she patted me on the cheek the way she might have patted a dog.

Soon Sandro and I were cruising amidst high speed traffic on the *autostrada,* singing along to soaring Italian pop anthems while fields and orchards and farm houses rolled past.

I shouted over the music and the noise of the open window. "I think your mother doesn't like me."

"What? Is sure she likes you. Maybe she is tired."

So he had noticed.

"Maybe I should give money for all the food I'm eating. Or do something for the family." Or maybe she was a traditional Catholic woman who knew about our little nightly encounters and thought the worst.

Sandro wiped his brow and put a hand on my knee. "No you worry. My mother and father is very happy you visit."

Maybe I was oversensitive, but "visit" seemed so cold. They—or at least his mother—did not want my presence to turn into a long-term matter. Did Sandro?

"Not to be sad," he said. "Sky is blue, sun is warm. You are young and beautiful. I am young and—ha! Tonight we look at stars."

I made him replay the last song and teach me the words. The jubilant voice and clanging guitars, the fresh landscape sliding by, the wind in my hair, washed the worry away. I felt free as a bird.

We stopped in Taranto to buy wine, then left the highway and I had the novel experience, for the first time in Puglia, of traveling uphill. We climbed over a craggy valley onto an unpaved mountain track, bouncing over boulders and stumps until by the time we stopped I thought I'd have to screw my head back into my neck.

We parked on a treeless summit of bald, crevassed white rock. And flies. The kind of place only an astronomer might find beautiful. In three directions, low, scrubby mountains pocked with boulders, which glowed red in the sunset like a fresh strike of meteors. To the southeast, a wide plain stretched out into the distance like a chiaroscuro carpet. It was Sandro's world, from this summit, across Italy's boot heel to the sparkling shores of the Adriatic and Ionian Seas. I wanted to reach down and scoop up this world in my arms. I wanted it to be mine.

While Sandro assembled his telescope's motors and gyros, I skipped around the mountain top, feeling like Julie Andrews in "The Sound of Music", minus the green slopes and wildflowers. I spun around and around, arms outstretched to embrace all of Italy, while the wind tried to sweep me into the sky, and I belted out the lines I remembered from a song I'd made Sandro play over and over in the car because it made me feel so good, which in English meant:

> *Let me breathe again*
> *Take me where you fly*
> *Where one never falls*

Yes! I could fly where I wanted. I could fly without falling. I ran against the wind across the naked rock, singing my lungs out to the sky, my open jacket flapping like a wing. I could breathe again!

Sandro had laid out our meal inside the car to keep flies off. We took our plates and sat on the hood, devoured rich tomato- and mozzarella-stuffed *panzerotti*, clinked wine glasses, watched the hills fade into the dark. We leaned into each other and kissed long and hard until the sky turned black.

It was a perfect, glassy clear stargazing night. He pointed to Mars and a bluish circle he assured me was Neptune. He asked if I wanted to view craters on the moon, but something gave me the feeling that for him, the moon was his equivalent of my taking out-of-town visitors to Hollywood.

"I want to fly a million light-years away," I said.

"Only? I take you more far."

Minutes later my jaw reached halfway to the ground. My eyes took in not only one, but two perfect spiral galaxies, like spiders spun from diamonds.

"What are their names?" I said.

He sniffed a laugh. "Not have pretty name. Big one she is M51. Twenty three million light-years distance."

He took me for a spin around the universe, lingering over globular clusters and strange colored nebulas. Some were tiny and blurred, others bursting with clarity. While they were beautiful and awe-inspiring, what struck me most were Sandro's little cries of delight each time he located a target and, like an eager little child, waved me over. One star cluster looked like exploding fireworks, another was shaped like a smoke ring. Red giants, binary star systems. He wrapped warm arms around me as I leaned into the eyepiece. He loved them all like old friends, or pets, or jewels he'd collected. I wanted to be one of his stars.

Later he attached a camera to capture the stars' night-long journey across the heavens, while he and I lay back on a pair of mats watching the same.

"I think I just saw the Starship Enterprise," I said, but he misinterpreted the joke.

"I am sorry, you are bored to look on too many stars," he said.

"Absolutely not bored. All I've ever looked through were toy telescopes when I was little. It's all so strange and beautiful." I turned on my side and stroked his arm. "Just like you."

"I also have a toy telescope when I am little. I stay outside all night to look, too many times. When I am twelve my father buys me good telescope. Not professional, but good. Every year I want bigger lens, more eyepieces, new motor. He says me, better if he gives me pornography, because is cheaper and I will stay in my room all night."

"I wish I had a hobby I loved so much."

"Hobby," he said, processing a new word. He raised his head to check the telescope, then leaned back, taking in the sky. "Have hobby is good. But many times I ask...how to say? *Aiee!* My English!"

I kept quiet while he rubbed his forehead, coaxing his thoughts into a viable translation. At last he spoke, to the stars: "I ask, why something you love must be hobby?"

I didn't understand immediately. Then I got it. "You also love your work, yes? The trees, the land, the heritage—sorry, the history. Making something so pure and perfect."

He turned to me, resting his head on his folded hands. "You love your work?"

"I love it. I do. Well, it could be better. I would prefer working in a classroom, or at least face-to-face. Like this." I touched my nose to his. "But I love to teach. I love to know people from everywhere. I love to see students blossom—you know, open like flowers, and go from little English, to...like you right now, saying what's in your mind. The world is so divided, and I'm so lucky, I get to help bridge that divide. I really feel that way. Do you understand?"

"I think." He spoke with such sadness, for a moment I thought he was jealous. Of me!

"If you don't love your work, then the oil won't taste good," I said.

"Yes, you are right. My father, he loves very much. Sometimes— you don't say him!—when we have the new oil, he kiss the first can, for luck. It's like he kiss a woman. For me, I work for father. It is what I must do. I do good job. But I don't want to kiss oil cans."

The bitterness in his joke he capped with a sigh.

"What do you want to kiss?" I said. "Besides me?"

Our lips came together. Then he sat up, sideways to me, facing his telescope.

"Okay, I tell you. When I am eighteen, I go to Padova. You know? It is city in the north, near from Venezia, I think you say Venice. Università di Padova have department of physics and astronomy. Know who teach there before? Nicolaus Copernicus! Galileo Galilei! True! I go in the room where Galileo was teach. I stand where he standed. I touch walls his voice touched. Sit in chair and close my eyes, and I think I hear him, I feel his...his..."

"Spirit?"

"Spirit! Yes. Then students come inside, and I am embarrassed. But they say me: stay. I listen to *professore* speak about astrophysics—too difficult for me, I understand only a little. But this I want! Learning about the universe—yes, this I want! After, some students invite me drinking. Padova is beautiful city, everywhere students, everywhere people talking intelligent things. Books, music, art, astronomy. Not talking only harvest. I tell myself, this I want! My new friend brings me to the university observatory, says me his project is for discover black holes. This I want! This I love! I love!"

Sandro hugged his knees to his chest, his lips funneled. It was getting cold, despite our jackets. I fetched a wool blanket from the car and tucked it around us.

I asked, "So, did you apply?"

He looked at me, uncomprehending.

"Did you try to get in to the university?"

His head bowed, gathering words. "In Padova, I go to office of *professore,* we talk long time. He say is difficult, too many people want there to study. But he say will help me. He get for me the papers…"

"The application for admission."

He shrugged and took a deep breath. "I think. I don't know English word. He write his name for *referenza.* I go home. I say Mamma and Papà, I study astronomy. My father is very angry, no will talk. Mamma says, 'What job is this, astronomy? Is hobby, not…ah…*carriera.'*"

"Career?"

"Yes, is not career, she say. Go to factory or bank and ask for astronomy job, they will laugh! Or maybe you want move to the moon!'"

"That's ridiculous," I said. "But you sent the application, didn't you?"

"I answer all of questions. I put the papers on my table in my room." Even in the dim moonlight I saw his face flush. "Tomorrow—I mean, next day I work the olive press, go back my room, papers are gone."

"What? Oh my God! Your mother?"

He shrugged. "Maybe she is right. Very many students, how many astronomy jobs in Italy? Maybe astronomy is better to be hobby. Here," he said, indicating the bald mountain top. "I bring my telescope any time, my private observatory."

"Your mother is wrong," I told him. "Anyway, it isn't too late. You can still go study, become an astronomer—teach, write, do research."

"Then who harvests the olives? Who makes oil? One day, my father is too old for working. I am the only son."

"Why couldn't you do both? Hire people to run the farm. You come back to supervise during the harvest."

He wrapped his arm around my shoulder. We sat quietly staring into the darkness.

"You remember what I promised you?" he said.

"I remember."

"I promised I show you God."

After a deep breath, I said, "I saw him. You showed me the universe."

He rocked, a full-body nod. "My problem, your problems, are little tiny."

I snuggled against him, rested my head on his shoulder. He stroked my hair.

I opened my mouth to speak, then shook my head, never mind.

"No more talking, yes?" Sandro said.

And there, on the mountaintop, beneath a scratchy blanket, in full view of the universe while God watched from above, our passion took its final course.

Hours later I lay wide awake, listening to night insects, the camera on the telescope clicking every few seconds, and the breath of the warm, beautiful man in my arms. A cold gust slipped under the covers. In his sleep, he squeezed me tighter.

I mouthed silently into his ear, with the stars as my witness:

"*Ti amo.*" I love you.

Chapter 25

*M*orning was nearly gone when we pulled up to the house. Sandro's mother rushed outside clucking like an angry hen. We had all been invited to lunch at the neighboring vineyard. Though Sandro's translation lacked enthusiasm.

"Don't you like them?" I asked.

"They are good people, make best wine," he said.

His mother hurried us inside. I had difficulty reconciling the stern matron who'd shattered her son's dreams, with the motherly woman who felt my hair between her fingers and shooed me upstairs with orders to shampoo and change as if I were a favored niece she wanted to show off.

I checked messages while towel-drying my hair. One from Jessie:

> *So? You having his baby yet?*

I swiped a quick response:

> *Wouldn't you like to know! The pasta's great though. Long and slippery.*

Next, one from Elias:

> *Remember you said you weren't experiencing culture shock? Here's proof otherwise. Don't say you weren't warned. PS hamsters fine miss their mom*

His link sent me to an article by some woman psychologist with a hyphenated name in Hong Kong, about the four stages of acculturation. By her definition I was in Stage 1: Elation. "One finds it rather stimulating that most things are so unlike back home."

That was putting it mildly. I'd just returned, by way of a 2700-year-old Spartan port, from a white mountain where I'd serenaded the Italian-speaking galaxies with pop anthems and slept with Adonis.

What worried me was Stage 2, Resistance: "...after several weeks, when the differences can turn into annoyances." If her Stage 1 definition was such a huge understatement, then what big, brash "annoyances" were in store?

I preferred the next stage, Transformation, when one swings to the other extreme, embracing the new culture and rejecting the old. Going native, I guess she meant. I saw myself forever chucking flat American English and microwave burritos in favor of musical Italian diction, home-pressed olive oil, and pasta washed down with the neighbor's wine.

According to the article, I'd have to wait nine months for Stage 3, and another three or four until I graduated to Stage 4, Integration. It all seemed so clinical, like the stages of grief. Forewarned is forearmed, I supposed. But the emotional roller coaster of culture shock seemed a small price to pay for this beautiful, modest man and this beautiful, modest place. I was almost ready to tear up my return ticket.

Oops, that was Stage 1 thinking.

When I came downstairs Sandro's mother insisted on re-doing my hair, teasing and pinning it just so. She rummaged in a drawer and offered me a sheer silk scarf to drape over my shoulders.

She was up to something. I just couldn't imagine what.

THOUGH THE GIAMPICCOLOS' PROPERTY bordered theirs, it was at least a mile and a half drive around the boundaries of both plantations before we turned through their gate. The house was another grand stone-walled *masseria* like the Buonaventuras', only it looked almost deliberately ancient, as though the roof tiles and window casings were crumbled by design. A teenaged boy shooed chickens out of our way and gallantly opened the car doors, greeting Sandro's family as they stepped out onto the gravel. He welcomed me last, not quite touching cheeks, calling me *Maestra* with a bemused expression, like he'd never seen an American up close and expected something different.

A heavy man with a thick gray mustache came out bearing a tray of drinking glasses. He was all Old World elegance in a vest and cuffed shirt, tucked into charcoal trousers belted around a boulder-shaped frame. He practically sang his greetings, leading us through the garden to a beautifully laid out table surrounded by flowering bushes. He set down his burden and walked straight to me with wide open arms.

"La bella donna dall'America!"

He nearly bruised my cheeks with his kisses, his brushy mustache tickling my ears while powerful hands gripped my shoulders as though deciding whether to lift me off the ground or crush the life out of me. *Bella donna,* he'd called me. Pretty woman. It's also the name of a poisonous weed.

Signor Giampiccolo excused himself to carry more food from the kitchen. Meanwhile I sipped soda water with fresh lemon slices and admired the view. Endless rows of grapevines extended in every direction like lines of contorted dancers, bordered on one end by a grove of fruiting lemon trees. Beyond ran hedges and fences which separated the two families' lands.

Sandro sat across from me, smiling but somehow distracted. "Giampiccolo children and me grow up together. Like sister and brother." He sipped his drink. "Sister and brother," he repeated, shaking his head like it was a joke.

I heard a car pull up, then the click-clack of high heels.

Sandro's father waved. *"Ciao, Loretta!"* I turned around in my seat.

She looked like someone had lifted her by her long perfect black hair and dipped her in a vat of Prada. From open-toed white leather pumps to her creamy white trousers and long-sleeved golden tan silk blouse which perfectly set off her flawless complexion—by way of designer cosmetics, no doubt—and jewel-like hazel eyes. Not to mention the short blade of a nose and lips so ripe they looked like they should be juiced. As she rounded the table, she swiveled a butt that could have been sculpted by Michelangelo.

She greeted Sandro's parents first, then approached me, but instead of the expected cheek kiss, she held out a hand. "This is how Americans greet, yes? Pah! Too aggressive, like wrestling." Then she leaned in and we touched cheeks. *"Ciao!* I am Loretta Giampiccolo."

Her English was too superb to compliment without it being taken as an insult. "Happy to meet you, Loretta. I'm Serena Young. Sounds like you've lived in England before."

She shrugged off the remark. "No, just learned their bloody language. Eh, you know, some of us have a brain to study." She settled beside Sandro, bumping shoulders and twisting his ear. *"È vero, bimbo?* No brain, so you need a pretty girl to teach you. Am I not pretty enough?" She pinched his chin and pecked him on the cheek, dangerously close to his lips.

Stage 2 Acculturation crept up my spine.

"Sorry to be late," she said to me. "My mother needed aubergines from the shop."

Aubergines? The precise cadence of upper crust English mingled with her Italian vowels, an absolutely unfair combination of sophisticated and sexy. I wished Sandro would say something already.

Loretta, besides having perfect looks, perfect dress sense,

perfect English, even perfect goddamned eyelashes, was also a mind-reader.

"Why don't you talk, Alessandro?" she said. "Are you too shy around so many gorgeous women? By that I of course include your sister."

Olimpia blew a razzie, earning a scold from her mother.

Sandro finally spoke. "My father say me, always let women talk, so they thinking they are smart."

"Ey?" Loretta delivered a playful slap. "I think Serena and I must kill you now. But no...you are too pretty to kill." She tapped her head against his and I thought I would vomit.

"I know Alessandro since we both ran around in nappies," she said, then cupped her hand beside her mouth and stage whispered, "He looks better without them, don't you think?" I wasn't sure whether I was expected to laugh or blush. She leaned forward on her elbows. "I heard you are from Los Angeles?"

I felt like I was being run over by a luxury sports car. Was this why Sandro's mother had dolled me up, to be less outshone by this splendid goddess across the table? That was clearly impossible. I was saved by an eruption of *oohs* and *aahs*. From behind me Loretta's parents carried bowls and trays overflowing with food. Sandro's mother stood up to help and I joined her.

"No need," Loretta said.

"My pleasure," I replied, without a drop of pleasure in my voice.

In the kitchen, Signora Giampiccolo put the finishing touches on a platter of roasted yellow peppers. I saw where Loretta got her looks. Her mother was a far-from-faded slender Italian beauty, who despite cooking up a storm didn't show a drop of sweat on her forehead or the slightest wrinkle in her fashionable cotton blouse. She and her husband, though mismatched in size, were the very picture together of handsomely aged European chic.

She hesitated at my mimed offer to take the peppers, then

shooed me away with a grin, though there wasn't a drop of friendliness in it. I wasn't family, or neighbor, or even from around here. I was not welcome in the intimate territory of her kitchen. Chalk up another cultural *faux pas?*

At last nine of us settled around the table. It was the living picture of one of those culinary travel shows where the narrator sits down to a country meal with local farmer *bons vivants.* They'd always appeared staged, cut from the same template— the picturesque setting, mountains of glistening food, oceans of wine, amidst laughing bonhomie. And don't forget grapevines somewhere in the frame.

Now here I was, facing a painter's palette of vegetables, meats, sauces, pasta and breads, with pride of place reserved for two jugs of wine raised from the very branches whose leaves now rattled in the breeze. I silently apologized for doubting all those traveling gourmets. *La dolce vita* was real.

I stood up and raised my wineglass.

"Grazie a tutti! Buon vino, buoni amici!"

My crude Italian drew applause and a round of glass-draining. All except Loretta's mother, whose eyes bore into me like power drills when she thought I wasn't looking.

"How do you like Puglia?" Loretta asked. "Very flat and boring, yes?"

"I'm absolutely in love with it. Anyway, it isn't all flat. *We* just got back this morning from the mountains." Emphasis on *we*.

She was all dazzling smiles, though there was no mistaking a quick flash of eyes at Sandro. "Pah. You must go to Rome or Milan, see some real culture and fashion. Here we are all dirt farmers."

"Your dirt makes delicious wine," I said, raising my glass for her father to refill.

"Loretta makes joke," Sandro said. "Here in Capracornea she lives like *principessa*—how you say?"

"Princess," said Olimpia.

"Cannot be true." Loretta kissed him firmly on the cheek. "See? He is still a slimy frog."

"Maybe I should try," I said.

"Careful, with you he maybe turns into a wolf!" she said.

Whatever she meant by that, it still made me laugh.

"Anyway, I am happy that you have a good impression of our region," Loretta said. "You will return to America with wonderful memories."

A tickle in the back of my skull intensified into a full-blown itch. This woman was eloquent, witty, and friendly, yet her every move and word seemed calculated to carry some sort of code. Her fingers creeping up to his shoulder, she was like a dog crawling all over him, or maybe a cat. Or a gorilla. *They're neighbors, I told myself. Practically siblings. Calm down.*

"What about you?" I asked her. "I should have said, I love what you're wearing. I guess Milan is probably more your style than here."

"For shopping, yes, and to see friends. But I could never live there. Even if I want to, how can I?"

"I take it you work for your father."

Loretta took in a tiny forkful of baked fish. "Ha. My father sometimes complains that he works for me!" She said something in dialect to her father, who laughed something back and lifted his hands in surrender. She raised her glass to me. "But he is happy that I manage the business, so he can stay outside making love to his grapes. You taste the love, yes?"

Right on cue, her father lifted his glass and blew me a kiss. More cultural differences, or was he just being creepy? As if to answer, Loretta's mother clucked in rapid-fire dialect to Sandro's mother, who shrugged something back at her, while both women snuck glances my way. Even Loretta seemed embarrassed at whatever they'd said.

"Too much talk," Sandro broke in. "We must eat before food is cold."

Rich food and richer wine warmed my belly. I asked about the Giampiccolos' vineyard business, answered questions about my family, about California. Maybe I'd drunk too much, but as the talk got louder, the living tableau painting I'd imagined being part of at the beginning of the meal began to seem as though the painter had dabbed a few sinister tones in the margins. The way Loretta's father aggressively refilled my wine glass throughout the meal as though he was trying to marinate me for dessert. The way both mothers pointedly ignored me the whole time while also clearly talking about me. But also the way Sandro's father listened to the other man's jokes, glancing aside at me with a shake of his head, the roll of an eye. He teased Signor Giampiccolo in broken English for my benefit, calling him a "newcomer" in Puglia, here for "only" four generations, practically as much a tourist as the *Americana,* his joke carrying an undertone that needed no translation. These two men disliked each other in that special way reserved only for neighbors.

At least the two dogs who'd snuck under the table had no agenda other than to hunt for fallen scraps.

As we were leaving, Loretta wished me a nice trip home, which struck me cold, what with my having another ten days to go.

IT WAS A RELIEF to be back alone in my room at Sandro's house. Scenes from lunch replayed in my head: Loretta sensuously laying slices of cheese on Sandro's tongue; Sandro calling me *Maestra* instead of my name; she and he having a peppery argument in local dialect which I was certain involved me.

It was early evening, around seven o'clock. After such a huge afternoon feast, we'd all agreed to skip supper. Sandro was out in the oil press building with his father. I went down to the kitchen to soothe my pounding head with a glass of water.

Olimpia walked in a minute later, in a turtleneck pullover and pajama bottoms, retrieved a slice of fig tart from the refrigerator and, after I declined an offered piece, she sat down to eat hers.

"Can I ask you something?" I said.

Her head shifted slightly in my direction.

"What is it with your brother and Loretta?" I said.

"Sorry. I do not understand."

"Are they...um...are they really just friends?"

A floor board creaked somewhere in the house. Olimpia's head whipped around to the kitchen door, but no one was there. She looked back at me with big eyes, licking crumbs from her lips. Then she stood up and went to the sink to rinse her fork and plate, her back to me.

"I do not know if I am allowed."

That was an answer in itself.

"Please come to my room, Olimpia. I won't tell anyone. Please."

She sat on my bed, her body as stiff as before, even after I shut the door. I pulled the chair over to face her.

"Tell me."

I waited for what felt like ten minutes, watching her legs bounce against the side of the mattress, hands stretching the collar of her turtleneck over her chin. At last she took a deep breath and exhaled.

"They will marry."

It was an effort to keep the hot acid bubbling up my throat from spewing out my mouth. Questions like bullets shot across my brain so fast they didn't have time to fully form. What did he think he—? What was I—? How much did she—?

"Tell me more," I said.

"He should told you."

"He should *have* told you." I couldn't help myself. She didn't take kindly to the impromptu lesson, hands pressing the edge of the bed as if preparing to leave.

"I'm sorry," I said. "Your English is great. Better than most of my students. Please."

I bit my lips in anticipation. This kid obviously knew the score. She knew what I was thinking, what her brother was thinking, what I didn't want, yet needed, to know. Her hands returned to her turtleneck, stretching the collar over her jaw.

"How to say? Everybody always know they will to marry. When I am a little child, I know my brother to marry Loretta."

"Huh? He must have been, what, twelve or thirteen when you were born?"

"He is twelve, yes. Loretta also. Birthday three months after."

I tried to form an acceptable scenario. Childhood friends and neighbors pledging to marry, the way I once rubbed pricked thumbs with a girl in sixth grade to be blood sisters forever—or until we entered high school, when she considered me not pretty enough to join her new clique.

I said, "I didn't see a ring."

"No ring. Only father's promise."

"What do you mean?"

Olimpia pulled her turtleneck collar over her mouth. "I am afraid I say too many—too *much*. If my brother knows..."

"I promise I won't get you in trouble."

She chewed the stretchy fabric, eyes wide, sizing up whether to trust me. The collar snapped back in place under her chin. "You must promise. So...I do not know when—before I am borned. My father and Signor Giampiccolo make agree. Alessandro and Loretta will to marry. Then, when my father stops to work—how you say it?"

"Retire. When he retires. Go on."

"When my father and Signor Giampiccolo retire, their two *masserie* make together to be one big business."

"You mean the farms will merge? I mean, join into one property?"

She nodded.

I was flabbergasted. An arranged marriage to unite two dynasties? It was a thing you read about in history books, between Medieval fiefdoms, not something that happened in the twenty-first century.

"Is this real?" I said. "That's what Sandro wants?"

She shrugged and thought about it. "Want, not want. It is so."

"Then why did he ask me—" I covered my mouth. I wasn't sure anymore that he had actually ever asked me to come here. I was a stupid naïve little girl who'd thrown herself at him. But no, he *had* said he wanted me to come, that his heart would break if I didn't, that he wanted to show me God. And there had been no reluctance in his kisses, and more, for three nights running. The story was not that simple.

"You are a very nice girl," Olimpia said. "Smart and pretty. You are new and, how I can say? *Esotica.*"

"Sounds like exotic."

"Si. Yes. I think is why he like you."

"But Loretta—"

"She also is smart and pretty. But maybe not so nice."

Footsteps mounted the stairs. Olimpia slipped out before whoever it was entered the hallway.

I wanted to lean out the window and scream and bellow so that Loretta might hear across the fields. I was so stupid. Used. Cheap. What was I, some last-minute fling before the wedding? I paced circles around the creaky floor. One thing I didn't get: why hadn't Loretta pulled my hair out? Surely she saw right through my reasons for coming here. Maybe she secretly wanted a way out?

I sat on the bed, gnawing my knuckles, trying to remember every word he'd said to me before I came. *Suffer.* He'd said he would suffer if I didn't come. Did he actually know the English meaning? Had I filled in the subtext for myself? Invented the whole thing? My hands squeezed my head. *Stop thinking so much, Serena! Stop it!* Thoughts turn into stories and stories turn into reality and reality turns into...what? Shame.

Or did it? I replayed Olimpia's words over and over. I was new and exotic. I would never have thought of myself, the plain suburban white girl from Orange County, as exotic, but to him I supposed I was. What did that imply? That here, among the same old people he'd been surrounded with his entire life, I was some whimsical fantasy?

And what about me? Maybe he was my exotic, whimsical Stage 1 Acculturation fantasy? How could that be? The way he'd treated me—the way we'd adored each other—these past few days, it felt so real.

Then there was Olimpia's remark about Loretta: 'maybe not so nice.' What did that mean? Nothing, probably.

Or maybe that I was the biggest, stupidest, self-deluding cursed-by-God fool bitch slut...I punched myself around the head.

At first I thought the knocking was the sound of my own fists on my skull. Until I heard door hinges squeak.

Sandro's voice: "Serena? *Posso?*"

Chapter 26

"When's the wedding?" I asked.

Sandro dropped onto the chair like a sack of wet noodles. He didn't even turn on the light.

"Tell me." The words trembled in my throat.

"Who said?"

"No one. It's just so obvious," I told him. "When?"

"I do not know."

A grown man who didn't know his own wedding date? "I don't believe—" I wouldn't be able to hold back the blubbering much longer.

"Serena, this you must believe. I do not know. Maybe never." He pressed his forehead with the heel of his hand. I desperately wanted to believe him. I wanted to believe that my coming into his life had somehow changed his destiny. If only he would step toward me right now with words of love and promise, I might resist the temptation to throw myself out the window.

"I'm very tired. Too much wine," I said. "Need to sleep."

"You are very angry."

I turned away. "I think you should leave right now."

"O-*kay*," he said with that boyish, almost happy chirp which tore at me like a vulture's cry. "Tomorrow is Sunday. My family, we go to church. Very boring, even you understand Italian. Maybe morning you stay here. After, we talk."

"Yes. Good idea."

I didn't move or in any way hint that he should stay.

"O-*kay.*"

He back-stepped to the door and let himself out.

And I learned that crying yourself to sleep wasn't just a romance novel cliché.

I WATCHED THE WINDOW slowly brighten to dull gray, unable to turn my head away, as though my neck, my shoulders, arms—everything—had turned into sandstone. Somewhere a floorboard creaked, but it wasn't a footstep, only a contraction as the ancient house came out of its nighttime chill. The family must have gone by now, leaving me alone in this cold hollow space surrounded by ancient twisted trees whose original planters had been dead for centuries. I shivered beneath the heavy wool blanket, alone among ghosts.

Maybe I should pack and leave before they returned. Drag my suitcase to the village, hop a bus to anywhere. Though maybe buses didn't run on Sundays. Besides, everyone in town knew of me. Word would reach Sandro before I'd taken twenty steps.

My phone had died overnight. I plugged it in and waited for it to restart. Whom to contact? It was nearly nine o'clock: midnight in California. Zuzie would be up. Except she was in Hawaii, probably body-surfing someone's body at this moment.

A message to Jessie got no reply.

My contact list showed Elias online. I could at least talk to my sweet little hamsters.

"You realize it's midnight?" were his first words. He tugged down his sloppy hair, as if that might freshen his appearance; his facial stubble looked like mildew.

"Somehow you strike me as the type who stays up until three watching sci-fi reruns and eating reheated pizza."

"Wrong about the pizza."

"Two-day-old enchiladas."

"Burritos. Close enough. Hey, hey, hey, look who's here. It's Mommy." He reached behind his shoulder and presented a hamster to the camera.

"What are they doing out?" I said.

"Huh? Me and the guys, we're one happy family now. Hey, no no no no no." Elias leaned off camera, then resurfaced with the other hamster, who had a string of shredded lettuce hanging from his mouth. "See? This one's eating me out of house and home." Elias held Hardy to his nose while he put on a goo-goo voice, "Aren't you, sweetie? You're a little piggie-wiggie, aren't you?" Then back to me: "I'm thinking of adopting them from you."

"No way. Sorry."

"What about visitation rights? Sundays and every second Tuesday?"

I sat back on the bed, tisked and sighed. "Elias, I'm not in the mood. They okay, though?"

"They're fine. Though I ain't so sure about you."

"Yeah."

"Listen, let me put the boys away. Don't hang up." I had a view of his ceiling while his voice sounded in the distance: "Bedtime for beasties!"

He returned and settled into his couch. "So, for someone enjoying a sexy Mediterranean dream holiday, you look pretty shitty."

"I'm stuck in Acculturation Stage 2."

"After four days? Not possible. According to Doctor Tsang—"

"Forget Doctor Tsang. Maybe I'm Level 2 of Dante's Hell. That's more what it feels like." I summarized the events of the last couple days, from being the Fool on the Hill to discovering I was the Other Woman. Elias listened patiently, nodding now and then; probably the way he paid attention to clients describing computer problems. If only he could program a fix for me.

"Let me ask you," he said. "You didn't once, before dumping

your life savings into this trip, not once did you entertain the possibility of this very thing? That some hot Latin charmer might only be looking for some quick and dirty entertainment with a disposable American chick?"

"Screw you!"

"Hey, let's not get started on my fantasies."

"What did you just say?"

His image turned into a pinkish blur; his hand blocking the camera. "Uh...uh...uh... Oh, man. I am such a... How about let's text instead of talking? Then I can blame my stupidity on autocorrect."

"Won't work."

"Why's that?"

"Oh, Elias. Because you're just being honest. Part of me admits you have a point. But still, part of me thinks Sandro was also being genuine."

"I won't say genuine what." Elias followed with a sheepish grin. "I mean, how well do you really know this dude?"

"I feel like I know him, even now. The things he told me..."

"Okay, stop. Let me test you, like on one of those dating games." He tapped his chin, then said, "What about TV shows? Who's his favorite on 'The Bachelorette'?"

"How the heck should I know? Do they even show that in Italy?"

"Okay. Music. What stuff does he like?"

"That I can answer." I tried to recall the singers we'd listened to in the car. "Well, I can't name them. They're all Italian pop singers."

"Lady Gaga, maybe? She's supposed to be Italian, I think."

"I didn't hear any Lady Gaga."

"Okay. We've established that he either hasn't heard of or doesn't like Lady Gaga. Do you?"

"Who cares whether I like her?" I said.

"Because at least you and me both are familiar enough with her output, that we can discuss whether or not she rules or sucks."

I shook my head at him. "Come on, be serious, dude. I take your point. But you don't have to count how many things you have in common to be with someone. I mean, it might even be the other way around. Can you imagine, if you and your partner knew the exact same things and agreed on everything, how boring that would be?"

"Uh huh. Let me ask you something else." His finger flicked his lip. "Did you just call me *dude?*"

"No. Yes. What's it matter?"

"'Kay, here's what I think. Time to clear up the mystery of the alleged betrothal once and for all. Maybe it has to come from the horse's mouth. Or in this case, the mare's."

I sat up straighter. "You think I should confront Loretta?"

"That her name?"

"Loretta Giampiccolo."

Elias whistled. I described in detail how she dressed, how she spoke, her shopping trips to Milan.

"Sounds like she's more at home in a Ferrari than a farm," he said. "And she obviously senses what you're up with her supposed fiancé and didn't scratch your eyes out—that tells you something. She might even be looking for a way out."

"I don't know. What difference would confronting her make?"

"Man, I thought I was the one who's stupid with people. Let me put it this way: you have *what* to lose?"

He was right. How could I just walk away? I was fired up now. "You know what, Elias? For once, you're right? I can't give up so easily. Something like this happens to a person once in a—"

"Once in an olive moon?"

"Ha! Thanks. I mean it. Thanks for listening."

"No problem, *dude.* And Serena?"

"Hm?"

"In case things don't work out, yeah? There's this other guy I know who also has absolutely nothing in common with you."

"I miss you, too, Elias," I said.

"Really?"

I didn't know what had prompted those words. But there was no use in lying.

"Really."

I KEPT TO THE shade of olive trees until the grove came to an abrupt end and trekked across a parched and dusty field. In a sweat by the time I reached the border hedge, which I followed for at least a quarter mile until finding what I needed: a gate to the Giampiccolo vineyard. I pushed open the heavy wrought iron with a loud rusty squeak.

Hysterical basso yelps shot through the vine rows. I slammed the gate just as two black and brown mongrels lunged against the bars. So much for my plan. I'd have to walk the long way around and wait outside the road entrance. But then the barking subsided and turned to whimpers. Both dogs pressed their snouts through the gaps, sniffing my legs while black tails waved like metronomes. Either these were the world's stupidest watchdogs or they recognized me from yesterday's feast. I ventured a hand through and cautiously patted one's head. Their response was ecstatic.

The dogs escorted me through the vineyard to the front door of the main house, where, after no response to my several knocks, they followed me around back. I parked myself on a wooden bench to await the Giampiccolos' return from worship.

Surrounded by roses and lavender and decaying grape leaves, I tried to piece together my reason for sitting here in the first place and what I intended to do with my falling-apart-at-the-seams heart. He *had* asked me to come to Italy. Practically begged me, with those sad, sweet eyes and his talk of suffering without me. That night on the mountain had been a true merging of souls, not just body fluids. Hadn't it? I wanted to ask him right now! Surely the feelings which coursed through me also simmered inside him, like his mother's sauce on the stove—all the ingredients in place, just needing to stew a bit longer. Maybe it was too soon for words of love and the commitments they implied, especially in a second language.

An old Sociolinguistics lecture popped into my head, one of those typical academic logical roller-coasters oozing with theory and of no practical use in the outside world, but right now it felt like an oracle speaking.

The fact that learners struggle with certain verb tenses in other languages proves that time perception is cultural, not hard-wired into our brains. Teachers can explain over and over the differences between past forms such as, "He ate", "He was eating", and "He has eaten," yet students routinely get them wrong. Then there are constructions like "I will have eaten"—sticking the modal future *will* onto the past perfect *have eaten*—to form a hypothetical statement about the future, which even advanced non-native speakers find difficult to understand, much less formulate on their own.

Why is the present tense the only one that never poses a problem to second language learners? Why is it the one that we naturally fall back to in other languages? The logical explanation is that time isn't real—that past and future, as physicists confirmed, are elastic concepts, upon which each culture imposes its unique perceptions.

Maybe the same thing is true about love. Does 'Ti amo' carry different subtexts through the air than 'I love you'? Do *amare* and *love* imply the same commitments of the heart, now and in the culturally-perceived future? Would an Italian receive such words as understatement, or would they be loaded like bullets and scare him away before he was ready? Which was why I'd been afraid to say them out loud up on the mountain, and maybe why, in all his expressiveness with words and hands and fingers, they hadn't yet formed on his tongue. Could I ever love him and he *amare* me in ways that we would fully, commonly understand?

I'd never felt this way with a man before and that was good enough. I had no reason to give up. I would declare this to Loretta if I had to.

The dogs raised their heads and kicked up dust toward the house. The family was returning from church. I waited until I heard car doors open, then strolled into view as casually as I could pretend.

Signor Giampiccolo, in his dark Sunday suit, did a double-take when he saw me.

"Maestra!" He opened his arms; I wasn't taking the bait. His wife pressed her palm to her cheek and rattled off what sounded like prayers to ward off the Black Death. Loretta stepped from the car, engagingly chic in black and white, with a look of concern that seemed genuine. "Serena! Is there a problem at the Buonaventura house? Are you all right?"

"Everything's fine. Tell your parents I'm sorry to intrude. I went for a walk."

Loretta explained to them. Her mother shook her head as though she would have preferred better news, such as a war or pandemic. "My parents insist you join us for lunch. Please," Loretta said.

"No, no, I couldn't—actually, I came to see you. Do you have a few minutes?" I flicked my head toward the garden. I wanted to talk outside, overheard only by the flies.

Again Loretta filled in her parents. "My father says after, you must eat with us. Moment, please. I need better shoes for garden walking." She raised a spiked heel and rolled her eyes.

When she returned she'd changed more than shoes, dressed in slim denims and a red and white checked cotton shirt under an open white cardigan; the picture of a farm girl...if that picture was on the cover of Italian *Vogue*. We followed a graveled path toward their lemon grove.

"So you manage all this," I said, with a sweep of my head.

"Yesterday I was joking. My father, he is an excellent vintner." Loretta stopped for a moment, taking it all in. "My job is at the computer, on the telephone, try to bring this business out of the Nineteenth Century into the Twenty-first. Sometimes I fight him like cats and dogs."

"But you always win."

She smiled at the suggestion. "I've traveled to California, you know. Wine trade fairs. Some very good vineyards there. Of course, it was Italians who created the California wine industry."

We stopped between trees heavily laden with yellow fruit. Loretta raised one, scraped the rind with her fingernail, and held it to her nose. "Soon to harvest. Here we are not so famous for lemons like in Sorrento. I want to plant more, produce limoncello in commercial quantities with our own label. But my father says it needs too much land, too much work. So, again we fight." She locked her eyes on mine and said, with many possible layers of meaning, "But later I will have victory."

"You don't ever think of leaving Puglia, going somewhere with more...culture? Fashion?" I said.

"Come, sit." She indicated a bench fashioned from a planed tree trunk. "To answer your question with honesty, no. What will I do? Marry a man, make his babies, walk around the city to shop all day? Or work in an office?" She swatted the idea away. "I think such life is more boring than sitting under these trees. Because these are my trees, one day is my business, my fortune. If you have money, any time you can fly or catch the train to find art, fashion, music. And you? California is very good, yes?"

"I suppose it is." Should I tell her about the vanished citrus groves of Orange County? If only I had it in me to wax lyrical about my home and its long-buried heritage. If only I could think of a way to deftly change the subject. I hadn't planned to reveal much about myself. How could I compare to her? There was something about this woman which dominated not just the conversation, but the very air around her. She shifted her body to face me at an angle, her knees nearly knocking mine, then slapped her thighs and spoke through a smile loaded with knives.

"So you are sleeping with him? I hope so. Otherwise, what a waste, coming all the way around the world." She must have seen the shock on my face, because she gave a little chuckle and patted my knee as though we were best of friends. "In fact, I am very happy that Alessandro found a nice, clever American girl. Yes, truly I am happy."

My heart stopped trying to crack through my chest, my legs muscles thawed. Maybe I'd been misjudging her. Maybe all this talk of marriage was simply a running family joke. "Thank you," I said. "I think he's great. Funny. Sensitive."

"Yes, yes, I know, I know. I hope you have a very good time with him here—you said you are leaving when?"

"In ten days."

"Ah, too short. Well, I wish you big passion with Alessandro for these ten days. Then you will return to America with lovely memories to keep you warm at night. You know what I am talking about, yes? Ha. And Alessandro will have wonderful memories of this time. It is so good to let a man have his fun and—how do you Americans say it—get it out of his system?"

Either all the air in Puglia suddenly evaporated into space or my lungs turned to ash. High-pitched ringing filled my head; not the village bells, but my brain neurons popping. I couldn't fathom any woman even thinking such a thing, much less saying it out loud. Perhaps I'd heard wrong?

"He never mentioned me, did he?" Loretta said.

I couldn't sit still any longer, not so close to her. I walked to the nearest tree and examined its bulging fruit. I wanted to yank it off and throw it. "Let me ask you something, Loretta. Are you bullshitting me or what? I mean, if this is a joke, that's fine. You got me. But—"

"Do you think I will joke about this?" Loretta sat with hands folded in her lap, more vulnerable than I'd previously seen her. Her eyes swelled, her mouth shrank as she spoke. "Alessandro said to me you are coming. I can not stop him. I can not stop you. So what can I do? Cry like a hurt animal, like maybe you cried after you met me? That is not me. That is not how I do my business, is not how I do my life. If I discover a problem, I must fix. And the best solution to a problem, in business or in life, is if everyone can go away with something. So, you have your *favoloso* European romance like from American movies, yes? Alessandro has his delicious affair with the high-spirited American beauty. And for me, I can watch him enjoy his little fun while I am his friend, so I do not have to when I am his wife. At the end, we all are happy if we choose to be."

I tried to dull the hurt in my chest, but the stab of her words was too sharp. "What makes you so sure that's what he wants?"

"Oh, Serena, please sit." She patted the bench. "You don't like me. And I should hate you, yes?"

"Well, I don't hate you. Why should I? But I think you're wrong about Sandro."

"*Dio mio!* I *wish* I can be wrong about this man! I know him too well."

"But do you love him? Because I do!"

Loretta released a deep breath, then patted the bench again and bade me over with a flick of her head. I sat down and waited for her to speak.

"Alessandro and I grew up together. I think you heard this too many times already. Everybody says we are like twin brother and sister. Always every day we play, never apart." She hooked both index fingers together. "Since we are children, everyone expects we will marry. Oh, sometimes I am so sick of hearing this! Since we are five years old—uncles, cousins, schoolmates, teachers—'Oh, you will marry! Yes, you must marry. God put you together.' Maybe all the loud and crazy talk was like—how do you call it—I don't know the word. Influence? One day we started to believe it. I know I will never marry someone else, and he is the same. Of course, our families both like it. Join two farming dynasties, yes?"

"Wait. Stop."

"I don't stop! You listen to me! You think I'm happy to have you here? I tolerate you. I even find it a tiny bit amusing. Until you appear at my home wearing his mother's scarf. Then I realize what a danger you are, that maybe you actually think you can move in here."

"Maybe I will!" So that had been his mother's game, like waving a red cape at a bull, to knock away whatever complacency Loretta must have felt about their arrangement. I guessed flames were shooting from my eyes, because for once she seemed taken aback.

"Oh, you will? Are you of Catholic faith? How can you expect he will marry you or that his family will accept you for one moment, even if I disappear?" Loretta swallowed her little show of histrionics. "This is what I want. It is what I am having. I wish to be honest with you, even if he is not."

I hid my face in my hands. I would not allow myself to weep in front of her. "I'm sorry, but this is so strange! All I hear is expectations and merging businesses," I said. "Where's the love in this picture? Don't you want someone to love you? Doesn't Sandro deserve someone who really loves him? Don't you also—?" My throat seized up. I thought I might suffocate.

Loretta took my hands, and I let her. I couldn't imagine what was in this woman's heart. They certainly had appeared at ease with each other yesterday, like an old married couple. But not like two young people in love. I felt more sad for her than anything else, until her hand brushed my cheek.

"I let him have you to play with. And I let you have him, as long as it is temporary. Is that not love?"

I got up and ran. "No one needs your stupid approval!"

The dogs chased me through the long rows of vines, barking happily, like it was a game.

Chapter 27

Silent Uncle looked up for once when I stamped dust off my shoes outside the open door. The family was in the middle of lunch. I took small servings of chickpeas and ribbony noodles, which the ever-mindful linguist part of my brain noted they called *tria*. The Buonaventuras had already changed out of their Sunday clothes but remained in church whisper mode. I recalled Sandro's remark that everyone within a hundred kilometers knew what everyone else had eaten for breakfast. I had a creepy feeling that he and his family knew exactly where I'd been and for what reason, though I couldn't imagine Loretta calling to report. Maybe her dogs had told their chickens.

I mentioned that I'd gone for a walk all the way to the Giampiccolos' house and back. Sandro avoided looking at me. His parents remarked what fine weather I'd had. I tried making small talk about the Giampiccolos' beautiful lemons, which Sandro's father dismissed with a sarcastic speech accompanied by a dizzying hand pantomime.

Sandro explained: "My father say, lemons make money only if have many more trees, so can make more *limoncello* than one fat man himself can to drink." Similar to what Loretta had said. I guessed that the neighbors had their eyes on portions of Buonaventura land as part of the nuptial arrangements. Maybe Sandro's father wasn't completely keen on the fine print of the engagement.

Mamma served coffee and sweet biscuits, remarking more than once that I must have been exhausted after such a walk. Something in her voice made it sound like a hint, in this case one I was happy to take.

I piled my dishes together. "How do I say, 'take a nap'?"

Olimpia answered: *"Fare un pisolino."*

"Io fare—"

Olimpia clicked her tongue. *"Faccio* for first person singular."

Lousy teaching manner. Though now I had no need to say a word, merely smile to the parents and carry things to the kitchen. As soon as I was out of their view, I ran up the stairs.

I threw myself face down on the bed, heaving sobs into the fat, suffocating pillow. What a fool I had been to come here. What an idiot to fling myself at Sandro, to have the audacity to insert myself into this family and feed off them for two whole weeks. Loretta had made it brutally clear: all I was to any of them was a disposable plaything for Sandro to spew his wild seeds into before settling down to a lifetime of businesslike marriage. Maybe that was why his father was so friendly toward me, so jovial and easy with his hands. Perhaps he'd done the same as a young man, or maybe he fantasized a little piece for himself.

I reached under the bed for my suitcase. Fingers froze on the handle. Why should I quit? There was no ring. This entire engagement was a commercial arrangement, which even his father didn't seem to entirely accept. Sandro didn't show Loretta the affection one might expect toward a fiancée. Then there was that night of stars and magic on the mountaintop, a sense of infinity linking us. Nothing would ever diminish that. And this place: the earthy beauty, the food, and sense of history and culture that had been absent in my life, not to mention the fascinating language and dialects. Everything I'd ever dreamed of was here.

I stared out the window at leaves drooping in the windless afternoon. A chicken wandered past.

I turned on my computer, checked work messages. A notice about a Business English curriculum update. Reminders about Daylight Saving Time. Invitations to submit papers for next year's TESOL, the international English teachers' convention. Sure, I'd send in mine: *Comparative asemantic phonations of second language teachers who fall in love with a student and drown themselves in a vat of oil.* Including a scatterplot of his bilingual fiancée's brain after being pounded to smithereens with a wine bottle. I'd start the research tomorrow. Someone else would have to write up the findings.

Below, a message dated just a couple hours ago. From Bieber:

> *Dear Teacher Serena, I wish*
> *you come back soon.*

I checked the student contact list. Green light beside his name. What time was it in Shanghai? It didn't matter; the poor kid never slept.

He picked up on the second ring, his face lighting up while he fumbled to straighten his glasses.

"Teacher Serena!"

"Hello, Bieber. How are you? Wait, what time is it? Am I interrupting your tutoring?"

"Aiya!" He laughed. "Today Sunday. Basketball and tennis lessons only, finish six o'clocks."

I shook my head. I'd read somewhere that thanks to Yao Ming and Li Na, every Chinese parent wanted their kid to have a backup plan, so that if they couldn't make it as a banker or corporate CFO, they'd become a multi-millionaire basketball or tennis star instead.

"I miss you," I said. "How's your substitute teacher? In fact, who did they give you?"

"Barbara. She is from Ohio." He said it as though it was the worst thing in the world.

"Is she too strict? If she goes too fast, you can ask her to slow down."

"She is good teacher, I think."

"So what is the problem?" I said.

"She is not you."

I pressed my hand over my lips, but that didn't stop my cheeks from twitching or the tears from welling. What timing he had. Such a simple declaration of being needed by another person opened a gusher in my heart.

"Teacher, what is the problem?"

"Nothing, Bieber. Never mind."

He rested his cheek on his fist as if playing counselor.

"Really, it's nothing," I said. "Tell me about school. Any English exams?"

"No talking of school. Teacher Serena looks sad." He held a fist toward the camera, with the little finger hooked outward. "Pinky promise. Remember?"

His finger hovered in place. His eyes hardly blinked. He wouldn't give up.

What a silly game. But this little boy wanted someone to trust. And I guessed so did I. I held up a curled pinky. "Pinky promise."

I told him, in as simple English as I could muster, about picking olives, making oil. His eyes lit up when I described riding the motorcycle, the police, watching galaxies on the mountain. But he wanted more.

"Your boyfriend? Is why you sad?"

I sighed. "No boyfriend." Bieber went bug-eyed when I described the arranged marriage, making me repeat many details—which family produced olive oil, which made wine.

Then he asked with disarming innocence, "You want to marry him?"

I ought to have stopped. Why was I telling all this to a kid? "I don't know. Maybe eventually. If he wanted."

"Maybe you give him flowers! Or chocolate."

"Bieber, you're sweet. But that isn't how it works."

He clapped his hands. He had the solution: "You must fight her, like in movies—what you call? Just moment... *Duel!*"

"Good idea," I said.

"What is her name?"

"The woman? Loretta."

"Loretta," he repeated back, sounding more like *Noretta.* "What family name?"

"I think maybe I'm saying too much. Finished."

"Please? I like to hear." His raised his hooked pinky as his bond.

"Anyway, you'll never be able to say this one. Giampiccolo."

"Jam—*aiya!* Spell for me."

I heard his keyboard click as I spelled it out. He made a couple attempts, *"Gee–am–pee*...Wah! Can not say. What about boyfriend's family name?"

"Why do you need to know?"

He offered his familiar toothy grin. "It is funny for me to speak Italian."

I spelled out Buonaventura. He seemed to be typing a lot more than I was telling him.

"Wait a second, Bieber. What are you doing? I have no more photos in my image folder."

The keyboard clatter stopped. He showed his hands in a gesture of innocence.

"I think if Noretta not rich, maybe he does not want her," he said.

"I'm not rich either, Bieber."

"But I think he loves you, not loves her. Only marry because their families thinking money."

This was going too far. I didn't need relationship advice from a cloistered Chinese boy barely in his teens. Time to end this discussion.

"Sandro and Loretta have known each other since they were children."

Bieber shrugged off this argument. "Han Yun, girl in neighbor flat, I know all my life. If my mother says I marry her, I will jump from the window!"

"Is she pretty?"

He stuck out his tongue and snorted, making us both laugh. Then he resumed typing.

"What are you doing, Bieber?"

He appeared not to hear me while his fingers kept working.

"Bieber, what are you typing? What are you doing? Do you hear me? Bieber? You're scaring me. Whatever you're doing, quit it."

"Sorry. Text to my friend." A bald-faced lie. Unless his life had undergone some radical upheaval in the past week, as far as I knew, Bieber had no friends.

"Bieber, I think I should go."

He fixed me with a caught-in-the-headlights stare.

"Teacher, please, I want you be happy."

Chapter 28

I woke the next morning with the urge to run.

Not home. Out of this house, away from this drama, just for the day to clear my head. To see this place—Italy, Puglia—with only myself for company, through my own eyes and heart.

Sandro had to work anyway. His family would be happy to have me out of their hair for one day. I asked to borrow a Vespa and that most underused commodity in this part of the world: a helmet. One was eventually found and, after a little trickery with the straps, fit snugly on my head. Meanwhile, my head's inside was stuffed with enthusiastic, contradictory travel advice from the whole family.

I zipped down the drive, spinning into the dirt only once before reaching the gate.

Everyone had agreed that I should turn right, so I turned right. At the next intersection my hotly debated itineraries diverged. Another right toward the white sandy coast or straight ahead to a medieval castle once home to a flying monk?

There was something metaphorical about idling at a crossroad in the middle of nowhere, engine growling like a restless bear. All the significant choices in my life hadn't been choices at all—where to study, who would employ me, which students to teach. Nearly every decision I'd ever made for myself had been a letdown, from where to live to my choice of car to my cheap phone.

Including coming here?

I twisted the throttle to keep the sputtering engine alive. Straight ahead: what if the castle was big, cold, and boring? Turn right: what if the coastal towns were touristy kitsch? What if I made no decision? What if I simply stopped worrying about "what if...?" In a weird Zen way, deciding not to decide ensured there would be no letdowns, only surprises.

Maybe getting lost was the best choice. Allow the universe to decide.

I turned left.

With the crossroad behind me, all those jabbering thoughts of Loretta and Sandro, marriage and work and money, vanished in the wind while I raced down the long straight country lane.

Ten or twelve minutes later I hit a deep rut and the front tire burst. Damned universe.

The dusty road was deserted. My phone had no signal, but the GPS indicated a village somewhere ahead. I pushed the heavy, crippled machine forward over pitted pavement, arms and back aching. Twenty minutes later, ready to lay down and wait—days if necessary—for a car to come along, a house appeared around a bend. A village, and someone who might repair a tire, couldn't be far. The linguist nodule of my brain felt a jolt upon discovering Greek letters on the gate, and again on a rusted sign hanging from a fence. I leaned the bike against a tree across the road and wiped off sweat. Plus I had to pee.

I stepped from behind the tree, fastening my jeans, and found myself in the sights of two chesty young guys, who right then were climbing over the wall, jabbering in some rough argot that sounded neither like Italian nor the local dialect. One sprinted straight at me, the other circled behind. Biting back a scream, I stood my ground, fumbling in my pockets for a weapon. My mind searched back to the introductory jiu jitsu class I'd taken my freshman year; did I hook my arm around the neck or under the armpit? How to take on two strong men?

But I wasn't their target. One seized the Vespa's handlebars and pushed it away.

I tripped in a pothole while jabbing S-T-O-P into my dictionary app and screamed the first word that popped up: "Arresto!"

They halted dead in their tracks and stared back with big, toothy grins. One waved, gesturing for me to catch up. What an idiot I felt like. They had only come to help.

"Do you"—I caught my breath—"do you speak English?"

Both burst out laughing.

"No Een-ga-leesh-oo! No Een-ga-leesh-oo!"

Ten minutes later we stood outside a village hardware and machine shop. A squat older man emerged, examined the damage, scratched his stubbled chin, then traced a circle around his wristwatch: come back in an hour.

"Quanto?" I said. With only around fifty euros in my pocket, I braced myself. Another Italian mechanic about to ruin me.

"*Cinque euro.*"

I must have heard wrong. Five euros? He said something, indicating my companions and slapping his chest. From what I gathered, the price was based upon my being their very close and dear lifelong friend.

My new best buddies led me to a white-walled restaurant on the side of a house with signs in Greek and Italian, where I spent the next two hours—the repair took longer, since the mechanic joined us—savoring thick coffee and sticky pastries so sweet they made my teeth ring, answering the usual questions by means of the translation app. "Leonardo DiCaprio!" they all repeated in reverence.

As word spread of the Hollywood starlet in their midst, half the village squeezed into the restaurant. I learned that most considered themselves *Griko,* descendants of the region's original ancient Greek colonizers, their dialect heavy with archaic Hellenic terms which stumped my poor phone. I could have sworn that the plump, tomato-cheeked lady claiming to be from a 3000-year-old family accused the elderly man from a 2000-year-old family of being a "newcomer".

The Vespa restored to its former glory and topped up with fuel and oil, I collected two dozen names and made as many promises for a return visit, waved farewell and, as before, ignored every suggestion for where to go next. The universe had so far been the best guide today.

MORE GRIKO VILLAGES, AND then at last the smell of the sea. I stopped in a weedy field and skipped over wildflowers until I stood at the edge of a bluff. Below, a fringe of stony beach stood between brown and yellow striped cliffs and an infinite blue expanse inhabited only by low-flying seabirds. I had no idea whether I was looking at the Adriatic or the Gulf of Taranto, and I resisted the urge to check my GPS to find out. I didn't want to know where I was. I didn't want to be found.

I had no idea how I'd come here. I'd lost track of time and place, choosing crossroads based on the sign with the highest Scrabble score or a name's oddity, heading onto unmarked lanes, zig-zagging where I should have zag-zigged. The sun had passed its meridian, so I figured I was facing south, and that was all I knew about where I stood, other than alone at the end of the world. I was neither lonely nor scared. It was like the feeling I'd had on the mountaintop, only earthbound, without a pop anthem soundtrack.

I sat on a boulder perched precariously at the edge of the cliff, imagining for a moment what it might feel like to tumble over the precipice and fly into the sea. Whatever move I made had its own unforeseeable yet unyielding outcome. Braking too late on the freeway, coming to Italy, falling in love with Sandro, confronting Loretta, taking random turns on a Vespa. There was a consequence to everything, but was there a meaning?

A sail appeared way on the horizon. Three thousand years earlier Ulysses himself had likely sailed past this same promontory. In those days people believed that the universe consisted of five elements. The first four—water, earth, air, and fire—surrounded me now: sea, rock cliff, the cool breeze, and the sun above. Then there was the fifth and final element, which the Greeks had called *ether* and the Romans *quintessence*—fifth essence. The substance the gods breathed, which bound the universe together. I took a deep breath and felt the quintessence roll down my tongue.

Like a douse of warm water, the answers to questions which had begun this morning at the first crossroads poured over me.

Every time I'd tried to control my life's course, events never went the way I wanted. But when I stopped worrying about consequences, I got more than I dreamed for. Had I followed advice that morning, I'd have probably whiled away the day wandering around cold, empty castles and deserted-for-winter beach resorts from a well-trodden tourist to-do list. Instead, I'd made crazy choices based on nothing but the feeling in my gut, and even a minor accident had turned into a celebration.

I stood up on the boulder, inches from the rim, fifty feet above crashing waves, yet completely unafraid, feet anchored to the earth and head aimed at the sky, my body an electric conduit between the two, bathing in the quintessence. What was coming over me? If I'd tried right then to describe the feeling to my friends, they'd think I'd transformed into some airy-fairy spiritualist and next I'd be sitting lotus position on a bamboo mat snacking on tofu chips.

It felt better not to think.

I pirouetted on one foot and leapt.

Away from the sea, into a patch of weeds. I had a crazy mission. I had to get back to Sandro's in a hurry.

I checked the Vespa's fuel level, then took out my phone. No more random highways. I needed the most direct route back from wherever the heck I was. I opened the map application, waiting for it to unblur, for the GPS icon to change from gray to red, the satellites to line up and mark my existence on the face of this planet. A couple urgent beeps.

And the screen went black.

I tormented the power button. The phone began a reboot, died halfway and ceased responding altogether.

THREE OR FOUR KILOMETERS down the road an old woman herding goats pointed me back the way I'd just ridden. A pair of amused schoolchildren practiced their English and showed me on a phone where I was. I stopped to buy water at a roadside shop, where three men and their cigarettes debated the quickest route to Capracornea. I never felt lost. While the Vespa sang beneath me at full throttle, I was running on pure quintessence.

Back at the Buonaventuras I wheeled the bike back into its shed and was struggling to untangle my hair from the helmet strap, when I heard shouting. A bitter quarrel between Sandro and his father inside the oil press house.

I stood like a voyeur by the half-open door. Soon it swung aside and Sandro marched out, a curt nod acknowledging my presence. He waved to say, *It's nothing,* and kept walking, leaving me puzzled as to whether I should follow. His father came out next and, seeing me, offered his own *it's nothing* wave, then turned back into the building.

I caught Sandro by the arm outside the kitchen door. "What happened?"

"Nothing. Business only."

He let me follow him up to his room. He switched on the light; was it that late already? I pulled the chair closer, restraining myself from stroking his cheek.

"Tell me the business problem. You looked so angry."

"You can not understand."

"Try," I said. I'd understood a lot of things today.

"How to say? Ai! What word?" He stroked his chin, trying to conjure the English genie from his stubble. "Is my mistake. Today press the olives, but one basket is not good."

"What do you mean?"

"Today the workers find one basket olives in the east grove, maybe Saturday harvest, forget to bring in. I say them, put in corner, save for...how you said it? Salt water?"

"Pickle."

"Pickle. But some workers inside, they don't know. They press these olives, and all goes together making oil."

"Why is that a problem?"

Sandro's forehead furrowed, squeezing drops of English vocabulary from drained-out synapses. "Olive must be fresh. If two days in the sun, can a little bit, how to say—*fermentare*. Now is mix together with other oil. More than one hundred liters no good."

"Are you serious? Can anyone really tell?"

"My father can taste. Me too. Little-little *rancido*. My father is very angry me."

"You also yelled at him." I squeezed his hand, which was moist despite the day's dryness.

"I say, but you speak nothing. Okay?" He waited for my nod. "My father says we put these oil in extra virgin tins. I am so angry to him!"

"If the inspectors..."

"Inspectors not the problem." He rubbed fingers against his thumb, indicating money. "Customers not the problem. Woman buys in Buenos Aires supermarket, she don't know. Problem is here." He punched his chest.

"You don't really think your father would do that? I thought he has such pride."

"I do not think he will do it. I think he is only saying because he is angry me."

"And the spoiled oil? You have to dump it?"

"Can sell, but cheap, lose money." His face dove into his hands. "Sometimes I am hating olives business."

How strange the universe was acting today. Sandro's disquiet fed right into my plan. I slid onto the bed beside him.

"Does that mean you sometimes love it?"

"It is my work."

"I know it's your work. But it isn't your passion."

He raised a hand to quiet me, but I wouldn't quit.

"Sandro, listen to me, please. Your whole life is stuck in these trees, while your heart is up in the stars," I said, finger stabbing the heavens. "No, let me finish. I know you now. You need to follow your heart or you'll never be happy. Your dream is to be an astronomer—"

"Stop. We talk this before. For me, is crazy thinking."

"Exactly! Sometimes you just have to do something crazy! It's like God is giving you signs, like for me today. He's simply waiting for you to follow your heart and make a totally crazy move—then all the best things start happening to you, better than you ever imagined!"

He stared at the floorboards, taking it in. "What crazy move God or maybe Serena tells me I must do?"

"Come here." I took his hands in mine and kissed his knuckles, kneading his fingers as I spoke. "We'll go to Padova. You and me, together. You'll study astronomy, I'll find work teaching English. I can support us for rent and food. After you graduate, you can get a job, maybe at an observatory or a museum, or as a lecturer. Maybe in Hawaii—they have that huge telescope on the Big Island! Can you imagine living in Hawaii? We can go anywhere in the world that you find work. I can teach English almost anywhere. I can start a school. It'll be wonderful! You'll be doing what you love. Both of us will, together! There's nothing crazy about it. It's following our hearts!"

His mother called from downstairs. My words had had their desired effect. I knew not to say any more, nor to demand any response. Let the idea sink in.

At dinner I told my story of getting lost, the burst tire, the Griko village, the cliff by the sea. When I told about the phone dying, Sandro's father laughed so hard he nearly choked on his wine. He pointed at me and said something with the word *coraggiosa*. Sounded like courageous, the last word I'd have ever attributed to myself, until possibly, just a little, today.

After dinner Sandro's father served brandy. A word out of my mouth about old photos led to him barricading me behind stacks of family albums—pictures sliding loose, old sepia tones and faded colors. Mustachioed men and stern women. Boys on donkey carts. Baby Sandro in the arms of his beaming, beautiful young mother, his father as a child leaning on a tree, his grand-father as a five-year-old in a sailor suit.

Sandro and I were both a little drunk by the time we staggered upstairs to my room. Our arms went directly around each other. He smelled like sweat and leaves and the tangy aroma of crushed olives. Our lips clasped. Desire practically bounced off the walls and ceiling, but neither of us moved beyond our little dance. After the events of the past two days, nothing was just for fun any longer. Either it was just a game or it wasn't, something confined to this moment or extending into the infinity of the stars. I thought my own illusions had been stripped away that day, but I needed a clear sense of what was in his heart. I'd said my piece. It was his turn.

I searched for clues in the way he held his shoulders, the swell and contraction of his chest. I searched for something beyond linguistics. My life had been focused around words and sentences, the subtle intricacies of syntax and idioms, but I'd never learned how to read another person's soul.

He leaned into me a little. A little sigh brushed my ear. I wanted meaning, damn it! No more secrets, no more hesitation.

Words—plain stupid words—flushed from the speech lobe of my brain, pumped by the beating of my heart, flooded onto my tongue.

A shouting match erupted inside my hollow skull.

Keep your mouth shut!

Say it! Be crazy!

Not the right time. Keep it shut!

Nine days left! Nothing to lose! Be crazy!

Keep it shut!

Be crazy!

Keep it shut!

Be crazy!

Keep your mouth shut! Keep it shut!

FOR GOD'S SAKE, KEEP IT SHUT!!

I opened my big, fat, stupid mouth.

And said, *"Ti amo."*

The air in the room froze. His breathing stopped. I wanted to pluck the words back out of his ears. I shoved a fist against my mouth to make sure nothing else escaped.

His eyes looked sadly into mine. "You are beautiful and intelligent and *coraggiosa*. When I am with you, I am happy. What you say today, it touches me here." He moved his finger to his forehead, then placed it on his heart. "And here."

I waited for more, but neither the words I wanted to hear nor any other followed.

"Run away with me?" I said.

He hung his head for a drawn-out moment with his hands clasped between his knees, then raised himself from the bed.

"I can not answer in this moment."

Chapter 29

On Tuesday I picked olives with Valerio's team. Again, he worked whatever tree was beside mine, a never-ending cigarette glued to his lip, relentlessly teasing and flirting and teaching me colorful Italian curses.

Sandro, meanwhile, spent the morning in the press house. He had to set up new systems to avoid repeat mistakes, he'd announced over breakfast, though I wondered if an ulterior motive was to avoid my questions.

It was killing me. Last night had made me more certain than ever that I was more than just a fling to him. Maybe he was mulling a compromise response to my proposal, where he could study and work the olives. Maybe he needed to confront his father first, before committing to a new life.

Maybe he didn't know what he wanted.

Or maybe I was dreaming.

We worked the northeast grove, where the trees were shorter and closer together, and it was easier to build a rhythm into the task. I couldn't believe I'd arrived only a week ago today. Already I was an old hand as an olive picker, while California felt like a past life. Time had flashed by in an eye blink. As would the next eight days before I had to leave. Eight days left to win his heart.

We took lunch as usual at the big outdoor table. Sandro clapped my shoulder like I was one of the crew, then kneaded my muscles between the blades, knowing exactly which spot needed relief after hours of picking. Valerio demanded the same for himself, triggering an exchange of playful profanity and dirty looks from Sandro's mother.

Sandro filled his plate and sat beside me. I took a chance and whispered, "Can we talk for a minute after lunch?"

His phone rang. A few words later, he left his untouched food and dashed toward the main house.

Sandro returned as I was mopping the last sauce from my plate with a hunk of bread. He spoke in low tones to his parents, then sat down to his plate of lukewarm pasta.

"Problem?" I said.

"Here no problem," he said between mouthfuls. "Giampiccolos having problem with computer and Internet. He asks me look if here is same."

"Maybe they have hamsters?"

"*Che?* Oh, ha! No 'amster. I think is—in English you say also *virus?* Paolo maybe can fix. Loretta's brother."

Valerio beckoned. No time left to talk.

That afternoon I threw myself into the work, nearly doubling my hourly olive yield, the only way to keep my mind off everything else. By five-thirty, all aching and sweaty, I hitched a ride on the mini-tractor with its trailer full of olive baskets. Rounding the corner past a storage shed, I recognized Loretta's car, its door hanging open with nobody inside. Then I heard her shouting. She stood in the press house doorway, waving her arms as though wracked with spasms. Sandro walked right past her with long, angry strides. He noticed me watching, then shouted back at Loretta in English: "Is not true!"

"*Cazzo!* Then whose children are they?" she demanded.

He picked up his pace, ignoring me, and disappeared into the main house. The door slammed.

"You want to know what happened, yes?" Loretta called to me. "This man you think you love so much, he has another family!"

My heart plunged like a bungee cord from my throat to my stomach. Loretta stormed over to me, waving her phone.

"You should know this," she said. "Today I get phone calls from a woman, says she is the mother of his children. Not just one. Two! I tell her she is crazy, and she calls me a bitch and a whore and some English words I don't know."

"English?"

"Yes. When I speak Italian, she doesn't understand. I hang up on her many times, but always she calls back with her filthy tongue!" Loretta's laser glare could have sliced steel. "First I thought it was you. But the country code is from Turkey!"

The hairs on the back of my neck shot up like porcupine quills. My heart stopped beating. Sandro rushed back out of the house, his face redder than I'd ever seen. *Io 'sta qua manco la conosco!*" I guessed he was denying that he knew the woman.

He lunged for her phone, but she wrestled it out of his grip.

"Tell me, Serena, is it proper American English to call him a lying, stinking sack of goat turds? If he doesn't know this *puttana*, this slut, where does she get these photos to send me?" She tapped her phone and held it for me to see.

My screen shot of Sandro.

Then another.

And another.

"Different shirts, different days." Loretta put on the righteous tones of a TV lawyer. "So happy, showing his little Turkish cow what to do for him!"

She rotated the phone for the benefit of the jury—that is, me—inches from my face. I knew this pose by heart, the crooked smile, finger in his mouth. I even remembered which lesson: Thirteen, Personal Care. We'd been playfully arguing about brushing teeth before or after breakfast.

"And what's this?" She swiped to the next photo.

Sandro in bed, his bare chest in all its glory, relaxed and

happy. It took all my willpower to resist punching myself in the face.

Sandro's hands flapped helplessly at his side. I wondered if he suspected the photos' true origins.

But Loretta wasn't through. "Show me her picture! I want to see your little Asian beauty!"

He uttered a curse Valerio hadn't taught me yet, spun on his heel and strode back to the house.

Loretta arched like a cobra about to strike. "You still want him? Go fight over him with his Turkish whore!"

I hurried inside, taking two stairs at a time, and locked myself in my room. The computer took a thousand years to start up—curse automatic updates!—then an eon-long minute to log in to the school portal. Bieber wasn't online. One o'clock in the morning there, he might still be up. I fired off messages:

What are you doing? Please stop it NOW

Then I checked Yasmin. Istanbul was one hour later than here. Her video chat was offline, but my e-mail to her received a response minutes later:

Hello Serena! You know all the special words
you teach me? The most very bad dirty
dirt words? Now she also knows them!

I wrote back:

You must stop

I heard my name called for dinner. I couldn't face Sandro and his family, yet not showing up would have been worse. At the table I learned the details of the Giampiccolos' cyber-attack. Each time they tried to open financial records and other business files, pop-ups appeared requiring a password. Same with their e-mail accounts. To make matters worse, their company website had been hacked, replacing every picture of vineyards and wine bottles with Justin Bieber videos. A computer specialist from Bari was driving down this evening.

I excused myself, pleading a headache and sore limbs from the day's picking. The moment I latched my door I dashed off another e-mail to Bieber:

> *Send me the password.*
> *And stop all this!!*

I GAVE UP AFTER the hundredth or so e-mail and lay back on my bed staring at the ceiling all night. The soreness in my arms was nothing compared to what was going on inside my heart.

At last I heard a telltale blip. A message from Bieber:

> *Can not stop. Already coming.*

What was that supposed to mean? I fired off another message and waited, but no reply. It was a bit past noon in Shanghai. As if being in school ever stopped a teenager from messaging. Who else was involved in this? I sent notes to all my students:

> *If you're doing something in Italy, please stop!*

I was helping Sandro's mother clear breakfast dishes when we heard deep rumbling in the distance, growing gradually louder until even the floor vibrated.

Everyone ran in the direction of the noise, louder now, like a tank platoon on the move. That direction happened to be toward the Giampiccolo property. I was among the first to reach the border fence. The first to see the source of the rumble.

Oh.

My.

Frigging.

God.

It was a platoon, all right. An excavator, a bulldozer, and something that looked like a Godzilla-sized buzzsaw on treads, which passed close enough to display a company name stenciled on its side in Cyrillic letters. Once upon a time I'd learned that alphabet for some long-forgotten linguistics course; I was pretty certain that the last line said *Bulgaria*.

I clung to the wire fence in helpless rage watching grape vines torn up by the roots and decapitated by the spinning claw. Three rows at a time, the Giampiccolo vineyard was being ground into mulch.

Sandro's family chased the machines, but their operators didn't pause their destructive tasks. Loretta and Paolo hurdled through the vines with metal pipes, succeeding in smashing the excavator's cab window before it rotated and threatened them with the giant claw of its digger.

While I watched the unfolding calamity, part of me was awe-struck at Vlad's ingenuity in transporting his heavy equipment halfway across Europe on such short notice. I doubted he was out there, or that his drivers would listen to, or even understand me.

The bulldozer turned toward the grape crushing shed. Things were about to get worse and there was nothing I could do except try to guess who else was enrolled in Bieber's plot to sabotage Loretta's engagement to Sandro. My Estonian student managed apartment buildings in Tallinn. What could he do other than issue an overdue rent notice? Then there was my Ecuadorian fitness trainer who, unless she'd hopped a flight from South America—

A gunshot crack put a brake to my thoughts. Signor Giampiccolo rose from a trench between vine rows, aimed a hunting rifle toward the bulldozer, and squeezed off another round. A harsh ping of bullet ricocheting off metal. Sandro ducked for cover as Signor Giampiccolo turned his sights toward the rolling buzzsaw. Another loud bang, and this time what sounded like an engine seizing. The blades ceased turning.

A horn sounded. The excavator turned around, leading a general retreat, though they managed to trample one more row of grapes along the way.

I squeezed through the gate, past the crowd of gawking olive pickers. I leapt over upturned earth, trying to make sense of the thoughts zinging like missiles through the Armageddon unfolding inside my head. Everyone was busy inspecting the damage, so Sandro didn't notice me until I bent down beside him to examine a severed trunk. He shook his head sadly.

"Looks maybe Mafia work. I don't know," he said.

I was almost relieved. "Really? This happened before?"

"Not here," Sandro said. "Some years before, near Brindisi. Olive groves. But..." He shook his head again. Before he could complete his statement, his father called him. "I think you go my house. I must with them."

I COLLAPSED ONTO MY bed and buried my face in the blanket. Everything drained from my body as though a vein had split open. Maybe it was only a nightmare. Maybe I'd wake up and find everyone cheerfully gulping breakfast coffee at the table.

But it was no dream. I forced myself up, clicked my laptop awake, and shot off another message to Bieber:

Video talk. Now. Please. Whatever is next, you must stop it.

His chat light remained dark. I leaned over and grabbed my ankles, hair sweeping the floor, and tried to think what to do. Go out and pick olives like nothing had happened? Hide here all day until they put the pieces together and drowned me like a witch? Pack and leave? How would I get anywhere unless I stole a car?

I checked the time on my phone: not yet one in the morning in California. Who to call? Zuzie was still in Hawaii. Miko? I didn't need her kind of analysis; I needed...I didn't know what. My mother? Chances were that if she were even awake, she'd be drunk senseless.

No other choice. I messaged Elias:

You busy?

Seconds later the video ringtone chirped, Elias's name flashed. I brushed back my hair and clicked.

"Hey! You and Miss Gucci Grape made it a threesome yet?" He looked sloppy and unshaven. Some TV show with a laugh track murmured in the background.

"I'm not in a joking mood."

"Gotcha. Calling to check up on the dudes?" The television noise ceased.

"How are they?"

Elias straightened himself and tucked hair away from his eyes. "Well, I was almost gonna call you yesterday. Hardy was, like, sleeping all day. Put him on his wheel, he just lay there. But seems fine now."

"You sure?"

"Sure I'm sure. Maybe the stimulation of my companionship wore him out. What's up with you? Any interesting developments?"

"'Interesting' is putting it mildly." I gave him a brief rundown about the Griko villages. "Though I determined their dialect is more rooted in Byzantine than Classical Greek, although the community apparently dates as far back as—"

"Wait wait wait, excuse me, Serena, do you mind me saying that I don't give a big fat Greek poop about them? But speaking of poop, that's how I'd describe how you look right now. What the heck is going on?"

I broke down and told him the whole story, from Bieber's hacking my image folder to organizing what amounted to international terrorism to impoverish Loretta's family so that the engagement would be broken off. Saying it out loud made it all sound ludicrous, yet at the same time worse than I'd even thought. By the time I finished, the computer was shaking in my lap.

"Wow, that is some uber-nerd of a kid," Elias said.

"Is that all you have to say? Admiring your fellow dork?"

"Sorry, didn't mean it like that. Man, I wish I could pass you a tissue."

"I wish a lot of things, Elias. I wish I'd never come here. I wish I'd never invented this stupid fairy tale in my head, that some handsome prince is going to kiss me and the old me disappears and I turn into some storybook princess and live happily ever after." I rubbed my cheeks with both palms and ended up smearing tears and snot all over my face. The bedsheet served as a cleaning rag. "But then I think, what's so wrong with wanting that? Some people, without hardly even trying, get to be video stars and marry a Scandinavian count. What's so wrong with believing in happily ever after?"

Elias kept silent for a minute. His face seemed frozen.

"You still there?" I said.

"Sure. I don't know what to say." He wiped his eyes, as though he'd teared up too. "I guess I don't believe in fairy tale endings. Sounds clichéd, but to me life is like a computer program. You encounter a bug, spend way too much time working it out, only to find that the fix causes a new bug. Rinse and repeat."

I nodded, while trying to stifle a hiccup outbreak. "Think you could undo what Bieber did to the Giampiccolos' computer files?"

"Not if he's encrypted them, which is how it sounds."

His answer prompted a new crying fit. I muted my microphone as primordial sobs erupted through my throat.

"Serena? Hello?" Elias said. "Can you hear me?"

I nodded.

"What if it works?" he said.

I cocked my head.

"What if they don't figure it out?" he said. "What if they actually believe it's a Mafia attack, and your guy's family doesn't want to touch them with a ten-foot olive branch?"

I clicked the microphone back on. "You really think so?"

"On balance...uh...maybe in a parallel universe."

The computer nearly slid off my lap. "Oh God. Everything was going so great. Or at least not this screwed up. And then—damn it! I'm such a loser. Everything I try to set up for myself fails. If this gets out, I'll be fired for sure. And even if not, what have I got to go back to? No money, a crappy apartment, stupid underpaid dead end job?"

"Could be worse."

I needed sympathy, not platitudes from some misanthropic computer technician. "You should talk. Living in your aunt's garage. Some dream life."

Whatever nerve I'd struck erupted all over his face. His eyes narrowed, his lips funneled. He cut off my attempt to apologize.

"Hey, don't knock it. Running around every day listening to idiots—not you, of course...well, maybe you too—screaming 'Emergency! My computer won't start!' And turns out they'd used the vacuum cleaner and forgot to plug the laptop charger back in. Or they just don't know what happened, all this porn popping up after they clicked on some Nigerian e-mail. And I'm the digital janitor cleaning out all the nasty yucky stuff. What more could I want out of life on earth?"

"Don't be so cynical."

"Cynical? *Moi?* Lemme tell you my sob story, take your mind off yours for a sec. So I had this roommate in college? I was helping him out on this coding project? Used to tease him for being an uptight teetotaler, once slipped vodka into his ginger ale. He was so angry, he kicked me off his project and went with another guy. They developed a weird algorithm for counting your eyelashes for facial recognition security. Yeah, did you know that's harder to fake than iris recognition? Your stupid eyelashes! So of course they dropped out of school, guy now drives a Lexus at his beachfront tax haven estate in Puerto Rico."

It was the first time I'd seen him seethe with such anger. He sat up straighter. He spoke without tripping over words. The teacher in me even noticed more fluid syntax and vocabulary. I nodded for him to go on.

"There's times I'm driving home after fixing some fool's home office network and he's tried to squeeze me on my fee, and I feel like missing my exit and just keep driving—drive all the way down to Costa Rica or someplace. Start a new life, grow weed, live in a treehouse. Because why not? But...well, you know me...I never had the guts to pass that offramp."

"You can still—"

"I know. But hear me out. Sometimes I think that maybe people like me serve a specific purpose. I mean, not everybody can be brilliant or successful or rich. Somebody's got to be a failure, and a lot of us have to be mediocre, because otherwise there's no reference point for success. So that's my function in life, to be a turtle so Yertle can be king—a plain schmuck who cleans up messes made by dumb old ladies and bartenders and secretaries."

"And English teachers," I said.

"And mixed-up, pretty English teachers. One who's not like me. She's no mediocre loser. She has the guts to up and go to Italy. And even if her dreams are all being run over by bulldozers, at least she has the...the..."

"Guts again?"

"I was trying to come up with a different body part."

"I'm a fine example. Look how those guts are working out."

"Serena, listen. You. Yes, you—you're a far finer human being than that asshole with the eyelash recognition. Or that bitch blonde at your work. Or a wine maker's stuck up daughter who's under orders to marry for money. Don't take this the wrong way—even though I might mean it that way too—but I'm in awe of you."

"Then tell me how to clean up this mess, Elias. Please."

"Sorry. To do that, I'd have to understand people."

He rubbed his eyes with his thumb and forefinger, knocking his glasses off. He leaned off-screen to retrieve them.

"Elias?" I said.

"Yeah?"

"I think you need to get angry more often. It becomes you."

His face reappeared, glasses on crooked, biting his lower lip. "You think?"

In the corner of my screen a green dot appeared. Bieber was finally online.

"Elias, so sorry. Gotta go. Call you tomorrow, okay?"

"Sure."

"And, and, and... Sorry. And thanks. For being a friend."

"Likewise."

Bieber didn't respond for eight, nine, ten rings. Then he came on at last, seated in his school uniform in front of a wall of books. He grimaced like a chimp.

"Hello, Teacher Serena."

"Bieber. Um...what is happening?"

"Just now school finish. I am in liber-erry."

"Library," I corrected. "That is not what I mean."

He looked away, then back at me, eyes made huge by his glasses.

"We want help you. If Noretta is not rich, then your boy-friend wants to marry you, not her."

"Bieber, listen. Thank you. But...but...do you know what a mess you've made?"

His smile puckered.

I asked, "Do you know what *backfire* means?"

He shook his head. I typed it in the text box and waited while he looked it up.

"Why didn't you ask me?" I said.

"Not only me!"

263

"I know, but you should have—" My look must have scared him.

"Teacher, please I can talk?"

"Sure."

He leaned closer; the camera distorted his mouth and eyes into a froglike droop. "Teacher Serena, you think I am stupid little boy. I think so. I am very stupid." He looked side to side, breathed deeply, and said, "I talk your other students. They are not stupid, they are adults. But we all are same thing."

"What?"

His lips tightened, his brow furled. I'd never seen him so serious. "All your students love you. All want you have love."

Was I ever going to stop crying this day? I squeezed my eyes shut. *I love you too,* I wanted to say. I love you, you crazy boy. And love makes us do crazy things. When I looked again, some other school kid was leaning into the picture, gawking at me. Bieber elbowed him away, uttering some brisk Chinese words.

"It's all over now, right?" I said.

He glanced side to side.

"Right?" I said again.

"Almost."

"What?"

He mumbled something to the shadows crowding around him. "I call him, he say too late, can not stop. Sorry, Teacher Serena! I must go."

The password. I forgot to ask him the password. He didn't pick up after that.

Chapter 30

alf the places at the outdoor lunch table sat empty. Sandro's father had posted sentinels around his and his neighbor's properties to watch for further bulldozer attacks and dispatched Sandro to warn nearby farms. Valerio attempted to lighten the mood with wisecracks I wished I understood. I picked at my food amid the crossfire of incomprehensible dialect.

I was glad nobody paid attention to me, not even when I walked around gathering dirty dishes, though I was unnerved by the unusual vigor with which Sandro's mother shooed me out of the kitchen.

Hiding inside all day would be not only unbearable but incriminatory. I made my way through the groves, found Valerio's crew, and claimed a ladder and a basket. There were no new emergencies all afternoon. Gradually I lost myself in the repetitive task of plucking olives.

I was one of the last to quit, gathering scattered fruits until it was almost too dark to see. Waving away Valerio's offer of a lift on the tractor, I walked alone back to the house.

Inside my room I tore off my dusty jeans and pullover and lay on the bed. I tried to find solace in the mild breeze cooling my body, the purple-red sunset framed in the window, but my thoughts kept spiraling back to bulldozers and severed vines and wracking my brain for clues about the password that Bieber still hadn't provided.

Calm down, Serena. There was nothing that connected me to the crime. No way they would suspect me, as long as I maintained a façade of wide-eyed, happy visitor. It might even give me the opportunity to offer sympathy to Loretta, to add my labor to repair the mess and bond with her family. They might even accept me as part of the community, and as Sandro's paramour.

A light rap on my door. Sandro whispered that I should come downstairs. I threw on my one remaining outfit not in need of laundering—a summery yellow dress—and straightened my shoulders on the way to the stairs.

The entire Giampiccolo family was lined up on a sofa like a court of inquiry. Sandro's parents occupied armchairs, while his sister Olimpia sat in a dining chair. Another dining chair in the center was obviously meant for me. Sandro stepped aside and leaned against the wall.

I took my place in the line of everyone's fire. The word "Inquisition" came to mind, though that had taken place in Spain. In Italy they fed martyrs to lions.

"Buonasera." I coughed to mask the tremble in my voice.

Signor Giampiccolo cleared his throat, like a power lawn-mower starting. Loretta clasped her hands on her knees and said, "What do you know about all these?"

"You mean this morning?" I put on my best look of innocent surprise, wishing that I'd taken that college acting class Jessie had tried to push me into.

Loretta's mother launched into an ear mauling diatribe, arms and hands providing subtitles, the gist, if not the details, of which were painfully clear, since half of them involved pointing, flinging, flicking and punching in my direction. Signor Giampiccolo and his son nodded along, while Sandro's parents sat in stony silence. Loretta patted her mother's lap; only then did the older woman taper off and lean back with arms folded like the vice she obviously intended to clamp around my neck.

"What did she say?" I asked. "Really. I want to know every word."

"Every word does not matter," Loretta said. "Some are not nice. But she says what we all are thinking. Since you are coming here, you are so crazy for Alessandro. Yes, of course everyone can see. He is a very handsome and passionate man, so it is natural for girls to like him. You remember you came to me, and what I have told you? I say I trust Alessandro so well, that I am happy for him to play with another girl before he is married? Do you not think I am generous to you, and to him, to let you have fun during your little dream trip to Italy? Do you?"

Her eyes gored into me, as though she truly expected an answer. "Go on," I said.

"Am I to think it is coincidence—one day later!—I receive telephone calls from a crazy woman with a sailor's dirty mouth, who tries to destroy my trust for him? Then my family computer is attacked—oh yes, the programmer specialist today traced it to China. Then next day our fields are attacked by Bulgarian machines. Who is this enemy with agents around the world? Who will receive advantage to destroy our business? Perhaps some person trying to make my family disappear?"

My jaw remained firmly clamped while Sandro offered a roundup for his parents. Signora Giampiccolo piped up again, but Loretta waved her quiet and continued.

"Then today afternoon we have visitors. Do you know who? No? Inspectors from the European Union Agriculture Commission! You look surprised. A very good actor you are. Yes, they have left two hours ago, and now we must discontinue to sell our wine until the investigation is concluded."

"I beg you to believe me," I said. "Why would I want to wreck your business? I had nothing to do with phone calls or hackers or bulldozers, or...or... EU inspectors."

"Is that right? You know, I truly want to believe you," Loretta said, far too calmly for comfort. "I honestly thought you're too stupid to do such things! I do not know how you might alert the Agriculture Commission in Brussels with a false report that our wine is contaminated. Except for one thing. They show us the report. The complaint origin is from our distributor in Fargo, in the American state North Dakota. I never heard before of North Dakota! Where is it? We have no customer, no agent, no distributor in some stupid city called Fargo!"

So that was the final stunt Bieber had been unable to stop. My dour Belgian student in the North Dakota oil fields obviously had friends back in Brussels. I turned to Sandro, but his eyes wouldn't meet mine. I looked back at Loretta. Her open-mouthed smile had all the warmth of a rat trap.

"I call them, you know," she said. "I telephone your school. I pretend I want to be your student. 'Please I am-a want-a speaking Eng-a-lish. Someone recommending me Serena.' Then I ask the lady, what is Serena's experience, where are her other students? That lady is so proud, so happy tell to me, Serena has students all around the world! Italy, like me! Shanghai! Istanbul! Bulgaria! Even in North Dakota!"

All four parents demanded translation, but Loretta hissed them into silence. The air thickened with accusation. Even the Virgin Mary's portrait at the end of the room seemed to aim incriminating eyes at me. Though I'd been raised without religion, unless you counted my mother's Liquid Church of Jim Beam, I felt cornered into making a confession. Or at least a statement that wasn't entirely false.

The stairway creaked. Silent Uncle watched from the bottom step.

"*È vero. Sono i miei studenti,*" I attempted in Italian. It's true; they're my students. "Wait. Listen, Loretta, Sandro. Tell your parents. I swear to you, I swear by *La Madonna* there, that I did not ask for any of these actions!"

I recognized too late my mistake at invoking the Sacred Virgin. Loretta interpreted my words for them with thick dabs of sarcasm, which made all four parents erupt, though at each other, not at me. Loretta's mother screamed at Sandro's. Sandro's father stood up, shouting and wagging a finger at Signor Giampiccolo.

I threw a pleading look to Olimpia and whispered, "What's he saying?"

"My father say, if their wine business so easy can to destroy, even by stupid little American—ah, then he say very bad word—maybe is not good idea for the marriage."

Signor Giampiccolo chopped one hand on the other, shouting back at Sandro's father, who rose with clenched fists. Sandro's Mamma wailed.

Loretta's mother lunged at me with her silver crucifix pendant clasped like a dagger.

I toppled backward. Sandro grabbed me before I hit my head and dragged me from the house.

Outside, night had fallen. He hauled me across the court-yard and ordered me into his car. Voices followed from the house even as the engine kicked into life and tires spun over gravel. We reached the gate before he remembered to turn on headlights.

"Where are we going?" I said.

His jaw remained clenched until the first crossroad. "I do not know."

Neither of us spoke as we sped through the dark, turning seemingly at random into unlit lanes, then onto a wider, potholed *stradone*. I rolled down the window and stared outside, trying to figure out what to say. The night was warm and dry, what Americans might call Indian Summer.

I had trouble making sense of what had just transpired, what I had done, what I might do, what I could possibly say to him. It was better to keep my mouth shut, while my hair whipped my face, wind screamed past my eardrum, staring ahead at endless stone walls and ghostly trees in the headlights' periphery. Until some insect smacked into my cheek. I closed the window, leaving the space around us cloaked in unbearable muffled quiet.

"I think I know the password," I ventured quietly. "For the computer files. He left a clue. Try different Justin Bieber song titles. I'd start with 'Believe.'"

Sandro coughed inside his throat. "Is true? All not your idea?"

He passed a slow-moving flatbed truck. I pressed back in my seat, seeking the shadowy refuge of its curve. "True," I said. "I promise."

I told him everything, as plainly as possible. The screenshots, which made him flinch. Bieber's hack. Even a little about Yasmin's "special words", hoping that might lighten the horror, at least for me. But he kept his stony silence, even as my speech deteriorated into gut-shaking blubbering. "I'm so sorry, Sandro! I made such a mess! I can't believe this is happening."

He took a hand off the wheel and slapped his own face. "Happening," he said.

I slapped myself so hard that he jumped in his seat. Then I pummeled my face with both fists and started to cry. "It *is* happening," I said. I was afraid to ask, but there was no more putting it off. Truly nothing left to lose. I let a minute pass to calm down, and said, "Did you think about the things I proposed?"

His hands strangled the steering wheel. "I did think."

I twisted to half-face him. "Sandro, you don't love the olives or the business. That's what you told me! I'm not sure you love Loretta, or her family, or your village, or even Puglia. What kind of life do you have here? Planned out until the day you die. Let's go—you and me—now. We don't even have to go home. Keep driving, all the way to Padova. Go study your stars, follow your heart, do what you love! Be with one who loves you. Even if it isn't me, I don't care. I just want you to live your dream!"

He pulled to a stop beside the road.

Sandro stared ahead into the night, his long, deep breaths see-sawing over the purr of the idling engine. "How to say you?"

He switched off the car and stared some more.

"Many times I look at stars and planets. Saturn, he is my favorite. Twenty-nine and half earth years for move around the sun. This means I am not yet one Saturn year old. I am lucky if I live three Saturn years. I am little. I am nothing. Solar system, galaxy, universe, God makes all perfect. All works together. Like Saturn's rings. Like my life here. But some people, they live like meteorites." His hand dove through the air. "*Psheeewww...Poof!*"

"You're saying that God meant you to stay here your whole life and make olive oil? What about God making you strong enough to choose your own life?"

He still wouldn't look at me. "What is strong? Throw away family, history, throw away the land because I have one small passion? Maybe Americans and Italians make different translation of this word, *strong*. If my father said to his father, 'I do not want make oil,' what happens? No house, no farm. What if I say this? You say this is strong? For which purpose? Seven generations work and tradition—*Poof!*"

The car felt stuffy. I opened the window a crack and let in the breeze, the chirps of night birds. "How can tradition be more important than your own happiness? That's prison, that's not living. Even you said: 'beautiful prison.'"

"What is your life, Serena? You once said me, you look in your computer, this way you see the world. Maybe you click a button or sit on the airplane and—*hoopla!*" He snapped his fingers. "New place! New life! All bad things behind you now? Is it really, yes?"

He dropped his head and drummed his fingers on the steering wheel, gazing through the windshield up toward the sky. "I look at the universe in my telescope. I feel I am not important, I know this is true. I see my farm, my village, Puglia, my history, my tradition. I know this is important. Is my *destino*—destiny. Not so bad. If every person do what only he wants? All these important things, everything—history, tradition, family, community—how I can say it?"

"Disappears."

"Yes. World disappears in one moment."

I tried to absorb what he was saying. I tried to understand it, to feel it in my own heart for just one second. Maybe he was right in his way, to embrace his life the best way he could, and I was right in mine, so eager to transform into something else.

"So you won't go to Padova to study?"

"I won't."

I kept the last question—the obvious question—to myself, but it inflated inside me until it threatened to flood the whole car and suffocate me. I worked my throat to not sound pathetic, but it did anyway:

"Then why did you sleep with me? Why did you encourage me to come here? Why did you say you'll suffer...?"

"Is because I am confused man, stupid man, not strong man. You here makes me question my life." He reached across and took my hand, pressed it to his chest. "One face of my heart will be always for you. In the same face where I keep also the stars and the moons and the planets and the room where Galileo was teaching. Now, every time I go to the mountain, I bring you, here, inside my heart."

I said the only thing left to say: "I'll be there."

"O-*kay*. We drive."

We passed a long warehouse-like building before entering a town. A few cars sped by in the other direction. Restaurants and bars sat mostly unoccupied. We drove past a brightly illuminated public square, where a crowd had gathered. I caught strains of music.

Without warning, Sandro slammed the brake, squealed around a corner back toward the square and stopped beside a church.

"Come. This you must see."

A furious drum beat reverberated across the open space. Sandro led me by the hand between people of all ages, everyone bouncing or twirling in place to an infectious rhythm. In front of the cathedral doors, a crop-haired woman sawed blizzards of notes from a violin. A bald accordionist raced her up and down the scales, backed on crunching acoustic guitar by a man in a vest. But most striking was a tall, bald-shaven man, head back, eyes closed, striking an enormous tambourine in a raw, primeval beat that sounded as though it rose direct from the stony ground into his blurred, palpitating hand.

In front of the band the crowd gave way to a man and woman dancing. In truth, the woman made nearly all the moves, while the man shuffled in pursuit with outstretched arms. She stamped across the paving stones with hands on hips, loose white skirt spinning, then paused coquettishly, hip thrust to one side, twirling a red chiffon scarf high over her head while the man stepped around her. The woman's moves were erotic without a trace of lewdness, teasing both man and crowd, while the music played both sinister and sweet, evoking images of angels courting with demons. She lowered her arms, encircling his head with the red scarf. Then, as he reached for her waist, she whipped away the cloth and pirouetted to the other side of the clearing. The band broke into a chorus, the violinist's voice as high and vibrant as her strings, while the man rejoined the crowd. People clapped and cheered and sang along.

Just when I thought it was over, the woman flicked her red scarf at another man and resumed the dance with a new partner. My knees took up the rhythm.

"What is it?" I asked Sandro.

"*Pizzica*. Also can say *tarantella*," he shouted over the music. "Puglia tradition. In old days, some women are bitten by the *tarantola*." He made his hand creep like a spider.

273

"Tarantula? The spider?"

"Yes! Spider. After they bite, woman becoming crazy with spirit of spider. Only can make spirit away with *tarantella* dance. But here, Salento, have special dance, little bit different—*la pizzicarella*. Maybe can say woman is like spider catching—" He pinched his fingers and imitated a fly.

The dance finished with the woman rushing back into the mass of onlookers while the drummer maintained a slow beat. I joined the applause. Whatever problems swirled inside and around me were eclipsed by the hypnotic rhythm and dance.

The drumming flared again, and the band raised a new tune. Another couple took the stage, the woman in a searing black and red dress.

I was too mesmerized to ask: the names of the songs, the name of this town, why tonight? The fewer words between Sandro and me, the better. Some onlookers sipped beers, but most seemed to find their intoxication in the music and dance. Men and women, young and old, waved hands and moved their feet, some couples circling each other in the crowd. I pushed forward for a better view, watching one woman after another take center stage and play spinning spider to a series of willing male flies. Everyone cheered loudest for a short grey-haired lady, who looped her scarf around a young man a third her age.

While she took her bows, a hand latched onto my elbow. A shout filled my ear: "'Ollywood!"

First one, then another grinning face stepped in front of me: my two rescuers from my Vespa day out. One had his arm around a woman, to whom he introduced me as *Star di 'Ollywood*. The guy holding my arm pulled me forward into the clearing, crying, *"Pizzicarella!"*

I tried to free myself, looked to Sandro for rescue, but he stood with folded arms and a hint of amusement in his eyes. The other guy's girlfriend tossed a red scarf my way. What was I going to do, let it hit the dirty ground? The moment I caught it, a cheer rose around me and the drumming began.

I closed my eyes and shut out the crowd. Today I'd lost every shred of dignity, every pretense to innocence, every hope of a life with Sandro. I'd snuffed out every dream I'd had in coming to Italy. What else could I possibly have to lose by doing a crazy dance in front of absolute strangers shrieking in some incomprehensible, melodious dialect? I placed a hand on my hip and twirled the red cloth as high as my fingers could reach. The accordion crunched a soaring, multi-hued chord. The violin burst into ecstatic arpeggios. I stuck out a leg. The crowd went wild.

Trying to recall the moves I'd seen, I stepped to the right, then—left—cross—right—cross—lift skirt and twirl with scarf outstretched. Guitar completed the sound. The tambourine rattled and pounded like a pouncing spider.

My partner reached forward. Like the women before me, I shuffled backward, right hand on hip, left twirling the scarf over my head, over his, over mine. Then I pivoted around and skipped across the floor, both hands behind my back, fluttering the scarf like a tail. The music built higher, the violin trilled up and down the scale in rapid spurts of triplet notes, the accordion chasing behind.

I spun in place, spun in place, hands on hips, I spun in place, shedding my troubles and pains. My dress rose around me, a blossoming yellow flower. Maybe my panties showed, but I didn't care. No longer a clearing, no longer a crowd. The music, deep drumbeats, humming guitar strings and accordion pipes, bound together with slithering fiddle; cocooned in a web of sound, just me and this man, the spider and the fly.

He taunted me with his dance. I answered with my hips. I gave his scalp a teasing swish with the scarf, then twirled away, earning a whoop from somewhere. Catching a glimpse of Sandro watching, I nearly lost my balance.

My partner encircled me in his arms without touching, and danced around me, spinning into my web.

Then he was gone.

The music continued. A man old enough to be my grandfather stepped forward, and the dance continued. Something came over me, a dark gauze around the edges of my vision. I was neither young nor old, my partner too was ageless, just a man. Both of us freed from the bounds of the body. My feet ached from the uneven stones. Sweat dribbled into my eyes, hair stuck to my cheeks. The older man spun away. Time to choose my own victim.

People moved aside as I stepped toward Sandro. He stood in place, waiting, daring me. I whisked the scarf across his face and he followed me into the clearing.

His dancing surprised me: light on his feet, playful in his dodges and feints. We orbited each other like a binary star system, him chasing me, me chasing him. I spun and skipped, spun and skipped—lights, faces, tiles, walls, Sandro's moving feet, a soft mass of moving color.

He danced in the shadows, eyes shining in his shrouded face, taunting me into pursuit. A voice in my head screamed at him to rot in his beautiful prison, that narrow box of his little farm, his little village, his little life that he'd locked himself into.

The world around me swooned and darkened, sucking me into a whirlpool. I was in a new universe, submerged in dance. I was no longer Serena the foolish, stupid, naïve believer in pop songs and pictures of Saturn. This was how life should be, I told myself. Free of age, free of ambitions, freed from hope and dismay, moving in place to express the beauty and vigor in my soul. To move across the earth like a spinning top as a testimony to joy. I pressed a foot back to steady myself.

The music dropped to a long, growling whisper, like a cat hunching for that big leap. The air stopped spinning. Something had changed. A beautiful man stepped side to side before me, as though stitching webs with his feet, always and forever bound to this patch of earth. I hooked the scarf behind his head, trapping him, pulled him close until we inhaled each other's panting breath, smelled the sweat from our scalps. He was still Sandro, but not the man of the phone cam, not the man whose gaze roamed the stars, nor the one from my daydreams who'd promised me a new life in fairytale land. He was Sandro the charming olive farmer. Alessandro, my student, my friend.

Drum and fiddle and accordion and guitar melded into an explosion of cascading notes and rhythms. Whipping away the scarf, I released Sandro from my grip, from my spell, from my ferocious beating heart.

I fell backwards onto the ground and kept on dancing on my arching back, whipping the scarf across my chest while my feet stamped up and down, up and down. I was in the birthing posture, something inside me pushing to be released, some sort of liquid, inky darkness pressing to escape. My body clenched: thighs, hips, breast. A black substance rose from my midsection, a dark miasma—the soul of the spider spirit escaping, ascending into the black sky of heaven.

The dance had worked. A spell had been broken.

The music coalesced into one last blinding white chord.

WE PULLED INTO THE courtyard of Masseria Buonaventura in total darkness. It must have been past one in the morning. I'd dozed most of the way back. The moon had set and a thin film of clouds obscured the stars. No light shone from any window.

Opening the car door took effort. The ache in my legs returned, fresh blisters shot darts through my feet. I limped toward the house, trying not to trip on stones.

Pain ripped my scalp. My neck wrenched backward. An animal shriek, then I was face down on the ground, gravel scraping my cheek. A fist slammed into my back.

Loretta's voice: *"Puttana!* Whore!"

She reeled in my hair and pressed my head into the sharp stones. A struggle behind me, Sandro prying her off. They exchanged heated dialect while I sat up, brushed pebbles from my face, and felt for blood.

"Choose now!" Loretta ordered Sandro in English. "Me or your little American girl?"

He approached her from behind; hands alighted on her shoulders, stroking her gently, soothing the wild beast. She growled but gave in, leaning back against him.

"I do you a favor not to tell your employer what you have done," Loretta said to me in a voice drained of expression. "So you have a job to return to. So you will get out of here. Out of my life." She shrieked like a wildcat and threw dirt in my face. "Out of my world!"

I ran from the courtyard with only one shoe, gravel torturing my blisters.

I ran through the dark, ran between black monster trees, over a wall, and kept running, ignoring Sandro calling my name, until his voice faded into the night.

Chapter 31

A large insect—a beetle or cockroach—crawled along the steel bedframe inches from my face. I didn't have the heart to flick it away. It, unlike me, deserved to live. It, unlike me, belonged here, on a sagging upper bunk in this stuffy, noisy budget hostel in the inner bowels of Rome.

My bunkmate below shushed me, for around the third time, possibly because I couldn't stop breaking into blubbering fits. Though I wasn't sure how I was any worse than the fog-horn-mouthed drunks in the bar downstairs, a zillion unmuffled scooters racing and beeping past, or even the squealing train brakes from the station just one street over.

I hugged my knees to my chest, desperate for sleep, despite chest-aching tiredness after a shivering night in the olive grove followed by half a day clinging to a hard fold-down seat in the corridor of an overpacked train. I had a week to endure until my flight home, which the airline agent had reminded me—before my phone died on the train—was a rock-bottom fare that was neither changeable nor refundable.

My bunk was a sagging raft sinking in an ocean of shame. Whatever had made me think that I could simply board a plane and insinuate myself into a man's life, his family, his neighborhood, his life-long commitments, all of which, like his language and culture, were alien to me? Or, more truthfully, to whom I was the alien. How stupid I was—how desperately naïve!—to imagine that he would absorb me into his world, this man I barely knew. To mistake hospitality for acceptance. To misinterpret sweet words and sex for love. And the more I'd been wrong, the harder I'd thrown myself at him! I should have jumped off that sea cliff at the end of the world; at least I'd have died happy in my delusions.

There were always the train tracks, conveniently nearby.

The woman below hissed, "Shhhh!" I blew her a razzie.

I MUST HAVE FINALLY dozed off, until a truck horn in the street below startled me awake. Daylight and a naked ceiling bulb stabbed my eyes. My sleepy-stupid brain took a moment to re-member where I was. All I knew was my ankle itched terribly; I sat up to scratch.

"Oi."

Sitting on the top bunk opposite mine, a girl waved. Young and thin, with nearly black, perfect skin like a doll, her eyes narrowed to slits when she smiled. I forced a smile back and scratched my bug bites, watching her feed herself with twig-like fingers from a small plastic tub. My stomach let out an angry snarl; I hadn't eaten in at least a day. The girl held out her con-tainer and offered a thumbs-up. Without waiting for a response, she slid off the bunk and stepped over to mine, borne on a waft of pepper and garlic.

I accepted a boiled peanut which set fire to my tongue and brought new tears to my eyes, the first in days not from sadness. After the initial shock, it was delicious. I had nothing to offer in return, but she insisted I take more, then brought over an open can of flaky, oily fish. I gathered from hand signals and a few recognizable words that she was from Mozambique and spoke some Portuguese, though not a word of English or Italian. She was alone in Rome, unable to communicate why she'd come. Yet she smiled as though she didn't have a worry in the world.

When we finished, the girl carried her empty containers to

the bathroom. I lay down again, stroking my gurgling belly. Her small act of kindness uncorked a fresh bout of sobbing. If only she knew how selfish I was, how heartlessly toxic I was toward other people's lives, she'd have saved her generosity for someone more deserving, like last night's cockroach. She'd wasted precious food on a worthless lump of flesh.

Fingers brushed my cheek. Soft, sibilant speech attempted to soothe me, though I didn't understand a thing. The girl's large eyes pleaded with concern. How I would have loved to unload my soul to this beautiful stranger. And how lucky she was to be safe behind the language barrier, so that I couldn't poison her wide-open heart!

Wait, which hypocrite issued such a thought? Wasn't my calling in life supposed to be enhancing communication between people from far-flung corners of the world? Great, I'd found something new to hate myself for.

The girl clapped three times and tapped her chest. "Halima."

I clapped back. "Serena."

I climbed off the bed and we hugged. Whatever hopes or demons had led her to Rome, she simply seemed happy. She seemed to be telling me to do something to stop myself from plummeting deeper into the abyss. I would go out. I would try to change my ticket. Then I'd buy food to share in return with this sweet young woman.

That's when I discovered my shoes were missing.

I hunted under bunks for signs of footwear, but not a sole in sight. The last thing I needed right now was the prospect of walking barefoot in search of new sneakers in the world epicenter of overpriced designer-brand accessories. I extended my search into the hallway. At the far end a big-boned blonde sat reading beside the window.

"Excuse me," I said. "Have you seen any shoes? Someone's stolen mine."

Without looking up from her book, she said, "They are not stolen." Her accent sounded Germanic.

"Then do you know where they are?"

Her face twisted as if that were the stupidest question ever asked. "It is neither proper nor hygienic to bring shoes into the place where one sleeps."

"Are you saying that you took them? Where the hell are they?"

"I do not respond to profanity." She held her book almost to her nose; conversation over and out.

I tried the second floor lobby. Two worn armchairs and nearly every bit of floor space were occupied by young backpacker types hunched over electronic devices, since this was apparently the only place in the building with proper Wi-Fi. Along the back wall were dozens of neatly arranged shoes. A bearded guy rolled his eyes to the floor above, and said to me in a Nordic accent, "Crazy shoe lady."

I settled on the floor beside an empty socket and plugged in my charger. The phone took its time firing up. Several messages came in, one with a photo: Elias smiling with a hamster on either shoulder.

I quietly mouthed, "My little family."

Wait...what did I just say?

Chapter 32

As attractive as the idea was of spending a week in the ancient capital of the western world, *spend* was the governing word. I had to get home.

The Middle Eastern-looking guy at the reception desk was no help when I asked where the airline office was. A lanky Australian in the corner of the lobby looked up from his tablet and waved me over. After a few false leads to offices near the airport, he found an airline service desk on the via Bissolati, fifteen or twenty minutes' walk from the hostel.

I headed outside, carrying everything of any remote value, in case another hostel inmate found them "improper" for me to keep. A light drizzle gave the narrow streets a dreamy Old World presence. It also made the pavements slippery as snot.

The city was noisy, traffic-choked, the air pungent enough to taste. At the Piazza della Repubblica I dodged across three or four lanes of speeding cars, delivery trucks, and certifiably insane Vespa maniacs, in order to view my first genuine Roman fountain up close: four young nymphs, naked to the world, fountains spitting at them all day long. I could relate to that.

I found the airline office—a counter inside a modern-ish building representing several airlines—where I queued for at least half an hour before finally being granted an audience with the perfectly groomed young woman behind the desk.

I unfolded my reservation printout and slid it across to her.

"I need to return earlier. Please, if there's any way."

She typed something into her computer, pursed her lips, then said in lightly-accented English, "I'm sorry, miss. This ticket may not be changed."

"Even if I pay extra?"

"I'm sorry." She pushed the paper back to me and glanced past my shoulder toward the next customer. I spied her name tag.

"Giulia, please. It's urgent."

"May I know the nature of the urgency?"

"I'm nearly out of money."

"I am sorry, miss. Exceptions only for medical emergencies. Perhaps your embassy can help you."

Giulia couldn't have been more than three or four years older than me, and her only ring was on the wrong finger. I decided to go for broke. "My stupid boyfriend in Puglia slept with me for a week before I found out he's engaged. See these scratches on my neck? Here, see? That's where his crazy fiancée beat me up. I've got to get out of here, Giulia!"

Her eyebrows rose and her lips funneled. She typed something. "I put you on a special waiting list. It's the best I can do."

I clasped my hands in prayer. "Thank you, Giulia. Thank you."

"If you see the asshole—" She made a chopping motion at her neck, an Italian hand gesture anyone would understand.

I FOUND A COFFEE bar and splurged on a double espresso, while watching people and traffic drift by. The sky had cleared to a rich powder blue.

I'd been *coraggiosa,* as Alessandro had said, in coming to Italy by myself, hadn't I? What good had it done me? What life did I have? What life did I want? I was in limbo in an exotic Purgatory, waiting to get on a plane.

Back home it was past two in the morning. I sent a brief text to those who needed to know:

In Rome. Hope to return early. Don't ask

Less than a minute later, a reply from Zuzie:

In Tustin don't ask either

Oh my God! She was supposed to be in Hawaii until Thursday. Maybe half an hour later, my last drops of coffee long cold, I was nodding off, thinking I might return to the hostel for a nap, when the message tone jolted me awake.

Can I ask something else then

Who was it from? Elias. I replied:

Long as it's not about olives

A few minutes elapsed before his next message arrived.

If you could choose anyone in the world,
who would you want as a dinner guest?

What was that supposed to mean? I thought for a moment.

I don't know. Jane Austen

She's dead

You didn't specify. Make it Steven
Pinker. Not for his polemics about
violence. His linguistics theories.

Nerd

Who would you invite?

Elias, a minute later:

Jennifer Lawrence. Not for her
tush. Her charity work

Me: *Go to sleep*

ON THE WALK BACK I found a small grocery, where I bought bread and cheese, a couple apples, sparkling water, and a bag of roasted peanuts, enough food for two.

But Halima was gone. Her bag wasn't there. The bunk was freshly made for the next guest. I hoped this was good news: someone had come for her. Sitting in a chair eating, getting crumbs all over the floor, I knew what real loneliness felt like.

With everyone out enjoying the sights of Rome, the hostel was quieter by day than during the night. I lay down on my bunk for a much needed nap.

A message alert startled me into consciousness. The ceiling was a blur; the light in the room had changed. Had I slept through the afternoon? I had trouble focusing on the phone screen until I sat up and let the cobwebs recede.

From Steve, a photo of a bouquet: carnations and roses.

> *Stopped by to bring you this. Your*
> *housemate said you're in Italy. Hope you*
> *don't mind I gave these to her, seemed like*
> *she could use them. Your friend, Steve*

What a good man he was. The believer in happy endings. Maybe I finally understood him a little. When you sorely needed convincing that life was good, you could simply go to the theatre and find happiness on demand, with dancing and singing you could whistle any time you wanted those feelings back.

I'd really hurt him, the poor guy. And myself, most likely. What was so wrong about going with a guy like Steve? He was honest, making his own decisions, carving out a life for himself, his feet on the ground, not like me.

And maybe just a little bit dull.

I could use dull right now. And a pee.

I carried my phone into the bathroom, thinking how to reply to Steve. Maybe: *I get it now.*

I prodded the screen to wake the phone, when it buzzed in my hand. A new text from Elias.

Would you want to be famous? How so?

I lingered on the toilet and thought about it.

Don't think I could handle famous.
Rich might work though

He had his response ready:

Famous would be cool, like Tim
Berners-Lee famous, guy who
invented the world wide web

Cute, I thought. While I washed up, another message:

When did you last sing to yourself?

I slipped on the slimy tiled floor, nearly banging my head on the mirror. Whatever game Elias was playing treaded dangerous territory. My fingers shook so much I had to correct myself three times to compose four simple words:

On a mountain top

I'd almost succeeded in flushing it from my mind. The memory made my body itch violently. Or maybe it was because I hadn't washed in three days. I pulled two cardboard-stiff towels from a cabinet and lay one across the bathroom floor. After a terrifying shower during which I worried the curtain rod, seemingly fixed to the wall by rust alone, would smack my head, I found another message:

Last time for me singing while watching
Americas got talent. I could of won

And another:

If you could live to 90 and choose either the
mind or the body of a 30 year old for the last
60 years of your life, which would you want?

I was so tired the walls pulsed and shifted color, like an opium dream. I threw my shoes onto my bunk and climbed up after them. Just in time: the door opened and in walked the blonde shoe thief, who dropped onto the mattress below. So she was my sensitive bunkmate! I threw the blanket over my offending footwear.

Though I was dead-tired, Elias's question tumbled inside my head until I knew that I would get no rest until it was answered.

I messaged:

> *Does that mean when I turn 30 I*
> *suddenly get a 90 year old body*

He: *I'd have to read the contract*

> Me: *I'll take the body. My mind*
> *gives me too much grief. You?*

He: *Body. But not this one. Trade with some*
surfer – he gets my mind I get his pecs

I was halfway into the land of dreams, when another message beeped.

Name 3 things you and I have in common.

Later too tired, I wrote back.

I switched the phone to airplane mode and curled up under the sheet.

Chapter 33

*M*y phone frothed with messages when I switched it off airplane mode in the morning.

U OK? From Miko.

You were right, I wrote back.

About the pervert?

He isn't a pervert

What was I right about

About trust

I spent the next day exploring Rome on my own. Every corner seemed to have its own statue or fountain or plaque referring to some historical person or event. The ancient Colosseum was overrun with feral cats—descendants of the lions which had once snacked on Christians? I almost wished they'd devour the chattering swarms of V-finger selfie Chinese tour groups. Outside, I dodged packs of underaged pickpockets and descended into the Roman Forum.

I fumbled with the photocopied guide borrowed from the guesthouse and wandered, awestruck among the ruins of the ancient center of world power. On these paving stones, Roman citizens had once gathered and argued, rushed to work, shopped for vegetables, taken the kids for a stroll. Each column, every monument, every arch boasted its own story and spectacle, until the very accumulation of awesomeness lost its impact. The grandiose sites of the Eternal City moved me far less than the potholed back lanes, rugged stone walls, and the grandfatherly olive trees of Puglia. Here in Rome, history pounded its chest at every turn. In Puglia, history shrugged and laughed and invited you for a drink. I realized with a lump in my throat how sorely I missed the place.

I rested on a pedestal in a little rose garden beside the House of the Vestal Virgins. Did they have such beautiful roses back then? My eyes feasted on the enormous waxy petals, red and bursting with life against the somber gray ruins. Inside that building and courtyard specially-chosen women had been confined most of their lives with the single task of keeping a flame burning for the goddess of fire. Anyone who broke their vow of chastity was buried alive.

My phone beeped. Would Elias ever stop? After my brief chat with Miko I'd replied to his question about three things we had in common: *Underpaid, nonsmokers, hate pineapple on pizza.*

His message read: *Boring answer. Here's mine. Nerds in our own way. Dreamers. Self-inflicted loners.*

Ouch. Tears spurted like bullets, and I had nothing in my purse to wipe them with. I cried over my spoiled fantasy, the humiliation I'd heaped on myself. I cried over the love I'd begun to feel for a flat, homely region at the end of the world, which I'd never belong to. Mostly I cried over his last three words, seated alone in a garden where women had been confined for life, all their passion and joy and dreams left to wilt like these lustful red roses.

A group of Asian tourists stopped to take pictures of me. Within minutes I'd be all over Chinese social media: white girl crying in ancient Rome. I barked, "Go away!"

On the way back I stopped at the airline office. Giulia didn't recognize me until I said, "Boyfriend," with the head-chopping gesture. Then she was all business, typing away. And then she was all pity: "Nothing yet. Sorry."

Another message:

What's the one thing you'd change
about how you were raised?

NEXT MORNING THE EMPTY bunks across from mine were filled by a pair of bubbly Irish women, Mary and Fiona. In the brief residential half-life of this hostel, I was now an elder veteran. I warned them about the shoe thief, gave instructions about how to coax a dribble of hot water from the shower; the secret socket I'd found to recharge electronics; which hostel staff were the least rude. Grateful for my survival tips, they invited me to join them exploring.

Mary and Fiona were less interested in historical sights than in following the old adage, "When in Rome..." After passing through a bohemian district—all eccentric little shops and exotic eateries—we found an unassuming working class restaurant, where we ordered unbelievably cheap pizza and house red wine, and talked.

As they put it, their home village was a misbegotten bastard of stones and sheep stuck to a tumor dangling from Ireland's left buttocks. They'd saved for two years to travel together for as long as their money lasted. They'd just spent a month in Portugal and Spain and were working their way through Italy. I told them I admired their guts to just get up and go.

"'Tisn't so very hard," Mary said. "All you need is to feel suffocated by your fecking backwards busybody little town. Right, love?" Fiona bobbed a nod.

I told them about Sandro and his very opposite response to being rooted down. I caught myself embellishing the details, as though the experience had already attained some distance, had taken on the trappings of a fable rather than a fresh gaping hole in my chest.

"Sorry to hear about your gentleman," Mary said. "Have you another man back home?"

"I was dating this guy, but I don't know..." I'd forgotten to text him, too.

Fiona spoke at last, but only to order another pitcher of wine.

"So what's wrong with him then, the guy back home?" Mary said.

"Nothing's wrong. That's what's wrong!" The wine, rather than fogging my head, seemed to be clearing it. "He's nice. Clean-cut—even his car's clean-cut. A little old-fashioned, holds the door for you, never swears, light drinker at most."

Mary and Fiona clinked glasses. "Not an Irishman, then. So far so good."

"I mean, he's got good, steady work, saving to buy a house. Makes no secret that he's eager to settle down, have kids someday. The kind of guy you can just tell would be a great dad and a great neighbor..."

Fiona nodded and said in a scratchy voice, "Living death."

"Truth!" Mary said. "Drop the fellow. You'd be a bird clipping its own wings before she ever had a chance to fly!"

We all clinked glasses. "Here's to flying," I said.

Mary and Fiona leaned into each other and kissed, oblivious to the stares from the mostly workingmen diners. I confessed to them how jealous they made me. And now all I wanted to do was get home and start over again, to reboot my life.

I paid my share and left, and was soon back in the familiar queue at the airline office.

"I'm afraid there's no change" Giulia reported. "Very difficult with such kind of ticket."

The next customer started to wedge in front of me. I elbowed him back.

"Meet me after work, okay? I buy you a drink," Giulia said.

"I don't want to make this into your problem," I said.

"What problem? A glass of wine, girl talk. Problem is for the waiters who must hear us."

We met outside promptly at six and walked two blocks to a wine and coffee bar in a busy side street. I was still light-headed from lunch, but Giulia insisted on red wine: "The color of broken hearts."

She told me she'd trained to be an air hostess, until she discovered how scared she was of flying, and preferred this desk job. She'd been going out with the same guy for two years. They were talking of marrying next spring.

"He must save up some money if he wants me," she said. "Oh, but even if he doesn't, I will take him. But don't tell him that, please."

A new text came in. I thought Elias had quit his little game, but instead he'd advanced a level.

If a crystal ball could tell you the truth
about yourself, your life, your future,
what would you want to know?

Giulia asked why I was rolling my eyes.

"Nothing. This guy, just a friend, keeps sending me ridiculous questions. This is a toughie." I showed her the text.

"What else does he ask you?"

I scrolled through his last few questions. She nodded knowingly.

"I think this man is very clever, tries to reel you in like a fish."

"He's just being a nerd."

"Is he handsome?"

"No-o-o-o," my voice laughing.

She toyed with her napkin, regarding me for a moment with an imperceptible smile. "I think this is a good man for you."

"Why? Because he's not handsome?"

"First I ask you: your man in Puglia. Is he handsome?"

"Like Adonis."

Giulia held out both arms as though to say, *See? Argument over.* "Okay. I explain to you. You know how men always think a beautiful woman must be stupid? Dumb blonde, yes? We know this is bullshit, right?"

"Of course."

"But for men, it's true. The more handsome is a man, the more stupid and asshole he is."

"Oh, come on. You don't really believe that?"

She flashed a dirty look to the eavesdroppers at the next table, then leaned in and half-whispered, "Okay. Dalai Lama. Good looking?"

"Not particularly."

"What about Bill Gates? Gandhi? Mister Bean. Frodo. Stop me when I name a hottie."

"Uh..."

"See? The smart, good ones, not so handsome. Now you consider the assholes. So many lover boys! Loki. Tom Cruise. Draco Malfoy. Stalin as young man...*cara mia!*" She fanned imaginary post-coital heat from her face.

"But Alessandro...he isn't an asshole."

Giulia caught the waiter's eye and tapped her empty glass. She turned back to me, mirroring my seriousness. "Yes, I understand, Serena. If you insist he is not an asshole, then you are a fool. But I do not think you are. So we try another word. In Italian he is *stronzo*. In English it means 'piece of shit.'"

The waiter appeared with a bottle and poured us both refills. When he left, Giulia said, "Our server—not bad looking, right? Future serial killer."

"And your boyfriend?"

"You decide." She pulled up a picture on her phone. He had kind, laughing eyes and mouth. But not even his athletic upper body compensated for a too-small nose and too-wide jaw. "You know how I know it's real, him and me? We cut each other's hair. Like chimpanzees who groom one another."

Some chimpanzee. Giulia's hair was shoulder-length, ruler-straight, parted to one side, immaculately cut and perfect for her diamond-shaped face. We clinked glasses and drank.

"So tell me what happened with your handsome asshole," she said.

For the second time that day I told the story. It was starting to take on legendary proportions. When I came to the bulldozers, she covered her mouth and laughed. The waiter, taking an order at the next table, turned his head like he'd been listening in.

"I know," I said. "It sounds like I made it all up. I wish I had! Then I could have written a happy ending." My eyes burned. I tipped some wine into my mouth, choking as it went down.

"Happy endings are bullshit, don't you think?"

I lifted my glass into a beam of light from the window. The wine took on a gem-like color, sparking a pleasant memory of a garnet bracelet my mother gave me as a child. "I don't know. But don't you ever dream that life was really like that—everyone gets their wish? The girl gets the guy, the guy gets the job. Everyone goes out singing and dancing, like in Broadway musicals, know what I mean?"

God help me, what was I turning into?

"Yes, I know. This is very charming, very American, believing in such sweet stories, always the good guy wins. In Italy maybe our thinking is different. We don't have your musical theater. Here we think life is like our operas, always such grand and beautiful tragedy. They also are fantasies. But perhaps more close to reality than your American good-guy-always-wins."

The waiter came by again. I waved no. Giulia had another.

"I'm afraid I haven't seen any operas," I said.

"Ah, you must! Do you know my favorite? *Madama Butterfly*.

Do you know the story? No? I tell you, okay? In Japan there is a lonely young woman who meets a handsome, rich foreign man."

Uh-oh.

"He is so good to her, he is her dream. Such love they speak! They sing a duet of great passion, then he takes her to bed."

Singing along to Italian love ballads on the car radio. Lovemaking under the stars.

"Of course he leaves her, making sweet promises to return and she will be his bride. Then she sings the most beautiful aria in the history of music—oh, I love this song—about her dream of a wonderful life she will have with this man."

I caught a choke in my throat. "Uh, let's change the—"

"But all along, he planned to marry a woman of his own nationality. And—*oops la!*" She slapped her mouth and actually blushed.

Yes, let's not go there, I thought.

"No, let's hear the end," I said.

"Well, she...she meets the wife. Then Butterfly sings another gorgeous song, and..." She mimed holding a dagger.

"She kills the wife?"

"That would be your happy ending, yes? I'm sorry. In the original version she cuts her own throat, but now many performances, she stabs herself in the stomach, which I believe has more drama."

I downed the last lingering drop in my glass. "Aren't there any, like, happier operas?"

She counted on her burgundy fingernails. "Mm. *Rigoletto,* the girl dies in the end. *La Traviata,* the girl dies in the end." Looking back up: "It appears not."

"Right. Can you ask the waiter for a butcher's knife?"

Giulia placed her hand on my arm. "Oh, Serena, I am so sorry to give you pain. But this is what I'm talking about—art is art and life is life, and I love both. It is useless to wish your life can be like a story. This man does not deserve your dreams, and he is not worth to punish yourself."

We sat in silence for a moment. I was tempted right then to tap out my forgotten text to Steve, with an apology attached. Not that he would understand. To think that *I'd* criticized *him,* in my mind at least, for loving his happily-ever-after musicals. At least he could differentiate them from real life. I was the one guilty of living inside a half-formed romance novel daydream. And then losing the plot.

Giulia spun her glass between her fingers, finished the wine, and broke into a grin.

"So how do you answer his question? Your friend."

I looked at her, uncomprehending.

She pointed at my phone.

"Oh, that. Him. I don't know. What would I ask a crystal ball? How about...Is there ever such a thing as a happy ending?"

She shook her head. "Wrong question. Better you ask: Can you have a happy new beginning? I believe there is such possibility. So, I see you tomorrow, yes? Hope I can have good news."

BACK AT THE HOSTEL that evening, Elias's texts kept me company, his questions progressively more probing, less whimsical.

> *If you could wake up tomorrow with*
> *one new ability, what would it be?*
>
> *Do you think your childhood was*
> *happier than most other people's?*

I lay on the bunk starting at the spots on the ceiling, composing answers in my head. His questions had hijacked my thoughts; I'd hardly given a thought to Alessandro since yesterday. How had he done that? Were these some kind of hypnotic suggestions, designed to play with your mind? No, they didn't feel that way. My little breakdown in the ancient rose garden had been cathartic. Since that moment my soul had lightened—I still wasn't exactly delighted with where my life had brought me, but I no longer wanted to run into the slaughterhouse traffic around the Colosseum.

His confessional replies to his own questions had made me know him too. Maybe he wasn't just an awkward, irritating nerd. Or maybe he and I both were. Maybe he was just like me, desperately seeking someone to trust.

Maybe this was what it felt like to have a true friend.

I drifted into warm slumber seeing his face in the mold stains in the ceiling paint.

Chapter 34

*I*n the morning the first thing I did was grab my phone. Sure enough:

What do you value most in a friendship?

Honesty? Too obvious. Same dress size? Too flip.

I went downstairs to the bar and lingered over a coffee while I composed answers to questions that had moved beyond banter to deeply-felt inquiries.

What's your most terrible memory?

I described the day I discovered my father had left without saying goodbye, and then finding my mother passed out drunk and nearly drowning in the bath. Elias told me about showing up for school in his pajama bottoms.

*What's one thing that's too
serious to joke about?*

Genocide, I wrote, then deleted. Cancer? Suicide? I considered carefully before I sent my response.

Love, I mean real love, not dating

His answer to the question:

You

Rather than feel ruffled by his remark, I was totally sucked into the dialogue. Little by little, one drop at a time, he was pulling things out of me that I'd never shared with anyone. Maybe it was the timing. Maybe right now I simply needed this letting go. Things I thought I'd be ashamed to reveal instead exhilarated me by letting them see light. And like it or not, I was learning more about Elias, such a strange, and strangely clever, guy.

A few minutes passed. I was about to order another coffee when an oddly-worded message came in:

> *Tell your partner what you like about them; be very honest this time, saying things that you might not say to someone you've just met.*

Another immediately followed:

> *Last one a misfire. Disregard!*

What the heck was that about? I copied the text and put it into a search engine. But the bar had no Wi-Fi. I ran up to the guesthouse, grabbed my computer and headed to the lobby. The search result popped up within seconds:

"36 Questions to Make Anyone Fall in Love with You."

This was no frivolous *Cosmopolitan* list, but developed and tested by a team of research psychologists to "explore whether intimacy between two strangers can be accelerated," using a system of "sustained, escalating, reciprocal, personal self-disclosure." I checked my chat history. His questions matched up exactly, in the prescribed order.

I screamed, "How goddamn sleazy desperate can you get?"

Every eye in the lobby swiveled up. Fiona's voice trilled across the room: "Your man the house painter or the olive farmer?"

"Another one."

"My, the lass gets around!"

I hammered out a furious message:

Was that number 28 or 29?

The apologies started pouring in immediately. I deleted each pathetic one without a glance.

I shut off the phone and went out. I walked along the Tiber River, crossed to the Vatican, crossed back again and traversed the city center until my legs couldn't carry me anymore.

I found a bench and pulled out a beat-up novel borrowed from the hostel's bookshelf. But I couldn't concentrate, my thoughts consumed with anger and confusion and betrayal and more than anything else, humiliation. I felt so used! I gave up and found my way to the airline office. Giulia leaned around her current customer and gave me a sad shrug.

That night I couldn't sleep again. The shoe thief snored, while Mary and Fiona lay tangled in each other on the opposite bunk. Elias's abortive question remained stuck in my head. *Tell your partner what you like about them.* Presumably "your partner" meant him.

Be very honest, the question had said. That he was a stupid, immature, manipulative, bumbling shit? The truth, and nothing but the truth. Okay, granted, he was generous, at least with me. But generosity was easily contrived. Smart? Big deal. Most people I knew qualified as smart.

One of the Irish women released a flutey, contented sigh in her dreams. I turned to the wall, letting the hubbub of bar patrons through the window lull me like so much white noise. It occurred to me that this was the second night in a row that I hadn't paid a thought to Sandro.

MARY, FIONA, AND I set out together in the morning. I was angry at myself for allowing my visit to one of the grandest cities on earth to become smothered in gloom. Although I was down to my last few euros, I was determined for just one day to have fun. Tomorrow I could rummage garbage cans for food or drown myself in the Trevi Fountain.

We shot a thousand lewd selfies in front of every nude statue we happened upon, had lunch in a greasy kebab place, then in the afternoon wended our way to the Piazza di Spagna, parking ourselves halfway up the Spanish Steps among other tourists and couples and students and weirdos. There probably wasn't a real Roman anywhere in sight. But the air was brisk, the sky dotted with puffy clouds.

A group of Lithuanian choral students rose right in front of us and gave an impromptu *a capella* performance while jugglers and break dancers did their routines in the square below. Fiona bought us gelatos from a street vendor. This was the Rome I'd wanted to experience: spontaneous, playful, the air filled with music. My friends held their ice creams to each other, and I made it a giggling threesome for pictures. We vowed to stay here all day.

A phone message beeped. I almost didn't check. Elias hadn't sent anything since yesterday, so I figured he'd gotten the hint. But the status bar revealed that it was indeed from him. I was about to shove the phone back, until my eyes caught the preview line:

grandparents

I sighed. Another stupid question about ancestry? The scrolling preview replayed:

We're going to be

My eyes blinked like they'd caught some dust. The message preview replayed a third time:

We're going to be grandparents

I unlocked the screen and checked the full message. That was all it said. I wrote back:

WTF?

Seconds later the phone rang. Elias. I hesitated, then decided, why not?

"What are you talking about?" I said.

"Well, first thing is we gotta rename a hamster. Whaddaya think of Laurel and *Harriet?"*

He kept quiet while the meaning sunk in.

Finally, I said, "Are you sure?"

"Heck, I been going all night. It's like four a.m. here and I think by now I may be the world's leading expert on hamster midwifery."

"But how did you—?"

"He—I mean, she, like, made this little nest in the corner. I mean my living room, not the cage. And then just sat there all day. I picked him—her!—up and could feel the fetuses—or is it *feti?*—like little tiny lumps. Before she bit the shit out of me."

My eyes welled up. "Have the babies come?"

"Not yet. From what I'm guessing, could be another three, four days."

"I...I...gotta go."

"Right. You want to buy cigars or should I?"

"Really. I better go."

A rumbling formed in the pit of my stomach and rose like magma into my throat. My darling, sweet, innocent little Hardy was about to be a mother. Which made me... Elias was right! I sprang to my feet.

"I'm going to be a grandmother!"

People around me cheered and applauded. The Lithuanian choir huddled, then broke out into Handel's Hallelujah Chorus.

Mary tugged my shirt. "What's going on?"

"Explain later. Gotta run!"

I bounded up the steps two at a time, groups and couples splitting to let me through. Then I ran and ran and ran, dodging around pedestrians along the via Sistina. A guy on a Vespa pulled alongside and called, *"Dove vai?"*

Cue the most adrenalin-pumping ride of my life around buses and cars hurtling every direction, capped by a careening U-turn across three honking lanes before screeching to a halt in front of the building. I rewarded him with a peck on the lips and dashed up the steps.

I flung the doors open with both arms.

"Giulia! I'M GOING TO BE A GRANDMOTHER!"

Twenty heads turned to look me up and down. Giulia beckoned me forward, apologizing to people in line. I gave her the story through gulps of air, then: "You gotta get me home!"

She spoke into her phone at lightning speed: *"...emergenza familiare...nonna...si, si, è vero..."* She called another number, arguing back and forth while jabbing her keyboard, nose to the monitor. With a final, *"Molte grazie,"* she put down the phone and typed frantically, waving away my questions. Then she nearly smothered me with a printout.

"Your flight departs in three hours forty-five minutes."

"Oh my God! I don't know how to thank you, Giulia!"

"By not talking. Go!"

"Come to California for your honeymoon!"

"First you come to my wedding. Now go! *Vai! Vai!*"

I went.

Chapter 35

I refused contact with all non-rodent life forms until further notice.

Elias left the cages outside the door so I wouldn't have to deal with him. Hardy—Harriet, for now—had blown up like a pear.

I spent the whole next day in bed. My suitcase and its contents lay scattered on the floor, reflecting my own state of being: split wide open, guts exposed for nobody to see or care about. Gaping at the four stark walls of the "home" I'd been so anxious to flee back to: a whitewashed prison of my own making. Serving a sentence I deserved for blind stupidity in mismanaging my life.

I scrounged a can of macaroni in the kitchen, then shoved it back. Beans had fewer connotations. I ate them cold on my mattress, then fell into a doze.

My eyes cracked open to an almost-full moon beaming at me through the window. I shut the curtains so violently that two hooks popped off. I never wanted to see the moon or stars or planets ever again.

Italy already seemed far, far away in the remote past. My only reminders were trinkets: a stone from the seaside cliff, a pair of espresso cups with the Lecce civic coat of arms, and the red chiffon scarf I discovered to my horror I hadn't returned to the Griko guy's girlfriend. Somewhere I had a paper scrap with his scrawled address; I would mail it to him.

The one person I couldn't avoid was Zuzie, who by my

second day back had lost patience. She caught me en route to the bathroom.

"Don't know what happened to you over there. Unless you got mixed up in murder, I don't quite get what you're hiding from."

Zuzie guided me to the kitchen counter. Steve's wilting flowers sat in a plastic pitcher at the end. She filled two glasses from a box of wine and forced one into my hand. "Here. Drink and talk."

"In Italy they spit out crap like this," I said.

"So would I if I gave a shit," Zuzie said. "Now spill. What happened?"

"No, you tell me. Did you even *go* to Hawaii?"

"Sure did. Then Professor Lover Boy's wifey decides to surprise him. Sitting there waiting in his room when we come back from a reception drunk off our ass."

"Oh my God."

Zuzie finished her glass with one gulp and went for a refill. "Didja know Hawaiians used to toss virgins into volcanoes? All I know is, thank Pele I ain't no virgin, cause that's what that bitch surely had in mind."

"I don't think that legend is true," I said. "But anyway, you seem pretty calm about it."

She fished something from her wine with a fingernail. "I dunno. I guess you fool around with a married guy..." She shrugged. "Shoulda known better, right? Have a few laughs, break a few hearts. Have a few clumps of hair torn out... What about your guy?"

Whatever showed on my face made her eyes bug out.

"No. Don't tell me," she said. "God's sake. Bastard's married."

"Engaged." I turned away, hating being so transparent, hating being unable to simply shrug it off like her.

Zuzie reached across the counter and stroked my arm. "Hey, hey. Tell me you had some good moments. I mean, *Italy!* Wasn't it wonderful at least for a while?"

"More wonderful than could ever be real. Stupid! I'm so stupid!"

"Shut up, Serena. It was real. It. Was. Real. That's the part you keep here." Her fist thumped her heart.

I sipped cheap red wine, remembering my last bittersweet glass before this, in a Roman bar with Giulia. "The color of broken hearts."

"I guess I just need a few days, that's all."

"That long? Your dude's obviously less of a jackass than mine. Took me around eighteen, max twenty-four hours. Come here, sister."

We leaned across the counter and gave each other a big, warm, rocking hug, neither of us letting go even when our elbows knocked both glasses onto the kitchen floor.

"Hate to say it," I said, "but that's where that swill belongs."

THAT NIGHT TINY SQUEAKS intruded into my half-waking dreams. For a moment I thought I was back in Puglia, someone treading the hallway floorboards. Then a louder squeak, like a whistle.

I exploded from the covers. In the pre-dawn light I counted four little squirmy pink creatures. Then another crawled from under Harriet. So cute I wanted to scream, but covered my mouth for fear of frightening them.

I followed Elias's printed instructions: fetched a dish of water, stuffed blankets around the cage for warmth, then I lay on the floor watching Harriet groom her newborns. They were beautiful, innocent, wriggling joyfully through their first daybreak in this big, strange world.

I willed them long hamster lives. I willed them happiness. If baby hamsters could face this struggle that is life, I supposed so could I.

I filled my four remaining days off by searching for classroom teaching jobs. Most wanted a higher degree than I possessed, minimum two years classroom experience, professional references. That didn't stop me from blasting applications, with my old student testimonial video, all over the country and the world. I was barely easing off jetlag, yet already I wanted to run away again.

THURSDAY NIGHT I COULDN'T sleep. In a few hours I would face my students. What would I say to them? What would they say to me? I genuinely felt neither anger nor resentment. All that they'd done—other than hundreds of thousands of euros in damage—was hasten the inevitable. I fully expected no one to show up.

In the morning the hamster pups were so adorably frisky, I forgot to check the clock until three minutes before my first lesson. No time to do my hair; I tied it back with the red tarantella scarf.

Bieber was right on time; I supposed his mother left him no choice. We stuck strictly to the textbook, no unscripted dialog, which was just as well, since his substitute teacher had obviously been way too lenient. He flubbed the subjunctive all over the place.

I prompted: "I insist you—*blank*—here tomorrow."

"I insist you are here tomorrow."

"No, Bieber. I insist you *be* here tomorrow."

He put on his familiar nervous grin. "Aiya! I don't understand!"

"You don't need to understand. It's something you'll get a feeling for." Aggression crept into my voice. "I'm sure subjunctives will be in your TOEFL exam. Come on, let's work. Try making a sentence."

"Mother wants I be a banker."

"No. You can't form a subjunctive with *want,* because, um... it requires a complement and...oh, God, English is so *screwed up!*" I pressed my eyelids. I wasn't ready for this. I wasn't in the mood for lessons at all.

"I insist..." Bieber spoke softly, tentatively, "...the teacher...stop...feeling sad."

308

My body let go like a deflating balloon. I leaned in toward the webcam, that conduit carrying me across the world into the room of this innocent, warm-hearted boy who'd just made a correct subjunctive.

"And I insist that the student listen to my words. Bieber, I want you to know that I am not angry. I am not upset at you. What you did, you and my other students—how can I say this? It made Alessandro understand what he really wants. That isn't subjunctive, by the way. You did him a favor. And a bigger favor for me. Because I learned the truth about him. And myself."

All I got from Bieber was a head-hanging nod.

"And now it's over. Finished," I said. "We continue with lessons, same as before."

He wouldn't look up. Something wasn't right.

"Bieber, is there something you aren't telling me? Did anything else happen that I don't know about?"

A faint head shake.

"Bieber?" I raised a curled pinky to the camera.

A moment's hesitation. He raised his.

"No more bad things," he said. "I insist that Teacher Serena believe me."

"Good subjunctive. See you Monday."

YASMIN WAS MORE LIKE a wound-up spring, eager to zip through Lesson 30, avoiding every topic except the text. I left time at the end for "special words", but for once she didn't ask, merely fidgeted with her headscarf, wished me a good day and signed off.

Vladimir, whom I dreaded facing, should have been next, but his name had vanished from my calendar, today, tomorrow, next week. I tried to send him a message, but his contact information had been locked.

I had one more scheduled at the usual time of noon: A. Buonaventura. Why hadn't he canceled or requested a change of instructor? What if he suggested we just be teacher and student? Or what if he claimed a change of heart, claimed to want me back? That would be worse because I might give in.

The second hand on the kitchen clock circled to two minutes past twelve. I stared at the screen, rigid as a monk, not even brushing an annoying hair from my eye. I inhaled and exhaled, in and out, counting breaths, not even fidgeting my butt, adjusted my headset, checked the computer's clock, checked the wi-fi connection.

By ten minutes past the hour I knew he wasn't coming.

I put a call through to the office. I would ask Marisa to remove Sandro from my calendar. I'd tell her I wasn't making progress with him, he needed a stricter approach, every detail outlined in advance for the rest of his life, like his work, like his marriage. Marisa didn't pick up. She sent a text reply:

In meetings. Don't forget your 4:00.
Call me after. Need to talk.

My last time slot had been blocked out in yellow: a free intro lesson for Y.L. Chamiak in Minsk. A freebie on my first day back? It seemed unfair. Though the way the trip had ravaged my bank account, I desperately needed the students.

My three o'clock Ecuadorian fitness coach welcomed me back by teasing that I'd gained weight, then I punished her with grammar the way she liked. Afterward, I had eight minutes to prepare for the free student. His profile showed male; employer: military; self-assessed English level: intermediate; reason for study: professional purposes. I opened the Intermediate Business English sample lesson. Then it struck me: a foreign military officer using a cheap online language school in America? Plus, I hadn't bothered to check before, but it was two in the morning in Minsk.

No time to think further. The student was online. I clicked the call button.

He wore a heavy glued-on mustache, a too-large officer's cap covering half his ears, and a khaki jacket festooned with medals. Wait...one of them was a star-shaped badge that said *Sheriff*. The shiny insignia on his hat bore the words "Intel Inside".

"Goot effternoon. I am Yevgeny Lukozadovich Chamiak, Under-Vice Edmiral in Belarus Imperial Navy. Your name, lady professor, please?"

Elias's accent was an atrocious hash of Borat and Count Chocula, his mustache already peeling on one side. I was in no mood to play. Why was I unable to tear myself away?

"Serena Young. Come on, let's—"

"Yang? Is sounding like Chinese name. You are also can to teaching me Chinese?"

I shook my head. "Let me refer you to a Mandarin language school."

"Nyet! Is time of waste, learn Chinese. One hour later, you must learning words all over again."

What was it about this guy, dragging me into his silly games? And this name, Chamiak? I ran it through a translator. Cute. It was Belarusian for *hamster*. I could hang up...or maybe play along, just for a few minutes.

"What is your purpose for learning English, Admiral?"

"Ah! Is very help when to interrogating arrested foreign journalistniks. Also for pick up chickens."

"Chickens?"

"Yes. Once I am being in America, am going to pub. There I am seeing one very, how you say, hot-temperature chicken who is karaoke singing. Very bad voice, machine exploding. Can being top secret weapon! I must recruit for Belarus army!"

"Navy, you mean."

"Yes, navy." His mustache drooped over his mouth.

"And did you pick her up?"

He pressed back the mustache, which began another slow

curling descent. "Misfortunately she is running away. Like Russians during war against victorious Belarus. Is sad story, yes? Is why you are cry?"

I dabbed my eye with a knuckle. "Please stop making me not feel sad."

"I am doing? Is good! My military training is defend against our enemy Russia, who has invented Russian novels, in which characters always feeling sadness and melancholic. Therefore if you are sadness I must to shoot you."

The exhausted and weepy part of me wanted to wrap up his little prank and sign off. But another part felt like I was hurtling down a wild amusement park ride, giddy about where the track might lead.

"So, let's start our lesson," I said. "Today we'll do Intermediate Business English, 'Discussing a contract.' If you'll open the document I sent you to page five—"

"Nyet, nyet, nyet." When he shook his head, his mustache flew clean off. He picked it up and held it in place with a finger. "No business. Must to use regular textbook."

I couldn't figure out what he was up to. I scrolled through the lesson titles on my screen. "Fine. Let's start with Lesson—"

"Thirty-two."

Eyes glistening like a puppy's, he held up a stack of papers: a printout of Lesson 32.

Now I had to laugh. "How did you know—?"

"We heff ways..."

He was taking his games to a new level. I could stop anytime I wanted. If I wanted. My heart thumped so fast I worried he could see it through my clothes.

"Okay, let's begin," I said. "Lesson 32: Dating and Romance. Let's start with the dialogue. You be Jason and I'll be Linda."

"Hello," he read, gargling the *h* like he was preparing to spit. "Is this seat taken?"

"Yes. But my friend appears to be late."

"Your *boyfriend?*" He played up the highlighted vocabulary like a bad actor.

"I was in a *relationship,* but we *broke up.* So I became *single.*"

"I also remain *unattached.* Are you *free* later? May I *take you out?*"

"You sound very nice, but I don't feel ready for *dating* right now." This was already too strange. Though I'd been through this dialogue a hundred times, I couldn't prevent a laugh escaping.

"What funny?" he said.

"It's the Romance chapter, and, um—every verb so far is from a class called copulatives."

"Is English teacher joke."

"I suppose."

He frowned at this. "Question. Why is woman speak copulatives, but play hard to getting? Man is very charmful, I am thinking."

"Maybe this man hasn't figured out the right way to impress her. He is awkward with people. His best friends are computers."

"Ah! Same Leenda! Without computer she is cut off from world. They are perfect match."

"Okay, stop. Enough." I held my hand in front of my webcam. "I don't want to play this game."

"Then we can to talking—"

"No no no no no. Here, I'll do a little English teacher magic. When I snap my fingers, you can speak perfect American English."

I snapped. He drew in a breath, but I shushed him and said, "And when I snap them again, you're not Admiral Hamster. And can you please take off the stupid mustache?"

I snapped again. He twitched his lip and the mustache fell.

"Game's over," I said. "Elias, what do you want?"

"I—oh...um...I guess I want to clear the slate."

"What slate? What the hell are you talking about?"

Elias picked glue off his lip. "You never answered my last question."

"Huh?"

"See message dated 3:23 pm Tuesday the—"

"You've got to be kidding me. I still haven't gotten over how you manipulated me with all your trick-someone-into-falling-in-love-with-you questions! You're an ass, you know that?"

"I do know that. But it was working. A little bit. Right?"

We stared at each other's webcam images. His face appeared to have changed since I'd last seen him. His cheeks had lost some of their roundness; a jawline had emerged. As silly as it looked, a uniform—well, a jacket with actual shoulders—gave him a definite masculine boost. With some judicious wardrobe advice, he might even verge on attractive. Whether he noticed me examining him or he was examining me, his lips spread into an impish smile.

"You remember it?" he said.

I shrugged. "Maybe."

He shrugged back. "Nu?"

"Three things I like about my partner—that was the question, right? That's making the bold assumption that he's my actual partner."

"I withdraw the assumption."

"Good. That clears the way for an answer." The answer that had been ringing in my head since Rome.

"Okay. One—he's always generous to me, even when I'm doing something stupid and breaking things and have nothing to give in return. Number two..." The words had trouble forming. Then a dam broke. "You make me laugh. Not *at* you—well, maybe sometimes. But you do make me laugh at myself, in a way that's...that's...it's like a solvent that eats through all the layers of crap gunking up my life. It makes me feel smart. Feel appreciated. You make me laugh and when I'm laughing that's when I feel alive. And...and..."

"Yes...?"

"And I wish you'd keep making me laugh, making me feel."

"What's number three?"

"Wasn't that three? Oh. Give me a sec. Um...you're a good father—and grandfather now—to our hamsters."

He caught the word *our* and nodded appreciatively.

"Your turn," I said.

"Okay. Three things I like about my, er, *buddy* Serena." He raised a finger like an orchestra conductor. "One. I like that every time I talk with you I get the impression you're not just listening to my words, but critiquing their syntax and ascribing punctuation and even double spacing between my sentences. No, don't deny it. "

He raised the first finger of his other hand, then entwined both index fingers together in an unmistakable embrace.

"Two. I like that you're always doing the most irrational things for the most rational reasons—wrecking cars for hamsters, running halfway around the world to look through a telescope at the moon. Lecturing me on Byzantine Greek verb endings when your heart's exploding. It's like you're this knot which holds the whole world together, and if you untie it, the planet will split in two."

His words flowed through me like an invisible ribbon which wrapped itself around my heart. If that's how he felt about my personality disorders, what did this man think of the rest of me?

An incoming e-mail alert dinged. I nodded at Elias to continue.

"So finally we get to big number three." He drew in a deep breath, gathering courage for whatever momentous thing he was about to declare.

The e-mail preview scrolled in the corner of my screen. A Japanese-looking sender name. No, I told my eager touchpad finger, now was the absolute worst time to multi-task in my entire life. Until I read the subject header.

"Um...Elias? This is the rottenest timing ever. But can I call you back in, like, maybe an hour?"

"Minsk is very late already."

"You can immigrate in the meantime. One hour."

Chapter 36

Ten minutes later I put a call through to Marisa.

"Long time no see," she said. Her latest hairstyle resembled a teased and hairsprayed cross between a bird's nest and a helmet. "So how was, uh, Spain—where was it you went?"

"Italy. It was okay. Love your hair. We need to talk."

"That's what I said." She cleared her throat. "So, look, I've got bad news and good news. The bad you'll have guessed, so I'll give it first. One of your students went AWOL. Never showed up for his substitute. Italian. Interesting coincidence." She shot me a funny look.

"Oh yeah, him. His English was beyond repair."

"Right." Her eyes turned quizzical. "For once no breaking down in hysterics. This is progress."

"Listen, Marisa, without getting into detail, I've had enough hysterics in the past two weeks to last a lifetime. Anyway, what I wanted to talk about—"

"Sweetheart, I'm not through." Her fingers drumming the desk popped in my headphones. "You want the good news or not?"

"Why not?"

"Hm. Somebody's in a funny mood. So anyway, we did a little student survey about their satisfaction with the programs, the textbooks, the interface, and naturally their teachers. Not sure if it'll come as any surprise who took the number one spot."

"Please spare me. I am not interested in hearing more accolades for Victoria the Great."

"Who said anything about Victoria? Oh, that's right—you weren't here! She's no longer with the company."

Zuzie shuffled out of her room, giving me a little finger wave on the way to the bathroom. I looked back at Marisa. "Not sure I heard right. She quit?"

"Oh, sweetie, you missed the circus." She pushed her office door closed behind her. "Compliance guy caught her in a random audit. One of her lessons, right there on video, she stripped down completely topless in front of a student."

"What?"

"Yeah, and I'll tell you what's worse. He paid her for it. Fifty bucks!"

Now I knew what had happened to Vlad. Part of me was incensed that they'd assigned Victoria as his substitute teacher. But most of me was sorely tempted to message her: *He offered me 120, you cut-rate slut.*

"So, what...you actually fired her?" I said.

"She's lucky we're not suing for damages. But, I mean, the poor girl's suffering enough. Her fiancé called off the wedding after he heard."

I covered my mouth in time, I hoped, to hold back a gasp. Too many heartbreaks going on around here. A twinge of sympathy for poor, ice queen Victoria knocked on the door of my heart.

"So, back to the subject at hand," Marisa said. "You're number one."

My mouth still hung open when I dropped my hand. *"What?"*

"By a wide margin. I guess you're doing something right, because your students love the heck out you."

"Oh my God, that's so sweet! That's the nicest..." I reached for a tissue.

Marisa rolled her eyes. "Okay, I'm going to wait for you to

quit blubbering, then lay it out. Ready? First and foremost, this means a raise. Don't get too excited—only about eight percent. Any more and we'd have to up our fee."

"Uh huh."

"You're cool as a cucumber today, ain'tcha? Anyway, the catch is: it also comes with a cut in teaching hours—that is, if you want it."

"Why on earth would being ranked number one mean a cut in teaching hours? That makes no sense!"

Zuzie's head leaned from the bathroom, shooting me a concerned look.

Marisa reveled in my confusion for a moment, then said, "That's what our meetings were about earlier today. With your best buddy Vicky out of the picture, we need someone to film all those video lessons. So...number one teacher, a hit with students, not too shabby looking if she finally did something about the hair. A little crazy and prone to histrionics now and then, but that can be edited out. I made a case for you."

"And?"

"You think I'm telling you all this just to say the board voted it down? Unanimous, honey. How does it feel being a video superstar?"

I didn't remember ever losing the ability to speak, like right now. I barely remembered my name—my mind had emptied to make room for everything she'd just told me.

Marisa continued, "While you're letting flies into your mouth, let me point out this is an ongoing project. If this first set sells, there'll be more. Then there's promo videos, other web extras, things like that. So figure two, three days a week on this. Base pay to be discussed, and some residuals on sales. Oh yeah, and we need you on the home page to do the little iEnglishU wiggly walk. That pays separate. You're the new face of the company. This is long-term, you know. Of course it means spending time up here in the Bay Area. Might consider moving. What do you think, sweetheart?"

"I...wow...oh my goodness...."

"Lost for words?" Marisa steepled her fingertips, pleased as a mother hen. "So, maybe while you're letting that sink in, you can say what it was you wanted to tell me?"

"Oh. Yeah. So, Marisa? Um. I quit."

Chapter 37

"*You what??*" Elias's face filled the screen, still wearing his military cap pulled down to his ears.

"I said I quit my job. Take off the dumb hat."

He flicked it from his head. My jaw must have plummeted to the floor, because he responded with a sheepish grin, turning side to side to let me admire what he'd been hiding underneath. His hair had been freshly styled: cropped along the sides, a shaggy tease on top, one wayward lock dangling rakishly over his forehead.

"Wow," I said.

"Yeah, well, I got tired of you nagging me to get a haircut."

"Next time let me style it." Not that I knew how. I'd e-mail Giulia for advice.

"So you gonna maybe explain what's going on?"

"Let me forward it to you. I was hoping to get your feedback." I clicked send.

He got it a few seconds later. I toyed with the red tarantella scarf drooping from my hair, while Elias's face flexed through a kaleidoscope of expressions before settling into a frown. "This is one heck of a long contract," he said.

"I know. Skip to the remuneration bit on page 4." I clicked there myself. "It isn't huge money. I mean, it's just a community college. But it's a real salary. Should be enough to get by if I share a place."

Elias stared into the camera, blinking so hard he could have extinguished a fire. "You're moving to Seattle."

It was a plaint rather than a question. I should have guessed how he would take it.

"When?" he said, almost a whisper.

"They want me in two weeks. They had an urgent opening, and my application was lucky good timing—for the first time in my life. They even said they'll cover some moving costs."

"Uh huh. What happened to the person you're replacing?"

"I don't know. Maybe found a higher-paying job. Maybe run over by a truck. Doesn't matter. It's all legitimate. Teaching refugees and new immigrants—real people in a real classroom! The department head's Japanese. You can help me check them out if you want. But...well, they need an answer by tomorrow."

"Right. I notice the digital signature field's already been filled in."

I carried my laptop to the sofa and lay on my side with my head propped on my fist. "Oh, Elias. This is what I want—to teach real flesh-and-blood people, not pixels. Go to a brand-new place and see what happens. To do things my way for once! In some ways I feel my life is finally just beginning."

"Okay. So, objectively speaking, I'm delighted for you. I mean, who wouldn't be?"

Him, obviously, judging by the way he removed his glasses and pinched his eyes.

"On the other hand," he continued. "How can I put this? We were just talking, you know...before." He sniffed and wiped his nose on the back of a finger. "I was kind of forming a perhaps overly optimistic impression of you and me. Of *us*."

"Now that you mention it," I said, "we didn't finish the game."

"Game."

"Tell your partner three things you like about them. You still need one more."

"So now we're partners."

"For the purposes of the game," I said.

"Right." He checked my face for possible ridicule, then let out a long, sad sigh. "May as well start by revising my previous answers. I told you two things I like about you. Well. I lied. I should have said they're what I *love* about you. No, I don't need a tissue. You know me, a sleeve will do. Oh, all right."

His head leaned off screen for a moment. He had the decency to mute his microphone while he blew his nose. When he returned, his glasses were clouded with mist.

"So. Number three. You're the most beautiful woman I've ever met or imagined or...or even fantasized." I felt the warmth in the timbre of his voice, even through the tinny laptop speakers.

"I know," I said. Because finally I did know. The world as I'd seen it from a webcam and an airplane window and on the ground here and nine time zones away, all possessed a beauty I'd finally begun to believe I also was capable of. Now *I* needed a tissue. "Tell me something interesting."

"Ah...what? I guess there is one more thing. Number four, for extra points. But, uh...see, I'm a tech guy, so the only way I can phrase this is in the context of what I know. There's hardware on the outside, like my hair—you've seen it—and software on the inside and—"

"Just say it."

He ran a hand over his scalp, while his eyes fixed with a glow that penetrated the screen, which penetrated the short distance between us.

"Serena, for lack of a better word, you make me want to upgrade myself. For you. But also for me."

Then to my surprise, he stood up and all I saw was an orange t-shirt through his unbuttoned jacket. "I guess that finishes the game, and maybe I gotta go."

"Wait! Can we talk?"

"I don't feel like playing anymore. Good luck up in Seattle. Don't forget to write."

The call ended. His status switched to offline.

ZUZIE WAS OUT. JUST me and the hamsters. I cleaned their cages, wrote to Jessie and Miko, checked my phone messages—none. I sipped a solitary glass of wine while the light faded around me.

He'd told me he loved me. Or something approximating that; he'd used the word *love*. What was happening? Elias wasn't Mister Stability and Security like Steve, or Alessandro's romance movie fantasy, or the hot bodied surfer in Huntington Beach. There were no logical arguments in support of loving Elias back. Then why was that word, that four-letter word, lodged so deeply in my chest?

Maybe love has nothing to do with logic. Or fantasy. Or ripped pecs.

I tapped a message:

> *New round. My turn to ask a question.*
> *If your partner decided to move 1200*
> *miles away and asked you to come with*
> *her, tell her how you'd respond.*

I waited through half an hour and one and a half more glasses of wine, but he didn't reply. I'd hurt his feelings. He thought I was toying with him.

I tapped out one more message:

> *Did you get my question*

I heard an incoming message tone, but not from my phone. From outside the front door. My toe snagged the carpet on the way.

He stood on the welcome mat staring down at his phone. "Yes. To both."

"Have you been standing outside there this whole time?"

"No. About to ring the bell, but then this message came in and—"

"Um...want some wine?"

"No. I mean, yes. Please."

He'd changed his shirt before coming: a lavender button-down fastened up to the neck. His haircut looked even better in person. There was something new and confident in his stance. He stood by the counter while I shook the last dribbles from the wine box. I'd filled a third of a glass when a message beeped. Miko, suggesting cupcakes.

I held the phone out of Elias's view and pecked out:

Sorry busy

Miko: *With what*

Me: *Elias*

Miko: *That nerd?*

Pots calling kettles black, anyone? Or did Miko self-identify as a normal human being? Perhaps there was something new to learn about my friend. I handed Elias his glass and reached for a misshapen hand-blown goblet, the only clean drinking vessel left. Another incoming text beeped. Elias raised his wine and a curious eyebrow. I responded with an apologetic eyebrow of my own and tapped Miko's message.

Us nerds deserve love too <3

Indeed we do, I tapped back before turning off the phone and filling my goblet with water. Elias and I clinked glasses.

"You're not just talking about me coming with you to the airport, right?" he said.

I leaned against the counter, facing him, shook my head and laughed.

"Because this whole idea is really dumb," he continued. "Seattle's got more nerds than slugs on the ground. They don't need to import any schmucks like me. I'll end up begging in the streets. And I might be allergic to rain."

"If you think it's a dumb idea, then why are you—"

"Hold on, I'm not finished." He swallowed his wine, made a sour grimace, and set down the glass. "I needed someone to turn to for advice. So naturally I asked Van Damme. My desktop, remember? He's usually more open-minded than Conan. And right there on his home screen is this photo you sent me of you on that Vespa."

He stopped for a moment, swallowing back whatever was welling from inside him. I reached for the tissue box at the end of the counter, but he waved his hand: no.

"Made me remember what you told me about finding yourself at that crossroads in the middle of nowhere and taking the path that nobody told you to take, that it made no logical sense, but felt right, like it was a voice from above. Am I right? Maybe I need to listen to voices too—who says computers don't talk? Know what Van Damme said?"

"Tell me."

"He said, 'Maybe it's your turn to do something wild, take a risk, break out of your gloomy little garage fixing old ladies' computers,' and...and..."

"And?"

"'And if you really love her, you idiot, don't you dare say goodbye.'" His mouth twitched and twisted into a smile so unsure it was like watching a baby take its first steps.

I yanked the red chiffon scarf from my hair, looped it around his head, and danced him, a willing fly, onto the cushioned web of the living room couch, where we surrendered to each other's hungry embrace. His kiss tasted of breath mints over a trace of nacho cheese flavored tortilla chips.

Chapter 38

*H*ere's what I hate about my life: saying goodbye.

My final Friday with iEnglishU. Bieber showed up for his lesson several minutes late. I dove right in to the current exercise until he cut me off.

"Teacher Serena, I must say something." His eyes were as big and alarming as I'd ever seen them.

"What's wrong?"

"After you I am quit," he said, almost a whisper.

"What? What did you say?"

He glanced aside, avoiding my eyes. "I quit English lessons. I am sorry."

"But why? I know prepositions are confusing, but you'll start with Rhonda next week, and she's a really great teacher."

"No next week." His eyes rolled side to side in that look I knew so well: avoiding the answer. "Time you are in Italy, I need help read Italian words."

What was he talking about? "Bieber..."

"I meet somebody."

He looked away again, grinding back an embarrassed grin. A new window popped up on the screen, showing an angelically pretty girl of twelve or thirteen with light complexion and long, straight, milky brown hair. I thought it was a photo, until the face came to life.

"Buongiorno, Maestra. Mi chiamo Cristiana." A voice sweet

as a flute trilled through rows of perfect pearly teeth. Had I been a thirteen-year-old boy I'd have been in love by the third syllable.

"*Salve, Christiana. Dove abita?*" I said. Where do you live?

"*Sono di Torino. Spero di vedervi a casa mia.*"

I believed she had just invited me to visit her home in Turin.

"Oh my God, Bieber, she's such a sweetheart!"

His face beamed, all hesitation gone. "From now I study Italian."

"But your mother—"

"Angry like monster!" He imitated Godzilla with clawing hands and a duck-lipped snarl, making Cristiana laugh so hard she broke into hiccups. The girl really liked him! Bieber defiantly folded his arms, more like a Transformer robot. "I tell her I don't care what she say! Is my life, yes?"

I wished I could reach through the screen and hug this boy. "Yes, it's your life! Your life! I'm so proud of you, Bieber!"

"Oh," he said, that embarrassed eye roll again. "Not Bieber. I change name. Now I am Luciano."

"Luciano! I like that."

"I will miss you, Teacher Serena."

I squeezed my eyes closed as hard as I could. I'd seen this boy every day for nearly a year, more often than anyone else in my life. I felt like a big sister, swelling with pride for where he'd come, not only with his English, but as a soulful human being. Sure, for a few days I'd thought he'd ruined my life. But in fact he'd changed it for the better. What heartbreak to say goodbye.

"Oh, Bieb—*Luciano*. This is...I'm going to miss you so much! Oh, my God. We'll speak again. *Arrivederci!*"

I had to sign off so he wouldn't watch me cry.

THAT WEEKEND MY ROOM turned into a jungle of old clothes and mountains of papers, half-filled boxes and suitcases. I wanted a midnight bonfire, maybe find some tarantella music and dance my old life farewell. I opted for boring and responsible instead, sorting out piles for donation and recycling.

I had my foot on an overstuffed suitcase, with one end of a binding strap between my teeth, when the doorbell rang, then rang again. Wasn't Zuzie home? I stomped to the door.

It opened to Steve, all dressed up in a camel hair jacket, bearing a small bouquet of roses.

"Serena. Oh. Hi..." He as uneasy as I was. He couldn't have chosen a more awkward moment. I never had sent him that text.

"Hi, Steve. I, um, didn't expect to see you. You look good. Uh, I'm a bit of a mess right now, but if you want to—"

"Hey, there he is!" Zuzie's voice sailed across the room. "Whoa! Those for *moi?*" She butted me aside, her green silk dress shimmering as she reached for Steve's flowers.

I asked, "Will someone please tell me what's going on?"

Zuzie took Steve's arm and waltzed him into the living room. "Stephen and I are attending the thee-*ate*-er."

"A Funny Thing Happened on the Way to the Forum," he said.

"Huh?"

"Name of the musical," Steve said.

"Yep," said Zuzie. "You ain't the only chick gets a trip to Italy."

This did not compute. Steve...and *Zuzie?*

He nodded me toward the kitchen to talk in private. "Listen, Serena, I never got to tell you: no hard feelings. Hope you're the same. But you know, that night? I overheard your roommate talking about 'The Music Man'—I mean, she was kinda shouting it to the whole neighborhood. Then when I came by with those flowers for—well, she was just so emotional. Took her for a drive listening to soundtracks. 'South Pacific', 'Bye Bye Birdie'—hey, you know that one has a song about an English teacher? Anyway, we kind of bonded, you know? So when I saw these tickets to the South Coast Rep—hope you don't take any offense—but I thought Zuzie might appreciate—"

"Damn straight," she said. "I'm a true dame of culture."

"What offense?" I told him. "You two get going. Have a great time!"

They hooked arms and marched to the door, singing together:
Something for everyone,
A comedy tonight!

Then Zuzie ran back inside and swept me up in a thick embrace. "Sayonara, girl," she said, kissed my cheek, and let go.

"Steve, if I don't see you again..." But the latch clicked shut.

Elias showed up early Monday morning to finish loading his car, though there was barely room for my stuff, what with his boxes and boxes of electronic junk.

It had taken him less than a week to receive one potential job offer in Seattle and another three interviews scheduled. He was over the moon about the move, until I brought up one eensy little thing.

"No way," he'd said. "I am not sharing a house with that...that *insect*."

"Then we're not sharing a house with anybody or each other. Even on your pay and mine, there's no way can we afford it without Miko."

"We can camp in a park."

"Funny. Ha ha. Look, she barely finished bootcamp, and she walks right into this crazy job. She doesn't have time to look for anything else. Anyway, it's a house! With a backyard! Where you gonna find that in Capitol Hill?"

I kept secret my own reservations: the small lemon tree in the garden. But if Elias and Miko had to learn to stand each other, it was only fair for me to expunge my own demons. Maybe I'd try my hand at making limoncello.

That was last week. Today we were off. Barring a volcanic eruption or engine breakdown, we'd be moving into that house tomorrow, at the end of an eighteen-hour drive.

Elias came back inside holding a package. "Delivery guy just dropped this off. For you."

It was the size of toaster oven, bound in twine. With Customs documents in Italian.

I carefully slit it open on the kitchen counter. Buried in packing confetti, a small wicker basket held a little bottle of red wine and another of olive oil, flanking a fancy embossed wedding invitation. It seemed that the two families hadn't wasted any time.

I deposited the whole thing, box and all, in the garbage can.

Elias lifted it back out. "What? You're gonna waste these?"

"I'm not going to risk being poisoned."

"Then I have a better use." He grasped the wine bottle's neck and brandished it like a club.

I followed him outside, not exactly happy. "You're going to put a dent in it."

"Excuse me, who took a semester of mechanical engineering?" He circled his car, testing potential impact points with his knuckles until he stopped at the rear bumper. "I hereby dub thee *Enterprise 3,* going where no goofy English teacher has gone before!"

The bottle made a loud thud which I felt in my teeth. He swung again, harder. It exploded in a shower of red liquid all over our clothes.

"Damn! Shoulda guessed it was spumante," he said.

"And it made a dent." I patted his shoulder. "She has that effect on people."

I had one last student that morning before I could leave. Yasmin's head was wrapped in wild colors, which made me ponder: if the whole point of headscarves was to make women appear demure, then how did one explain the riot of swirling hues that brought out her intense beauty?

Yasmin shook with excitement. She had finally made it to the long-anticipated Lesson 32. She made a big performance of the dialogues, playfully coquettish when she was the woman, putting on a tigerish growl when she played the man. I didn't dare mention copulative verbs. In the end, though, she confessed disappointment.

"I do not think man and woman really talk such way. Maybe in America?"

"No," I said. "Only in textbooks."

"Then I don't understand. Why not write real English? This rubbish dialogue—no use!" I felt bad for her, all hopes dashed of springing lines on an unsuspecting foreign guy in a tourist cafe. She asked me for some "real" romantic dialogue. I hesitated a moment, then sent her a link to the 36 Questions.

Yasmin's eyes popped and she chirped like a bird. "Now you tell me whole story, how you and this boy hook up."

She squealed and clapped at each twist in the tale. It didn't matter that Elias meanwhile walked right past carrying the hamster cages. I'd defend myself if challenged for revealing personal data to a girl across the world—it was for educational purposes.

Yasmin applauded. "Is funny story, but good story. Because you first know to love this boy when you are far away. Then coming home, you first speak love through computer."

"It is a bit funny," I said, though I didn't get her point.

"That means—is possible!" She clapped again. "Can fall in love through the webcam!"

I threw my head back and laughed. "I hadn't thought about it, but you're right."

She pumped her fist. "I am having hope! Thank you, God! Thank you, Internet! Thank you, Serena!"

"Okay, Yasmin, time's up. I have a long trip. I'm afraid that it's time to say—"

"Wait! Special words!"

Elias popped his head inside and waved. We were all ready, except for me and my computer.

I wiggled two fingers at him, then told Yasmin, "Sure. Two minutes."

She drew in a loud breath. "I want tell to you, Serena. As my very good teacher, as my very good friend...you *kick ass!*"

"Thank you, Yasmin." I pressed my thumbs hard into my eyes. "That's the nicest, the sweetest—"

"But why? Why in English violence kicking ass is good? So stupid! You *kiss* ass sound much more friendly. Explain me, please! English does not make sense!"

I smiled at my student. The horn beeped outside. Time to take wing.

This, and everything else on all sides of the world, is what I love about my life.

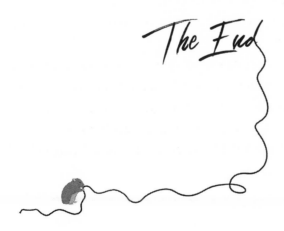

The End

On Love and Olive Oil

SOURCES FOR THIS BOOK

The 36 Questions to Make Anyone Fall in Love with You were created by a research team headed by Prof. Arthur Aron. Read the full academic report:
journals.sagepub.com/doi/pdf/10.1177/0146167297234003

The Four Stages of Acculturation are adapted from clinical psychologist Dr. Cathy Tsang-Feign's book *Living Abroad*. Read a summary: cathyfeign.com/articles/culture-shock.html

Yes, **copulative verbs** are a thing. They are a class of verb which joins a subject to an object or adjective. For more information: eltnotebook.blogspot.com/2010/11/an-elt-glossary-copulative-verbs.html

And is **iEnglishU.com** a real language school? Judge for yourself!

Finally, about **olive oil**. Not all the "extra virgin" oils in your supermarket are real. I've written a brief guide, **HOW TO CHOOSE AN EXTRA VIRGIN,** which can save you worry and maybe save you money. Simply join my mailing list at the link below and I'll send it to you for free, as well as occasional news about travel, languages, and my books.

EXTRAVIRGIN.JRLAURENCE.COM

Acknowledgements

The AUTHOR IS INFINITELY grateful to my dear friends and outstanding writers, Pat Dobie, Leigh Camacho Rourks, and Lorin Wertheimer, who dissected this novel with surgical precision, good humor, and warm-hearted encouragement.

Grazie mille to Mauro Italiano, who corrected my Italian dialogue and patiently replied to every nitpicky question about colloquial and regional usages.

Blessings to the original Serena, an assigned name which she peeled off to reveal herself as Grace, whose offhand remark about traveling the world every day through a webcam sparked the idea for this story, and whose extracurricular confessions about the routines, challenges, and unrequited dreams of an online language factory worker moved my heart.

Above all, love and gratitude to Cathy.

About the Author

J.R. LAURENCE IS A writer and artist who has worked in news media and broadcast entertainment in North America, Europe, and Asia, with Time Magazine and Walt Disney Television, among others. Passions include cycling, fountain pens, and daydreaming in foreign cafés.

JRLAURENCE.COM

Made in the USA
Las Vegas, NV
28 March 2022

46441887R00199